No One But You

Leigh Greenwood

sourcebooks
casablanca

Published by Sourcebooks Casablanca, an imprint of Sourcebooks
P.O. Box 4410, Naperville, Illinois 60567-4410
(630) 961-3900
sourcebooks.com

Printed and bound in the United States of America.
POD

ONE

Texas, 1867

NO ONE KNEW BETTER THAN SARAH WINBORNE THE IMPORTANCE of appearance when a woman needed to attract the attention of a man, but the barren countryside which still lay in the faltering grip of winter offered limited opportunities to tidy her appearance. A sharp wind had made it necessary to wrap her head in a wool scarf. Her ill-fitting wool coat disguised the soft curves of her body. Heavy boots contributed the final touch that made her appearance about as alluring as that of an escaped convict.

"Can I take the reins?" her daughter begged. "Just for a little while."

The aching muscles that arched across Sarah's back and down her shoulders nearly caused her to give in to her daughter's wheedling, but Ellen was only seven and her experience was limited to their plow horse. "We're almost there."

Ellen slumped down. "I don't see why we have to hire anyone to help us." She pouted. "I'm big enough."

Six years of dealing with hired hands who were lazy, stole from her, or watched her with hungry eyes, had convinced Sarah she needed more than a hired hand this time. She needed a husband.

"You're a big help," Sarah said to her daughter, "but we can't do everything ourselves."

"I can help," her son offered. "Not like Ellen, but I can do some things."

Jared and Ellen were twins, but that's where the similarities ended. Ellen was well-grown and sturdy. She enjoyed nothing better than working alongside her mother or the series of hired hands her mother had employed since their father went off to the war. Jared was as tall as his sister, but he didn't have her strength or her solid build. But what set him irrevocably apart from other boys his age was his withered leg. The doctor said it came from the umbilical cord being wrapped around his leg before he was born. Her husband had never forgiven her for giving him a disabled son. He didn't seem to care that she had given him a perfectly formed daughter.

"I know both of you will do all you can," Sarah said to her children, "but you're still too young."

"And I'm a cripple," Jared said. "Everybody knows a cripple is useless."

Sarah had tried her best to help Jared build self-esteem, but it was hard on a boy to have to watch his sister do all the things he was supposed to do. It wrung her heart to watch his struggle to be like other boys, to witness his efforts to mask his disappointment, to pretend he didn't care when all he wanted was to be normal.

The war had been over for two years. Her husband was one of many who hadn't returned, who'd died on some distant battlefield, their bodies unclaimed and unidentified. By the time he'd been officially declared dead, she'd managed to adjust to life alone. She had wanted to remain a widow, but food had to be bought and taxes had to be paid. She couldn't do that *and* pay a hired man. She decided to marry again because a husband wouldn't require any wages.

The idea of marriage cast a chill over her heart. She didn't want to be beholden to a man ever again, but her children needed a father as much as she needed a man to do the labor that was beyond her. But this time would be different. This time she would do the choosing. She would set the terms. She would have the upper hand.

"Why are we going to see the Randolphs? Do you know them?"

"In a way."

She had never met any of the Randolph men, but she'd heard how they'd come back to their ranch after the war bringing a bull to improve the quality of their herd, had stood up to a clan preying on their cattle, and had taken part in a successful cattle drive to Missouri with Richard King, the famous cattle baron and owner of the King Ranch. She'd also heard that the Randolph crew included several honest and responsible war veterans. She hoped to persuade one of those men to become her husband.

"What are they like?" Jared asked.

She knew he was really asking if they would like him. She'd heard that the oldest Randolph brother had been an officer in the war and that two younger ones had held the ranch against all comers. That didn't seem like a recipe for understanding a boy with a withered leg. She had to be honest with Jared. Trying to protect him had only led to more hurt.

"I don't know what they're like, but from what I've heard they're honorable men." They both knew honor seldom included an understanding of anyone who was different. She loved Texas and Texans, but the men seemed to feel that anyone unable to participate in typically male pursuits wasn't welcome to share their company. She could only assume they were too embarrassed, or incapable, of allowing themselves to show emotion. Emotion was considered feminine, and no Texas man could live with the thought that he might be anything less than thoroughly masculine.

Ellen pointed to a post that had a seven enclosed in a circle carved into it. "Is that their ranch?"

Sarah's stomach cramped and her chest felt tight. The idea of approaching the Randolphs had been daunting when it first occurred to her. Now that she had reached the ranch, her anxiety escalated, as did her doubts about her sanity in considering such a course of action, her fear that her mission would be fruitless, might even be seen as begging, asking for pity. Yet she would endure anything because she was faced with losing their home, her only means of supporting her children.

"It's their brand," Jared pointed out. "And the trail branches off here."

The trail was broad and well-worn, an indication that a lot of business was conducted from this ranch. That encouraged Sarah as much as it made her fearful. Why would a successful, probably even wealthy family be interested in helping her? Being a war widow didn't give her any special distinction. There were thousands of them in Texas, many in worse circumstances than she. Nor would she trade on Jared's limitations. That would only make him feel worse about himself.

But she had no choice. She hadn't found anyone in Austin who would work for the wages she could afford to pay. That's what had propelled her on the desperate course of deciding to hire a husband.

"I don't see a house," Ellen said.

"Ranchers like to live in the middle of their land," Jared said. "That way they don't have to ride so far each day."

"I wouldn't care how far I had to ride," Ellen said. "That's the best part of owning a ranch." The girl loved horses.

The landscape felt as threatening as the circle of debt closing in around her. While they passed some areas of open grassland, much was a tangle of mesquite, chaparral, prickly pear, wild currant, cat's claw, and a dozen other varieties of low-growing trees, bushes, and vines, nearly all armed with vicious thorns. Come spring they would be covered with sweet-scented flowers. Some would produce succulent berries in summer that could be made into jam if one was brave enough to risk the thorns. All provided a hiding place for the longhorns on which most Texans depended.

"I don't see many cows," Jared said.

"That's because there won't be much graze here until spring," his sister said. "The cows probably stay near creek bottoms."

Sarah was more interested in looking for calves sired by the bull the Randolphs had brought from Alabama. She was hoping she could find a way to buy one of the bull calves eventually. She needed to improve her herd if she was to provide her children with an inheritance. She wasn't worried about the ranch surviving while she was gone. There was nothing left to tend except cows and horses. Since the cows were wild and horses practically so, they could take care of themselves better than she could.

The mere thought of marrying a man she'd never seen was enough to make Sarah turn around, but she had to think of her children. Her daughter could look to a husband to take care of her future, but it was essential that Jared have a way to support himself. It might have been different if he'd been interested in learning a profession or becoming an apprentice, but he liked the ranch as much as Ellen. Sarah suspected he'd never be happy anywhere else.

"Is that their house?"

Ellen was pointing to a building that had just come into view. It was too far away to see any detail, but there was no question that, despite its size, it was a house and not a barn. Who'd ever seen a barn with a front porch?

"It's big," Jared said.

Huge was a better word. It made her feel small, unworthy, presumptuous even to be here much less asking the Randolphs to give up one of their valued employees for her. Especially since her offer was rather unusual.

"It looks new," Jared said.

"It's made out of boards instead of logs," Ellen observed.

"It would have to be," Jared told his sister. "It has two floors."

"How many rooms do you think it has?" Ellen asked.

Sarah didn't know how many rooms, but maybe a family of so many brothers needed a house that big. She didn't know how many might be married, how many might have children. It wasn't unusual for whole families to live in the same house, especially since the war.

"I bet they have hundreds of horses," Ellen said.

"They would only need that many for a drive," Jared said. "I doubt they have more than thirty or forty."

Ironic that though Ellen was the physical child, she was the one most likely to exaggerate or romanticize a situation. Jared was the practical child, the one who wanted facts, who was likely to correct you if you were wrong.

As Sarah drew closer, she was able to identify several structures, the most imposing of which was a barn. She could understand the chicken coop, the sheds, and the bunkhouse, but she couldn't recall seeing a barn in Texas.

At first she thought the house couldn't be new because the boards had had time to weather, but as she drew closer, she realized it had been painted a soft gray so it would blend into its surroundings. She liked the cleared yard, the trees planted for future shade, the beds she could imagine being full of flowers in the spring, the porch provided with several chairs for rocking in the cool of the evening. How was she going to convince any man to leave this ranch for a place so rundown the bank president had done everything he could to keep from having to foreclose on it?

"Do they have any kids?" Jared asked.

"I don't know." She hadn't been able to find out a lot about the family without asking questions that were bound to raise unwanted curiosity. One man who'd quit had spread such an unflattering description of her ranch that no one would talk to her. Even taking into consideration the economic depression that had gripped Texas after the war, the wage she could pay was not enough for a man to feel he was getting paid for his work. Again, a husband wouldn't expect to get paid.

"Do you think we can find anybody here who'll work for us?" Jared asked. "They have a bunkhouse."

Her ranch didn't have a bunkhouse. The men had to sleep in the shed. They hadn't liked doing that, but she'd refused to let any of them sleep inside because there were only two bedrooms. More than one man had implied he'd be willing to work harder with more encouragement. Sarah had never had any doubt of what kind of encouragement they meant.

"I hope so," Sarah said.

"No one in Austin would."

She hadn't told the children what she intended to do. She was too afraid of the questions they would ask. She was even more afraid of what she would have to settle for. She was a realist. She didn't have much to offer besides herself.

But she refused to think about that yet. She still believed there were honorable men in Texas. She had no one else to fall back on. Her parents were dead, and Roger's family had turned cold when Jared was born. When Roger didn't return from the war, they cut her off completely. All she had to show for the bargain her father had made with Roger's family was a piece of land that was too large to be a farm and too unsuccessful to be a ranch. She had held out against the compromise nearly every widow faced—marry the first man who offered or risk starvation—but now she had no choice.

She had come too far to turn back, but now that she was here, she wondered if she hadn't been an idiot to attempt such a crazy plan. Regardless of any agreement she might make, it would be her husband's legal right to expect her to behave as his wife. She didn't want to be any man's wife ever again, but she would do it for her children. There was nothing special in that. Thousands of women were forced to do it even when there wasn't a war.

"I bet they have a dozen beds in that house," Jared said to his sister.

"I'd rather sleep in the bunkhouse," Ellen said, her eyes glowing.

"We'll sleep in the wagon just like we have since we left home," Sarah told her children.

"What if they offer?" Ellen asked.

"We'll politely decline. I don't want to be beholden to strangers."

"Wouldn't it be rude to refuse?" Jared asked. "You always said Southerners never turn away a stranger."

"I said they would offer them something to eat if they were hungry and a bed if they were sick. We're neither hungry nor sick."

"I'm hungry and Jared has a bad leg," Ellen said. "Doesn't that count?"

"We have our own food, and I don't want anyone pitying Jared," Sarah told her daughter. "We're here to find a man who can help us, not beg for favors."

"It's not begging if they offer," Jared said.

"They won't."

Sarah wondered why she thought the Randolphs would be willing to help her. She had nothing to offer them, and she was asking them to give up one of their most responsible and dependable workers. Just because she was desperate didn't mean people would feel they should deprive themselves to benefit her. She looked up at the house that loomed before her. It practically shouted at her to turn around and go back. The feeling was so strong she pulled the horse to a halt.

"Why did you stop?" Ellen asked.

"We shouldn't have come," Sarah said to her children. "We have to turn around."

Jared looked around, apparently trying to find what had caused his mother to change her mind. "Did something scare you?"

The odds were stacked heavily against her, but what kind of mother would she be if she quit? It didn't matter if she was so scared she could hardly breathe. It didn't matter that she was practically selling herself to a man she'd never seen. No one else would take care of her children. Both were looking at her now, waiting for her to say something.

She was about to shake the reins and start the horse again when a voice stopped her. "Are you folks lost?"

Sarah spun around to see a man with broad shoulders and a lean body approaching with an easy, swinging gait and a hoe resting on his shoulder. Apparently he'd been working in a grove of fruit trees whose leafless limbs looked like outstretched fingers against the pale gray winter sky. She didn't know how she missed seeing him. He was as tall as the trees themselves.

Oddly, he gave her the impression of being as sturdy as a tree, able to bend when necessary but keeping his roots firmly attached to the ground. Maybe it was his expression that was an engaging mixture of curiosity and cheerfulness. Maybe it was his unhurried gait, the way he stood calmly waiting for her to reply. Or maybe it was simply clothes that fit his body comfortably without being baggy. Maybe it was his broad shoulders and powerful forearms she could see below his rolled-up sleeves. His voice had a low, slow, and distinctly Southern accent; his gaze was forthright. His gray eyes seemed to welcome her. Or it could be that she was so afraid of being spurned that anything less than outright rejection seemed like an invitation.

"We're not lost," Ellen told the man. "We've come to look for a hired man."

The man's brow creased. "Why would you think he was here?"

Sarah pulled her scattered wits together. "I need to find a man to help me with my ranch. I was hoping one of the Randolphs would know of someone I could hire."

The man's expression cleared. "You ought to go to Austin. You'll find plenty of men there looking for work."

"I've been to Austin."

"How about San Antonio? It's a far piece, but I'm sure you can find lots of men there."

She could find lots of *men* just about anywhere, but she didn't want just any man. If she had to marry him, he had to be someone special, maybe someone like this helpful stranger.

The man switched his hoe to the other shoulder, stepped forward, and extended his hand. "Howdy. My name's Benton Wheeler but everybody calls me Salty."

Sarah took the proffered hand. It was big and rough-skinned with long fingers. His grip was firm but gentle. "I'm Sarah Winborne. These are my children, Ellen and Jared."

"Pleased to meet you." Salty shook hands with both children before turning back to Sarah. "You have a handsome family. They must take after their mama."

Sarah wasn't immune to a compliment, even one she was certain she didn't deserve. "They had a very handsome father."

"A lady like you doesn't deserve anything less."

This man's voice was like a fragrant oil, slipping sweet compliments by her in a way that made it feel like he meant every word.

"He died in the war," Ellen said.

"I'm mighty sorry to hear that. Children deserve a father."

They'd never had one, but that wasn't something Sarah was willing to share with a stranger, even an intriguing stranger who had succeeded in making her *feel* pretty when she knew she didn't *look* pretty.

"He never did write," Ellen said. "Do you think that makes him a bad father?"

"He couldn't write if he died."

"I suppose so," Ellen agreed with Salty, "but Mama wanted at least one letter."

Sarah loved her daughter dearly, but the girl had no idea when to keep her mouth shut. She was as open and uncomplicated as the horses she loved so much. "I would like to speak to Mrs. Randolph," Sarah said to Salty. "Is she at home?"

"She sure is. I'll walk you up to the house."

"You don't need to do that."

"It's no trouble. Besides, my mama told me to be nice to pretty ladies."

The only reason this man couldn't be happily married to an adoring wife would be that his silver tongue had gotten him into trouble with the law and he was hiding out.

"I expect it was your father who advised you to offer them soft soap."

Salty grinned. "You have to be a Southerner to know what that means."

"Because I'm a Southerner, I know just how much it's worth."

She liked his laugh. It was easy, genuine, and was accompanied by glistening eyes that said he was a man who enjoyed a woman's company. She was certain women were equally charmed by his company. He had a way about him that was dangerous because it made a woman feel all manner of things were possible even when she knew they weren't.

"Ma'am, I think you just accused me of being a purveyor of untruths."

Sarah couldn't resist laughing at his mock chagrin. "Nothing so serious. Just a matter of exaggeration."

"But only a *slight* exaggeration."

His assumed look of hopefulness, like a little boy hoping to escape punishment for some small transgression, almost made her laugh again. This man could have turned her head if she weren't a serious woman in need of a capable and responsible husband. It must be wonderful to be able to wake up each morning knowing that your world was unthreatened, that the day would provide you with reasons to be glad you were alive.

"It would be ungracious of me to disagree with you so I won't. Now you'd better introduce me to Mrs. Randolph before you give me reason to go back on my word."

"Your mother is a hard woman," Salty said to Ellen.

His accusation provoked Jared into breaking his silence. "No, she's not. She's nice to everyone, even the men who left us."

Sarah could tell from Salty's sudden lack of expression that an explanation was required. "Two of the men who worked for us left before fulfilling their agreement. It caused us to lose most of our crops last year." Which was the reason she was in such a desperate situation.

"I must apologize for my gender," Salty said. "Only a low-down skunk would do something like that."

"Arnie wasn't a low-down skunk," Ellen protested. "I liked him."

"You liked him because he let you ride with him everywhere he went," Jared said. "I told you he wasn't nice. I just didn't know to call him a low-down skunk."

Salty's glistening eyes were at work again. "It seems I've made an addition to your son's vocabulary," he said to Sarah. "Do I have to apologize?"

If she didn't get away from this man, she was going to do something foolish. He probably wasn't married after all. He enjoyed flattering women too much to settle down and get serious with anyone. Yet there was something genuine about him that made her believe a woman could depend on him. Despite the flattery and the laughter, he seemed solid, unshakable. Still, she couldn't afford to be dazzled by his smile or thrown off balance by his kindness.

"I won't ask you to apologize if you'll stop dragging your feet and introduce me to Mrs. Randolph. I could almost believe you didn't want me to meet her."

"Why would I want you to meet her when it means I'll be denied the pleasure of talking to you?"

She didn't know why Mr. Randolph had hired this man, but she doubted it was for the amount of work he got done. It would be nice to be with someone who had the power to make her feel her life wasn't such a burden, but she couldn't afford that luxury. She needed a man who knew how to fix things, to make things work, who wouldn't be put off by the hours of backbreaking labor it would take to put her ranch in order. She needed a man who could fill the role of a father to her children. She needed a man who would honor his commitments and respect her.

She needed a miracle.

"Somehow I think you'll survive. Now if you'll excuse me, I'll introduce *myself* to Mrs. Randolph."

"I said I'd walk up with you, and I will." He ambled to the horse's head, secured a grip on the bridle, and clucked for him to start walking. "Rose—that's what Mrs. Randolph insists everybody call her—doesn't get around much these days, so she'll be tickled to see another woman she can talk to."

"Doesn't she have a mother, sisters, sisters-in-law, even aunts who visit?"

"None of that. Just herself, and believe me, that's more than enough."

Sarah wasn't sure how to take that.

"When she speaks, everybody jumps," Salty continued. "Yes, sirree. The best way to get thrown off this ranch is to mess with Rose. She won't have to do a thing because George will kill anyone who bothers her. Not you, ma'am," Salty said, glancing back at Sarah. "George wouldn't lay a hand on a lady. Of course, I'm not sure about Monty. He doesn't hold much with women, at least not in a romantical sort of way."

Sarah had never met a man who barely paused long enough to allow someone else to get a word in edgewise. She had no doubt he could maintain a whole conversation by himself.

"Maybe I shouldn't have come," she said. "I don't want to upset the family."

"It's too late now. You're trapped."

Sarah cast nervous glances on either side and behind but didn't see anyone else. "What do you mean?"

Salty pointed toward the house. "Rose has seen you. You can't back out now."

TWO

Sarah looked toward the house where a woman stood on the porch beckoning to her. She noticed two things right away: the woman was very pretty, and she was very pregnant.

"Rose is expecting her first baby," Salty told her. "George has tried his best to convince her to stay in the house, but he gave up. People usually do when they go up against Rose."

"Maybe I should talk to her husband instead."

"If you think Rose is going to let you leave without talking to her, you don't know Rose. But of course you don't know her. You couldn't. But you'll love her like everybody else."

Could Salty mean everybody did whatever Rose asked because they loved her? Sarah had never heard of a woman who had that kind of power over men. Such a skill would be more valuable than gold.

Rose came down the steps to meet Sarah before Sarah's wagon came to a stop. She didn't act like a woman who needed to stay inside. She glowed with health and happiness as she said, "I'm Rose Randolph. I'd come down to meet you, but if I leave these steps, Salty will tell George and I'll be in for a lecture."

"I'd never tell on you," Salty protested.

"I know, but he'll ask me and I'd have to tell him the truth."

Sarah didn't know what to make of this woman. Maybe it wasn't "disobedience" in this case, just a difference of opinion. Not like it had been for her with Roger. Whenever Sarah had failed to live up to his expectations, he'd shouted at her, even struck her on occasion.

"Please don't leave the steps," Sarah said. "I'm capable of climbing far more than those."

"This hasn't slowed me down"—Rose rubbed her stomach—"but it has made me more clumsy."

Sarah remembered her own pregnancy only too well. Roger had been furious at the change in her appearance, that she couldn't do as much work as before, and that she was unable to satisfy his physical appetite as often as he wished. In the last months he had found her so unappealing he had gone elsewhere.

"It's a matter of balance," Rose said as Salty helped Sarah down. "If I turn too quickly or lean over too far, I lose my balance."

Sarah remembered stumbling, even falling to her knees. "Let me give you a hand up the steps," she said.

"Nonsense. I'm perfectly fine holding on to the railing. Tell your children to get down and come in. Salty will take care of your horse and wagon."

"I don't mean to stay. I just need to ask a few questions."

"I'll have none of that. You're staying for supper. And if you have more than a couple of questions, you can stay overnight and ask them tomorrow."

Sarah felt like she'd been run over by a freight wagon, but she had a feeling a lot of people did when they met Rose Randolph. If she herself had been more like Rose she wouldn't have been forced to marry Roger.

As was her habit, Ellen jumped down from the wagon without waiting for assistance.

"This is my daughter, Ellen Winborne."

"How do you do," Ellen said to Rose. "I'm pleased to meet you." She had good manners when she remembered to use them.

"You're going to be tall," Rose said. "I bet you're a big help to your mama."

"Not really. I prefer working outside."

"So do I," Rose confided, "but none of these men can cook."

"I don't like cooking."

Rose's gaze narrowed on Ellen. "Stick to your guns. There are a lot of men who make good cooks. Now I'd like to meet your brother."

"It's difficult for Jared to get out of the wagon by himself," Sarah said to Rose. "He was born with a withered leg."

"I'll lift him out."

Sarah had forgotten Salty was still there. She turned to decline his offer, but Salty had reached over the side of the wagon, hooked his arms around Jared, and lifted him out like he weighed nothing at all.

"Can you stand on your own?" he asked the boy.

"If I have something to lean on," Jared said. "I can hop with a stick, but I can't go very far."

Sarah knew it embarrassed Jared to have to confess his weakness to yet another person, but she was proud of him for facing up to it.

"Bring him into the parlor," Rose said to Salty. "He's probably covered in bruises from being bounced to death in that wagon."

Sarah wanted to protest that this was unnecessary, that a chair in the kitchen would be fine, but Salty climbed the steps carrying Jared in his arms like he did this every day. Rose pelted Jared with questions and Salty with orders. They all disappeared inside the house, leaving Sarah and Ellen to turn when they heard the sound of an approaching rider.

The man who rode up a moment later was the best-looking man Sarah had ever seen, even better looking than Roger. He swung down from the saddle when he reached them. Sarah could tell he was looking at her closely, probably trying to figure out if he was supposed to know them. He smiled and extended his hand in welcome.

"My name is George Randolph. There can't be a good reason why you're standing outside in this wind."

Sarah collected her badly scattered wits. "I'm Sarah Winborne, and this is my daughter, Ellen."

"Let's save the rest of the introductions until we get inside."

He appeared to be the kind of gentleman Roger had thought himself to be. But Sarah was certain George would never hit his wife or turn his back on a crippled son. She looked down at her dirty boots.

"Don't worry about your boots," George said. "You should see what the boys look like when they come in."

Sarah felt like a beggar in her worn coat and threadbare scarf, but there was nothing left to do but acquiesce to the invitation. She and Ellen climbed the steps and went inside.

The hall that ran from the front to the back of the house was empty of furniture, but what looked like a dozen pairs of shoes and boots lined the wall.

"The men change in the bunkhouse before they come in to eat, but sometimes their boots get muddy getting here. Keeping extras is easier than trying to scrape the mud off."

On the immediate right was a doorway which appeared to lead to an office. On the left was an open arch. Looking through it, Sarah saw that Salty had settled Jared on a couch. Rose was busy putting pillows behind his back while Salty propped his leg on an ottoman.

"Are you comfortable?" Rose asked Jared. "I've got more pillows. And blankets if you're still cold."

"I'm fine," Jared said, slightly flustered at being the object of so much attention. "The fire is very warm."

Heat from a cast iron heater on the right side of the room had made the large room almost too warm after the cold of the outside.

"If no one needs anything else," Salty said to Sarah, "I'll bring in your bags and unhitch the horse."

"I can do that," Ellen said.

Salty grinned at her. "I could use some help. No telling what that horse might do if I turn my back on him."

Ellen wasn't amused. "You're making fun of me."

"No, I'm teasing, but I won't do it anymore. Friends?"

"I guess so. It's just that people think I can't do anything because I'm a girl and I'm only seven."

"I never thought that. Now we'd better get the horse rubbed down and in the barn."

"Take off your coat and get comfortable," Rose said to Sarah after Ellen and Salty had gone.

Sarah was exhausted, more from worry than from the strain of handling the reins all day.

"You must be tired," Rose said. "Come sit by me. You can commiserate with me about being pregnant. The men around here seem to think everything ought to be the same as before."

"This is nothing compared to what it will be like when the baby gets here," Sarah said.

"Rose has been preparing us for that day," George said with a fond smile at his wife, "but I'm still looking forward to it."

"You'd better," Rose said with an equally doting smile. "If I go to all this trouble, you'd better like the results. Now tell me about yourself," she said, turning to Sarah. "What could have compelled you to travel this far in this weather? You don't live around here, do you?"

Sarah hardly knew where to begin, but she decided to start with the easiest question. "I have a ranch below Austin."

"You poor woman! What a long distance. Where did you sleep? What did you eat?"

Sarah decided it would be easier to start at the beginning.

It took only one trip for Salty and Ellen to carry into the house, and set down in the hallway, the few belongings of the Winborne family. He glanced into the parlor before turning to go outside. He'd been rather glib when he met Mrs. Winborne and her two children because he didn't know what to say. One look at her clothes had told him she was down on her luck. No woman as proud as she would dress like that except out of necessity. She wasn't a beauty, mind you, yet she was pretty in a way her bedraggled clothes couldn't hide. There was something very appealing about her despite the stubborn set of her jaw. If he were to guess, he'd say it had taken all her courage to come on this errand. He hoped Rose or George would be able to help her, but she wasn't going to hire anyone away from the Circle Seven. Every man here knew he was fortunate to be working for the Randolphs. Fighting rustlers as well as Cortina's bandits was hard work, but he had a place to sleep, plenty to eat, and he even got paid.

He felt especially sorry for the boy, Jared. Having a useless leg was hard on a kid, and no woman was going to marry a man who couldn't walk by himself. How was the poor kid going to find a job? He knew how people felt about cripples. His whole family had found out after his pa's accident.

"Can I help unharness the horse?" Ellen asked as they started down the front steps.

"You ought to stay inside where it's warm. I expect it's going to rain soon."

"I don't care. I like rain, and I like horses. I bet you got hundreds."

Salty halted at the bottom of the steps. "Not that many, but we probably have close to forty counting the foals we had last year."

"Sam—he was one of the men who worked for us—said big outfits had hundreds of horses."

"We only need that many when we do a cattle drive. You need to ask your ma if you can go with me to the barn."

"She won't mind."

"She doesn't know me or anybody else here. You've got to ask her."

Ellen's shoulders sagged and she turned back to head inside to the parlor. Salty assumed that meant she thought her mother wouldn't let her go, but she was back in less than a minute with a smile on her face.

"Mama says I can help you as long as I don't make a pest of myself. She's going to ask you later, so you got to tell her I was good."

Salty's eyes crinkled in amusement. "What if you're not?"

"I will be," Ellen assured him. "If I'm not, Mama will make me stay inside and wear a dress."

"Come on. I want to get done before the rain hits."

On the short walk from the house to the barn, Ellen barely stopped talking long enough to take a breath. Salty had never had a little sister or even a young female cousin. His father's farm had been rather isolated so he'd never met a girl like Ellen. All the females he knew wore dresses, and rarely talked about anything except babies and taking care of their men. Unless she changed a lot, Ellen wasn't going to be much interested in either.

"Hold up," Salty said when they reached the barn. "I want to put your ma's wagon inside."

"I wish we had a barn," Ellen informed him. "I could sleep there instead of in the house."

Salty opened the two big doors. "You wouldn't like it much. In summer it doesn't smell too good. In winter it's cold, and sometimes mice and snakes like to snuggle up for warmth."

"You're trying to scare me," Ellen said.

"Nope. Lead the horse in. We'll unharness him inside."

Once inside, Ellen's attention was caught by the stalls and the sections that housed ranch equipment. While Salty unharnessed the horse, she checked saddles, bridles, and harnesses. She spent longer inspecting several pairs of chaps before moving on to a wagon unlike any she'd ever seen. "What's this?" she asked.

"It's a chuck wagon," Salty told her. "It's for our drive this spring."

"I wish I could go on a cattle drive. Have you ever been on one?"

"Nope. The boys can't wait, but I'll take care of things here."

"Why would you do that?" He'd obviously come down a notch in Ellen's estimation.

"Because I don't like sleeping on the ground, breathing dust, eating food with grit in it, spending the whole day in the saddle, fighting off Indians and rustlers, or trying to break a stampede."

"Did you really fight Indians and rustlers?" Her eyes glowed with excitement.

"Yes, and it's not something I want to have to do again."

"Why not?"

"I did enough shooting and saw enough killing during the war. Do you want to see the bull? He's the reason George built this barn."

They went through a door at the far end of the barn. A chute led from the barn to a large pasture. "It took the better part of a month to fence in the pasture," Salty explained, "but the bull is too valuable to let roam free. We bring him in every night to keep him from being stolen."

Over the next twenty minutes Ellen peppered him with questions that made it clear she had become accustomed to doing the work that would normally have been her brother's. What's more, she seemed to like it. That confused Salty. He'd never seen a female who acted like she wanted to be a man. There wasn't much Rose couldn't do, but she didn't like cows and she was perfectly happy to confine herself to work around the house. He had no problem with a girl wanting to ride a horse or chase cows, but he didn't understand why a girl wouldn't want to be a *girl*. It would be tragic if doing what her brother couldn't do made her think of herself as more of a man than a woman. There was no place in Texas society for a woman like that.

"I think it's time you headed back to the house," Salty said after he'd explained a cattle drive in as much detail as he could provide. "If you want to know more about cows, ask Monty when he comes in. Hen can tell you everything you want to know about fighting Indians and rustlers.

They're George's twin brothers. I'm just a cowhand who likes working around the ranch."

He was sorry if that disappointed Ellen, but he never wanted to have to defend his ranch against Indians or rustlers. He didn't have to worry about that because he didn't have a ranch. Or the prospect of getting one. He didn't even have enough money to buy a pitifully small farm. He would probably end up working for George Randolph for the rest of his life.

———

"Now that my wife has satisfied her curiosity," George said to Sarah when she'd finished recounting her journey, "would you like to tell us what prompted you to undertake such a long trip? Am I right in assuming you meant to arrive here, that we're not merely a stop on a longer journey?"

Sarah had known this moment was coming. She had prepared what she was going to say, but she hadn't expected to meet a couple like George and Rose Randolph. She'd been invited into their home, had her comfort and that of her children made a priority. She didn't have to be told to know they would take a personal interest in her story.

"That's rather awkward to explain, and a little embarrassing."

"Then don't explain."

"I have to, or you won't understand why I need your help." She picked at an imaginary string on her dress. "I live on a large ranch I inherited from my father. My husband didn't come home from the war. I've hired several men over the last six years, but that hasn't worked out. I don't even know the size of my herd because they never had time to count them. Now I can't afford to pay anyone enough to work for us. If something isn't done soon, I'll lose the ranch." She paused. Once she uttered the next sentence, she could never take the words back. "My only alternative now is to marry again. A husband won't require the wages I can no longer afford to pay."

"Are you sure you have to do this?" Rose asked. "Don't you have family you could turn to?"

More embarrassment. It wasn't her fault Roger's family had abandoned her, but it felt like it. "My parents are dead, and Roger's family has turned their backs on us." She refused to embarrass Jared by disclosing that he was the reason for the estrangement.

"I would have thought you'd have had better luck finding a suitable husband in Austin," George said. "There are only a few single men working on ranches this far from town."

Sarah wanted to avert her gaze, turn away, leave the room, but she had come this far. There was no point in losing courage now. "I interviewed quite a few men for the job without letting them know that I had something more in mind. I stayed in Austin for nearly a week without finding a man I felt I could accept as a husband."

"It's not as simple as that, is it?" George asked. "You want someone who can help bind the family together."

"That's right." Sarah was immensely relieved that George understood. "I need someone who can help me make Ellen believe she might be happier growing up as a young woman than the son she thinks I need her to be. I'm more guilty than anyone else because I've depended on her so much." She turned to Jared. "And I need someone who can understand that Jared is a wonderful boy even though he can't do the things most boys can."

"That's what Rose did for my family," George said. "We wouldn't be here without her."

"Yes, you would," Rose contradicted. "Probably still fighting, wearing dirty clothes, and choking down Tyler's cooking, but you'd still be here."

Sarah wondered if it would ever be possible for a man to look at her the way George looked at Rose. She could cook, clean, wash, mend, and sew. She could work in the fields, put up food for the winter, dress meat, and make sausage. She could dance, sing a little, and carry on a conversation if it didn't wander too far from ordinary life. She believed she was capable of satisfying a man's physical appetites. Surely no man could expect more.

"Go on," George encouraged. "I didn't mean to interrupt you."

Sarah jerked her thoughts away from the impossible. "When I asked if there were any other men I might interview, I was told you employed the most capable and dependable men in the area. So that's why I'm here, to ask if you will help me convince your most capable and dependable man to marry me."

"Why should I do that?" George asked.

"You have no reason at all," Sarah said.

"Yes, we do," Rose said. "You need help, and we can give it to you."

"How?" George asked. "We don't have anyone who fits her requirements."

"We have the perfect man." Rose flashed a very satisfied smile and announced, "Salty. If you choose him, nothing will go wrong."

Sarah hoped her face didn't show her surprise. She'd found him attractive, but she didn't want a man she found appealing. That wasn't supposed to be part of the bargain. She didn't want any emotional attachment while they were married…or any emotional entanglement to deal with when she divorced him. Divorce wasn't common, and divorced women were often looked upon with a jaundiced eye, but Sarah was willing to take that risk rather than find herself and her children bound to a second husband like her first.

"I had someone older in mind, someone who'll be willing to commit to at least five years," Sarah said. "Salty is young enough to want to marry and start his own family."

"Salty's twenty-seven," George said. "There's only one older on the ranch. All the men who work for me were soldiers during the war."

She didn't want a soldier, either. The two she'd hired had been bitter, cynical, and given to drinking up their small wages. Worse than that, they'd had no understanding of Jared's handicap. They acted like he was faking. Their scoffing had driven him to a dangerous attempt to saddle a horse. He'd fallen in the corral, unable to get up. It was a miracle he hadn't been stepped on or kicked. She'd fired both men immediately, but the real damage had been done to Jared's self-esteem. How could he respect himself as a man when he couldn't saddle or ride a horse, something his sister did every day?

"I admit I barely know Salty," Sarah said, "but I don't think he's the kind of man to be interested in taking such a job."

"Why not?" Rose asked.

What to say? No one knew she didn't want to be married again. She'd been forced to marry Roger who'd mistreated her, turned his back on his son, then deserted his family. The physical side of their marriage had been a painful and humiliating experience she never wanted to repeat. The men in her life, from her father through to the men who'd worked for her, had been hard and unemotional with no respect for women beyond the creature comforts they could provide and no interest in children beyond the free labor they supplied.

Salty was different. He didn't have the age and experience necessary and didn't appear to have the gravity she preferred, but he had been respectful to her and kind to the children. A man like that would be dangerous. She might come to like him, to hope he wouldn't leave.

"I can't give you a concrete reason," Sarah said. "It's just the feeling I got."

"I think we ought to ask Salty," Rose said.

"Ask me what?"

Flushing with embarrassment, Sarah turned to see Salty standing in the archway.

THREE

"Mrs. Winborne is looking for someone to help her on her ranch," Rose explained. "I told her you were the perfect man for the job."

"Why me?" Salty asked, turning to George. "Are you dissatisfied with my work?"

"Of course not," George said. "I'd hate to see you leave, but I wouldn't want to do anything that would stand in your way."

"Stand in the way of what?"

"Mrs. Winborne's offer is a little out of the ordinary," Rose said. "I'll let her explain it. George, why don't you take Jared into the kitchen? I made gingerbread, which he might like. Then you can round up Zac and Tyler to help me with dinner."

Salty would have been happy to look for George's two youngest brothers himself, but it looked like there was no way out of this interview. He didn't know whether it would be kinder to tell Mrs. Winborne right away that he wasn't interested in leaving the Circle Seven, or allow her to explain her offer and then turn her down.

"I can tell you're uncomfortable with being put on the spot," Sarah said.

"A little," Salty agreed.

"I am, too, because I don't think you're quite what I'm looking for."

Salty had been prepared to say just that, but hearing the words coming from someone else affected him quite differently. Much to his surprise, he found himself saying, "Maybe not, but why don't you explain your proposal? I might be able to offer some suggestions."

What was he talking about? He knew nothing about this woman and her situation. Still, he entered the parlor and sat down in a straight back chair at a safe distance. He had a weakness for people in trouble, but he didn't want that to get him tangled up with Sarah and her brood.

"I own one of the largest ranches in Caldwell County," Sarah began. "My husband didn't come home from the war, and it's too big for me and the children to operate alone."

That was a familiar story, but most women in Sarah's position would have married again or sought refuge with family. He wondered why she hadn't.

"I've hired a succession of men to help with the ranch, but they never worked out for a variety of reasons."

"Why?" Knowing the problems she'd encountered might help him find a logical reason for turning her down.

"Some didn't want to work hard. Others were rude or rough with the children." She averted her gaze. "Some appeared to be more interested in me than in their work."

He had no trouble believing that. She was a very attractive woman. Any man working on a secluded ranch and seeing no other woman for weeks on end could be forgiven for becoming more than interested in her.

"Couldn't you find anyone in Austin to work for you?"

Sarah kept her gaze averted. "I'm not in a position to pay a wage that would induce anyone to work for me."

"Have you offered to let the men share some of the profits?"

"There haven't been any profits to share. Unless the situation improves, I'm going to lose the ranch. The bank president has done everything he can to hold off, but he can't much longer."

"Maybe it's time to ask your family for help."

Sarah's gaze locked with his. "My husband's family will only help if

I put Jared in an institution. If you've ever seen one of those places, you know why I could never do that."

Salty did know, but he also knew what it was like to have to deal with a handicapped person day after day. "So what do you propose to do?"

Sarah glanced away before turning back to Salty. He could practically see her gather her courage. That stiffness in her jaw returned. She sat up straighter, her back firm, her head up. "I'm proposing that the man marry me."

If she was willing to remarry, why hadn't she done so before now? From the look in her eye, the thought either frightened her or was repugnant. He felt sorry for any woman forced to barter herself in this fashion, but he couldn't think of a better inducement for a man to take on the responsibility of a failing ranch. Knowing he would have such a woman in his bed at night would be more than enough incentive for hundreds of men. He didn't understand why she hadn't been able to find anyone to accept her offer.

"There are two conditions," Sarah said. "First, the man will not share my bed."

Salty's eyebrows rose. Now he understood why she didn't have any takers. Working like a farm horse all day and being denied the comfort of your legal wife's body at night would be enough to drive a lot of men to do something drastic.

"Sorry, ma'am, but I don't see that you have any incentive to offer. It sounds like all work with nothing in exchange."

"That's not all. The man must agree to divorce me when the ranch has reached a certain degree of profitability."

Salty threw up his hands. "Whoa. You've just given a man every reason *not* to accept your proposal."

"In exchange for the divorce, I will give him half my ranch."

Surprise caused a quick intake of breath, a sudden jump in Salty's heart rate. What was left of his parents' farm had been directly in the path of General Sherman's march through Georgia. When the Union army moved on, they left nothing standing. Salty had been trying to accustom himself to the prospect of working for someone else for the rest of his life. He wasn't a tradesman and had no desire to live in a town. He'd saved everything he'd earned working for George, but the only land he'd be able to afford in the foreseeable future was much farther west where the Indians still roamed and it was too dry to farm.

"I can't believe you can't find anyone to take you up on your offer. Most ex-soldiers will never get the chance to own land."

"I haven't made the offer because I haven't found anyone I felt I could trust."

"Do you trust me?"

"I don't know you well enough to answer that question."

She was being evasive, not meeting his gaze, her hands twisting in her lap. She even shifted in her seat. Something was nagging at her, and he meant to find out what it was.

"Why did you come here instead of going to San Antonio? Surely you could have found dozens of men there eager to take you up on your offer."

She looked directly at him. "Nine men have worked for me in the six years since my husband left, but there wasn't one among them I would trust enough to marry. I came here because I was told George Randolph had hired some of the most trustworthy and dependable men in the area."

"If George thinks I'm dependable and trustworthy—you can ask him and Rose if you like—then you can, too."

She was avoiding his gaze again. He liked looking at her eyes. They were so large they seemed to dominate her face. They were an indeterminate shade that could go from blue to green depending on her setting. Or mood. They were impossible to ignore. They pulled you in.

"It's not just a matter of trust."

"What else?" She was hiding something, something she didn't want him to know.

"I don't think you're the right person."

"Why?" He wasn't going to give up easily. This was the chance he'd been hoping for since he left Georgia.

"You're too young."

"I expect I'm older than you."

"Probably, but you're young enough to want to marry and start your own family. I need someone who's beyond that. Besides, being young could present other problems."

"What problems?" He had an idea where she was going, but he wanted her to spell it out. She dropped her gaze to her lap and her hands started to twist again.

"Young men have...needs. I understand that, but it would be embarrassing to have a man presumed to be my husband consorting with women of that type."

"It wouldn't be a problem if everyone knew our marriage was simply a business arrangement."

She looked up. "You would be my legal husband. Who would believe you never entered my bed?"

She had a point. Women had few legal rights, wives virtually none and no protection against a husband.

"Why not make the same offer without marriage?"

"I have my reputation to consider. No one is going to believe a man can live with me for several years without..." She left the sentence unfinished. "If my reputation weren't enough, I have two children to consider. Anything that hurts me would hurt them even more. An older man, especially one who has had children of his own, would be better able to control his appetites and understand my children."

"Not every man is going to be able to understand your children's very different needs regardless of their age or if they've had children of their own. Jared needs to believe he's as much a man as anyone with two good legs. You've allowed Ellen to act like a boy for so long she doesn't know how to be a girl."

"She's only seven. She has plenty of time to learn to be a girl."

"Not when she's been brought up to value herself according to what we expect of a boy. Have you told her how pretty she is? Put her in a frilly dress?"

Stung by his criticism, Sarah met his gaze squarely. "I do *not* treat her like a boy, nor do I value her only for the work she does. I tell her she's pretty a dozen times a day. I've made dresses for her, but she won't wear them. *She* is the one who has decided that she must do the work that would normally be expected of Jared. *She* is the one who insists on taking care of him. When I've asked her why she feels she has to do so much, she tells me it's because she's been given the body Jared should have had. She knows better than anyone what being crippled has done to him." She didn't speak again until her breathing had slowed. "I'm sorry if I've spoken too forcefully, but I won't allow anyone to criticize my children."

Salty did a little mental backpedaling of his own. He hadn't meant to criticize her, only point out what he saw as problems. "I don't think my lack of years will be a bar in understanding your children," Salty said. "It might even be a help. They wouldn't see me as so different from them."

"For a seven-year-old, thirty is old."

"I'm only twenty-seven."

"You're older than I am."

"A man should be older than his wife."

"We're not talking about a normal husband-wife arrangement," Sarah reminded him.

"What if they start to like the man and feel about him as they would their father? Do you mean to tell them it's a marriage in name only?"

"Yes."

"How are they going to react?"

He could tell from her confusion she didn't have an answer to that. "I don't know, but I can't lie to them."

He had to give her credit for bedrock honesty. If she agreed to accept him, he would never be in doubt of where things stood between them. He didn't want any emotional entanglements, either. He believed people were incapable of living together peacefully. Sooner or later there would be another war somewhere. He had no intention of fathering sons to die anonymous deaths on some battlefield, be it distant or near.

"Are those your only objections to me?" he asked Sarah.

She stood and crossed to a window that provided a view of the lane leading up to the ranch house. Right now it was a rough path cut through the stark landscape. George and Jeff had already outlined plans for plantings of trees, shrubs, and flowers that would meld the house and its setting. They were still discussing what to do about the other buildings.

"This is rather difficult to say," Sarah said without turning around to face Salty. "I don't wish to hire anyone I find attractive. I'm no different from other women. I get lonely. You seem to be a very nice man. Once I get to know you, it's possible I might begin to think of a different kind of relationship." She turned around, her expression set. "My life has been controlled by men who took no thought for my comfort, wishes, or happiness. Things have been difficult since my husband left, but it has been *my* life. I want it to stay that way."

Salty was surprised a woman as pretty as Sarah would find him attractive. That hadn't occurred often. When it came to expressing any feeling that was important to him, his tongue would promptly tie itself in knots, and nothing he said would make any sense.

"Since you've put your cards on the table, it's only fair that I do the same," Salty said. "I think you're a very pretty woman, but I'm not much for romance. I can never think of sweet things to say, and I can't imagine why a man would want to sit out of an evening in the moonlight unless it's summer and it's hotter inside the house. You can stop worrying that I'll turn into some kind of lovesick calf. Even Rose says I'm a hopeless case."

Sarah's smile was strained. "It can't be that bad."

"Probably worse, but that's not all I wanted to say. Everything my family had was destroyed in the war. Taking you up on your offer is the best chance I'll ever have of getting some land of my own. A man needs something of his own just to call himself a man. If you'll pick me, I promise not to have a single romantical notion in my head. And if you start getting them, I'll be so cold and mean you'll get shut of them faster than a calf with a wolf on its tail can bleat for its mama."

Sarah's smile seemed genuine, but it didn't look like anything Salty had said had caused her to change her mind. He got to his feet.

"I've said my piece so I'll go. There are other fellas here, all good men. Maybe you'll find one of them more to your liking."

"It's not a matter of liking. It's—"

"I understand. I'm just not what you want."

She appeared about to say something else but didn't.

"I expect you'll want to join everybody in the kitchen. It's the last door down the hall on your right. You can't miss it. There's always some kind of commotion wherever Rose happens to be."

Salty left the room before she could say anything else. He had lost his chance. He practically ran down the front steps and was halfway to the bunkhouse before he could take his first full breath. He hadn't realized he was so tense. Sarah's proposal had taken him by surprise. He'd thought he'd accepted that he wasn't going to have the kind of land he wanted where he wanted it. He'd thought he was even looking forward to working for George. The brothers were a difficult and restless bunch, but he liked all of them, even Jeff. Sarah's offer of half her ranch had knocked over his carefully pieced together acceptance of what the future held for him because he wanted a chance to earn that land.

He knew the chance she was offering would mean years of back-breaking work. He was certain there would be times when he questioned his sanity in being married to a woman he found attractive but couldn't touch. There were already nights when need racked his body so hard he couldn't sleep, and being close to a woman like Sarah would intensify it several times over. Why should he set himself up for that kind of torture?

Because of the land, the chance to own something of his own.

He entered the bunkhouse and headed for the corner that had been his home since the last board was nailed in place a few months earlier. He'd thought he could be happy here, would be content to have his own bed, a place for all his belongings, and some wall to decorate if he wished. No more sleeping out in all kinds of weather. No more eating meals cooked over a campfire. He was working for a family he liked and a man he admired. What more could a penniless ex-soldier want?

He plopped down on his bed. It would take very little to make him happy. First was a place of his own. Next would be friends. He really didn't need anything after that. He knew what kind of responsibility a wife and family would be. If things had been different, he might have thought differently, but they weren't so there was no point in thinking about it.

His thoughts were interrupted by the sound of the bunkhouse door opening.

Walter Swain came in shivering and rubbing his hands together. "I was hoping you'd have a fire going. That wind is as sharp as a knife."

"No point in heating the bunkhouse when George will probably ask us to hang around after supper."

"I hope so." Walter walked to his bunk to take off his heavy coat and hang it up. "I get a chuckle out of some of the things Zac says."

Walter Swain, a forty-seven-year-old widower with two grown children, was a big, burly man who was as strong as an ox and as easygoing as a summer breeze. He never complained. He could work from dawn to dusk and get up the next day and do it again. He would work as hard as he must to make Sarah's ranch successful, would probably grow to be fond of her children, and was the kind of man who would be respected in any community. He didn't drink, saved his money, and never seemed to feel the loss of female companionship. He would become so much a part of her family she'd probably never ask him for a divorce. He'd be a friend and companion, a partner and confidant, but he'd never be the kind of husband a woman like Sarah deserved.

Of course, Sarah didn't want a husband. She wanted a friend and companion. She wanted a partner and confidant. Salty could be all of those, but he wouldn't get the chance because Sarah was attracted to him. It didn't seem fair that something which should have brought him pride would make him unhappy.

He had to figure out how to talk Sarah into changing her mind. She was too young to turn herself into a middle-aged woman, which was what marrying Walter would do. He didn't want her need for security to cut her off from being open to finding a man she could love and want to marry.

"Whose horse and wagon is that I saw in the barn?" Walter asked.

"A war widow and her two kids," Salty said. "I expect you'll meet them at supper."

"Any particular reason why she stopped here?" Walter pulled off his boots to put on the shoes he would wear up to the house.

"She's looking to hire someone to help her on her ranch."

"This is cow country."

"I expect she has cows, too."

"Why has she come here instead of Austin or San Antonio?"

"You'd better let her tell you that. I just met her myself."

"I'll look forward to meeting her. Maybe she'll have some news."

Walter didn't ask if the widow was young or pretty. That's why he would be perfect for her.

———————

Sarah had remained in her chair after Salty left, more shaken than she cared to admit. She had never had any trouble telling a potential hand that he didn't fit her needs. Nor had she had any trouble replacing them when they failed to do their job. So why did she feel bad about telling Salty he wasn't what she was looking for?

Okay, so she found him attractive. It wasn't like he was so handsome she'd dream about him tonight. She probably found him attractive because he seemed very nice, had a sense of humor, and had been kind to Jared and Ellen. She was, however, annoyed at him for thinking she'd treated Jared like an invalid while forcing Ellen to do the work usually expected of a boy. She'd done everything she could to treat her children normally, but her situation wasn't normal. There was no sense in taking herself to task over Salty's disappointment. If he was as hardworking and dependable as Rose said, he'd find a way to own his own land.

Rather than give herself an opportunity to continue to think about Salty, she left the parlor and headed for the kitchen. The voices coming through the open doorway made it easy to find. She paused in the doorway. Jared was sitting on a stool next to Rose. Ellen was on her other side, as interested as her brother in what Rose was doing.

"I don't usually do this," Rose was saying, "but you're company so I have an excuse."

"Don't people like them?" Jared asked.

"They like them too much. If Zac had his way, I'd never cook anything else."

"It sounds fascinating," Sarah said, entering the kitchen. "Who's Zac, and why wouldn't he want you to cook anything else?"

"She's making doughnuts," Ellen said, turning to her mother with a big smile. "She said she'd teach me how if I wanted."

"Zac is my husband's youngest brother," Rose told Sarah. "He's the same age as your children and spoiled beyond redemption."

Ellen and Jared were cutting the holes out of doughnuts and handing the dough back to Rose.

"You can see why I don't do this often," Rose said. "George has five brothers and we have three hands just now. With the three of you, that makes twelve. At two doughnuts each, that's two dozen."

"You have that many already," Sarah pointed out.

"They'll want a couple more before they go to bed. They'd eat a dozen apiece if I'd let them."

Sarah felt a pang that she'd never made doughnuts with her children, but there had been no time or money for anything as frivolous as that. Over the next half hour, Sarah helped Rose cook the doughnuts in a pot of boiling fat. As soon as the doughnuts were laid out to cool, Jared and Ellen sprinkled them with sugar. When they were done, the children counted forty-two.

"I think that's enough for one day," Rose said, surveying their work. "Now we have to put them in a tin before Zac and Tyler come in to help me with supper. Jared, I'm going to put you in charge of the tin. You're not to let Zac or any of the others have a doughnut until after supper. Would you do that for me?"

"How am I supposed to stop them?"

Rose handed over a large wooden spoon. "Give them a whack with this. That ought to slow them down."

Jared looked at the spoon like it was a rattlesnake.

Rose pressed it into his hand. "I haven't been able to figure out how to keep Zac and Tyler from stealing sweets," she said. "Zac has mastered the art of putting a whole cookie in his mouth and still being able to talk. I tell him he's got pouches in his cheeks like a squirrel."

Sarah couldn't imagine having a child behave like that. She had done exactly what she was told as a child. On the few occasions she hadn't, the punishment had been quick and harsh. Her own children had never required punishment. Jared wasn't able to get in trouble, and Ellen never thought of anything except helping take care of her brother and helping with the ranch in any way she was able.

"It's time to think about fixing supper," Rose said. "I wonder where the boys are."

"I'll be glad to help," Sarah offered.

"You're company."

"Company that wasn't invited. I insist on helping."

"I'm not sure I could get anything done with that many people in the kitchen."

"Let Zac and Tyler have the day off."

"If I did that, they'd be wanting a day off all the time. You don't know what it's like having to deal with six Randolph men. You can't give them an inch."

Sarah didn't know quite how to take Rose's remarks. She doubted Rose was one to suffer mistreatment. Besides, she'd made her complaints with humor instead of rancor.

A commotion caught her attention, and she turned just in time to see a handsome but disheveled urchin burst into the kitchen. "I smell doughnuts," he announced. His gaze swept the room looking for the source of the tantalizing aroma.

"Rose said she was never making doughnuts again after you stole so many last time." This from a tall, skinny boy who entered on the first one's heels.

"I smell them," the boy said. "I know they're here."

"They're in this tin," Jared announced, much to Sarah's surprise. "Rose said I'm to whack you with this spoon if you try to steal one."

The boy turned his full attention on Jared. "I don't know who the hell you are, but get ready to die."

FOUR

Rose took the boy by the ear. "This impudent rascal is Zac," she said to Jared. "Pay no attention to him. His bark is worse than his bite."

"I don't bark and I don't bite," Zac announced as he wiggled free. "I just shoot people."

"Go get the wood," Rose said, pointing to a box in the corner, "or I'll give your doughnuts to Monty."

"You can't," Zac protested. "He'd eat 'em."

"Then you'd better hurry with that wood. The sooner I fix supper, the sooner you'll get your doughnuts. The tall one who's going for water is Tyler," Rose said to Sarah. The boys had left as quickly as they'd entered. "You've probably heard the only words he'll speak all evening."

Sarah had never been allowed to run outside much less inside the house. She'd had to keep her voice low and speak only when addressed. She had no idea what her mother would have done with a boy like Zac. Her father would have broken an endless string of sticks on his back until he'd broken his spirit. It was clear no one had broken Zac's, though he obeyed Rose without question.

"I really would like to help," Sarah said.

"Okay," Rose said, relenting. "I'll tell you what I'm planning to fix, and we can divide the dishes between us."

The next hour was unlike anything Sarah had ever experienced. It was soon obvious that Rose knew what every person in the kitchen was doing even though she never seemed to take her eyes off her own work. She kept Zac and Tyler busy fetching and carrying, setting the table and filling glasses with milk or water, and setting out cups for coffee. Tyler made the coffee while Zac brought out bowls and laid out serving spoons. The whole time he kept an eye on Jared and the tin containing the doughnuts. Once everything was done and on the table, Rose told Zac, "Tell everybody it's time to eat."

Remembering how the two boys had entered the kitchen, Sarah was prepared for a stampede, but seven men entered quietly and waited for Rose to explain the new seating arrangement. Sarah could tell the men had washed, combed their hair, and put on fresh shirts. It was a revelation. These men were so different from her father and husband. Could she come to like a man like that?

She put that question out of her mind. She'd already decided against Salty.

Rose introduced everyone at the table. It was hard to take her eyes off the twins—they were as striking in their similarity as in their differences—but she forced herself to concentrate on Walter Swain. She eliminated George's other cowhand because he was even younger than Salty.

As the meal progressed, she was more and more favorably impressed by Walter. He was open, genial, and apparently well-liked. His looks were average, but she wasn't looking for an attractive candidate. She was impressed that he didn't give her any more attention than he would any other stranger he was meeting for the first time. His enjoyment of Zac's high spirits led her to believe he might become a good father figure for Jared and Ellen. He wasn't as tall as Salty, but he was solid and well-built. He looked like a man who could hold up under the hard work necessary to save her ranch.

She was aware that Rose and George had noticed the direction of her gaze. George surely couldn't like the idea that she was hoping to take away his best and most dependable man. Still, she hadn't seen any indication that he was angry or upset over her proposal.

"Why doesn't everyone move to the parlor while the twins clean up?" Rose said when the doughnuts had been eaten and everyone started to leave the table. Zac was out of his seat before the last word left her mouth. "There are more doughnuts for everybody, so no sneaking off to the bunkhouse. Walter, Mrs. Winborne has a proposal that might interest you. Why don't you show her into George's office and let her tell you about it?"

Even though Sarah had been trying to think of a way to speak to Walter, Rose's suggestion took her by surprise. She didn't know why she should have looked at Salty at that moment. She turned away just as quickly, but not before she read his expression. Resignation. He was certain she was going to choose Walter. There was no reason for her to feel she was taking something from him, but she did.

"I'll be happy to speak with Mrs. Winborne if George has no objection," Walter said.

"It could be a good opportunity for you," George said.

Walter had to be curious, even a little confused, but if he felt it, nothing showed. Sarah considered that a good sign as well. He was a man who could take surprises or unexpected turns in stride. That was good because there would be plenty of both.

Sarah was surprised to find she didn't feel entirely comfortable being in a room alone with Walter. There was nothing she could put her finger on, but being alone with him lacked the ease she'd felt with Salty. Walter settled into a chair a comfortable distance from her and waited for her to begin.

"I feel a little awkward talking to a man I don't know," Sarah began.

"Would you like me to start by telling you something about myself?"

"I'd appreciate that."

His background was exactly what Sarah was looking for, but she found herself comparing it to Salty's. That was stupid and pointless, but she couldn't stop herself.

"That's about it," Walter said when he'd brought his story up to the present. "Is there anything else you wanted to know?"

"No. Thank you for being so open."

Walter's smile was fatherly. "There's nothing unusual about my story. There are probably a hundred men in Austin and San Antonio like me."

Maybe, but she hadn't found any of them.

"Now how about you telling me about this proposal of yours."

Sarah didn't want to have to bare the story of her life, but he had a right to know why she was in the position of having to hire a pretend husband. It was hard to tell him about her marriage, but Walter showed nothing but sympathy for her situation. By the time she was finished, she felt like she was talking to an old friend. "I think that's everything. Do you have any questions?"

"Are you sure you want to do this?"

That wasn't the question she'd expected. "After what I've said, why do you ask?"

"A pretty young woman like you should be looking for a husband, not a man old enough to be your father."

"I don't want a husband. I mean, not a *real* husband. I don't want any man to control my life ever again."

"Not every man is like your father or your husband. I'm certain you could find a dozen young men who'd treat you like a princess."

Sarah didn't want to be treated like a princess, either. She wanted to be treated as an equal, one whose opinions would be listened to, whose wishes would be valued. She'd been in control of her life for six difficult and frightening years. She wasn't willing to go back to being treated like a possession.

"Giving up your chance for a normal marriage is a big step," Walter said.

"I'm determined to be the only one in control of my life. I'll need something in our agreement that says while you're legally my husband, you'll have no authority over me."

"That might be awkward to put into some kind of legal language. It would probably be easier to keep it as an understanding between us. Or the man you choose."

It probably *would* be difficult to find the right language, but she wanted something in the agreement that protected her. She had no reason to distrust Walter, but she had plenty of reason to distrust men.

"Would you be interested in my proposition?" she asked.

"Any man would be interested," Walter said with another of his fatherly smiles. "I hadn't been thinking of having a place of my own again, but a man likes to feel he's in control of his life, too. I'll need to talk to George first though."

"Take your time. I haven't made up my mind yet."

That seemed to take him by surprise. "I didn't realize you'd talked to anyone else."

"Just Salty. The other cowhand is younger than I am."

"Salty is a good man," Walter said. "And much closer to your age."

"That's not a consideration."

Walter paused a moment before saying, "I guess that's all I need to know. You'll let me know when you've made your decision?"

"Of course."

He rose. "You're fortunate to be able to call the Randolphs your friends."

Sarah nearly blurted out that she'd never met the Randolphs until a few hours ago. She wasn't sure what kept her quiet. She nodded and waited for Walter to leave the office.

The moment he closed the door, she fell back in her chair. He couldn't have been nicer, and he was exactly the kind of man she was looking for, so why had she been so tense? Why did she feel relieved he was gone? Maybe she was tense because she was about to make a decision that would affect her family for years to come. Maybe it was the result of meeting so many new people in such a short time. It could be that she was tense because she was on strange ground. Perhaps she was simply exhausted and would feel much more like herself tomorrow. More likely she was worried because she didn't know how her children were going to react when she told them what she had done. In some ways, her choice would have more impact on them than her.

Giving up all hope of figuring out what was bothering her, she was about to get up when she heard a knock on the door and Salty came in.

"I saw Walter leave. Do you want to join the rest of us?"

She would have preferred to be alone so she could clear away some of the fog in her mind. "Are you sure the men wouldn't prefer their own company?"

Salty smiled in a way that caused a flutter in her chest. "We have more than enough of our own company. Visitors are always welcome, especially when they're as pretty as you. Since we've *never* had a visitor like you, that makes you really special."

No one had ever told Sarah she was special. It was a concept she had difficulty absorbing. Was she special only because she was a female and reasonably attractive? Probably, but she intended to enjoy the feeling. It wouldn't last long.

"What do you do in the evening?" Sarah asked Salty.

"Sometimes we talk about things we did during the day or ranch business in general, but mostly we listen to the twins tease Zac. It'll be a real treat to listen to someone else."

Sarah felt something akin to panic. She had nothing to say that could interest a man like George Randolph. Zac and Tyler probably knew more about running a ranch than she did. Neither her father nor her husband had ever wanted her opinion. Everything she knew had been learned by trial and error or by picking the brains of hired men who made no attempt to hide their disgust at her ignorance.

"I'm sure they don't want to listen to me."

"That's where you're wrong. Ellen and Jared have made everyone curious to know more about you."

What could her children have been saying? She'd always cautioned them to be careful what they said around strangers, but they had virtually no experience with strangers, especially not a woman like Rose who treated both of them as normal children and fed them doughnuts. They'd never been around a spirited child like Zac, a charming boy who was bubbling over with enjoyment of life. He made everyone laugh and want to join in the fun. You wanted to throw off all restraints because Zac had none and was having more fun than you had ever thought was possible.

"There's nothing interesting about me," she said.

"How often do you have women showing up at your ranch wanting to hire a man to marry her?"

She wouldn't have put it quite that way, but she could see his point. "That makes me unusual, not interesting."

"Ma'am, anything unusual is interesting. Now are you going to join us?"

More than ever she wanted to be by herself, but apparently she was to be the night's entertainment. "Only if you promise not to expose my ignorance."

She couldn't quite make up her mind what she thought of Salty's expression. It could have been a mixture of surprise, amusement, and disappointment that she would think so badly of him. Deciphering the expressions of people she didn't know was a guessing game that was liable to put her in the wrong more often than not.

"If we don't hurry, Rose is going to send somebody after us. If we're lucky, it will be Tyler. He hardly ever talks. If we aren't, it will be Monty.

He makes up stuff just for the fun of it."

"Come sit by me," Rose said when Sarah entered the room. "Everybody has joined forces against me."

"She says she hates cows and doesn't think much of horses," Ellen said to her mother. "And she has a whole ranch full of them."

"I've tried to point out that I married my husband *in spite of* his cows and his horses," Rose clarified.

"I think she married George in spite of us," Monty said.

"She certainly married him in spite of you," Jeff said.

Sarah had noticed at supper that Jeff was missing his left arm. She wondered if he'd lost it during the war. She wanted to like him, at least be sympathetic, but his expression was so forbidding even some of his brothers avoided him.

Rose laughed. "I married him in spite of *all* of you."

"She didn't marry George in spite of me," Zac announced. "She loves me."

Everyone laughed, but Sarah hadn't missed the angry glance Monty threw at Jeff, or the glance George gave Jeff that caused him to shrug his shoulders and look away.

Sarah enjoyed watching the brothers tease Zac because it was so clear he enjoyed the attention. It made her sad that Jared had no older brothers whose love was strong enough to overlook his physical imperfection. Neither Jeff's injury nor his bitterness had been enough to prevent him from being a valued member of the family.

"Did you find anything interesting when you were in Austin?" George asked Sarah during a lull in the conversation.

"I don't know much, but I do know I don't like the Reconstruction. They tried to tell me I owed a lot more taxes than I did."

Monty's laugh was angry. "They did the same to us, but Rose sent them packing."

"What did you do about the taxes?" Rose asked Sarah.

"I told them they'd have to see the president of the bank because he held the mortgage. They never bothered me after that."

"That was right clever," Salty said.

"Of course she's clever," Rose said. "She's a woman."

That got a good-natured laugh from everybody, as well as a slighting remark from Monty and a spirited rebuttal from Zac.

"I knew you'd defend Rose," Monty said, teasing, "because she spoils you."

"She'd spoil you too, if you weren't so mean."

That generated another round of mirth.

The talk turned general with all the brothers except Tyler taking a part. It wasn't hard to see that though there were many sharp edges in the brothers' relationships, they were bound by a love that enabled them to look beyond their differences. Sarah had never known it was possible for men to do that. If her father and husband had been like any of these men, her life would have been immeasurably different. She was still thinking of that when Rose announced she was tired and was going to bed.

"We haven't had our doughnuts," Zac reminded her.

"You don't need me to eat doughnuts, do you?" she asked the boy.

"You have to eat *your* doughnuts."

"I think I'll save mine."

"If you don't eat them now, Monty will get them."

"Tell on me, will you?" Monty grabbed for Zac, but knowing where to find the safest place in the room, the boy had already ducked behind Rose.

"Salty, will you get the doughnuts from the kitchen?" Rose asked. "I wouldn't trust Zac or Monty not to eat half of them before they got back. Jared will show you where I put them."

Sarah's heart jumped into her throat. Her gaze flew to Jared, who looked stricken. Why would Rose do something that would expose Jared's weakness to everybody in the room? She was about to make an objection when Salty got up, went over to Jared, and held out his hand.

"Let me help you up."

Sarah held her breath when Jared reached for Salty's outstretched hand. Taking a firm grasp, Salty pulled her son out of the chair and to his feet. Once Jared had his balance, Salty picked him up. Sarah couldn't decide whether she was still angry or whether she was so relieved to see that no one seemed to pay any attention. She had always tried not to draw attention to Jared's leg, while keeping him busy with the things he could do. The Randolphs had apparently done the same with Jeff's arm. She wondered if he rode a horse or was limited to a buckboard. He didn't have the look of a man who avoided hard work. She wondered how he did it. Maybe Salty would tell her.

She was reassured a moment later to see Salty and Jared return. More important, he had a look of happiness on his face. Salty allowed Jared to settle back in his chair before handing him the tin.

"Jared is going to parcel out the doughnuts," Rose said. "He has my permission to penalize anyone who tries to take more than two."

"You'd better watch Monty," Zac warned. "He likes doughnuts better than girls."

"I don't like anything better than girls," Monty said, "but Ellen is too young and I'm afraid of her mother."

Sarah raised an eyebrow, but Monty only winked at her.

Zac jumped in front of everyone else, but the brothers kept picking him up and passing him back to the next person in line. Even Jeff entered into the fun. Zac made it known that he thought it was unfair that he was the last one to get his doughnuts, but when he looked in the tin and found there were only three left for him and Jared, his attitude changed. He took one doughnut, broke a second and handed half to Jared.

"I don't mind sharing." He cast an evil glance at his brothers. "The littlest kid never gets treated fair."

That brought an outcry from his brothers who promptly offered him part of their doughnuts. Zac ended up with twice what anybody else got, but he was generous enough to share his bounty with Jared. And Jared was greedy enough to accept.

Watching the whole exchange brought tears to Sarah's eyes. She had never imagined families could be like this. There were differences of temperament and inequities all around, but their love for each other bound them together. She didn't know how she was going to do it, but that's what she wanted for her children.

"Is anything wrong?"

FIVE

Sarah had forgotten that Salty had been watching her closely since she and Walter entered the parlor. She wiped away a tear. "No. I'm just a bit emotional. I don't think I realized how tired I am."

"Then you'll go straight to bed," Rose said. "If your children want to stay up a little longer, I'll make sure they get to bed."

"I couldn't ask you to do that."

"It's no problem. Jared is going to share a bed with Zac. I'm putting Ellen in the room I'm saving for the baby."

"Whose bed am I taking?"

"I offered up mine, ma'am," Monty said. "I don't mind sleeping in the bunkhouse. That way I don't have to listen to Hen snore."

"Hen doesn't snore," Zac said, "but you do."

This time Monty caught Zac before he could take refuge behind Rose or George. Monty tickled him—Zac shrieking he was going to pee in his pants—until Rose asked him to stop.

"Next time I'll catch you when neither Rose nor George is around," Monty threatened.

"I'll hide in the henhouse."

"Behave," Rose said. "What will Sarah think of you?"

"Just that I wish I'd had brothers like them."

Much to Sarah's surprise, that embarrassed the men so much they scrambled to get ready to leave.

"Men don't handle emotion well," Rose explained to Sarah as she was showing her to her room. "They show their affection for each other by verbal abuse and wrestling. Don't ask me to explain it. Men are strange creatures, my men probably strangest of all."

"I hate to force Monty to sleep in the bunkhouse."

"You're giving him a treat," Rose said with a laugh. "Living inside and having to wash and watch what he says is a severe trial to him. If I didn't keep his room straight, you wouldn't be able to get past the door."

The room Sarah entered was too Spartan for her taste, but it was clean and neat. There was nothing on the walls, and the only furniture was a plain bed, a plain wardrobe, a small table, and a single chair. The only object out of place in the room was her own small valise.

"Monty insisted on minimal furnishings. I saw no reason not to indulge him. I'll have one of the boys bring up a pitcher and basin. Monty prefers to use the pump outside."

"You don't have to bother."

Rose grinned. "It's no bother. I'll have Tyler do it. What's the use of doing for eight men if you have to run your own errands?"

After Rose left, Sarah set the small kerosene lamp on the table. Since she had to wait until Tyler brought the water to begin undressing, she crossed to the window and looked out. The sky was clear except for a few small clouds that rolled slowly from west to east. A three-quarters moon provided enough light to make out the dark hulk of the bunkhouse. It seemed like an unlikely place for a man to prefer to a room in his own house. She wondered if Salty preferred it.

She turned away from the window. Why was she thinking about Salty when she should be thinking about Walter? He filled every one of her requirements as well has having none of the disadvantages. By asking him to meet with her, George and Rose had vouched for his character. She should be relieved and grateful rather than trying to find an explanation for this increasingly strong feeling she was making a mistake. She had found exactly the kind of man she was looking for, and he seemed interested in accepting her offer.

She dropped down on the bed with a grunt of disgust. In actuality, she didn't have to look far for the source of her disquiet, her dissatisfaction, her inability to focus her thoughts on Walter; her attraction to Salty was so strong it had thrown her thinking out of balance.

Sarah got to her feet, determined to put Salty out of her mind. She picked up her valise, placed it on the bed, and opened it. There wasn't much inside beyond her night clothes. Neither she nor the children had more than three complete changes of clothes—two for work and one for company. Everything else had been worn out by hard use and frequent washing.

She was relieved to hear a knock. She opened the door to find Tyler standing there with the promised water and basin which he held out to her. When she took them, he turned and left without speaking. An odd boy, made even more unusual by being so tall and thin.

It didn't take long to wash and put on her night clothes. After putting out the lamp, she let her body sink into the mattress with a sigh of pleasure. She couldn't understand why Monty would prefer the bunkhouse to this bed. It was so soft she was sure she would oversleep if she didn't leave the curtain open for the morning sun to wake her.

Grateful for the barrier against the night cold, Sarah pulled the thick quilt up to her chin. She was afraid she would lie awake fretting over her fascination with Salty, but once her body heat had warmed the bed, she sank blissfully into a deep sleep.

She was mortified to find that everyone was up by the time she got dressed and down to the kitchen. "Why didn't you wake me?" she asked Ellen who was busy cutting out biscuits, something she never did at home.

"Mrs. Randolph said to let you sleep."

Jared looked up from where he was cracking eggs into a large bowl. "Mrs. Randolph said with all of us helping, you'd only be in the way."

Zac was cutting sausage while Tyler was grinding coffee. The aroma of roasted beans that filled the room brought back memories of Sarah's mother's kitchen when she was a little girl. But rather than the atmosphere of cheerful industry that filled Rose's kitchen, Sarah remembered an urgency to get the meal prepared quickly, the fear her father would find something wrong with it.

"I could set the table."

"That's my job," Zac said without looking up from his work.

"Put food in bowls and carry them to the table."

"I do that." Tyler sounded as protective of his job as Zac.

"You can cook the eggs as soon as Jared is finished cracking them," Rose said. "I have to fry the rest of the sausage and keep an eye on the apples to make sure they don't burn."

Not to mention what looked like a pot of grits and a pan of beef and gravy. Sarah had never seen so much food, nor had she ever had to cook about two dozen eggs. Even after dividing them into two batches, it felt more like she was stirring a pot of soup. When the first pan was done, she turned to ask for a platter only to find Tyler had already placed one at her elbow. By the time she finished the second batch of eggs, the first biscuits were out of the oven and the rest of the food was on the table.

The men, who'd apparently been waiting to be called, came in talking and laughing. In a matter of moments everyone was seated, every platter or bowl had been passed around the table, and hot biscuits were dripping with butter or wrapped around a sausage. The sound of talk and laughter had been replaced by that of spoons in bowls, forks scraping plates, and of sugar and/or cream being stirred into cups of hot coffee.

"I hope you aren't bothered by the quiet," Rose said to Sarah. "To a cowboy, nothing is more important than eating."

"I'm not bothered at all," Sarah replied. "I'm used to it." Her father had never allowed conversation when he was eating, and Roger had been interested only in his own opinions.

The quiet ended as soon as everyone was through with their first servings. Sarah was intrigued to note that while everything had been passed only to the right when the meal started, bowls and platters were passed the quickest way when it came to seconds. Or thirds. Monty seemed to have a hollow leg.

As soon as their appetites were satisfied, the men turned back to their conversations over coffee. George parceled out the duties for the day. He listened to suggestions or objections and made a few changes. Once the work assignments were settled, the men swallowed the last of their coffee and left as a group.

"What can we do to help clean up?" Sarah asked Rose.

Rose surveyed the kitchen. "Zac can hand the plates to Jared. Once he's scraped them, Ellen can stack them on the counter."

"I can wash the dishes if Tyler will dry while you put away the food," Sarah suggested.

"Ellen can help Zac put the food away. Meanwhile, I'll set Jared to shelling some dried peas for supper."

It was impossible to have six people in a kitchen without getting in each other's way from time to time, but everything was washed, dried, and put away in a short period of time.

"Now it's my turn to relax with a cup of coffee," Rose said to Sarah. "Want to join me?"

Sarah would have liked nothing better, but that would keep Rose from the nap she'd promised George she would take.

"There's nothing much to do until it's time to fix supper. Until I have this baby, the men have to clean their own rooms. The twins stay home on the day I do the washing, and Zac and Tyler do everything else before they can join their brothers. George will help any time I ask."

"That's all the more reason I shouldn't be causing you extra work," Sarah said.

"Pshaw," Rose said. "When you have to cook for ten, three

additional mouths don't make much difference. Besides, it's worth it to have a woman to talk to. Do you know what it's like to be confined to a ranch with only men for months at a time? George and his brothers do their best, but they understand their cows better than they understand women."

From what Sarah had seen, she'd have traded any one of them for her husband. "I think you're fortunate."

"Oh, I know that," Rose said, "but I can't let them know it. I wouldn't get half as much work out of them."

Sarah had seen enough to know it was love rather than guilt that caused the men to help Rose. She felt guilty for being jealous that Rose had something in such abundance that she'd never had at all.

"Now stop worrying. Tyler is taking Ellen to see the horses, and Zac has offered to show Jared around the ranch in his pony cart."

Sarah gave in. "You sit and I'll get the coffee. I'm as starved for female conversation as you. A seven-year-old girl is no substitute."

For the next hour Sarah talked about things she hadn't talked about in years, and over the course of that time their conversations moved from the general to the particulars of having a baby. It eased some of Sarah's burden of guilt that she could, in a small way, step into the role of the sister or cousin Rose didn't have.

Once they'd exhausted the subjects of childbirth, breast feeding, teething, and the best time to start toilet training, Rose asked Sarah, "Have you decided which man to choose?"

The abruptness of the question caught Sarah by surprise. "Yes, I have."

"But you're not happy about it?"

By now she shouldn't be surprised by Rose's powers of perception. "No, I'm not, but I'm just acting silly."

"Does that mean your brain and heart aren't in agreement?"

"How did you know?"

"It's a situation every woman finds herself in sooner or later. Men figure out the most practical solution and they're happy. We women want to go with our hearts first and hope the practical follows along."

"And if it doesn't?"

"I can't answer that."

"What did you do when you married George?"

"I followed my heart, but I took the job of housekeeper because I didn't have another choice."

Sarah was getting married because she didn't have any other choice. For that reason she had to be very careful when she chose the man to marry. She would be handing over a lot of legal rights she was depending on him not to exercise.

Rose lifted her bulk from her chair. "It's time I took my promised nap. George is going to want to know how long I slept. Why don't you take a nap, too?"

"I'm too keyed up."

"Then take a walk. If you'd like to ride, Tyler will saddle a horse for you and show you around."

"I don't want to get in the way."

"You won't. We don't get many visitors out here so we like to enjoy the ones we have."

"You've been more than generous."

"Nonsense. You saved me a trip to Austin to restore my sanity."

After Rose left the kitchen, Sarah washed the cups and rinsed the coffeepot. Once she had looked around to make sure there was nothing else she could do, she decided to follow Rose's suggestion that she take a walk. She'd spent her whole life on her father's ranch, but she still felt she didn't know enough about running one. Maybe she could learn something here that would help her turn the corner. Even a small advantage could be crucial to their survival.

The weather had changed overnight and the day was clear and

bright with only a mild breeze. It was one of those refreshing days when the sun was warm, and the air was crisp, when it felt good to be alive. Standing on the front porch, she let her gaze sweep over the land from the packed dirt that formed the yard to the hills that met the distant horizon. Seeing the land lie quiet before the burst of cosmic energy that would bring it to life in a few weeks, it didn't look like a place that would harbor hostile Indians or Cortina's raiders. It appeared far too welcoming to conceal poisonous snakes, nearly impenetrable thickets of bushes and vines armed with vicious thorns, or arid soil that refused to support the nourishing grass her cows needed or the fruits and vegetables her family needed.

Shutting out the dispiriting images, she walked down the steps and turned toward the barn. She was less than halfway there when Salty came out. She had thought her attraction to him was something she could easily overcome, but this morning it hit her with numbing force. She stopped, hoping he wouldn't see her, but there was nothing to conceal her from his view. When he waved, her arm didn't wait for a conscious command before giving an answering wave. She started forward, dragging her feet, because each step increased the attraction she was trying to forget.

"What are you doing out here?" he asked when she drew near.

"Just looking."

"I can show you around. What would you like to see?"

"I'm not sure." She wasn't thinking. "The barn," she said, latching onto the most obvious. "Why did George build it? I've never seen anything like it in Texas."

Salty turned toward the rectangular structure. "George grew up in Virginia where everyone had barns. He's not comfortable without one, but it was also practical. The bull is too valuable to be left out, and a shed doesn't offer much protection. It's also where we keep the saddles, bridles, chaps, and all the equipment we need for the ranch, as well as

Rose's buckboard." Salty pushed open the door. "Take a look inside."

A medley of aromas greeted Sarah. Leather and saddle oil competed with the odor of manure. Less prominent were the smells of new wood, moist earth, and hay. The door at the far end was open, giving a contrast of bright light, shade, and deep shadows.

"I let the bull out every morning before breakfast and bring him in before I go to bed. We're pasture breeding him."

Sarah could see the bulk of the animal resting in the shade of a live oak. She recognized some of the cows as longhorns, but the others were unfamiliar. "What kind of cows are those?" she asked.

"They're some we got from Richard King in exchange for our bull's calves. King is experimenting with new breeds."

She tried to concentrate on the rest of the barn rather than trying to think of a way to pay for one of this bull's calves. Even that frustrating exercise was better than allowing herself to think of the effect on her of Salty's nearness. What was it about this man that wouldn't allow her to ignore him? He wasn't devastatingly handsome. He was too tall and thin to be a grand physical specimen like George Randolph. He didn't have a commanding way about him. He wasn't so full of energy that it radiated out from him. He was just a man. You could pass him on the street and not notice him.

Well, somebody else could, but it was obvious she couldn't. Being with him in a barn talking about saddles and manure was the most exciting thing that had happened to her in years. What was wrong with her?

"Do you want to see the bunkhouse?" Salty asked.

Sarah collected her wandering thoughts. "I doubt the other men would like that."

"They won't care."

She allowed him to show her the bunkhouse, the corral where they kept their horses, and the shed where the bull used to stay. Even the chicken house. She probably would have followed him to the pigpen, but he said he thought it was better to skip that. The more she listened to him, the more she wanted him to keep talking. She loved his enthusiasm, his optimism, the pleasure he took in his work. Most of all, she loved his laugh. She couldn't remember the last time she or her children had laughed.

It appeared Salty could find a reason to laugh at anything. At the small pair of chaps Rose had given Zac on his last birthday. At the lazy bull showing no interest in the cows he was to impregnate. At a pullet fleeing the attentions of a rooster. The only time she'd seen him frown was when she told him he didn't fit her requirements. They ended up in a large garden where the fruit trees were beginning to bud.

"George leaves the garden to Rose and me. He says he got enough blisters digging the first one to last a lifetime."

Salty showed her where beans, peas, squash, and a dozen other vegetables would be planted in the days ahead. "Not everything we had in Georgia likes Texas soil or the heat, but I'm determined to find a way to grow apples and peaches."

Sarah had never seen an apple or a peach. The only fruits she had tasted were berries that grew wild.

"I expect I'll have the garden pretty much to myself until George hires someone else," Salty said.

"Why?"

"Rose will be busy with the baby, and Walter will be with you."

Sarah could hear the disappointment in his voice. She wanted to say something, do something, but nothing came to mind. She knew what she had to do. Despite her attraction to Salty, she had to choose Walter.

"I'd better get back up to the house," she said. "I promised to help Rose." Did he look disappointed? "Thanks for showing me around. I know it was time you'd probably have preferred spending doing your work."

"My work will always be here. I haven't had a chance to spend this much time with a pretty woman since before the war."

"I intend to tell Rose what you said." It was a poor effort at humor, but it was the best she could do. Fortunately, it earned a smile.

Salty corrected himself. "I should have said 'a pretty woman who wasn't married and expecting a baby.'"

"You're a very nice man. I hope you find a woman who's as nice as you," Sarah said impulsively. Then she turned and hurried toward the house before she could see Salty's reaction. Whatever it might have been, she didn't want the burden of remembering it.

Sarah had grown increasingly nervous as the meal progressed. An afternoon spent helping Rose hadn't been able to distract her from the decision she kept making over and over again. It seemed she only had to think *I will do this*, and a dozen reasons why she should do the opposite would spring to mind.

Other than saying that Salty had shown her around the ranch, she was spared questions at the supper table about her decision because the children were so full of what they'd done that day they couldn't stop talking. While she was pleased that Ellen had been allowed to ride any horse she wanted, she was thrilled that Zac had taken Jared over what sounded like half the ranch. Jared had rarely been a hundred feet from his front door. He must have felt like he'd been given the world.

"Tyler said I could ride better than him or Zac," Ellen told her mother.

"She hasn't seen me ride," Zac protested.

"I have," Tyler said.

Zac looked willful. "I don't care about horses. I'm going to New Orleans when I get big."

"If you don't stop yapping and eat, I'll send you there," Monty warned.

"Leave him alone," Rose said. "The day will come when you'll wish he was still here."

Monty laughed. "I'm not crazy."

"Jared said he'd like to go to New Orleans, too," Zac informed everybody. "We plan to open a gambling hall together."

Sarah didn't know whether Jared's flushed cheeks were the result of embarrassment over Zac's obvious exaggeration, or pleasure at being included in such an undertaking, which was something that had never happened to him before. She hoped it would be possible to invite Zac to visit someday. That would be wonderful for Jared.

"What are you going to do when you grow up?" George asked Ellen.

"I'm going to own my own ranch and run it myself," Ellen told him.

"Won't you let your husband help?"

"I'm not going to get married. Mama says men are lazy and undependable. And that's just the best ones."

The heat that flamed in Sarah's cheeks wasn't cooled by Rose's unsuccessful efforts to hide her laughter. Even George had difficulty repressing a smile.

"She must have heard Rose talking about me," Monty joked. "She says no woman in her right mind would have me."

"*I* said no woman in her right mind would have you," Hen corrected. "Rose said you'd drive a sane woman out of her mind."

"Sounds like the same thing to me," Monty said. "But I agree with Ellen. I'm not getting married either."

"For that we can be profoundly thankful," said Jeff.

Monty turned to Sarah. "George tells me that you want to hire one of our men."

"That's not exactly what I mean to do, but I do hope I can convince one to come work for me on my ranch."

"Have you decided which one?" Rose asked.

She had decided and undecided at least a hundred times. She would be relieved to be forced to state her choice. She was a sensible woman, a rational woman, one who made decisions based on facts and not emotion. She couldn't understand why this time had been so different.

"Yes, I have decided," she said.

"Who is it?"

SIX

"Salty."

Sarah couldn't believe her own ears. She'd intended to say Walter. His name was practically on her tongue. How could she possibly have said Salty? The man himself was so surprised he nearly knocked his coffee over.

"I always thought he was the perfect choice for you," Rose said. "I'm glad you agree."

Sarah's gaze swung from Walter to Salty, back to Walter, then again to Salty. Both men showed surprise, but not in the same way. Walter appeared surprised but sanguine. He must have guessed she favored him, though she hadn't said anything.

Still confused, Salty asked, "Are you sure you really mean to choose me? You said I didn't fit your requirements." He was handing her the perfect opportunity to allow her brain to correct the mistake her emotions had caused her to make.

"Don't you want to be our father?" Jared asked. "Is it because I'm a cripple?"

Sarah's gaze flew to her son, but he was turned toward Salty, a look of hopefulness on his face that she had never seen. What had Salty done to cause Jared to form such a strong attachment so quickly? How had she missed it? She held her breath waiting for Salty's answer.

"You're not a cripple," he said. "You have some trouble getting around, but there are lots of things I could teach you to do."

Jared turned to his mother. "Are you going to let him?" The longing in Jared's eyes would have pierced the resistance of a much more hardened soul than hers.

"Does your sister like Salty?" Sarah asked.

Ellen favored Salty with one of her rare smiles. "Tyler says he can ride a horse better than anybody except George, Monty, and Hen." In her daughter's mind, Salty needed no further qualifications.

Sarah turned to Salty. "What do you say?"

The ranch hand's gaze rested on Jared for several moments before turning to Sarah. "I'll be happy to accept your proposal."

Apparently unaware of the tension in the room, Monty said, "This calls for a celebration!"

Some of the tightness left Salty's face as he turned to ask, "Why? Because you're getting rid of me?"

"Damn right. Rose likes you more than me."

The lighthearted mood that quickly enveloped the room covered Sarah's discomfort and allowed her to avoid meeting Salty's gaze.

It wasn't much of a celebration when you could toast only with coffee, water, and milk, but that didn't seem to dampen anyone's spirits. Sarah was relieved to see Walter enter into the fun, yet she couldn't help but remain concerned about what Salty might be thinking. When he'd spent a long moment looking at Jared before answering her, she'd believed he was going to refuse. No doubt he'd accepted because of her son rather than her.

She wasn't prepared for how much that upset her. She put down her fork so no one would see how badly her hand was shaking. She believed she'd gotten her attraction under control, but hearing his name on her lips had forced her to realize *it* controlled *her*. Now she had promised to marry a man who wanted her land, who wanted to help her son, and who had shown no interest in her as a woman.

It was a devastating blow, but it wasn't too late. She could still change her mind until they were married.

One word—his own name—had changed the course of Salty's life. One minute he was an ordinary cowhand with little likelihood of any other future; a minute later he was a soon-to-be stepfather and landowner with the responsibility of making a bankrupt ranch profitable. Yet he could only achieve this by marrying a woman who didn't want to be married, and who didn't want to marry him because she found him attractive. This was made worse because he was attracted to her. If she found out—if she even suspected—she'd probably back out of the agreement.

He took a drink of coffee to loosen his throat, which had become dry and tight. It was difficult to smile at Sarah, to laugh at Monty's jokes and ignore his innuendo, while his brain was working feverishly to come up with a way to survive the coming months. *Years.* He wasn't particularly strong on marriage, but he was very strong on women. It was easy to avoid temptation when there were no eligible women around, but how was he to avoid falling victim to his needs when the object of his attraction was his legal wife? There would be no cold streams to dive into when the temptation grew too strong. There wouldn't always be wood to split, post holes to dig, or cows to be wrestled to the ground, either.

The sensible thing to do would be to turn down Sarah's offer. Walter would be good with the kids and kind to Sarah. He'd told Salty that marriage had taught him his need for women was counterbalanced by his need to avoid being reshaped and reformed by them, so he would have no trouble with Sarah's requirement that they live apart. But it took only one glance at the brightness of Jared's smile, the sound of his laughter, for Salty to know he couldn't go back on his promise to the boy. If any good was to come of the years spent dealing with his father's disability, it would have to be in what he could do for Jared.

"Stop looking like you've been sentenced to ten years of hard labor," Monty said to him. "If you're having second thoughts, I could take your place."

Jeff's voice was hard, his tone caustic. "I doubt Sarah wishes to add a third child to her household."

The amiability drained from George's face. "I'd like to look over the ranch accounts with you later this morning, Jeff. They aren't finished yet, are they?"

Jeff's mouth tightened with anger. "I know when you're trying to get rid of me."

"I'm sure you do. If you spent more time on your accounts and less searching for hurtful things to say, I wouldn't have to."

Jeff pushed back his chair and got to his feet. "Adding up numbers is all a cripple is good for."

"No one here believes that. Now before you leave, apologize to Jared for making such an insensitive remark."

Salty was pleased to see Jeff flush with embarrassment.

"I'm sorry," Jeff said to Sarah's son. "I have a nasty temper, which isn't improved by having a seven-year-old brother who can do things I can't."

Jared regarded Jeff solemnly before responding. "I can't do half the things Ellen can, and she's a girl. Mama says I should look for things I can do and not spend so much time thinking about what I can't. It'll just make me unhappy."

"I've been given the same advice, but apparently you're better at following it than I am."

Jared's eyes glistened with unshed tears. "I don't know. It's hard sometimes."

Salty's anger ebbed. He had gotten so used to Jeff's disability he forgot how hard it was on him to be faced with it every hour of the day. He, of all people, shouldn't have made that mistake. His father had never let him forget for as much as a day what he suffered.

"It's hard all the time," Jeff agreed. "Now I'd better get to work. The way this family eats, we need to make a lot of money."

"I could shoot more turkeys," Monty offered.

"No, you can't," George said. "You've nearly wiped out the population. Besides, Rose doesn't need any more feathers for pillows."

They even had feather pillows in the bunkhouse. Salty doubted he'd have that comfort at Sarah's place. But no use wondering what it would be like; he'd find out in a couple of days. Better to spend his time gathering his few belongings. And he'd ask George for his wages. He expected he'd need them soon.

"When are you going to leave?" Monty asked Sarah. "I was thinking I'd take Ellen out with us tomorrow if they were going to be around that long."

Ellen's excitement was evident, but Jared's lack of enthusiasm had an even greater impact on Salty. He said, "I'm not sure it's my place to make suggestions yet, but if it's okay with Sarah, I'd like to leave first thing tomorrow morning. It's going to take a couple of days to get home."

Home. When was the last time he had used that word, and why had he used it now?

"I agree with Salty," Sarah said. "We've been away too long already." She glanced at her daughter. "I expect Ellen will have plenty of opportunity to ride with Salty."

"You all will," Salty promised. "It's a family ranch, isn't it?"

He didn't yet know what Jared could do, but he was determined the boy wasn't going to be left out. There was no way he could make the leg normal, but he intended to help Jared focus on what he could do and then *do it*. Jared needed a reason to be proud of himself. Salty remembered how loss of pride had destroyed his father. He was determined that would never happen to Jared.

Rose got to her feet. "Zac has some clothes he's outgrown," she said to Sarah. "Do you think Jared or Ellen might be able to wear them?"

Salty hated the look of misery on Sarah's face. She must be feeling embarrassed to accept clothes, yet aware that her children needed them. Salty made up his mind right then that she'd never again be in that position if he could do anything about it.

"That's kind of you, but—"

"I have no one to give them to. If you don't take them, I'll have to cut them up for rags."

"If Zac has outgrown them, they're probably rags already," Hen said.

"They're a little worn," Rose admitted, "but if you don't have lots of work clothes, you'll spend half your time washing the same ones over and over again."

"Don't glare at *me*," Monty said. "*I* don't want my clothes washed."

Monty's inability to realize the world didn't revolve around him allowed Sarah time to get herself in hand. Salty was glad of it. When Rose turned back to her, his new bride-to-be showed no sign of emotional discomfort.

"We'd be glad of some extra work clothes. Ellen has practically worn hers through."

Rose gestured to Zac. "You can help me decide what to keep."

The boy shrugged. "I don't care. Give them everything."

Rose placed her hands on her hips for emphasis. "You're not getting anything new until after the drive to Abilene, young man."

"And then only if we get the prices we're hoping for," George added.

"I never get anything new," Zac complained, following Rose from the room.

Monty turned to Jared. "You'd better wash any clothes you get from Zac before you wear them. If you don't, you'll get cooties."

"Zac cooties," Hen teased. "They're the worst kind."

Salty was pleased to see the twins make Jared laugh. He was sure the boy had had little reason for most of his life. Probably Sarah hadn't, either. It couldn't have been easy struggling to hold on to her ranch during the war. It must have been made worse by losing her husband. It had to affect the children as well.

The more he thought about the situation he was about to step into, the more clearly he realized he had let the vision of owning land obscure the enormity of the task he was taking on. It was more than taking a failing ranch and making it profitable; his biggest task would be trying to restore hope to a family that had very little reason to have any.

George turned to him. "Want me to give you a hand with your packing?"

"Sure." Salty didn't know what his boss had in mind, but George never did anything without a reason.

"I'm coming, too," Monty spoke up.

George shook his head. "With Rose and me gone, you have to stay and entertain our guests. Just try not to embarrass your family."

"That means Hen has to stay," Monty said.

"I hadn't considered leaving these nice people alone with you and Tyler," Hen replied. "Tyler won't speak, and you should avoid it at all costs."

To the amusement of Jared and Ellen, the twins kept arguing. Salty and George left them.

"Did Mrs. Winborne really tell you that she wasn't going to choose you?" George asked as they left the house.

"She sure did," Salty replied.

"What was her objection?"

Salty gave a wry grin. "She was attracted to me."

George laughed. "I've heard a lot of reasons for not giving a man a job, but never that for not wanting a man to be your husband."

Their boots made scratching noises as the rocky soil compacted under the weight of their footsteps. Now that the sun had set, the air was cold and dry. The fruit trees wouldn't be budding for a while yet. Salty wondered who would take care of the garden here.

"From what she said, I gather she had a bad marriage and doesn't want to take a chance on the same thing happening again. We're to have no physical contact with each other, and I'll let her divorce me as soon as the ranch turns the corner. In return, I'll get half her land."

"Yet you're going to get married and pretend to the rest of the world it's real." George laughed as he opened the barn door. "I always thought you were intelligent, but I may have to reconsider." He reached for the lantern they kept just inside. "That's a recipe for failure."

Salty was taken aback. "What do you recommend I do?"

George shrugged. "Don't ask me. I had no intention of marrying Rose, even though I thought she was pretty as a picture the first time I saw her. I'm no better at romance than you." He lit the lantern and held it up. "Now let's see what I want to get rid of."

"Can we start with the bull?" Salty joked.

George enjoyed a belly laugh. "I can't do that—but I'll give you a calf as a wedding present."

"I was kidding!"

"What's one calf between friends?" George gave him an even look. "Besides, if that woman is desperate enough to take on a husband she doesn't want, you're going to need all the help you can get."

Salty was certain of that. Only the kind of help she needed had to come from inside of him. He didn't know that he had what it took to go from being a cowhand to being the manager of a ranch on the brink of collapse, as well as a husband to a woman who'd lost her faith in men and a father to two children who needed the man their mother didn't want. What had made him think he could handle such a challenge? He'd spent his whole life taking orders—from his father, from officers during the war, and from George. He'd never had the opportunity to do anything on his own, never had the chance to prove he could.

Well, now he had the chance. He'd been saying he wanted it, and now he couldn't fail. People more vulnerable than himself were depending on him.

The full impact of what she'd done hit Sarah when she walked out of the house the next morning and saw Salty standing by her loaded wagon, two horses tied behind it. She was going to marry a man she'd never seen before two days ago and hope he could come to love her children though he felt nothing for her. To raise her gamble from the reasonable to the unlikely, he was supposed to turn a failing ranch into a profitable enterprise.

She was crazy. She had to be.

She could say she'd made a mistake, that she'd changed her mind, but Jared was already seated in the wagon, smiling in that way which was so new to him. His eyes didn't hold the fear she'd seen so often in their depths. A boy with that smile must be looking to the future with less foreboding and possibly even a little hopefulness. If nothing else, Jared counted Salty as someone who saw him as a boy, not as a withered leg.

Ellen stood at the head of the horse hitched to the wagon, her hand gripping its bridle, proud that she'd been entrusted to keep him calm and under control.

Rose had followed Sarah outside. She moved closer and lowered her voice. "You know you got the best man, don't you? George will never find anyone to fill Salty's boots."

Sarah didn't know how to reply. How could she tell her she didn't *want* to think he was the best man, because that might make her want him to stay after the ranch was profitable once again? How could she say she was intending to marry a man she didn't want when that wasn't true? "The children like him already."

"Everybody likes Salty. We're going to miss him."

Guilt. Between that and fear, Sarah didn't know whether she had made the best or the worst decision of her life. How was it possible to have made a decision she didn't want to make, feel guilty for having done it, yet be determined to continue on? Her thoughts were so muddled she didn't know whether she was just confused or about to lose her mind.

Her thoughts clarified as Zac and Tyler marched out of the house and down the steps to deposit two large bundles in the wagon. She turned to Rose and said, "I can't take that much."

"Take them," Zac pleaded. "If my drawers are full, George will say I don't need any new clothes, even if I've outgrown everything I have!"

Sarah was caught between relief that her children would have enough clothing to get them through the next year, and embarrassment that her need was so great. This was another grievance to be added to the accounts of Roger and his family. There seemed to be no end to the ways their lack of love was still hurting her children.

Rose didn't meet her gaze. "I added a few things I don't need any longer. If you can't use them, give them to someone who can."

Sarah felt like a beggar. "I can't take all that."

Rose grasped her hand. "Since the war, nobody in Texas has had everything they need. George and I want to share what we can. When things are better with you, I expect you'll do the same for someone else."

Sarah couldn't imagine being in a position to help others as Rose was helping her, but she would find a way to do *some*thing.

Jeff came out of the house. George and the twins appeared from the direction of the barn, Walter and the other cowhand behind. Everyone had gathered to see them off.

Rose gripped Sarah's hand harder. "I'm going to miss you and your children. Promise me you'll come see us again."

Sarah felt tears begin to well up in her eyes. "Thank you for your kindness."

"Pshaw," Rose said. "I'd keep you here for the company if I could." She released Sarah and stepped back. "Now you'd better go. Salty looks anxious to start."

The abrupt reminder of what lay ahead halted her tears. From this moment on, Sarah vowed not to be swayed by emotion. It had gotten her where she was now. Only rigorous control could make anything good come out of it.

"Write," Rose called as Sarah descended the porch steps. Her feet felt weighted, her stride slow, her body resistant. She didn't know whether she was walking toward the familiar love of her children, toward an uncertain future with Salty, or away from the reassuring safety of the Randolph family. It didn't matter, she decided, because she was doing all of that.

"No need to wish you a safe journey," George was saying as Sarah reached the wagon, "because Salty will see to that. But I do wish you success and happiness."

Monty edged forward and winked. "Salty will take care of that, too."

Hen belted his twin and stepped in front of him. "Let us know if you have any trouble with rustlers, ma'am."

"Yeah," Monty said. "With those thieving McClendons gone, it's been too quiet around here."

Sarah allowed Hen to help her into the wagon, while Monty and George showered Salty with last-minute advice. "Your family has done far too much for us," she told Hen. "Please don't feel you need to worry about us anymore."

Hen shook his head. "George can't stop trying to take care of everybody, and Monty gets bored if he can't find some trouble."

Trouble? She had enough to keep both men busy, but she and her family had to do this on their own.

Salty climbed up in the wagon and sat next to her. He reached for the extended hand George offered him and said, "Thanks for taking me in."

"You more than earned your keep. I'm going to check on you, so don't be surprised when you see me ride up."

Salty grinned. "I expected that. Now I'd better get going. I want to get halfway to Austin today."

He untied the reins. Ellen quickly scrambled over the back of the wagon and perched on one of the bundles of clothes. They all waved as he turned the wagon and headed down the lane toward the Austin road.

"Why are we going to Austin?" Ellen asked. It was Sarah's question as well.

"I want to buy a few things."

Sarah tried not to show the surprise she felt. Salty hadn't mentioned this to her, or she'd have told him she didn't have any money.

"What things?" Ellen asked.

"I won't know until you tell me something about your ranch."

"What do you want to know?"

"How much milk does your milk cow give?"

"We don't have a milk cow. A wolf got her one night, and Mama didn't have money to buy another one."

"How about chickens? Do you have plenty of eggs?"

"I don't know. Ask Mama."

Sarah was mortified to admit to so many failures. "It's hard to keep chickens with coyotes around."

"We can fix that. How about pigs?"

"I have two sows." One of the hired men had shot their boar, saying he needed something to eat.

"How do you breed them?"

"I turned them out so they can breed with a wild boar." She'd have had to turn the pigs out anyway, because she didn't have any feed for them.

"At least we've got the horses covered," Salty said.

After a moment Ellen asked, "Is there anything else we have to do in Austin?"

"The most important thing of all," Salty replied.

"What's that?" Ellen sounded excited.

Salty laughed. "I know your mother knows, but why don't you ask Jared? See if he knows."

SEVEN

"You and Mama have to get married," Jared said. "Is that what you mean?"

"Of course. What could be more important?"

Sarah thought Salty would have considered survival of the next twelve months his first priority. They needed to get all her cows branded and some rounded up to sell. Then they needed to find a way to protect a milk cow and chickens, locate her sows, and plant a new garden. Marriage was just a piece of paper, and in this case it signified nothing.

"Where are you going to get married?" Ellen asked.

Sarah didn't look at Salty as she answered, "We'll go before a judge."

"I thought you had to get married in a church."

"Marriage is a legal contract, which is why you need a judge," Salty said. "People get married in a church so they can share their happiness with family and friends."

"Mama married Papa in a church," Jared remarked. "But I don't think she liked it."

Sarah flushed with embarrassment. It was difficult to hide things from children. It was impossible to watch every word, the tone of her voice, her expression, when her life was gradually falling apart. How could she worry about such details when it took every bit of strength, every ounce of courage, to stave off panic, to keep them from knowing how close they were to disaster? At least they didn't know their father had been a dreadful husband and father and that she'd *hoped* he wouldn't come back. She still felt guilty for that.

If it didn't have something to do with horses or cows, Ellen quickly lost interest. "Can I sleep on the ground tonight?"

"You'll have to ask your mother," Salty said.

"She made us all sleep in the wagon," Ellen told him. "I didn't even have room to turn over."

"The ground is dry, and I have a bedroll," Salty said. "Maybe your mother will reconsider."

Sarah felt a twinge of irritation. Ellen was her daughter; the decision about where she slept belonged to her, not Salty. She hoped he didn't think that just because he would become her legal husband he had a right to tell her what to do with her children.

"Salty will need his bedroll for himself," she told her daughter.

Ellen wasn't ready to give up. "I'm tired of riding in the wagon. Can I ride one of the horses?"

Sarah was tired of riding in the wagon as well. The uneven road had jarred her body until her joints ached. Her discomfort was partially relieved by the bright sunshine that penetrated her clothing and warmed her body. The sun felt so good on her face it would have been easy to relax and let Salty take care of everything, but she was Ellen's mother.

She was about to object, but Salty spoke first. "They're not used to anybody but me."

"Do they buck?" Jared asked.

"Sometimes."

"A lot?"

"No. Just enough to show they don't like you on their backs."

"Our horses never buck," Ellen said. "I wish they would."

"You'd change your mind after you'd been thrown a couple of times."

"Did you get thrown?"

Salty laughed easily. "More times than I want to remember. I grew up a farm boy, so I didn't really learn to ride until I went to work for

George."

"I wish I could ride," Jared said.

Sarah knew that was the thing that, more than any other, set her son apart from other boys his age. Most would have their own horse by now. To have a sister who could ride as well as any boy their age just made it worse.

"I'll have to give that some thought," Salty said. "In the meantime, I'll teach you how to handle a buggy."

Sarah swallowed her protest. She would have to talk to him about making promises he couldn't keep. She wanted Salty to do whatever he could to help Jared, but she couldn't have him raising hopes he couldn't fulfill.

"Now, why don't you and Ellen think of a game to play," Salty continued. "I need to talk to your mother about the ranch."

Sarah wasn't sure whether to relax or grow even more dispirited. By the time he fully understood the job he had promised to do, he might change his mind about marrying her.

─────

"That was a mighty good supper," Salty said. "I'll have to take you along when we trail cows to Abilene." They were seated around the dying embers of their cook fire.

Salty sat between the two children, cradling his coffee cup between his hands. Jared, lying on his side and leaning on his elbow, followed every move he made. Ellen sat cross-legged, her attention equally centered. Across from them, Sarah knelt to stir the coals. The smell of wood smoke and countless stars twinkling in the limitless expanse of the Texas sky provided a peaceful respite from the stress of the day.

"I want to go to Abilene, too," Ellen said.

"Salty was teasing," Sarah told her daughter. "Women don't go on cattle drives."

"Why not?"

How did you explain the conventional reasons for keeping men and women apart in certain situations to a girl who defined herself by the work she liked to do? Ellen liked horses and cows; therefore, she didn't see any reason why she shouldn't be included with men who liked the same things. She'd had little opportunity to see other children, so she didn't know that what most people expected of girls was very different from what they expected of boys.

"We don't take boys or girls," Salty said. "You would be away from home for several months, and it can be very dangerous."

"What's dangerous about herding cows?"

"There are Indians who don't want you crossing their land. Sometimes rustlers will shoot anybody who tries to stop them, but the most dangerous thing is a stampede."

Sarah listened to Salty explain the dangers of rounding up, branding, and trailing a herd to market. He had an incredible way with children. During the long hours they were forced to spend in the wagon, he'd kept up a steady conversation that made the miles pass so quickly it hadn't seemed long before they had to stop for the night. Though it wasn't possible for Jared to help as much in setting up as Ellen, Salty kept him enough involved that he wouldn't feel left out.

Now he was explaining the intricacies of a trail drive like he expected Jared to head out on his own the next day, and the best part was, the boy was so interested he seemed able to forget that such an undertaking wasn't possible for him. It wasn't something Sarah wanted to do, but she could see the excitement in both of her children's eyes. For them, it was like listening to a fairy tale, and Salty was the magician who spun the magic.

She took all the dirty plates to the nearby stream to scour them with fine sand. Listening to the conversation without being able to understand what was being said was like listening to soothing music. The low, easy flow of Salty's bass voice served as a foundation for the children's eager sopranos that rose and fell like sparks in a capricious wind. Sarah couldn't remember the last time her children had been so excited. The worst men she'd hired had caused them to withdraw into long periods of silence. It was a relief to know that wouldn't happen with Salty. It was doubly important because once they were married, she couldn't just fire him.

She'd begun the day worried she'd made a serious mistake in choosing Salty. Sitting next to him in the wagon had made her so tense it had taken her over an hour before the muscles in her shoulders could relax. When she managed, she started to worry that he would try to take over the decision-making. But that fear had been soothed, too. It wasn't so much one big thing as several little ones that led her to believe he wouldn't act like nearly every other man she knew. But no sooner was that worry relieved than the physical attraction was back.

By the time they'd stopped for the evening, she was relieved to have something to think about other than Salty. By the time they had finished eating, she felt almost normal again. Or so she thought. She wasn't aware of her own disquiet until she realized she had been scrubbing the same plate for several minutes.

She put it down and picked up another. What was wrong with her? Why was she feeling so unsettled? Her children were being entertained. They'd had a pleasant trip. They would reach Austin in plenty of time tomorrow to manage all their business and start home early the next day. Salty had been cheerful and pleasant. She couldn't have found a nicer man, or one who was better with children. Her errand to the Randolphs had been more successful than she'd had any right to expect. What was bothering her?

The plate fell from her slackened grasp and clattered noisily on a rock. Merciful heavens! She was jealous! Of her own children!

How could she be? They were wonderful children who'd had few occasions to act like normal seven-year-olds. They'd never laughed or played silly games with other children. They'd never gone to parties or stuffed themselves on desserts and sweets. They'd never had nice clothes or two parents to tuck them in bed at night. Nor did they have the usual family of aunts, uncles, cousins, and doting grandparents. And despite these deprivations, they never complained and worked as hard as they could. How could she possibly be jealous of them?

Because Salty was paying more attention to them than to her.

It was ridiculous. She couldn't possibly be jealous of somebody she didn't want. And yet, apparently she could. She could have understood it if he had been as handsome as Roger, but Salty's looks weren't what attracted her to him. He was just an average man, and she was a grown woman who'd been on her own for six years. She had more reasons than she had time to catalogue why she didn't want to be attracted to any man, so it irritated her that she should be so foolish.

She picked up the last plate, scrubbed vigorously, then rinsed it in the stream. The forks were cleaned similarly, driven into the sand a few times. Sarah washed her cup and glanced over at her children as she dried it. They were still focused on Salty, their eagerness visible even in the dimming evening. Occasionally a reflection of firelight flashed in their eyes. They looked so happy, so full of hope, she couldn't remain apart from them a moment longer.

It took only a few more minutes to complete her task. When she rose to her feet and turned to go back to the wagon, the children were seated on either side of Salty. He was speaking softly, but they listened with rapt attention. Maybe that's why she was attracted to him. Any man who could cast such a spell over her children in so little time could probably do the same to a grown woman. Familiarity would cure that. It was easy to be entranced by someone you'd just met, but it was difficult to be equally interested months later. By the time a year had passed, she'd probably wonder what she'd ever found so fascinating.

Having worked her way to that conclusion, she wondered why she didn't feel better.

———————

"Salty has an extra bedroll," Jared was telling his mother. "He said I could use it if it was all right with you."

Salty had spent several hours on the long trip trying to think of things he could do to help Jared feel better about himself. He'd told both kids stories, talked about roundups, and made secret plans for a surprise for Sarah. All of these things had included Ellen. Now, Salty didn't want to slight the girl, giving her brother something she herself had asked for, but Jared needed an association with a man that didn't depend on his sister. Salty also hated to put Sarah in the position of perhaps denying her son something he wanted, but it was a risk he needed to take. He hoped she would see it as an opportunity for Jared and consider it on that basis alone.

"Did you ask Salty if you could use it?" Sarah asked Jared.

"No, but Ellen did," Jared said.

Sarah turned to her daughter. "It was sweet of you. Not every sister would do that for her brother."

Ellen looked sulky. "I didn't ask for Jared. I asked for me."

"What did Salty say?" Sarah asked.

"He said it wasn't proper for young girls to sleep out with men. When I asked him why, he said I had to ask you."

Sarah's face flushed and she stammered, as though unsure of how to respond. As Salty suspected, she hadn't explained some of the basic facts of life to her daughter. He regretted having put her in such a difficult situation. He couldn't remember that anyone had ever had to tell him the facts of life; it seemed he'd always known them. But he'd had a group of guys to hang around with. Ellen and Jared didn't have anyone.

"That's not a very easy conversation," Sarah said. "Let Jared sleep out with Salty tonight. You and I will sleep in the wagon, and I'll explain."

"Explain what?" Ellen pushed.

"The birds and the bees."

"What do birds and bees have to do with sleeping outdoors? It's night. Everything's asleep!"

Salty couldn't help himself; a sputter of laughter escaped before he could stop it. He almost lost control when Sarah shot him an angry look. She was so darling when she wasn't sure what to do. Not that she looked helpless. She was about as helpless as Rose, and everybody knew George's wife could handle anything. Sarah had some of the same appeal: strength combined with vulnerability. Salty had no interest in a woman who would cling to him like a vine, depending on him to do everything for her except breathe. Nor was he attracted to a woman who had to prove she could do everything as well as a man. He felt a man and a woman could be versatile without forgetting what Mother Nature intended.

"I'll get the bedrolls," he said to Jared. "You can lay them out while I empty the wagon for your mother and sister."

"I'll help." Ellen climbed into the wagon. "I can hand stuff to you and Mama."

With the three of them working, the wagon bed was cleared in a matter of minutes. It would have been even sooner if George and Rose hadn't given Sarah so much. Salty didn't know what Rose had put in those two bags, but he knew that *all* of Zac's clothes wouldn't take up so much space. He wondered how Sarah was going to react when she got home and found out what was inside.

Ellen looked with envy at the bedding Jared was struggling to spread out on the ground. "I wish I had a bedroll."

"I expect our quilts are more comfortable," her mother said.

"I still wish I had a bedroll," the girl replied.

Salty had never known anyone like Ellen. He had a feeling Sarah's explanation of the different expectations for boys and girls was not going to change her daughter's desire to do all the things boys were allowed to do. How was he going to help Jared gain greater self-esteem if Ellen continued to do everything he did and do it better? Yet he couldn't help Jared at Ellen's expense. And maybe Sarah wanted her daughter to have the freedom to do anything she wanted, to be anything she wanted, without the fetters of conventional boy/girl roles.

Rose was the strongest woman he'd ever known, but she'd done everything from within the role traditionally expected of a woman. Was there anything wrong with doing things Ellen's way? Maybe he ought to stick to solving the problems with the ranch and leave Sarah and her family alone. Despite what she said, she probably didn't expect him to do anything beyond make the ranch profitable. Most likely she would resent it if he tried. It would certainly be easier if he backed off.

"I've got our beds all laid out!"

Salty turned away from the pile he and Sarah had made of the wagon contents to where Jared sat on one of the bedrolls. The boy smiled, clearly proud of having accomplished his task without help or supervision. The bedrolls were perfectly parallel, the corners squared, with the folded blankets at the bottom. Salty didn't know how Jared had managed all that on his hands and knees. He really had to find a way to help the boy. He couldn't fail him like he'd failed his father.

"I need to make sure the horses haven't pulled up their stakes," he said.

"Let me!"

Ellen was out of the wagon and running toward the horses before Salty could look to see if Sarah would offer an objection. The girl's mother smiled weakly and shrugged. Salty was beginning to see why she and Jared depended so much on Ellen: the child was so anxious to help that she didn't wait for permission before throwing herself into the next job. He hoped she didn't value herself only according to how much work she could do, but she seemed a happy child who genuinely wanted to help her mother and brother.

"The knots are still tight," Ellen announced when she returned. "I checked every one."

Salty was sure of that. "Then I think it's time for everyone to get some sleep. We should be up at dawn."

"We always get up at dawn," Jared told him.

So much for thinking he was a step ahead of this family. It was beginning to look like he'd have to hurry to catch up.

———————

"I'm ready," Ellen said.

"Ready for what?" Sarah settled down in the wagon next to her daughter. The two quilts that formed their bed cushioned them a little, but the underneath was still hard and unforgiving.

"For you to tell me why I can't sleep out with Salty like Jared can. Don't you like Salty?"

Sarah had known this day was coming, but she'd hoped to put it off a few more years. She didn't know where to start.

"This has nothing to do with Salty," Sarah began. "It's just that little girls stay with their mothers and boys with their fathers."

"But Salty isn't Jared's father."

"Then it would be brothers, uncles, cousins—some male relative."

"Jared doesn't have any of those, either."

This wasn't working. Her words were raising more questions than they were answering. "It's not just relatives. Men stay with men, and women with women."

"Why?" Ellen asked.

"Some of it has to do with custom," Sarah said, "but most of it has to do with the normal division of duties. Men are usually stronger than women, and most of the time they're bigger and taller."

That answer didn't carry any weight with Ellen. "I'm stronger than Jared," she told her mother. "The last hired man said he was sure I'd be just as big when I grew up."

"Maybe, but there are things you can do that men can't."

"I know," Ellen said. "Have babies."

How did she explain that having babies wasn't as simple as wearing a skirt rather than pants? Or that young girls were never allowed to be unchaperoned with men who weren't family members? Furthermore, how did she instill understanding without instilling fear, or explaining physical needs that a child of seven had never experienced and wouldn't understand? Most of all, how did she explain that either a woman was seen to be above reproach or she was beneath contempt?

"It's more than just about having babies," she said.

"What's so special about having babies, anyway?" Her daughter was growing impatient. "I don't want babies. I don't want to get married, either."

"Why don't you want to get married?" Sarah asked.

"I don't want any man telling me what to do."

"Maybe not every husband would try to tell you what to do."

"I've heard the hired men. They said it's not right for a woman to tell a man what to do. They think there ought to be a law against it, even if the woman's husband is dead and she owns the ranch."

Sarah sighed. She shouldn't have allowed Ellen to work with the hired men so much, especially considering the caliber of crew she could afford, but it had been impossible when they all had to work together. "I think that's enough for tonight. I'll tell you more after we get home."

But Sarah still didn't know how. She might ask Salty, but the mere thought caused her to blush. She'd never spoken to any man about what husbands and wives did together. She and Roger had lived through their whole marriage without seeing each other naked or talking about what they were doing. Her mother had told her it was natural, that everybody did it, but that nice women didn't talk about or enjoy it. If it was so natural that everybody did it, why didn't people talk about it?

Ellen had lain down, but she turned back to Sarah and asked, "Will you and Salty have a baby?"

EIGHT

Sarah was glad she hadn't lain down yet; she might have choked.

What could have possessed Ellen to ask about babies? Sometimes Sarah wondered what *she* knew about the topic. The experience was supposed to be a natural part of the development of an emotional relationship between a man and wife, but Sarah wasn't convinced a man and woman could have an emotional relationship more intense than friendship. If the man treated his wife the way Roger treated her, she couldn't even envision friendship. How was she supposed to convince Ellen there was something important between a man and a woman when she herself had never felt it, wasn't sure she believed in it? And how could she manage to weave this into an explanation of why young girls weren't allowed unlimited access to male company?

She settled on: "I'll never have that kind of relationship with Salty."

Ellen's brow furrowed. "What do you mean?"

"That's part of what I'll explain after we get home."

Ellen turned back and lay down. "I hope it has nothing to do with having babies, because I'm never going to have one."

Sarah felt relieved, and she supposed most mothers in her position would feel the same. She told her daughter, "You won't have to decide that until you're about ten years older."

"I don't want to get married, but if I do, my husband can have the children."

Sarah couldn't keep from laughing at the thought of Roger having to deliver Ellen and Jared. Just picturing him with a rounded stomach caused her to giggle. Roger had been vain about his looks. He'd checked his reflection in ponds, once even in a puddle after a rain. She'd had to hold his shaving mirror many times so he could step back to see himself.

She said, "We can talk about this in a few years. Right now we need to go to sleep." The sound of soft breathing told Sarah her daughter needed no prompting.

It was time for her to sleep, too, but Ellen's question left Sarah wide awake. Her feelings for Salty weren't the same as what she'd felt for Roger. He had been the son of her father's best friend. She had known him most of her life. She hadn't wanted to marry him. She'd begged her father not to force her, but their marriage had been the wish of both families. Roger had wanted it, too. When her parents died unexpectedly, she had inherited the ranch. Roger had been excited about having his own spread, of being out from under his father's control, but his enthusiasm had waned once he discovered how much work was required. It had waned further when the morning sickness started and Sarah's body grew unshapely. He was downright furious when his son was born with a withered leg. He'd probably thought going to war was preferable to being responsible for a ranch and a family he disliked.

Salty wasn't like that. He didn't have a handsome face or a bewitching smile. He *wanted* to work hard to have a ranch of his own. He'd already shown great kindness to Jared and respect for her and Ellen. He was cheerful, adept at taking charge and yet seemed conscious of not usurping her authority. Probably equally important for the months to come, he was easy to talk to. She hoped they could become friends. If he was going to be around for several years, that was probably best for all concerned.

Especially since he wasn't attracted to her. That would be the extent of their relationship.

"You can't buy all of that," Sarah exclaimed. "You know I don't have any money." When Salty showed her the list he'd made up, she'd had no idea he intended to buy everything now.

"I have enough," he told her.

Sarah hardly knew whether to protest or ask where he'd gotten it. "I didn't mean for you to use your own money to buy things for my ranch."

"It's going to be half my ranch one day, so maybe it's time to start thinking about it as *our* ranch." He was probably right, but she wasn't prepared for that jolt. Nor for his next statement, which stopped her cold. "As soon as we're married, it'll be legally my ranch, too." Again, he was right, but it was a scary thought. What exactly was she doing?

"Will you be my father?" Jared asked.

"I'll be your *step*father," Salty said.

"I want you to be my *real* father."

Sarah nearly dropped the coffeepot she was holding.

"Your mother would have to agree to let me adopt you before I could be your legal father," Salty told the boy. "But I can be your just-as-good-as-father right now."

"Would you let Salty adopt me?" Jared asked her.

Ellen spoke up. "I want him to adopt me, too."

Things were moving too fast for Sarah. She hadn't fully reconciled herself to the marriage. All the way to Austin she'd kept telling herself she could still decide not to marry Salty. Now, while she was trying to accept that he was thinking of the ranch as *theirs*, her children were asking if he could adopt them.

"We can talk about that later," Salty said. "Right now, your mother and I have to get married, buy what we need for the ranch, and find a place to stay tonight."

Married! The years she'd spent with Roger had scared her down to her bones. Marriage was the same as putting on a yoke she had no power to remove. The thought made her sick to her stomach. However, she couldn't put this off any longer. If she was going to change her mind, she had to do it now.

Stop! She was fooling herself if she thought she had a choice. This was no longer about her preference or her comfort, no longer about what she wanted. It was about her children, their security, their future, their happiness. She had tried, but she hadn't been able to secure that by herself. She had chosen Salty as the man to help her. She had no choice now but to follow through.

"Let's get married first," she announced. The sooner she got married, the sooner she could rid herself of the idea that she could change her mind.

All too soon she was standing before a bored judge who rushed them through the process with no more interest than he might have in selling a wagon or a horse. With only her children and the judge's wife and clerk as witnesses, Sarah repeated marriage vows for a second time. She found it unfair that she was required to promise to love, honor, and obey, while Salty was only required to say he would provide for her in sickness and in health. There was also the part about her endowing Salty with all her worldly goods, plus the comfort of her body. He was only expected to provide shelter and succor.

"Do I have to give you my horse?" Ellen asked as they left the judge's home.

"Why would you think that?" Salty asked.

"The judge said Mama had to endow you with all her worldly goods. I figured that meant she had to give you all her stuff."

"It just means we share what we have."

"Then why didn't the judge ask you to endow Mama?" Jared was leaning on Salty's arm. Salty walked slowly enough for the boy to keep up.

"It has to do with a lot of lawyer stuff," Salty explained. "When women get married, their property belongs to their husbands."

"Then I *know* I'm never getting married," Ellen declared. "I'm not giving all my stuff to a man."

Salty continued: "Even though a man isn't legally required to give all his stuff to his wife, he's expected to use it to take care of her and the children they'll have together. So it's really like they share everything."

Sarah almost scoffed. Roger had felt everything belonged to him, even her parents' ranch, and he'd been the only one who could make any decisions about what would be done with it. If he hadn't left for the war, he likely would have sold it.

"Does that mean you'll share your horses with Mama?" Ellen asked.

Salty tweaked her nose. "You don't care about what I'll share with your mother," he accused. "You just want to ride my horses."

Ellen jumped back but laughed. "Can I?"

"If your mother says it's okay we'll give it a try, but we have to go slow. They're not used to anybody but me."

Sarah noticed Jared was trying to pretend he wasn't listening. It seemed life in Texas conspired to make her son feel useless.

"We can talk about horses when we get home," Salty was saying to Ellen. "Right now we need to purchase some supplies."

He bought a buggy and a horse to pull it, two male pigs, a small flock of chickens, and a milk cow. He also made arrangements for a quantity of lumber to be delivered to the ranch as soon as it could be sent from the sawmill. He bought wire fencing as well. If it didn't have to do with horses or cows, Ellen wasn't interested.

"What are you going to build?" Jared asked.

"I expect the first thing I'll build is a chicken pen. I'm against feeding them to the coyotes."

"They'll eat the pigs if they can."

"We'll have a pen for them, too. But first I've got another purchase I want to ask your mother about."

"What's that?" Sarah asked.

Salty turned to her. "What do you think about a dog?"

"I always wanted a dog!" Jared said, excitement in his eyes. "Can we have one?"

Roger had insisted on bringing his into the house even when it was filthy. Sarah didn't dislike dogs, but... "Why do we need one?"

"The right dog would keep the coyotes away, as well as help with the cows."

Salty had mentioned cows, so now Ellen was interested. "How?"

"It can chase cows out of thickets where it's hard for a man on horseback to go. It can follow a scent when there's no trail, and they can catch rabbits that eat grass you'd rather keep for your herd."

"Where could you find such a dog?" Jared asked. Roger's had never done any of that.

Salty winked at Sarah. "I just happen to know a man who has one he wants to give away."

"Why does he want to give it away?" Jared asked.

"He has to move to San Antonio, and he doesn't think the dog will be happy there."

"Do you think he'd give the dog to us?"

"We just might ask him," Salty said.

Jared turned to Sarah. "Can we?"

She resented Salty putting her in this position. If he had mentioned the dog earlier, they could have talked and she could have made up her mind before the children knew anything. Now she was going to come across as a villain if she decided they shouldn't have it. "I'll have to wait until I see the dog," she said.

"When can we see him?" Jared asked.

"We can do it now."

Sarah simmered and fretted during the time it took to walk to a small house on the outskirts of town. Jared hadn't stopped asking questions the whole time. It was becoming increasingly clear that as long as the dog wasn't vicious or otherwise unacceptable, she was going to have to let him have it, whether she wanted the darn thing or not.

The dog the old man pointed out didn't come anywhere near the beast painted in Sarah's mind by Salty's description. He was lying in the shade of a fig tree. He didn't bother to lift his head, just watched them out of half-open eyes.

"He's depressed," the old man explained. "I can hardly get him to eat."

Sarah could believe that. He looked like a collection of bones held together by skin. There was some hound in him but probably a half dozen other breeds as well. He had short, dull brown hair, long bony legs, and a flat head. Sarah thought he was one of the ugliest critters she'd ever seen.

"What's his name?" Jared asked the old man.

"Bones," came the amused reply. "He's always looked like he was starving."

Jared let go of his hold on Salty's arm and managed to hop over to the dog on his own. He dropped to his knees. "Hey, Bones," he said. "I'm Jared. If Mama says it's all right, you're going to come live with me."

The dog lifted his head and began to pound the ground with his tail.

"Want to smell my hand?" Jared asked. When he held it out, the dog got up, came to sniff and then lick it. When Jared tried to pat him on the head, the dog licked the boy's face. Jared laughed before turning a beaming smile on his mother. "He likes me already!"

Her son was already in love with a frightful animal that didn't look capable of moving faster than a lumbering walk. How could this miserable beast drive off coyotes or help herd cows? Sarah said, "Salty says we need a dog who can work for us. This dog—"

"His name is Bones."

"Bones doesn't look like he can do much work."

"Don't let his looks fool you," the old man said in defense of his dog. "He's not one to waste energy when he doesn't have to."

"I'm sure he's a sweet dog—" she began.

"Sweet? Why Bones will tear the throat out of any coyote or wolf that comes near this place. During the last year I had my ranch…"

The old man gave her a list of achievements which would do credit to three dogs. It was difficult to believe Bones had accomplished even a fraction of it. Except for licking Jared's hands and face, the beast hadn't moved.

"What say we take the dog for a week or so and see how he works out?" Salty said.

"You can save yourself the trouble," the old man said. "I'm not giving him to anybody who doesn't want him."

"I want him," Jared pleaded. "He likes me."

The old man's expression softened. "Seems he does. I don't remember that he's ever taken to anybody like he's taken to you."

Sarah could feel the ground giving way under her feet faster than quicksand. She would take the dog because Jared wanted him. That's why she'd taken Salty, too. Wasn't it? When was she going to stop letting guilt and pity make her do things she didn't want?

She turned to Salty. "Are you sure about this dog?"

"Yes. I've seen him work."

She couldn't imagine the dog doing anything she would call work, but she only had to look at the happiness in Jared's eyes to know Bones had already proved to be of some worth. She turned to the old man and said, "If you're willing to give him to my son, we'll see your dog has a good home."

The old man didn't answer right away. Rather, he watched Jared and the dog. It was as though each had sensed a need in the other.

The thought flashed through Sarah's mind that this was similar to what happened when she first met Salty. She hadn't understood then what drew her to him, but now she began to. There was a kindness there that permeated everything about him. It wasn't just in the things he did. It was in the way he spoke, the way he smiled, the way he made a person feel at ease around him. The way he made people want to be around him. That's why she'd chosen him rather than Walter. It wasn't Jared at all. It was her. She wanted that kindness for Jared, of course, but she wanted it for herself, too. She hadn't realized how intense was her need until it overwhelmed her intellect and caused Salty's name to come out of her mouth.

The old man swung his gaze from Jared to Sarah. "I'll give you Bones. I know you don't want him, ma'am, but you'll be good to him because of your boy." He turned to Salty. "You've had your eye on Bones ever since you heard I was giving up the ranch. Now that you've got a ranch of your own, I guess you need him more than I do."

Sarah began to feel invisible. She had been Roger's widow and Jared and Ellen's mother for a time, important in her own right, but now she felt like just a wife again. Before her first marriage she'd been Frank Pettishall's daughter. She wanted to yell that she was not Mrs. Benton Wheeler any more than she'd been Mrs. Roger Winborne. She was Sarah, a strong, independent woman who had held her family together for six years on her own, a woman who'd chosen this man to be invited into her family, not the other way around. But she didn't say any of that because it would have been unfair to Salty.

"We'll take good care of Bones," her new husband promised the old man. "We'll come by for him early in the morning."

"Can't we take him now?" Jared asked.

"The hotel won't allow dogs," Salty explained.

"What hotel?"

"The hotel we're staying in tonight."

Ellen had lost interest in the conversation, but she perked up now.

"I've never been inside a hotel!"

Salty set a time to pick up the dog, and they left. Sarah had to talk to him about doing things without consulting her first. He'd bought all that stuff for the ranch on his own initiative, cornered her into accepting a dog she didn't want, and now he was going to spend money to stay in a hotel when there was no reason they couldn't sleep outside just as they had done all the way to the Randolphs' and back. He seemed sensitive to her feelings but still he kept making decisions without her.

Their walk back through town was slow because Salty insisted Jared walk alongside them. By leaning on his arm, the boy managed. Jared tried not to show it, but Sarah knew how much the effort of limping cost him. She was grateful to Salty for stopping several times to give her son a chance to rest.

Salty kept up a running conversation with the children about all the buildings they passed, and about what they could buy here or there, or about what kind of business was conducted inside. Her children had only a vague idea of the importance of a newspaper, lawyers, and the bank. Jared found it incredible that anyone could be rich enough to have someone else bake their bread, while Ellen thought women were foolish to want dresses like the fancy gown she saw in a dress shop window. Isolation had deprived them of the knowledge and experience that nearly every other child their age took for granted. That made Sarah feel like a failure—a feeling that only intensified after seeing where Salty insisted they eat supper.

The Bon Ton Restaurant was over half full when they entered. Compared to everyone else, Sarah and her children looked like beggars. Her dress was faded from too many washings, and thin from too much use. Her children's clothes had been patched to cover wear and tears in the fabric. Even Salty looked like a common cowhand.

The children were too excited to be aware of the stares, but Sarah couldn't understand why Salty seemed equally unconcerned. The three settled happily around a table. From the way the waitress looked at them, Sarah wouldn't have been surprised if she demanded proof they could pay before taking their orders.

Jared's eyes grew wide when the waitress listed all his choices. "Can I order anything I want?" he asked.

"Sure," Salty said. "Everyone can."

"How much is it going to cost?" Sarah asked.

"It don't make no difference whether you get chicken, pork, or beef," the waitress told her. "All the plates cost the same. Children's plates cost half."

Sarah was so agitated she doubted she could eat much. She sat in hard-held silence while Jared and Ellen discussed their choices with the waitress, who grew impatient with their questions. She wanted to explain that her children had never been in a restaurant, that being given a choice was an experience to be drawn out and savored. Ellen settled on pork chops in gravy, while Jared wanted baked chicken with sage dressing. When the waitress told him that would take about thirty minutes to prepare, he offered to order something else, but Salty said they would wait.

Sarah itched to kick Salty's ankles under the table until he couldn't walk. She'd rather eat a rabbit stew cooked over an open fire than be stared at by the other customers and practically sneered at by their waitress. Didn't he have any pride? How could he sit here knowing what everybody thought of them?

The waitress turned to Sarah. "What do you want, ma'am?"

"My wife and I will have the meatloaf," Salty said. "George Randolph tells me it's the best in Austin."

The change in the waitress's attitude was instantaneous. "You know Mr. Randolph?" She actually smiled. "Folks here haven't forgotten the ruckus he kicked up when he met his wife in here. Every time Dottie hears he's in town, she swears she won't let him through the door, but she always does. I think she's got a soft spot for him."

Sarah felt more lost than ever. What exactly had George Randolph done when he met Rose, and why did Dottie—whoever she was— object to him coming into the restaurant?

"George had a little disagreement with a man who was mistreating her," Salty explained. "It might not have meant much, but Rose's father was a Union officer and a friend of General Grant. When George married her, it made quite a stir."

The waitress left, and Salty filled the following minutes with stories about growing up on his father's farm, a few tales about funny things that happened during the war, and plans for what he hoped to do when they got back to the ranch. Sarah was thankful the children were so interested in his stories they missed the interest their presence in the restaurant had created.

After what seemed an eternity, their food arrived. The meatloaf was very good, but Sarah couldn't enjoy it. She couldn't escape the feeling that everyone around them believed she shouldn't be here. She thought it was significant that none of the departing customers spoke to them on the way out.

"Aren't you going to eat your supper?" Ellen asked.

"I'm not hungry."

"Can I have your meatloaf?" Jared spoke up.

"I asked first," Ellen said.

Sarah divided her uneaten meal between her two children and watched them devour every morsel. That made her feel like she never fed them enough, or that what she cooked wasn't good enough to excite their appetites. She knew Salty wasn't trying to show her how she'd failed to provide for her children, but he'd done so just the same. Both kids were looking at him like he had the answer to every question, that he could change any situation and make it better. Hadn't he turned their waitress's attitude from scorn to cheerful helpfulness? Hadn't he convinced a gruff old man to part with his treasured dog? Now he'd taken them to a restaurant and was going to pay for them to stay in a hotel. The difference he'd made in their lives was already so great they were bound to start turning to him rather than her.

Sarah thought she might feel better after they left the restaurant, but she didn't. Salty handing over the money for their two hotel rooms so casually you'd think his pockets were bulging with it made her feel worse than ever. Her children were so excited that not even full stomachs after a long, tiring day could slow them down. Both inspected every corner of the lobby, trying out the chairs and sofas, picking up magazines to look for pictures, and then paused longest in front of a buffalo head mounted on the wall. It was nearly as big as they were.

"Will I have my own bed?" Ellen asked.

"You'll have to share with your mother," Salty told her.

"What about Jared?"

"He'll share with me."

Sarah could practically see Jared stand a little straighter. It was probably the happiest he had felt about himself in ages, and someone other than his mother had been the one to do it.

All of her anger and frustration spilled over. "I want to speak to you," she told Salty. "Now," she added, when he didn't respond immediately.

NINE

Sarah tried to keep her voice level so the children wouldn't realize she was upset. They were unlikely to have another day like this for a long time, and she didn't want to ruin it for them.

"Do we have time to get the children settled into their rooms first?" Salty asked.

"We didn't bring anything from the wagon," Sarah pointed out.

"I had everything sent over from the livery stable when we left the horses and the livestock there."

Ellen looked around. "I don't see my clothes."

"Everything is in your rooms," the clerk told them. "Mr. Wheeler had the man from the livery stable reserve the rooms when he brought over your luggage."

Sarah knew if she wasn't able to get things off her mind soon she was going to explode. "It shouldn't take more than a few minutes to settle them in their rooms."

"I'll be ready when you are," Salty said.

Unable to say any of the things burning on the end of her tongue, Sarah took the key and headed up the stairs. Her room was on the third floor in the back. It was small and minimally furnished with a bed, chest, a ladder-back chair, and a stand with a bowl and pitcher. Their luggage and one of the bags Rose had given them had been placed on the bed.

"I don't know why they put this bag here," Sarah said as she moved everything off. "It should have gone to Jared's room."

"Maybe Mrs. Randolph meant these clothes for me." Ellen walked over to the bag and opened it. "I can wear anything he can."

Sarah began taking out things they would need for bed. "She said she regretted not having anything to give you."

"Then why did she give me this?"

Sarah turned to see her daughter holding up a dress that was clearly meant for a woman, not a child.

"There are more of them," Ellen announced.

Sarah tossed aside the nightgown she was holding and took the bag. Inside were two more dresses. Rose had given her some of her own clothes.

"Are they for me?" Ellen asked.

"No," Sarah said.

"Good. I don't want any dresses."

Neither did Sarah. Rose hadn't told her what she was doing, because she probably guessed Sarah wouldn't accept them. This wasn't Salty's fault, but it just added to her grievances. Was everybody determined to show her just how badly she'd managed her life since her husband deserted her? She was caught between appreciation for Rose's kindness and impotent rage at her own helplessness.

"Can you get ready for bed on your own?" she asked her daughter.

"I'm not a baby, Mama."

Of course she wasn't. It was proof of how upset Sarah was that she had forgotten Ellen had gotten herself ready for bed all year. "Good. I have to talk to Salty."

Ellen jumped up on the bed. "I'm glad you married him. I've never been in a hotel before."

Sarah burned to say there were many things more important than staying in hotels, but Ellen was seven and things like that made a big impression on her. "I'm glad you like him."

"So does Jared."

So did that waitress and the old man. So did everybody. Why was it everything worked for Salty but not for her? "See if Jared needs any help, and tell Salty I want to talk to him."

Leave it to children to sense what you were trying to hide from them. "Is anything wrong?" Ellen asked.

"We just need to talk over some things. Now, hurry. We need to get to bed because we have a long day tomorrow."

Uncharacteristically, Ellen left with dragging feet. She must have sensed that her mother was unhappy with Salty and was reluctant to carry the message. What had she done?

Sarah tossed the dress aside. She hadn't asked for it and didn't want it. She wasn't helpless, was she? Yes. Even worse, she was inadequate. She'd had to marry a man to do all the things she was unable to do. That he seemed to do everything effortlessly just made her failure seem worse.

She heard a knock at the door. "It's Salty. Can I come in?"

"Yes."

She had expected her frustration to burst forth from her and bury him, but when she started to speak she didn't know where to begin. She couldn't accuse him of trying to make her feel useless or of trying to steal her children's affection; she was sure he was only doing what he thought would help—which was why she'd married him. Yet she couldn't stay quiet or she'd snap. "We need to talk."

"What about?"

"About everything."

She wished she knew what was hiding behind that limpid gaze. A lot more than Salty let on. He gave the appearance of being easygoing and content, but his eagerness to have some land of his own, his disappointment when she said he didn't fit her requirements, and his shock when she chose him, were all signs of a deeper well of emotion he kept out of sight. Just as indicative was the connection he'd made with Jared. He had managed to make her son feel he understood the limitations of that withered leg, but that those limitations didn't in any way affect his estimation of Jared as a person. No one but she and Ellen had ever been able to do that.

"In that case we'd better sit down. Do you want the chair or the bed?"

"I'll take the bed."

But she felt silly perched there, preparing to have a formal conversation with a man she'd married that morning. Everything was out of kilter. She wondered if her life would ever feel normal again.

"I'm feeling left out of all the decision-making. I know it's your money you're spending, but it's my family you're spending it on and I don't understand why. I know this sounds ungrateful, but I'm not sure I want it."

"Is that all?"

Is that all? His response was so unexpected she wasn't sure how to respond. "Isn't that enough?"

"I thought something important was worrying you." He started to rise. "We have a long day tomorrow. I'd better—"

"Something important *is* worrying me."

He sat back down. "What?"

"I feel like I'm losing control of my life." That sounded a little like a child whining. "You're making all the decisions. I either have to agree or sound like an ogre." That sounded petty and ungrateful. "What I'm trying to say is, you're making decisions without consulting me. I'm not saying I disagree with them, but when they involve me and my children, I want to be consulted."

"Since I'm your husband now, everything I do will involve you and the children."

"Then I want to be consulted about everything."

Salty's gaze narrowed. "I was under the impression that you wanted me to stay as far away from you as possible." He averted his gaze. "You felt your attraction to me could be a problem."

She felt heat rush up her neck and suffuse her face. "I don't see how that applies."

"If I'm to discuss everything with you that involves the ranch or the children, as well as work with you, we're going to be spending most of our time together." His gaze met hers. "It's possible that being around me that much would end any attraction you feel. However, it's possible the reverse might happen."

Not if she continued to be as irritated with him as she was now. "I admit that I find you attractive, but since my desire to be consulted about everything involving my family is greater than my attraction to you, I don't think that will be a problem."

She wished Salty wasn't so good at keeping his emotions from being reflected in his face. Even his eyes, usually the window to a person's inner thoughts, gave nothing away. Maybe this was part of his plan to kill her attraction for him.

If so, it wasn't working. She was more intrigued than ever. He was good, kind, generous, fun to be around, and her children liked him. He was dependable, capable, and utterly truthful. There was nothing to dislike about him. And like any woman, she was intrigued by what she couldn't figure out. Furthermore, she was convinced there was some sadness in his past that still affected him. She had a feeling his cheerfulness was partly camouflage to keep people from sensing that hurt. Like so many men, he'd chosen to bury his pain rather than bring it to the surface.

Salty stood. "I'll do my best to remember to consult you before I make any more decisions. If I forget, remind me. I'm used to being on my own."

That was a strange thing to say, since he'd been working for the Randolph family, but she didn't challenge it. She'd already let herself become too curious about him. But she couldn't let him leave with nothing but complaints ringing in his ears. "I don't want you to think I'm ungrateful for what you've done. You've more than lived up to your part of the bargain so far. I'm sure you'll continue to do so. I just want to be included."

"I understand," he said. "Now I'd better go. Jared has some ideas about the ranch he wants to tell me."

"Are you sure you don't mean Ellen?"

Salty flashed her an amused smile. "Ellen already told me what she thinks we ought to do. Jared has ideas, too, but he's afraid they won't be taken seriously because his leg has kept him from knowing as much as Ellen."

Sarah wondered what she'd done to make Jared think she wouldn't listen to him. "What does he want to talk about?"

"I don't know yet."

"Then how exactly do you know he wants to talk?"

Salty smiled. "Every seven-year-old boy wants to talk. They're so full of discoveries they're spilling over with things to say. I suspect Jared feels it's hard to be listened to when he's with you. I saw it in his eyes when we were talking about the ranch."

"So you don't *know* he wants to talk."

"No, but I've got a feeling he does. I learned from George Randolph never to ignore my feelings. They won't go away, so ignoring them just makes it harder to get to where you're supposed to be."

Sarah couldn't shake the feeling Salty was talking about her, but he didn't know what it was like to be married to Roger. No attraction was worth that, no feeling powerful enough to make her change her mind. She knew where she wanted to be. She intended to get there with Salty's help, and then she would divorce him.

"Mama likes you."

Salty turned from where he'd been putting things back into his bed-roll. Jared was sitting up in bed, watching him with an eagerness that told him there had been too few men in his life he could trust.

"What makes you say that?" He wasn't asking because he wanted to know what Sarah thought about him; he already knew that. He wanted to know what Jared was thinking.

"She lets you do things."

That was a little too vague for Salty. "What things?"

"She never let us stay in a hotel before. We never ate in a restaurant, either."

"I paid for both."

"I know. I don't think we have any money. Does that mean we're poor?"

"You're not poor, because you have a ranch."

"I heard Arnie—he's the last man Mama hired—say the bank was going to take our ranch if she fired him."

"What did your mother say?" Salty asked.

"She said if Arnie didn't pack his bags and leave within the hour, she'd set the sheriff on him."

That sounded like Sarah Winborne: gutsy even when she didn't have a leg to stand on.

"I was glad he left. I didn't like him."

"Why?"

"He wanted Mama to marry him. He said he'd make the ranch prof-itable if she did."

"Why didn't she marry him?"

"She didn't like him. Ellen did, but I didn't."

"Why did Ellen like him?"

"Arnie let her do things Mama said were dangerous for a girl, even a girl like Ellen."

"He shouldn't have done that."

"That's what Mama said. I think he must have been right about the bank. That's why Mama married you."

Salty was surprised she would discuss something like this with two seven-year-olds. "Did she say that?"

"She said we didn't have enough money to pay a man to work for us. She said she would have to marry again, but she was going to divorce him as soon as she could pay the money she owed the bank."

Apparently Salty had underestimated the ability of seven-year-olds. Jared had no difficulty understanding the situation.

"Why wouldn't you want your mother's husband to be your father?"

"I wouldn't want Arnie, but I wouldn't mind you."

The conversation was moving along lines Salty hadn't anticipated. It was time he got to bed.

He hadn't shared a bed with a seven-year-old since he was a child himself, but he figured Jared would fall asleep within minutes after he blew out the lamp. He stripped down to his long underwear and admitted, "I'm not sure I'm cut out to be anybody's father. But if I was, you'd be my first choice for a son."

"Why would you want a cripple for a son?"

Salty was about to blow out the lamp, but he figured this was one question that needed to be answered in the light. He sat down on the edge of the bed and turned to face Jared. The boy didn't look upset. Just curious. That said a lot for Sarah's determination to help Jared think of his leg as a simple problem that could be dealt with, not something that made him a lesser person. Salty was glad of that.

"There's a lot about you that's more important than your leg. I know that must be hard to believe sometimes, especially when it keeps you from doing things other boys can do, but it's who you are inside that makes me say I'd be proud to be your father." Jared had probably heard that so often he had started to think of it as an excuse people used when they couldn't think of anything else to say. "I'm not going to tell you that your leg won't make life harder for you. It will. I'm not going to tell you it won't keep you from doing things you want to do. You already know that. Nor am I going to tell you that people won't think less of you because of it. You know that, too."

"Then how could you be proud to be my father?"

It was time to share a bit of himself. Salty didn't want to revisit the past, but he would if it could help Jared. "My father was a big, powerful man. There wasn't much he couldn't do. People used to brag on him, come to see him lift some log or bend iron with his bare hands. He was disappointed in me because I took after my mother's side of the family. She was so slender I used to be afraid she would break when my father wrapped his big arms around her."

"Were your brothers big like your father?"

"I didn't have any brothers, but that's not what I wanted to tell you."

"What was?"

"There was an accident. My mother died, and my father was paralyzed." Salty felt his throat tighten at the memory of the pain he'd suffered at losing his mother. "From that day until he died, he was so bitter that he made everybody around him miserable. He was still a strong man, but he used his strength to break things when he was in a rage. He blamed me for the accident because if I'd been home when I should have been, I would have taken my mother to church instead of him. It didn't matter that he'd been angry and driven his buggy too fast on a slick road. It didn't matter that he'd taken a green horse instead of waiting until I got home with the older one."

"He shouldn't have done that," Jared said.

Salty sighed. "What I find so great about you is that you have the most positive attitude of any boy I've ever known. You don't blame anyone for what happened to you. You're not even angry about it."

Jared's head dropped. "I am sometimes."

"That's natural...but you don't let it get you down. You don't really resent that your sister can do things you can't. You don't whine or expect special attention. Instead, you look for things you can do."

"Mama says I do lots of things to help."

"I'm sure you do," Salty agreed. "And as you get older, there'll be more ways you can help. There are jobs where having a withered leg won't stop you from being successful."

"Is that man we saw at the Randolph ranch successful? He didn't look happy."

Salty paused. "Jeff is very good with money, but he lets his bitterness keep him from enjoying his success and accepting his family's love."

"They looked mad at him," Jared pointed out.

"Sometimes he's so mean they get angry and strike back, but they do love him."

"I'd never be mean to Ellen. She beat up a boy who made fun of my leg."

Salty would like to have seen that. The boy would probably never live down having been bested by a girl. "You wouldn't be mean to *anyone.*"

"I would if they did something to Mama or Ellen. I don't care if that's wrong."

Salty reached over and tousled the boy's hair. "It's all right to defend your family, just like it was all right for Ellen to defend you. Jeff's brothers would do the same for him, even when he makes them so angry sometimes they want to knock him down."

Jared thought about this. "I can't knock anybody down. I can't even stand up without holding on to something."

"That's okay. You tell me if you have anybody who needs knocking down." Salty flourished his fists in a parody of a fight. "I'm rather handy with these."

Jared laughed. "You can't knock down little boys!"

"I can dunk their heads in a horse trough."

Jared got serious. "Would you really do that?"

"Your mother and I are married, so everybody will expect me to take care of you and your sister. A good dunking never hurt anybody, and maybe it would make them think twice before doing things to hurt people."

Salty decided they'd better stop before Jared thought up something else to ask. He didn't know whether Sarah would be angry that he'd shared such a personal talk with her son, but how could he consult her beforehand when he had no idea what Jared was going to say next? The ground would be even more treacherous with Ellen. People had all kinds of ideas about what could be said or done around little girls. He needed to tell Sarah what he and Jared had talked about, to make sure she understood that he couldn't anticipate what either child would ask. More than that, he needed to know how much latitude she would give him.

"We'd better get to sleep," he said to Jared. "We have a long day tomorrow."

"Will you let me handle the reins?"

He couldn't answer that without talking to Sarah, yet if he didn't answer now, Jared would think he was evading and stop confiding in him. "I'll have to talk to your mother first. She knows more about what you can do than I do."

"Mama says I'm too young, but I'm not. Besides, I can drive a cart even though I have a useless leg."

Salty agreed with the boy, but this was something he couldn't decide on his own. "I'll talk to your mother. If it's all right with her, I'll start teaching you how to handle the reins. Now go to sleep before you ask me something else that's going to get me in trouble."

"You won't be in trouble. Mama likes you."

Maybe she did, but Jared didn't understand that meant Salty was in for trouble.

They had been on the road for more than two hours the next morning, and Sarah still didn't know what Jared and Salty had talked about last night. He had questioned all three of them about their ranch, about what they'd done, what they hadn't done, and what they thought needed to be done.

She was surprised at how much Jared had observed despite his limited mobility. It was clear that he remembered practically everything he heard. It was equally clear that he'd thought through the information and come to his own clever conclusions.

Since they now had two wagons, Sarah held the reins of one and Salty the other. Most of the time the trail was too narrow for them to ride abreast, which forced one of them to ride behind. She didn't understand why this small separation bothered her so much. What was it about Salty that made her feel it was necessary to be near him? Right now he was explaining the intricacies of handling the reins to both of her children.

"If you have two horses, it's important to keep both of them equally in the bridle."

"We don't have harnesses for two horses," Ellen pointed out.

"That's because we've never had two horses," Jared added.

"Well, we have two now, so that's something to remember when we *do* have double harnesses," Salty said. "I'm going to pull off the trail and stop in the shade of that tree over there. I think it's time to give the horses a rest."

Sarah wondered why Salty was giving the horses a rest so much sooner than he had the previous two days.

"Ellen, why don't you and Jared get some fresh water from that stream?" Salty asked. "Be careful not to stir up mud when you do."

"I know how to get water," Ellen said. "I'm not a baby."

"I'll be sure to remember that." Sarah thought he was trying to hide a smile.

"Why did we really stop?" she asked when the children were out of earshot.

"Jared asked me if he could be allowed to handle the reins today. He said it was something he could do despite his leg."

Sarah was surprised by a stab of jealousy so sharp it shocked her. Why hadn't Jared asked her to teach him to handle a wagon? She should have realized this was something he could do that wouldn't be compromised by his leg. She also wondered why Salty was so much more concerned about her children than he was about her. Of course, she felt ashamed down to her toes for feeling this way. She should never have chosen him.

But she *had* chosen him, and she had married him, so she had to make the best of the situation. The only way to do that was to control her jealousy. So why did she open her mouth and say exactly the wrong thing?

"What if I say no?"

TEN

Sarah was wishing she could withdraw her words even before Salty's shocked response registered, but they were out and there was no getting them back. She felt like hiding in the catclaw thicket that bordered the trail. Instead she had to see if she could come up with something to keep Salty from thinking she was a spiteful, irrational woman who didn't have the best interests of her children at heart.

"You've put me in an awkward situation again."

Salty's startled expression receded, to be replaced by one of impatience. "I didn't put you there. Jared did, when he asked me to teach him to drive the wagon. I couldn't say no, and I couldn't say yes."

"But you said you'd teach him if I said it was okay."

"Of course I did. Would you have preferred I outright refuse?"

She *was* acting like a jealous, irrational woman. Salty would have every reason to think he'd married a shrew and wish himself back at the Circle Seven. A failing ranch, two challenging children, and a complaining wife. She'd be lucky if he didn't ask for a divorce immediately.

"I'm sorry," she said. "I don't know why I'm acting like this. You must think you've married a loony female who says one thing and then does another." She turned away from him so the sun wouldn't be in her eyes.

"Why would I think that?"

She thought it significant he hadn't said *I don't think that.* "I don't normally act like this. I guess fatigue of the trip, worry of not knowing if I would find anyone who could help me, and the strain of trying to accustom myself to having a husband I have to include in my decision-making have stretched my nerves until I feel wound so tight I'll explode. Move over some, so I can see you without squinting."

Salty relaxed, and a slow smile curved his lips. "Considering the circumstances, I wouldn't be surprised if you weren't ready to throw up your hands and do a little screaming. I'm told Rose overturned the supper table on her first night at the ranch."

Sarah was so surprised the imperturbable Rose would lose her temper so dramatically that she momentarily forgot her own difficulties. "Why would she do something like that?"

"Ask Zac if you want the embellished version. The short version is that she worked all day to clean the kitchen and prepare supper. The men came in without washing, sat down and started grabbing for food, everybody talking at once, and no one bothering to recognize her presence. I think it was Monty feeding the dog from the table that was the last straw. I'm sure you will feel better when you get home. Everybody feels more comfortable when they're in familiar surroundings."

"But you won't be in familiar surroundings," she pointed out.

"That doesn't matter. For the last ten years, I haven't been anywhere long enough to call it home."

She wondered if he'd like her ranch enough to feel at home—and if she *wanted* to him to feel at home. She also wondered why, after knowing her own mind for her whole life, she should be unable to string together more than two rational thoughts. All because she'd accepted a man who'd promised indifference to her. Only, he wasn't indifferent to her children, and her attraction for him only seemed to have increased.

Sarah made a decision. "I'd appreciate it if you'd teach *both* my children the proper way to handle a wagon or buggy. I don't know more than how to stop, start, and hold the reins in between."

"That's the important part," Salty replied. "Everything else is mostly a matter of style."

Apparently no one had told the man that maintaining indifference didn't include smiling at her in a way that caused her heart to flutter and her breath to feel shallow and insufficient. He might think that was the way people reacted to each other when they were just friends, and his smile might appear ordinary to most people, but to her it communicated warmth and welcome, genuine and readily given. There was more, too, but it was hard to decide exactly what. It was like a promise of understanding, of compassion, of loyalty, fidelity, esteem—all the things a woman looked for in a man but never found. Sarah was probably imagining all of this because Salty had promised to rescue her and her ranch. A deluge of relief. Rebounding hope. Overflowing thankfulness. And continuing disbelief that she might have found someone who was as good with her children as she wanted.

"Here they come with the water," Salty said. "I'd better help. I don't want them to give the horses too much."

When he'd sent them off together to fetch the water, Sarah had wondered how the children would manage to carry two buckets, since Ellen had to support Jared as she was doing now with her right hand. But each carried a bucket in their outside hand.

"This bucket is for the horses," Ellen said handing hers to Salty.

"This one is for us," Jared said to his mother. "The horses aren't the only ones who're thirsty."

Sarah held the dipper for her son to drink while Salty watched Ellen water the horses. She wondered what it was about this man that had enabled him to move into the heart of her family so easily. Ellen and Jared had felt varying degrees of fondness for the men who'd worked for her, but they'd never liked the same man, and they'd never liked any man the way they appeared to like Salty. Jared confided in him. Ellen wanted to be around him.

Her children had been the very best part of Sarah's life. Their love and devotion had carried her through many a dark moment, just as her love for them had given her a reason to carry on when she felt so tired and dispirited she thought she couldn't take another step. They were a family, a single unit. Maybe that wasn't enough, though. Mother Nature had decreed that it took a man and a woman to create a child. Maybe she'd also decreed that a child needed both a mother and a father, that one wasn't complete without the other.

Or maybe it wasn't Mother Nature at all. Maybe it was just that men and women weren't the same, and that children needed that dissimilarity because they learned different things from each.

Or maybe it was just Salty. He was kind and gentle, thoughtful and generous. Yet there was a strength about him that bred confidence, instilled a sense of security. There was nothing hazy about his thinking or confusing about his actions; you knew exactly where you stood with him, something every child needed.

Sarah was the one who couldn't make up her mind what she thought or felt. No, that wasn't true; she knew what she felt. She just didn't want to feel it. Her father and her husband had convinced her that life would be better without a man in it. She was sure that a strong, intelligent woman could succeed as well as a man. Their bodies were different, but their brains weren't, and it was the brain that provided all the answers.

Getting to know the Randolphs had caused her to question her conclusions. The love in that family was easy to see, even if there were moments of conflict. Was it possible that Salty was strong enough to carry a family on his shoulders, too, capable of a love that would cause him to put their happiness before his own?

Laughter scattered her thoughts. Salty had said something that caused Ellen to giggle. When he dipped his hand into the bucket and flicked drops of water on her, she shrieked with delight and tried to wrench the bucket away. He responded by holding it out of her reach and flicking water on her until she hid on the other side of the horse.

When he reached across the horse to continue sprinkling water on her, she ran laughing to her mother.

"Salty threatened to drown me!"

Even though Jared was laughing, too, his practical nature asserted itself. "There's not enough water in that bucket to drown you."

Salty hadn't left his position by the horse, but he was regarding them all with amusement.

"What did you say to make him flick water on you?" Sarah asked her daughter.

"Nothing. I was just teasing him because he was teasing me."

"What did you say?"

Ellen blushed. "I just said I thought Zac Randolph was cute and funny but spoiled."

"That doesn't sound like teasing to me."

"Salty said maybe I should marry him when I grow up and straighten him out."

"And what did you say?"

"I said I don't like icky boys because they grow up to be terrible men like him."

Sarah didn't know which surprised her more, Ellen thinking Zac was cute or Ellen comparing Salty to *icky* boys. She wasn't surprised that Ellen thought most men were terrible.

"You shouldn't say that to Salty," Jared spoke up.

"I was just teasing him for saying I should marry Zac Randolph." Ellen made a face. "Boys are awful little coyotes."

Salty came forward. "Does that mean men are awful big coyotes?"

"You're awful big *wolves*," Ellen said with a giggle before hiding behind her mother.

Having caught the tenor of the exchange, Jared was grinning. "I think you ought to dump the bucket of water on her."

"Will you help me?" Salty asked.

"Yes."

That was as close to a joyous sound as Jared had ever uttered. His eyes were wide and sparkling with happiness. He was so eager to partner with Salty he couldn't sit still.

Ellen uttered a happy shriek and plastered herself against Sarah's back. "You can't dump the bucket on me. You'll get Mama wet."

"What do you think we ought to do?" Salty asked Jared.

"You shouldn't wet Mama, but you can dump Ellen in the creek."

"Tell you what," Salty said. "I'll hold her, while you dump the bucket over her."

"Don't you dare, Jared Winborne!" Ellen shrieked. "I'll sic Bones on you."

Bones had been sniffing behind every bush and tree. Upon hearing his name, he abandoned his quest for game, barked, and trotted over.

Ellen peeped at the dog from behind her mother. "Bones likes me. Don't you, Bones?"

The dog barked. Apparently all one had to do was say his name to get a response.

"He's a boy," Jared reminded his sister. "Boys always like boys better than girls."

Sarah nearly laughed aloud at that sentiment. She was so astonished at finding herself in the middle of a silly game with both of her overly serious children acting like typical seven-year-olds that she hardly knew what to think. But apparently nothing was required of her beyond being a shield for Ellen.

"I think Ellen deserves to be punished for threatening you, don't you?" Salty asked Jared.

"Yes. Dump the whole bucket over her."

"That might be too much. Suppose I hold her so you can flick water on her."

There was a moment of hesitation when Salty looked at Sarah

asking for permission. She had no brothers or sisters, so nothing like this had even happened to her. Maybe this was how children growing up in a normal family behaved. Both the children were laughing, so she decided to trust Salty. She nodded her permission.

Salty gave a whoop and grabbed Ellen around her waist. She shrieked and clutched Sarah. Salty pried her hands loose and dragged her over to Jared. Ellen threatened her brother with all kinds of terrible retribution, but Jared just laughed and started to flick water on Ellen with both hands. Jared was getting as much water on Salty as on Ellen, but that didn't deter Salty. He urged Jared to keep it up until the bucket was empty.

Jared probably would have done just that, but the moment Ellen's enthusiasm began to wane, Salty changed course. He released her and picked up the second bucket. "Want to get Jared back?" he asked.

Ellen's energy rebounded. She started flicking water at Jared. For the next few minutes, the children filled the air with a virtual shower of water. Ellen was no more accurate than Jared, and Sarah was soon as wet as Salty. He grinned wickedly at her and licked a drop of water off the end of his nose with his tongue.

That caused something inside Sarah to snap, and she was suddenly seized with a compulsion to throw water on Salty. It was childish, it was ridiculous, it was something she'd never done, but she couldn't stop herself. She dipped her hand into Jared's bucket, scooped up a handful of water, and with a laugh that was completely unlike her, threw it at Salty.

His response was instantaneous. Devils danced in his eyes. His grin promised he was going to retaliate.

"Let's get them both," he said to Ellen.

For the next minute or so, the four of them sank into what Sarah would previously have characterized as a fit of insanity. They threw water at each other until they were all laughing so hard they were nearly helpless. That Bones punctuated their laughter with periodic barks only made everything funnier.

It was silly and childish but incredibly liberating. Sarah felt that she'd shed the weight of a lifetime of attempting to control her every thought and feeling, of being responsible for everyone's happiness. Anyone happening to come upon them would have thought they were lunatics, or at the very least immature and irresponsible. Sarah didn't care. The water was gone, her children were laughing like they never had before, and Salty was looking at her in a way that caused her to think that if this man could come to love her, she would be the most fortunate woman in the world.

The thought had a sobering effect. Had this unguarded moment, this small window in time when she'd thrown aside all control, revealed a need which had long lain hidden deep within her?

Ellen plucked at her shirt, which was plastered against her chest. "We're soaked," she pointed out. Water had run down and wet the top of her pants. So much water had landed on her shoes that it had washed off all the dust.

Salty collected the buckets. "The sun will dry us soon enough."

"Can we have another water fight someday?" Ellen asked.

"It was fun," Jared added.

Her children had never experienced anything as simple and joyful as this. It was a sad realization for Sarah. She'd been so overwhelmed by Jared's deformity and the struggle to keep the ranch going that she hadn't stopped to realize her children didn't know how to have fun. And it was because *she* didn't know how to have fun. It had taken Salty to make her realize what they were missing.

From now on, she would make certain her children had reasons to laugh. If she couldn't do it, she'd ask Salty. She was going to promise something else, too. She was going to start all over with him, pretend she didn't know anything about him. She was going to judge him by what he did, not by what other men had done. It was becoming increasingly clear that she wasn't able to control her attraction to him, so she was going to stop fighting it. She wasn't in love with him, exactly, and never expected that she would be. Still, it would be nice to have a man as a friend, one she could turn to when she had a question, needed some advice, or just needed a shoulder to lean on. She didn't want him to do everything for her, but she wanted something she didn't have now. She wasn't sure what it was. Maybe she would have to define it as it began to take shape, but she was going to take the risk.

She wondered if that's what most women wanted in a husband.

———————

Salty noticed Sarah's attitude toward him change after the water fight. It had been a silly thing to do, something he hadn't done since he was a child. Maybe he'd been around Zac Randolph too long.

Maybe he shouldn't blame it on Zac but rather on his own immaturity. He'd always given himself credit for a sense of humor, but he'd never considered himself immature. It was probably just a natural response to Ellen's *icky* comment. That was the first time she'd seemed in a playful mood, and he couldn't help but encourage her. From there things had accelerated until Sarah joined. Watching her throw water on him while laughing as hard as either of her children had been the biggest surprise of all. She was so serious, she made the air around her feel heavy. Now, as they neared her ranch—he had to start thinking of it as *their* ranch—he had to decide what his reaction was going to be.

"This is Mr. Wallace's land," Ellen was telling him. "He doesn't like us. He wants to buy Mama's ranch."

As they drew closer to the San Marcos River, the rolling hills had given way to nearly flat land covered with groves of elm, hackberry, cottonwood, and grassy meadows. Stagnant pools populated with frogs and sunning turtles alternated with open grasslands shared by cows and white-tailed deer. The air was softer, warmer, more moist. Spring would be here soon.

"Mr. Wallace doesn't want to pay enough for the land," Jared added. "Mama says he's a mean-spirited old skinflint."

He'd never heard Sarah make a derogatory comment about anyone except her husband, but Salty was convinced a spirited woman existed under the staid exterior. All she needed was the right reason to let that side of her come out. He didn't know what that reason might be, but he thought it might be fun to find it. Everyone ought to have a reason to smile from time to time. It was the good moments that made the bad ones bearable.

"Arnie said he was trying to steal our cows," Ellen said.

"I don't think he's trying to steal our cows," Sarah told her daughter, "but he has tried to make things so difficult I would give up and sell to him. Adding my land to his would give him the biggest ranch in the county."

They were riding abreast, Salty and Jared in one wagon and Sarah and Ellen in the other, but it was hard to carry on a conversation over the noise of the horses' hooves and the wagons rattling along the rough trail.

"Arnie said Wallace was so stingy he wouldn't hire enough men to take care of his herd," Ellen said. "He said we could steal from him if we wanted."

Arnie didn't sound like the kind of man who ought to be around impressionable children, but Salty supposed Sarah hadn't had much to choose from when she was looking for hired hands. Between the brutality of war and the loss of everything they valued, many men had become hard and cruel, not hesitating to take advantage of others. Women and children were especially vulnerable.

"Mama says only bad people steal," Jared told Salty. "Have you ever stolen?"

"Jared, that's a rude question." Sarah sounded shocked. "Apologize to Salty immediately."

"That's not necessary," Salty said. "I can't expect him to answer my questions if I'm not willing to answer his."

"He should take for granted that you're honest."

Salty turned to face Sarah. "None of us can take anything for granted until we've faced temptation that seems impossible to resist."

"Have you ever faced temptation like that?"

Salty turned to Jared. "Many times." He wasn't going to tell them about the times he had been tempted to suffocate his father and put them both out of their misery, or the times he was tempted to let him starve rather than fix a meal that would be thrown back at him. "Sometimes during the war we didn't have anything to eat or money to buy food. I didn't steal anything myself, but I ate food others stole. That makes me just as guilty."

"Mama says if the ranch doesn't get better, we won't have anything to eat. Will we have to steal?"

"No matter what happens with the ranch, you'll always have something to eat."

"Does that mean you're going to make us have a really big garden?"

Ellen sounded so horrified Salty couldn't repress a laugh. "Yes, it means we're going to have a really big garden. But we'll also have pigs, chickens, and a milk cow."

"I don't like pigs and chickens," Ellen told him.

"I don't either," Salty responded. "That's why we're going to eat them."

Ellen giggled. "If you eat the chickens, you won't have any eggs."

"We'll only eat the ones that are too lazy to lay eggs."

That started Jared and Ellen making chicken jokes. Salty glanced over at Sarah and was surprised by the look on her face. It was a bemused, sort of amazed, look. She probably thought they were all crazy, and she was wondering how she was going to get through the next ten to fifteen years.

"Is this the turnoff to your ranch?" The trail was faint, but Salty guessed it had to be.

"Can't you see the wheel tracks?" Ellen asked.

"Yes, but I don't see a house."

"That's because it's hidden by the trees," Jared told him. "Mama said Grandpa didn't like the wind whistling around his house in the winter so he built it in the middle of a bunch of trees."

"Sounds like your grandpa was a smart man. I guess that's why you and Ellen are so smart."

"Salty thinks Ellen and I are smart," Jared told his mother.

Sarah turned to her son with a softened expression. "Of course you are. How many times have I told you that you're the smartest children I ever knew?"

"You're our mama," Ellen said. "Arnie said mamas *have* to think their children are smart."

"You'd better be smart," Salty said. "I'm depending on you and Jared to help me with the ranch."

"Ellen can do that," Jared said. "I can't ride."

Salty was about to say that they'd have to see about that when Sarah's exclamation surprised him. "What's *he* doing here?"

Salty followed Sarah's gaze until he saw a man on the trail ahead who didn't look like a prosperous rancher.

"Is that Wallace?"

"No," Ellen said. "It's Arnie."

ELEVEN

ARNIE HAD BEEN LEANING AGAINST A TREE BY THE SIDE OF THE TRAIL like he was waiting for someone. He looked to be in his forties, stocky of build, and dressed in clothes that showed hard use. He stepped into the center of the trail when the wagons came into view.

"I thought you said Arnie quit," Salty said.

"He did," Sarah told him.

"Then what is he doing here?"

"I don't know."

Salty eyed Sarah. "Do you want him here?"

"No, and I intend to tell him so."

"Maybe it would come better from me," Salty suggested. "Knowing I'm your husband ought to convince him he's no longer needed."

He could see Sarah struggle with herself. "I want to know why he came back."

"Can't you guess?"

She might not have thought it before, but she did now. "Maybe it would be better if you talked to him."

"Pull your wagon behind mine. Ellen, jump down and ride with your mother."

He had expected Ellen to object or demand a reason, but maybe the tone of his voice told Ellen this was a time to do as she was told and save her questions.

"What are you going to do?" Jared asked in a whisper. He had caught the tenor of the situation better than his sister.

"That depends on Arnie." Like so many other times in his life, Salty was going into a situation virtually blind. He'd survived before. He expected to survive this time as well.

Arnie moved out of the trail to let Salty pass, but Salty brought his wagon to a stop next to him. Despite his downtrodden appearance, Arnie was a respectable-looking man who appeared to enjoy good health. His questioning smile showed good teeth; his cheeks sported a beard that was probably only three or four days old.

"Howdy. My name is Benton Wheeler. What can I do for you?"

Arnie's gaze slid past Salty and came to rest on Sarah. "Nothing. I'm here to see Sarah—I mean Miz Winborne."

Salty forced a smile. "She's not Miz Winborne anymore. She's Mrs. Wheeler now."

Arnie's gaze had been focused on Salty as he spoke, but now his gaze whipped around to Sarah. "You're married?"

"Yes," Sarah replied.

"But you didn't know him a week ago."

"I was introduced to him by someone whose opinion I respect."

"I would have married you." Arnie balled his fists in anger. "Why do you think I talked everybody in Austin out of working for you?"

"Considering the things you said before you left, there was no way I could have guessed the nature of your feelings."

"I was angry you didn't feel the same."

Salty decided it was time to stop this useless conversation. "I can sympathize with your situation, but I really can't have you talking to my wife like this."

"Did you really marry him?" Arnie looked like he couldn't believe what he was hearing.

"Yeah, she did," Jared answered for his mother. "Ellen and I were both there." The boy's confirmation seemed to deflate Arnie.

"How long have you been here?" Salty asked.

"Three days." Which explained why he didn't have a bedroll or a knapsack with him. "I thought Sarah would come back when she couldn't find anybody to work for her." Which would have put her in the position of having to accept him on his terms.

"Have you been taking care of the ranch?" Salty asked.

"What else would I have been doing?"

Besides plotting the downfall of an innocent woman? Salty thought to himself. "My wife and I appreciate your looking after the place. I believe standard wages are thirty dollars a month, so we owe you three dollars."

"You don't owe me nothing," Arnie growled.

"Yes, I do, and I like to pay my debts." Salty pulled out his money pouch and extracted three silver dollars, which he held out to Arnie. "I don't like to appear rude, but we've got a lot of work to do to get everything settled in before dark."

Arnie ran his gaze over the second wagon, the cow, the pigs, the chickens, and Salty's two riding horses. Salty wondered if he could tell Jared and Ellen were wearing some of the clothes Rose Randolph had given them.

"Looks like you found yourself a husband with money," he said to Sarah.

Salty didn't like what he said or the way he said it. A little more, and Arnie would find that Texas husbands didn't like it when men hassled their wives. He announced, "I think five minutes will be enough time for you to be saddled up and riding out. If it takes more than that, I may have to lend a hand."

"You fancy you can make me?"

Arnie was heavy and muscular, but his movements were slow. A man with Salty's wiry strength could wear him down while dancing out of range of his heavy fists. "I always had a reputation as a good fighter, and no jury would convict a man for defending his wife, no matter how he decided to do it."

Arnie hesitated a moment before uttering an oath and turning on his heel.

"I wish you'd hit him," Jared said.

"I had enough of fighting during the war," Salty replied. Enough of fighting the murderous McClendon clan and Cortina's rapacious rustlers. Enough fighting his father just to get through one day in peace. All he wanted out of life was a bit of land to call his own and someone to love. Sarah had given him a way to get the first. He hoped her children would provide him with the second.

He was relieved when he followed the trail into a grove of post oaks and found himself facing a small but well-built house. He brought the wagon to a halt, put the brake on, and wrapped the reins around the handle.

It was one of those crisp, late winter/early spring evenings when the air looked blue despite a weak sun's efforts to warm it. Despite the lingering cold, Texas mountain laurel was already showing flower buds, while bluebonnets and Indian Paintbrush were thrusting their heads toward the meager shafts of sunlight. A grandfather of yucca plants thrust its shaggy neck toward the sky, its crown of spiky leaves a sunburst of dull green. A chorus of birds, each looking for the best resting place for the coming night, quarreled among the treetops.

Sarah's house stood in the center of the open space within the circle of trees, its weathered wood, cracked and blistered with age, meshing with the background. A stone chimney rose only a few feet above a roof of shingles bleached gray from summers of harsh sun and winters of cold rain. A door and two curtained windows, looking unnervingly like a nose and two eyes in a weather-beaten face, welcomed the family home. It wasn't anything like his father's house in Georgia, but somehow it felt more like home than any place Salty had been in the years since.

"Ellen, you can help your mother take your luggage into the house. Jared and I will take care of the livestock."

"Jared can hardly walk," she reminded him.

"We'll figure something out."

Salty wasn't sure what he was going to do, but he was determined Jared wouldn't go on feeling he couldn't do anything except sit around the house. The first thing would be to devise something that would enable him to walk on his own, something like the various crutches his father had discarded without giving any of them an honest try. After that, he would tackle teaching the boy to ride.

"You need a hand?" he asked Sarah. She had climbed down from the wagon and was reaching for a bag of clothes Ellen was handing her.

"Ellen and I can take care of everything here. I'll start supper as soon as I get everything unloaded."

"There's no need to hurry," he told her. "It's still early yet, and Jared and I have a lot to do."

"I'll send Ellen to help as soon as we get everything unloaded."

"I want to take care of the horses," Ellen called out. "Arnie always let me."

"I'll save that job for you," Salty promised. "Now Jared can show me the shed where I'll be living." Sarah had already told him there was no room for him in the house. He lifted the boy from one wagon to the other, climbed up next to him then took the reins and started the horse forward. "You'll have to tell me where all the animals go."

"There isn't any place," Jared replied. "The chickens used to roost in the trees, and the sows go wherever they want."

"What about the horses?"

"We have a corral, but there are so many holes in it our horses keep getting out."

Salty had hoped to be able to start working with the herd soon, but it looked like he was going to be occupied around the ranch proper for longer than he wanted.

The shed had apparently begun as exactly that, open at the front and on both sides, the roof slanting down from front to back. Since then it had been closed in with ill-fitting boards. It had a doorway and single window in the front.

Arnie was coming out of it as they drove up. He threw an angry glance at Salty before heading toward his horse with two bundles under his arms. Once he secured the bundles on his horse, he headed back to the shed, only to emerge a moment later with a sack that sounded like it contained a collection of metal items—probably his coffeepot and everything else he used to cook and eat his meals. After tying this to his saddle, he turned and approached Salty. He looked over the livestock before he spoke.

"It's good you've got some money. It's going to take some to pull this place through."

"If you don't have any money, how did you think to marry Sarah?" Salty asked.

Arnie didn't answer. Instead he said, "There's not one man in a thousand who gets a chance for a woman like that."

"Then why did you leave?"

"I wanted to be her husband, not her hired hand. I never figured on her finding somebody like you."

Salty chastised himself for judging too hastily. From his tone, Arnie seemed to have a genuine affection for Sarah. "I'll take good care of her," he promised the man.

Arnie glanced at Jared then back at Salty. "The boy seems to like you. He never did me." Jared was leaning against Salty as though for protection. Arnie looked out over the expanse of grass at the tree-covered hill in the distance. "Tell Sarah I'm sorry I said the things I did. I never said anything bad about her, just about the ranch."

Salty and Jared remained silent while Arnie mounted and rode away without looking back.

After he disappeared beyond the trees, Jared said, "I still don't like him."

"That's okay," Salty said. "You can't be expected to like everyone."

"I didn't like the way he looked at Mama."

Salty could easily imagine that the hunger in Arnie's eyes was noticeable to a child as sensitive as Jared. He didn't have to understand it to be frightened by it. "He's gone now, so let's see what my home looks like."

"Ellen says she'd like to stay out here, but Mama says it's hardly fit for humans."

Salty lifted the boy down from the wagon. "Since I have to sleep here, maybe your mama doesn't think I'm human."

"Mama is afraid of men."

"Why?" The question was inappropriate, but he was so surprised by Jared's statement the word slipped out before he could stop it.

"I don't know." Jared's face wrinkled in thought. "Ellen isn't afraid of anybody. I don't think I'm afraid of anybody, either. But I don't like some people."

"That's perfectly normal," Salty assured him.

He opened the door and stepped inside the shed. It wasn't as bad as he'd feared, but beyond providing a roof and walls, it offered virtually nothing in the way of comfort. The meager light coming through the door and window revealed no bed.

"I hope your mother intends to let me eat at the house. If I built a cook fire in here, I'd die of smoke inhalation or burn the place down."

"All the hired men ate with us," Jared told Salty. "Mama said she had to make sure they had something to eat so they could work hard."

"Let's get my stuff inside. Then we can decide what to do about the livestock."

Jared propped himself up against the wall while Salty brought in his few belongings. He dropped his bedroll in the corner with an inward sigh over the lost comfort of his bunk bed at the Circle Seven. After a moment he told the boy, "I'll be back in a few minutes."

Outside, he unhitched one of his horses, jumped on the animal bareback and spurred him into a fast canter. It took only a few minutes to catch up with Arnie. "Will you do something for me?" he asked as he pulled alongside.

"What?" Arnie didn't appear too eager to help.

"I've got some lumber being sent out from town in a few days. Could you ask the man to bring a mattress as well and add it to my bill?"

"I slept on the ground for more than a year."

"I slept on the ground for four years during the war, and I'm not eager to do it again."

At first it looked like Arnie was going to refuse. But as nearly always happened, learning Salty was an ex-soldier altered people's attitude.

"I fought for two years until I was captured," Arnie told him. "They let me come home after I promised not to reenlist." Arnie nodded his agreement to deliver Salty's message then continued his journey.

When Salty got back to the shed, Jared asked, "Where did you go?"

"I asked Arnie to have the lumber man send me a mattress."

"You don't have a bed," the boy pointed out.

"I'll make a frame with some of the lumber."

"Can I watch?"

"You can help."

Jared didn't smile. "You don't have to keep pretending I can do things."

Salty knelt so he could look the boy in the eye. "There'll always be things you can't do. That's true for everybody. However, there are lots of things you can *learn* to do. I'm not ready to talk to your mother about it yet, but I plan to teach you to ride a horse."

"Do you think I can?" The hope and excitement in the boy's eyes were wonderful to see.

"It won't be easy, and you might have to grow stronger first, but we're going to try."

Jared let go of the wall and staggered forward to clutch Salty about the waist. "I'm glad Mama married you."

Salty had to swallow a couple of times before he could reply. "I'm glad I married her, too. Now, we'd better figure out what to do with these pigs and chickens until I can fix up pens tomorrow. I don't want the coyotes getting them before we get a chance to eat them ourselves."

"We can't eat the chickens, remember? We want them to give us eggs."

He winked at the boy. "Glad you reminded me. I'd have wrung their necks and had them in the pot before dark."

"I know you're teasing me," Jared said, "but I don't mind."

"Well, your mother won't be teasing us if we don't get our work done before she has supper on the table. If anyone is willing to cook for you, don't make them wait or you're likely to be cooking your own food."

Jared shook his head. "Mama won't starve you. You have to work hard."

"Which neither of us is doing, so we'd better get busy. We can leave the chickens in their cage, but what are we going to do with the pigs?"

———

"Do you like Salty?"

Ellen's question didn't exactly surprise Sarah, but she wasn't sure how she wanted to answer. While she tried to decide what to say, she carried the clothes Rose had given the children to the room they shared. Bare walls and floor cast their bunks in stark relief, quilts made out of scraps providing the room's only color. A single chest held their few clothes. Everything else had been sold.

"Of course I like Salty," she said. "I wouldn't have married him if I didn't."

Ellen tried on everything Sarah handed her. She might be a tomboy, but she had a woman's interest in new clothes, even if they were only new to her. "I don't mean like that."

"How do you mean?" Sarah didn't want to ask, but she had learned that both her children were tenacious in pursuing a question until they got an answer that satisfied them.

"Like Mrs. Randolph likes her husband."

Sarah had never believed it was possible for a woman to love her husband the way Rose loved George. She also had been certain there was no man in the world who would treat his wife as George treated Rose.

She told her daughter, "I hardly know Salty, and he hardly knows me. Two people have to be together for a long time before they care for each other that much."

"Oh." Ellen sank into such deep thought she didn't follow when Sarah went to her own room to open the bag of clothes Rose had given her.

Sarah's room was as bare as that of her children. The primary difference was that she had a real bed and a bureau that had belonged to her mother. A blue print dress from Rose's bag caught her attention. With her fair complexion and blond hair, blue had always been one of her favorite colors. She pulled the garment out, unfolded it, and held it up against her. She looked at her reflection in a small mirror on her bureau. It made her look younger. It was almost the same sky blue as her eyes.

"Why don't you put it on?"

Sarah whirled around to find her daughter standing in the doorway. She was embarrassed to be caught admiring her reflection in the mirror, just as she'd complained Roger used to do. "I was just looking to see if they might fit," she said.

"It makes you look pretty," Ellen said.

"It doesn't feel right." Sarah began to pack it away.

"If it's all right for us to wear the clothes Mrs. Randolph gave us, why isn't it for you?"

It wasn't a matter of right or wrong, exactly. It was a matter of pride—something that was as useless in this instance as it was vital in others. Sarah changed her mind, folded the dress, and laid it on the bed.

"I bet Salty would think you were pretty if you wore it," Ellen said.

That was exactly what Sarah didn't need to hear. "I don't want to make Salty think I'm pretty."

"Why not?" The hole under her feet was getting deeper and deeper.

"I only married Salty because I needed someone to help me with the ranch."

"I know, but he likes you."

Sarah sat down on the edge of the bed and drew Ellen toward her. "We have a business arrangement. He'll help me with the ranch, and I'll give him half of our land if he's successful."

Ellen stared at her. "Jared and I like Salty. How come you don't like him?"

Sarah shook her head. "Why is it so important that I like him?"

"We don't want him to go away like all the others."

Sarah glanced away from her daughter. "He won't leave. We're married."

"Papa left, and you were married to him."

Sarah sighed and put her arm around Ellen. She pushed the girl's hair out of her eyes. How could a seven-year-old look so grown up? It was impossible to explain why Roger's leaving was different. He hadn't been mature enough to take on the responsibility of a family, to do the hard work necessary to keep a ranch going, or accept the lack of adventure that accompanied going to bed with the same woman every night.

She reached for her daughter's hand, gave it a gentle squeeze, and settled on the simplest truth. "Your father left because he was needed to fight the war." Roger really left because he'd grown disenchanted with the work it took to run the ranch, had fallen out of love with his wife, and couldn't accept that he had a handicapped son. Sarah had learned long ago not to quibble over a little lie. It was more important to protect her children.

"I look like him, don't I?"

Sarah guided her daughter to the mirror. "More and more each day. He was a very handsome man. You're going to be a beautiful woman."

Ellen turned away from the mirror. "I don't want to be beautiful."

Sarah was surprised. "Why not?"

"I don't want a man to marry me then leave me."

Heart breaking, Sarah drew her daughter to her. "The war is over. Men won't have a reason to leave their wives and children." She prayed that was true.

"Salty won't leave?"

"No. He won't leave," Sarah promised. And he wouldn't. Not even after the divorce. He would have half of her ranch. He wouldn't be her husband anymore, but she'd be connected to him forever. Surprisingly, that thought gave her a feeling of security she'd never had before. There'd be someone to depend on, to talk to, to share her concerns about her ranch. And it would be even better because he was fond of her children.

She shook her head to dislodge these foolish daydreams. She had to stop letting her imagination run loose. She had no assurance he wouldn't simply sell his part of the ranch. She just hoped he wouldn't. She was hungry for someone she could talk to as a friend and confidant, an equal, someone she wasn't responsible for.

Ellen's countenance brightened. "I'm glad Salty won't leave. I hope he stays forever."

Sarah hadn't put the thought into words, not even in her own mind, but she hoped he would, too.

She thought about Arnie. She would never have married him under normal circumstances, but would she have done so for the sake of her children? Chills ran down her back. Despite the lies he told, Arnie had been her best hand. She would have married him if she'd had no other choice. After all, she'd married Salty, about whom she knew even less. Of course, Salty wanted her land more than he wanted her. Now that she'd gotten what she wanted, she didn't want it any longer, but how was Salty to know that if she didn't tell him she'd changed her mind?

"Do you think you could learn to like Salty a lot?"

Sarah had almost forgotten her daughter was still there. "I don't know. He seems like a very nice man, so I think I could. Why?"

"I want you to have a baby with him."

TWELVE

SARAH FELT LIKE SHE'D BEEN SLAMMED FACE-FIRST INTO A STONE wall. "What made you say a thing like that?"

"You had us when you married Papa," Ellen pointed out.

"That was different."

"How?"

Sarah felt so weak she sank back down on the bed. "I married your father hoping to start a family. But I have my family now, so I don't need to have any children with Salty." She breathed a sigh of relief. That covered the issue without involving any lies.

"Don't you *want* to have a baby with Salty?"

No. She didn't want that kind of relationship with a man ever again. It wasn't about having a baby, though. It was about the emotional commitment that would have to exist between them before she would consider entering another physical relationship. She hated to think of growing old alone, but that seemed preferable to the hell she'd endured with Roger.

She told Ellen, "I don't need any more family than you and Jared. Besides, when you two grow up and get married, you'll give me lots of grandchildren."

"I'm not going to get married, and Arnie said no one would marry Jared."

Sarah blamed herself for not being more vigilant, for not knowing more about what Arnie was saying to her children. She reached out, put her arm around her daughter's shoulder and said, "When I was your age, I didn't want to get married, either, but I changed my mind. I eventually wanted a family. Most women do."

"I don't."

"You may change your mind. As for no one wanting to marry Jared, that's nonsense. He's a wonderful boy."

"But he's a cripple."

"Lots of men have come back from the war without arms or legs, but their families are glad to have them back."

"Do you mean like that mean man at the Randolphs'?"

Sarah dropped her arm from Ellen's shoulder and looked her daughter in the eye. "I'm sure Jeff isn't really mean. But now it's time for me to stop chattering and see about starting supper."

"Can I go see about the horses?"

This was one of the many times she couldn't monitor what the children were hearing or saying, but there was too much work to be done to keep them by her side all day. She didn't feel so concerned about them with Salty as she had been about them with the other men who'd worked for her. "You may go. Ask Jared if he's ready to come to the house."

Ellen was through the door so quickly she could barely have heard Sarah's last words. Her daughter's love of horses brought a smile to Sarah's lips. She just hoped her daughter wasn't planning to join a cavalry unit when she got older.

It was a blessing that her children liked Salty, Sarah decided. That took some of the burden off her shoulders, because she no longer had to be both mother and father. They now had a man they liked and admired who would be part of their lives for several years to come. By the time of the divorce, they would be mostly grown, able to stand on their own feet.

Yes, she was grateful Salty liked her children and that he was making an obvious effort to be a positive part of their lives. She'd have to figure out how to thank him. One way would be to fix his favorite meals once she found out what he liked to eat.

Another might be to wear that blue dress.

———————————

Salty was ready to eat. He was hungry and worn out from both trying to do his work and keep two energetic seven-year-olds occupied. He'd never realized children could be so exhausting, even when they were helping! Ellen had so much enthusiasm it wore him out. Jared wanted to be involved, but there was very little he could do without assistance or some imaginative planning. At least Bones had the good sense to stay out of the way and just watch.

He drove the last nail into the last board and stepped back to consider his work. "I think this pen will hold the pigs until we can build something better."

"Will you put the pigs that ran away in the pen?" Ellen asked.

"Mama said we don't have enough feed to keep them in a pen." Jared was sitting on the chicken cage. Occasionally one pecked at him, but that didn't seem to bother him. "Enough pigs always survived before for us to have something to eat."

Salty tousled the boy's hair. "We'll need a lot more pigs now that I'm here."

Ellen giggled. "If you eat that much, you'll get fat."

"Wouldn't you two like to get fat?"

"I wouldn't like to be fat," Jared said. "I might hurt my leg even more."

That drained what little humor there had been in Salty's joke. "Your leg is going to get better," he promised, "not worse."

Jared shrugged. "A doctor told Mama it might get a little better when I got older, but he said I'd never be able to walk."

Salty had already picked out the piece of wood he would attempt to make into a workable crutch. "There's more than one way to skin a cat.

We just have to figure out how to skin your particular cat."

Ellen giggled again. "Jared doesn't have a cat."

Salty grabbed her and rubbed his knuckles across her head to produce more giggles. "Maybe I should have said 'particular problem.'" He tweaked her nose and let her go. "Now let's head up to the house. I can hear my stomach growling."

He started to let Jared lean on him for support, but he could tell from the boy's eyes that he was too exhausted to make it to the house. Hoping to make a game of it, he picked the child up and settled him on his shoulders. "Now you're taller than your sister."

"I want to ride, too!" Ellen cried.

"Maybe tomorrow, if your brother doesn't break my back." Salty pretended to stagger under Jared's weight. "I didn't know he was such a big boy."

Ellen bounded inside the house as soon as they reached it. Salty put Jared down and they followed.

The first thing to catch his attention was the aroma of sausage and corn bread. It smelled so good it caused his mouth to water. The second thing was Sarah wearing a blue dress. What that did to another part of his body was something he hoped no one would notice.

"Salty gave Jared a ride on his shoulders," Ellen announced. "He's going to give me a ride tomorrow."

Sarah looked up from the pan she was watching. "You're both too big to be riding on Salty's shoulders. If you give him a bad back, you'll have to do all his work." Then she winked at Salty, which caused his body further confusion. Maybe she was just teasing the children, but it looked more like a thawing in the stiff-backed resistance of the last few days. With the thaw, the wink, and the blue dress…well, if things continued in this direction, he was in for some sleepless nights.

"He says he needs lots of pigs to eat because he's real hungry," Ellen continued.

"Ellen said he'd get fat if he ate that much."

Sarah looked at her children then at Salty. "While you were doing all this talking, did you get any work done?"

"I took care of the horses while Salty made a pen for the pigs," Ellen replied.

Jared reached inside his coat pocket and pulled out three eggs. "I got some eggs our new chickens laid." He laughed. "They didn't like it, though. They pecked at me."

"What did you do with the chickens?"

"We left them in their cage. Salty says he's going to build a pen around one of the trees. It'll be my job to let them out in the mornings and close the pen in the evenings. He says he's going to make me a walking stick so I can do it by myself."

Apparently Salty could expect everything he said to be related to Sarah at the first opportunity. He could also tell from her frown she didn't like him making promises she wasn't certain he could keep. "My father was badly injured in an accident," he explained. "I made several crutches for him."

Sarah didn't appear appeased. "Ellen, set the table."

The girl moved quickly to help her mother.

"Is there anything I can do?" Salty asked.

"You can make sure you and Jared are washed and ready to eat in five minutes."

"Come on," Salty said to the boy. "You pump, and I'll put my head under the water."

"You'll get all wet!"

"That's the point."

"Do I have to put my head under the pump?" Jared asked.

"You do if you're dirty."

He turned to his mother. "Am I dirty?"

He looked like he hoped she would say no, but she laughed and replied, "Any boy who has had to fight with chickens for their eggs is bound to be dirty."

"I took care of the horses," Ellen said. "Can *I* put my head under the pump?"

"You can wash up inside," her mother said.

Salty had never thought of washing up before dinner as a game, but by the time he and Jared got through pumping water over each other, they were both laughing so hard they couldn't understand half of what the other said.

"It sounded more like you were playing in that water than washing in it," Sarah accused when they came back into the house.

Salty grinned at Jared, who was nearly as wet as he was. "I think we did a little of both. Dinner smells mighty good."

"What did you do with Bones?" Sarah asked.

"I left him to watch the pigs and chickens. Don't want anybody stealing them."

Sarah shook her head. "There's nobody but Mr. Wallace within miles, and I'm sure he's got enough pigs and chickens of his own."

"Don't tell Bones that," Salty joked. "He needs to feel useful."

That made the children laugh, but Sarah was now looking at him a little strangely, like she couldn't quite figure him out. It served her right for changing the rules of their relationship, because he couldn't quite figure things out, either.

That blue dress wasn't helping. It wasn't just the color. The garment was made to fit snugly at the waist and bosom. It was wreaking havoc with his thinking processes, as well as having physical effects on the rest of him. After many years of celibacy, he hadn't expected that. Apparently, all that had been lacking was the right woman.

He'd just married that right woman and promised not to touch her. He could foresee having to douse his head under the pump a lot more often.

The front half of the house was a single large room with space for the kitchen, a large table, and a sitting area focused around a fireplace. The kitchen area was made up of a cast iron stove, a larder built into the corner, and a work table. Long use had polished the surface of a rough-hewn supper table until it glistened in the fading sunlight coming in one of the two windows. A rough bench placed against the wall and two ladder-back chairs comprised the rest of the furniture. The walls were unadorned, and two doors led to what he assumed were two bedrooms.

As basic as this was, it was a step up from the dog trot Rose and George Randolph had occupied before the McClendons burned them out. Apparently Sarah's ranch had been successful at one time. He hoped he could make it so again.

That's what he should be thinking about, rather than Sarah's slim waist, her breasts, and the smile that still puzzled him. If he interpreted it correctly, she had stopped fighting her attraction to him. That could mean one of two things: she could have decided to admit her attraction and see where it would go, or she could have decided to admit her attraction but rely on his indifference to keep it from developing into something stronger. Which left him in a quandary. If it was the first, there was no problem. He would simply let his own attraction develop. She was his wife, after all. If it was the second, he didn't know if he could hold up his end of the bargain. When he'd made his promise, he'd been depending on her resistance to help him keep it.

"Serve Salty first," Sarah told Ellen.

"Why?"

"Because he's the head of the family now. It's a sign of respect."

Jared grinned at him before turning to his mother. "And he has to do the most work."

Life with his new family was proving to be more complex than Salty had expected. He was no longer simply a man contracted to manage their ranch in exchange for land; he was being incorporated into their family, not merely as a member, but as the head. He didn't know how that was going to fit with Sarah's need to retain control of her own life as well as be involved in all decisions affecting the ranch or the children, and least of all did he understand how it was going to affect the relationship between them.

"As soon as I make that crutch, you'll have your share of work," Salty promised the boy. But the words were hardly out of his mouth before he remembered Sarah's earlier reaction. The crutch had better make life better for Jared, or the recent thaw could become a chill just as quickly.

"Can I ride one of your horses?" Ellen asked. "We don't have any that good."

"I don't know," Salty said. "A man needs to rest his horses. I could use three or four riding horses instead of just two."

Ellen nodded. "Mama said Grandpapa had more, but they ran away."

"We've recaptured some of them over the years," Sarah said, "but they keep getting out of the corral."

Salty was reminded he had a lot of work to do before he could tackle the problem of the ranch's cattle.

"Before we worry about extra horses, we need to plant the garden," Sarah pointed out.

"I can sort the seeds and cut the potato eyes," Jared volunteered.

"I hate working in the garden," Ellen said. Salty would have guessed that.

The discussion of what to plant and when took up the rest of supper, but Salty wasn't so preoccupied he failed to notice Sarah had made the plain meal of sausage, corn bread, and beans taste a lot better than it sounded. He got the feeling she was embarrassed to serve him such a meager meal; she hadn't looked at him when she put the food on the table.

"I don't have any dessert." She flushed with embarrassment. "We ran out of sugar a while back."

He would have to start a list of additional things to have sent out when the man brought his lumber and his mattress. He couldn't think of a better use for the remaining money he'd gotten from selling the farm he'd come to hate.

"I found some honey," Ellen said, "but it didn't last long."

"That's okay," Salty said. "I don't have much of a sweet tooth."

"I do," the little girl replied.

"Me too," Jared added. "I really liked the doughnuts Mrs. Randolph made."

"Can you make doughnuts, Mama?" Ellen looked hopeful.

"I think so, but you'll have to wait until we get flour."

Flour, sugar, probably coffee as well. Why hadn't he bought staples when he was in Austin? Because he thought like a man. He'd bought pigs and chickens, a second wagon, lumber, wire, and seeds. Not once had he thought about food, clothes, shoes, needles and thread, or any of the things a woman needed to take care of her family. He'd make up that list before he went to sleep tonight.

"Are you through eating?" he asked Jared.

"Why?"

"It's time to start on that crutch I promised you."

Sarah stood. "Ellen and I will clean up."

Salty walked over to the piece of wood he'd set down just inside the front door. "The biggest problem is going to be finding a way to support your leg."

"I don't care, as long as I can walk."

"You'll care after the first few hours," Salty promised. "Lie down on the floor. It'll be easier to measure that way."

Jared got out of his chair, hopped to the middle of the room then dropped to the floor like a sack of coffee. "Any special way you want me to lie down?" he asked.

"No. Just get comfortable. I'll have to keep measuring as I whittle."

It was too dark in the house to see well. Salty guessed Sarah hadn't lit a lantern because she didn't have any oil or kerosene. One more thing to add to the list. "Let's go outside."

"It's too cold!"

"Not yet. Besides, I don't want to get wood chips all over the house. Ellen, when you get through helping your mother, run to the shed and fetch my bedroll."

"What do you want it for?"

"Jared can't lie on the ground."

Sarah didn't look up from her work. She told her daughter, "Go now, but don't dawdle with the horses."

Salty set a chair outside then helped Jared down the steps and to it. "Lean on the chair and stand up. That'll give me enough to get started."

Jared stood perfectly still, watching with avid interest. Salty's father had always yelled at him, had never stood still, had complained that Salty could never make anything that would enable him to walk. How different the two were.

Salty took a knife out of his pocket, opened the blade, and sliced a splinter off the long, slender piece of oak he was using to make the crutch. By the time he'd taken the corners off the wood, Ellen was back with his bedroll. He told her to spread it out. Once that was done, he picked Jared up and laid him down upon it, explaining, "I need to fit the wood as closely as I can to your leg."

It wasn't a crutch he was making, exactly; he had decided on a cross between a crutch and a peg leg. Jared's withered leg was capable of bearing a little weight, but it wasn't as long as his good leg. If he could position a footrest properly, the boy's weight could be shared by his leg and arm.

For the next half hour he worked on the general shape. Jared asked questions about it for the first several minutes, but after that he started asking questions about Salty's past. Salty was relieved when Ellen came outside and started asking other questions about his carving. He didn't want to answer questions about his past. He didn't want to remember most of it.

He noticed Jared shiver. "It's getting too cold to stay out any longer."

"Can't you finish it tonight?" Jared would have probably endured anything if Salty could have promised being able to walk on his own.

"It's going to take a couple more days. What I did tonight was the easy part. From now on, I'll carve a little then measure to make sure it fits. You'll be tired of me before I'm finished."

"I've been tired of not being able to walk my whole life," Jared replied. Sometimes children had a way of putting things into perspective.

Still... "This isn't going to make you walk like everybody else. It will be hard work."

"I don't care."

"I want you to care," Salty said. "You've got to promise to tell me if anything hurts. I'll probably have to make another one—maybe two or three—before I get it right." After years of being forced to make several kinds of walking aids that his father promptly destroyed, he'd promised himself he'd never carve again. But he couldn't think of a better way to help Jared.

"Can you carve anything else?" Ellen asked.

"I never tried. It takes a lot of work to run a farm or work a ranch. Doesn't leave much time for carving."

"Could you carve a bowl?" Ellen asked. "Mama's wood bowl cracked open last summer."

"Salty has more than enough work to do around the ranch," Sarah told her daughter, appearing from inside. "Don't ask him to spend time making things I don't need."

"You said you needed a bowl to keep the bread warm."

She laughed. "You and Jared eat it before it has a chance to get cold."

Probably because bread was the major part of their meal and they were too hungry to wait, Salty guessed. He would make sure they had plenty of vegetables this summer. He also needed to make sure the chickens and pigs were safe. They would be the major source of meat in the family diet.

"It's hard to find a piece of wood in this part of Texas that's big enough to make a bowl," he told Ellen.

"Could you carve a horse?" she asked.

"It's time to go to bed," Sarah announced. "We have to get up early tomorrow."

"We always get up early."

"That's because we always have a lot of work to do."

Jared got to his knees, and Salty helped him up. "Can I use the crutch?" the boy asked.

"It's not ready yet. There's nothing to rest your foot on."

"I can lean on it."

"I haven't built a cradle for your underarm. It'll hurt."

"It won't hurt long," Jared said. "I only have to go to the bedroom."

Salty wasn't sure he could walk with the crutch, but the boy settled it in his armpit and took a tentative step. Salty reached out to help him regain his balance, but Jared motioned him away. He kept stumbling, but he covered the short distance to the steps. Salty waited to see if he could pull himself up with the help of the rough rail. He was relieved when the boy managed to get inside on his own.

"If I had known he'd insist on using it tonight, I'd have started sooner," Salty told Sarah.

"It's the first chance he's had to walk on his own," she replied. "No one but you has been able to figure out a way to support his short leg."

"I'll work on it some more tonight."

"You've done enough for us today. There's still a lot that needs to be done tomorrow."

More than she realized, he'd bet. He reached down for his bedroll and was in the process of folding it when he heard Bones break into a series of barks followed by a savage growl. The noise could only mean one thing, so he dropped the bedroll and started for the shed at a run.

"What's wrong?" Sarah called after him.

"I think Bones has cornered a thief."

THIRTEEN

SALTY WASN'T USED TO RUNNING A HUNDRED FEET IN BOOTS, MUCH less a hundred yards, but he knew Bones wouldn't be barking without a good reason. He would have preferred to have a gun in his hand, but he'd left his in the shed.

He passed through the grove of trees surrounding the house and turned toward the shed. It was a dark night, the sliver of moon obscured by clouds, but he could make out a man struggling with the dog. The man struck at Bones. Whatever he held, it broke the dog's grip and the man started running away. Salty was torn between looking to see if Bones was all right and catching the intruder, but the decision was soon made for him. The man's horse was only a short distance away, and he leapt into the saddle and was gone before Salty could get close enough to identify him.

He was very sure he'd seen that horse before, however. Unless he was mistaken, it belonged to Arnie.

Salty turned back to Bones, who was inside the pen he had built for the pigs.

"What are you doing in there?" he asked before the reason was made clear. One of the new pigs lay in a pool of blood, its throat cut. The other was huddled in a corner. "Son of a bitch! Why did he want to kill the pigs?" A whine reminded him that Arnie had attacked Bones. Blood ran from a cut in the dog's side.

"What happened?" Breathless from her run, Sarah's words were barely understandable.

Salty knelt down next to Bones. "Arnie killed one of our pigs. He stabbed Bones, too, when the poor old dog stopped him from killing the other one."

"Why would he do something like that?"

"I'm not sure," Salty said, "but I have an idea."

It was too dark to see the extent of the dog's wound. He'd have to move Bones to the house to take care of him. He put his arms under the beast and lifted him gently. Bones whined, but he didn't try to get down. "I'm going to need a lantern."

Ellen came catapulting out of the shadows. "What happened?"

Sarah corralled her daughter. "Arnie killed one of the pigs and stabbed Bones."

Ellen looked stricken. "Is Bones hurt bad?"

"We won't know until Salty can get him to the house."

"I'll have the lantern ready." She disappeared as quickly as she had appeared.

Sarah sighed, watching her go. "My daughter never does anything slowly."

Salty laughed. "She's seven. 'Slowly' is a dirty word."

His aching feet made the walk to the house seem longer. Ellen met them at the door with a lantern. Jared stood just inside, using his crutch for support.

"Why did Arnie hurt Bones?" the boy asked.

"Bones attacked him. He stabbed Bones so he could get away."

"I wish Bones had ripped out his throat." It was easy for children to be vengeful, because they'd never seen what one human was capable of doing to another.

Salty laid Bones down near the stove, which was still warm. "Hand me the lantern," he said to Ellen.

Bones was lucky. It appeared the knife had found a rib rather than the soft tissue in between. The gash was about three inches long, but it wasn't deep.

"Is he going to die?" Ellen asked.

Salty shook his head. "It's not a deep cut. If we can keep it clean, he ought to be right as rain in a few days."

"I'll find something to make a pad to cover his wound," Sarah said.

"Jared, can you hold the light? I need Ellen to bring me a basin of water."

Sarah turned to her daughter. "I'll get the water. You bring the blue jar I keep in the back of the cupboard. I have a tea made of sage that will help stop infection," she told Salty. As soon as she returned from the well, she took the jar Ellen handed her and poured a generous amount into the basin.

When Salty tried to clean the wound, Bones whined and struggled to get up. "It's got to be cleaned to keep it from getting infected," he told Ellen when she asked why he was hurting the dog.

"Let me try." Sarah produced a length of fabric she had folded into a pad large enough to cover the wound.

Salty nodded and took the lantern from Jared. "Let me know where you want it."

"Hold it higher and a little forward."

Sarah took the cloth Salty had been using, dipped it into the basin and carefully pressed it against the dog's raw flesh. Bones whined softly but didn't move. With slow and careful movements, she continued to dip the cloth into the basin and press it against the wound until all the blood was gone. Once that was done, she squeezed some of the liquid directly onto the exposed flesh to flush out the remaining debris.

"Hand me that fabric pad," she said to Ellen. When her daughter complied, she soaked the pad in the solution, wrung out most of the liquid then placed it over the wound. "Now we need to find a way to keep this in place for a couple of days."

Salty was startled out of his reverie. Watching Sarah bent over the dog, deftly cleaning the wound with a minimum of pain, was like watching an angel bring about a miracle of healing. Sarah was a strong, independent woman who was capable of the gentleness and tenderness that men looked for in women. The sensitivity that soothed and healed without the need for words. He had just seen what he'd wanted without knowing exactly what it was, the answer to a question he'd been unable to put into words.

"I could fashion a bandage if I had enough cloth to circle his chest," he said to Sarah.

"I'll get some." Ellen was off like a shot.

"Do you think Arnie will come back?" Jared asked.

"I don't know," Salty replied. "I didn't expect him the first time."

"I never liked him," the boy repeated.

Salty turned to Sarah. "Maybe he thinks that, if I fail, you'll be forced to turn to him."

"Why would he think that after what he tried to do tonight?"

"You never know what a man who thinks he's in love will do."

Ellen returned with strips of bandage trailing after her. "Can I do it?" she begged.

"I think we ought to let Salty," Sarah replied. "If you watch closely, maybe he'll let you try the next time."

When the bandage was attached, Bones wasn't happy about having it around his chest. He tried to pull it off with his teeth. When Salty gave him an admonishing tap on the muzzle, he tried to kick the cloth off with his hind foot. "We'll have to watch him," Salty said.

"I'll do it," Jared offered.

"I'd better take him to the shed with me," Salty decided. "I can make sure he doesn't get out of it."

"Are you going to stay up all night?" Ellen asked.

"No." He couldn't do that and work all the next day, too.

"Then how will you know if Arnie comes back?"

"Bones will know." He hoped Bones would wake him. Arnie wouldn't come back unless he was planning to do some serious damage.

"What about the pig?" Sarah asked. "It can't be left lying in the pen overnight. We have to process the meat now."

Salty practically sagged against the doorway. He'd helped with hog-killings growing up. It was a long process that began at dawn and frequently lasted until midnight, and he was already exhausted. "We'll be up all night."

"The children and I will take care of it."

What kind of husband would he be if he went to sleep and left his new family to work through the night? Surely Sarah didn't think he would do that, even if he was her husband in name only. "While I take Bones to the shed, find me a big pot to boil water."

He trudged to the shed with heavy feet, thinking of the work ahead. How many times had he built a fire in a pit under a tub used to scald a full-grown hog? How many hogs had he scraped free of hair, struggled to hang so the corpse could be eviscerated and the processing of the meat begun? More than he cared to remember, especially because his father always sat close by, shouting that he was a fool, an idiot, that he was doing everything wrong. Knowing his father's anger sprang from helplessness had done little to ease the pain or calm Salty's anger—or expunge his guilt for feeling relief when his father died.

Ellen followed him. "Mama said I was to show you the pit we use to build the fire."

"How about the tub?"

"We don't have one. We just keep pouring water on the hog until it loosens the hair."

"I guess the wash pot will have to do."

Salty had filled it with water and started the fire before Sarah left the house with a handful of knives. Ellen trotted behind her with various pots and bowls. Jared was seated at the kitchen table they'd set up nearby. He'd been given the job of organizing the spices and the cans that would hold the lard which would cover and preserve the meat. Later he could help with grinding meat and stuffing sausages.

"Let's hope the clouds clear," Sarah said. "I don't have enough fuel to keep this lantern burning all night."

It wasn't easy when only half of the pig would fit into the wash pot at a time, but Salty finally got the thing scalded, scraped clean, and hung up. He was relieved when the clouds passed and the yard was illuminated by pale moonlight. But once he removed the pig's insides and got everything washed and cleaned, the real work of the night began.

He'd never liked hog killings because they required lots of people to work together. He'd always preferred to work alone. Yet, if he wanted to succeed with this ranch, he'd have to integrate himself into this family in a way that he'd never been part of in his own. Tonight was a good place to begin.

"What can I do?" he asked Sarah. By the time she got through telling him, he wished he hadn't asked. In Salty's father's world, once a man had cut up the carcass and taken the meat to the smokehouse or covered it with salt and seasonings, his work was done. The cleaning, cooking, rendering, grinding, and stuffing was women's work. The men sat around talking and eating cracklings.

He had to take the carcass apart. Some pieces would be cured in the smokehouse, some ground up, and some preserved in salt or lard. He helped Jared wash intestines to be used as casings for sausages. He boiled chunks of fat to render the lard. Through the long hours of the night, the four worked together, sometimes stopping to help each other before going back to their own individual tasks. They talked and joked. The children had never participated so fully in a hog killing, so they had lots of questions, most of which Sarah had to answer.

Sometime before dawn, Sarah got up from the table where she'd been working and said, "I'm going to fix breakfast. Do you think you can handle things for a while?"

Salty shrugged. "There's nothing left to do but fill the sausage casings."

Sarah put her hand to her back to stretch muscles that must have been tight and aching from bending over the table for hours. "My father never made sausages. He wouldn't have. I didn't know if you would."

"My father wouldn't have, either," Salty admitted. "But I disagreed with him about a lot of things."

Sarah's tired smile was more than enough to warm his heart. Her attitude toward him had unquestionably softened, but it was a long way from anything resembling love. Not that he wanted love. His mother had loved his father, who had made her life a misery. Liking each other well enough to be friends was the best way for a husband and wife to feel about each other, and that was what Sarah wanted in the first place. It would avoid the bitter pain of jealousy, the fear of believing the person you loved didn't love you, the torment of discovering you were interchangeable with other persons of your gender. George and Rose Randolph had found mutual love, but they were one in a million.

There was no denying the attraction between him and Sarah. He expected it to grow stronger. It was impossible to be around a woman like Sarah and not be attracted. But as long as he didn't confuse attraction with love—

"Are you going to help us?"

Ellen's question pulled him out of his abstraction. "Sure."

"Then why are you just sitting there staring at the house?"

He was staring at the doorway through which Sarah had disappeared. Was he hoping she would reappear, or was he merely remembering the way she looked as she walked toward the house? Either way, he had to stop thinking about Sarah and concentrate on work. "How are we going to organize this?" he asked.

"If you'll hold the casings, Jared and I can stuff them."

Salty looked at the two children, both calmly waiting for him to take the job they'd assigned him. He wondered if he'd ever been that assured as a child. His father had been prosperous, an important man in the community, yet Salty had felt worthless. These children were as close to being penniless as possible without starving. They should still be playing with dolls and pretend rifles instead of worrying about their next meal. And yet, because poverty had denied them the advantages he'd enjoyed, they had the experience of knowing what they did was important, that their contributions would always be valued, that their abilities were respected.

"Mama says I stuff sausages better than Ellen." Jared held up his hands. "My hands are smaller."

Salty's father would have ridiculed him if he'd been physically smaller in any way to a female. Here, Jared was able to take pride in it. Apparently there were advantages in growing up without a father and away from towns full of people who could only see the disadvantages of being different.

"Then I'll hold, Ellen will hand, and you can stuff."

Something about what he said, or the way he said it, caused the children to start giggling. In no time at all, all three of them were laughing.

"Are you going to get back to work, or do I have to find myself a switch?" Salty looked up to see Sarah standing in the doorway, hands on hips. But she was smiling.

Jared pointed to Salty. "It's his fault."

"Then I guess I'll have to switch Salty. Do you think I can find one big enough?"

That sent the children into fresh gales of laughter.

Salty poked them both in the sides. "Stop laughing, brats. Do you want to see me get switched?"

They managed a strangled *yes* then laughed even harder.

"It's their fault," he told Sarah. "I think I should switch them."

More hilarity, and Ellen hid behind Jared.

"No one gets any breakfast until the sausage is finished." With that announcement, Sarah walked back inside.

The children's laughter gradually died down. Ellen said, "I'm hungry."

"You're always hungry," Jared said.

"Then we'd better get to work," Salty advised. "I'm hungry, too."

Once they all settled down to their tasks, work went quickly. Soon the only question was whether to seal sausages in lard or put them in the smokehouse.

"I want some of this for breakfast." Ellen picked up a sausage made with seasoned meat and cornmeal and headed for the house.

"That's her favorite," Jared told him.

"What's yours?"

"Anything except liver," the boy said.

Salty chuckled. "I promise to eat the liver. Now, grab a sausage and let's head for the smokehouse."

He waited to see how Jared would do with the unfinished crutch, but the boy had already learned to use it. It must hurt having the end jammed into his armpit, but Jared didn't complain or hesitate. Salty decided he'd have to make the armrest as soon as he got enough sleep to not be a danger to himself handling a knife.

"Let me give you a hand," he said to Jared after they'd put everything in the smokehouse and started back. "You've got to have bruises in your armpit."

"It doesn't hurt," the boy said.

Salty gave him a knowing smile. "I made enough crutches for my father to know it does. I know you're anxious to be on your own, but it won't kill you to lean on me one more time." He held out his hand. "I'll finish your crutch tonight. Now let's get some breakfast. I think I have just enough energy to eat before I fall asleep."

Jared hesitated before giving up his crutch. "I'm not tired."

"You will be as soon as the excitement wears off."

"What's to get excited about making sausage?"

"It's not about making sausage as much as it is that things are different. Me being here, Arnie killing the pig, staying up all night. Even worrying about Bones."

"Are you sure he's going to be all right?" Salty's words had reminded the child of the dog.

"I expect he's already at the house wanting his breakfast."

"Will he still be able to hunt?"

Salty took Jared's arm and they started toward the house. "Don't worry about Bones. He'll be nosing around for rabbits long before it's time to take off the bandage."

Jared shook his head. "I don't understand why Arnie would kill our pig. I didn't like him very much, but he was always nice to us."

Salty wasn't sure how much to explain. "It's difficult to imagine why people do some things until you know more about them," he finally said. "Sometimes it's impossible even then."

Jared was limping worse than usual. The child had to be exhausted, staying up all night and learning to walk with a crutch that practically punched a hole in his armpit. He probably needed sleep more than he needed food, but breakfast was going to come first.

Both Salty and Jared washed up at the pump before heading into the house. Salty needed coffee and lots of it. He smelled it while he was still twenty yards away. It gave him a burst of energy, a lift in his gait.

"You hungry?" Jared asked.

"Yeah. Aren't you?"

"Sorta."

The child worked so hard and was so responsible, it was hard to remember he was only seven. "Your appetite will perk up once you get to the table. Your mom's a great cook," Salty said.

"I guess so."

Until the trip to the Circle Seven, the boy probably hadn't eaten anything that hadn't been cooked by his mother. Salty was quick to assure him, "Take it from me, she's a great cook. Better than *my* mom."

When they reached the back door, Bones was there finishing the last of what looked like corn bread and milk. "I told you he'd be right as rain before you know it," Salty said. "Isn't that true, old boy?"

Bones didn't respond until he'd lapped up the last of the milk. Licking his chops, he turned to Salty and whined softly, his tail wagging.

"That's right, stick to what's important. You can thank me for patching you up when you have nothing better to do."

Jared giggled.

"Go look for rabbits, but don't go too far. We only have one pig left."

The old dog headed off toward some brush. As they watched, Jared's grip on Salty's arm tightened. "Do you think Arnie will come back?"

"I doubt it," Salty said, hoping it was true. "Bones took a bite out of him."

The smells from the house caused Salty's stomach to growl. He gripped Jared under the arms and lifted him up the steps. Bowls of scrambled eggs, hominy, and a plate with new sausage were already on the table.

Ellen pointed to glasses of milk with obvious pride. "I milked the cow you bought. Mama said we can have butter for our corn bread tomorrow if she gives enough cream."

Salty had forgotten all about the cow. He'd have to remember to let the chickens out after he ate, too. He'd do a better job in the future.

Sarah came to the table with a three-legged griddle from which she put corn bread on each plate. "Sit down and eat while everything's hot. Once we get everything cleaned up, we're all going to take a long nap."

"What about building a pen for the chickens?" Ellen asked.

"What about my crutch?"

"Both can wait until the evening. Right now we need to rest." She returned the griddle to the stove, picked up a cup which she filled with coffee, and handed it to Salty. "Let me know if it's strong enough."

The coffee was hot and so strong it came at him like an angry range bull, which was exactly the way he liked it. With a sigh of satisfaction, he settled into his chair at the table. "Might as well hand me the pot. I intend to drink all of it."

"Can I have some coffee?" Ellen asked.

"In about ten years," her mother replied. "Now drink your milk and eat your breakfast. We're all tired and in need of sleep."

They didn't talk much while they ate. No one but his father talked during meals when Salty was growing up, but he'd gotten so used to the Randolphs all talking at once that the silence struck him as unnatural.

The children's energy picked up as they ate. Jared still looked tired when it was time to clean up and put everything away, but Ellen was nearly her old self. Salty wondered what kind of man it would take to win her heart and match her in strength and energy. He doubted such a man had been made.

"Did you stake the cow out?" Salty asked.

"No," Ellen said. "Mama said she'd do that later."

Salty shook his head, glancing at Sarah. "I'll take care of it. I need to look around for a good spot for the chicken pen. I want to get that done today."

"You can let the chickens run loose," Ellen argued. "They'll roost in the trees."

"Yes, but they'll lay their eggs all over the place, and we'll never find half of them."

"Jared is real good at finding their nests," Ellen said.

Maybe, but they needed every egg. It wouldn't take much to set up a temporary pen, just a few poles set in the ground and wire stretched around them. If he could set one up around a tree suitable for roosting, all he'd have to do later was make some nesting boxes. Of course, he'd have to enlist Jared's aid to find the chickens Sarah already had. He hadn't seen a single hen around the house or the shed.

He took one last swallow of coffee. "With a pot of this under my belt each morning, there's not much a man can't do," he said.

"You can pee a lot," Ellen suggested.

Sarah frowned at her daughter. "That's not a nice thing to say."

"You always tell me not to drink too much water before I go to bed because it will make me pee."

"It's okay for a parent to say that to a child. It's part of teaching them the consequences of their actions. Salty is an adult. He's old enough to make his own decisions."

"When will I be old enough to make my own decisions?"

"Not for several years yet. Now clear the table. I think we're all ready for a nap."

Salty started to ask Jared if he might suggest a good place for the chicken pen, but the sound of an approaching horse caused him to turn. "Are you expecting anyone?" he asked Sarah. It was too soon for his lumber to be arriving.

"No," she replied.

"I'll see who it is." But when Salty went outside, he didn't recognize the approaching horseman.

"That's Mr. Wallace." Jared had followed Salty to the door. "He's the man who wants Mama's ranch." Salty had no idea what could have brought their neighbor out so early, but he didn't appear to be happy about it.

Wallace regarded Salty with contempt as he brought his horse to a stop. He said, "Another one of those idiots Sarah hires hoping they can make something of this ranch. What's your name?"

"I'm Benton Wheeler, and I'm not another idiot hired man. I'm

Sarah's husband."

The news appeared to catch Wallace by surprise. At last he said, "I don't believe it. Sarah would never marry a man like you when she could marry me."

FOURTEEN

SALTY WAS SO SURPRISED HE DIDN'T KNOW WHAT TO SAY, BUT JARED wasn't similarly handicapped. "He *did* marry Mama. I saw him."

"Morning, Henry. What can I do for you?" Sarah had joined Jared in the doorway. Ellen wiggled through to stand next to Salty.

"You can tell me this man was lying when he said you married him."

"I can't because I did."

Henry Wallace was typical of many men who'd pulled together a successful ranching operation after the war. He was big, loud, and probably as strong as he looked. Dressed in a coat, shirt, and tie more suitable for time indoors than riding across open range, he appeared to be somewhere in his forties, with his thick brown hair and beard showing only a trace of gray. He rode a rawboned, piebald gelding, which he treated with rough impatience. His easily kindled anger was as apparent in his eyes as his contempt for people he didn't consider his equal.

"He doesn't look rich," Wallace said.

"He's not."

"Then why the hell did you marry him? He's not a looker like Roger."

"I like him," Jared said.

"Me too," Ellen echoed.

"What you brats like doesn't matter," Wallace snarled. "It's your mother who has to sleep with him."

Salty was tired of Wallace, and he was fed up with the man's treatment of Sarah and her family. "I assume you have some reason for being here other than to abuse my wife and our children?"

Wallace's grin turned wolfish. "Staking your claim, are you? Maybe you've grabbed for more than you can hold."

"Never happened before."

"I guess we'll see, won't we?"

Ellen moved closer to Salty, and he put his arm around her shoulder, something that Wallace didn't appear to like. The man turned to Sarah. "Your cows are on my range again."

"This is open range," Salty reminded him.

"*My* range isn't open, and I've told Sarah that lots of times before."

"Unless you've got a deed to that land, our cows have as much right to that grass as yours."

"I don't need a deed, because I control the range."

"That can change," Salty replied.

Wallace turned red in the face. "Are you threatening me?"

"Simply stating a fact. I've been hearing talk about a kind of barbed wire that can be used for fencing. Once they perfect it, that'll be the end of the open range. You'll have to own the land your cows graze."

"You *did* marry an idiot," Wallace said to Sarah. "I never heard a more ridiculous tale in my life. And if somebody *did* invent such a wire, ranchers wouldn't stand for it."

"Ranchers will be asking for it, because fencing is the only way to improve our herds."

"There's nothing wrong with the Texas longhorn," Wallace said. "It's the cheapest beef in the world."

"And will always sell for the lowest price. If you want to see the future of ranching in Texas, go see what George Randolph is doing."

"I don't need anybody to tell me how to run my ranch," Wallace snapped. He turned back to Sarah. "If you can't keep your cows off my land, I can."

Salty answered, "Tell me where to find them, and I'll make certain they're gone by tonight."

"I want them off now."

Salty's mouth twitched. "Since I'm not sure where the cows are and have no magic carpet that will get me there instantly, that's not possible."

Wallace appeared to lack a sense of humor. He turned redder than before and jerked the bridle so hard his horse half reared. "They're down by the creek," he said after he got his mount back under control.

"All the land on this side of the creek is mine," Sarah said.

"It would be if you could hold it," Wallace sneered.

"I'm not familiar with the extent of the land that makes up our ranch," Salty told him, "but once I am, I'll make sure our cows don't stray onto yours. I'll also make sure *your* cows stay on *your* side of the creek—if you don't do it yourself, which I'm sure you will."

"You talk big," Wallace said to Salty. "I'll be looking to see if you can live up to your boasts."

"I wasn't boasting," Salty said. "It's probably not a good idea to judge other people's actions by your own."

Wallace was so enraged it took him nearly a minute to stop fighting with his horse. The poor animal's mouth must be like leather. "I've had my say," he shouted at Salty. "Get those cows off my land, or I'll deliver them to you in the back of a wagon." And with that final threat, he turned his mount, drove his heels into his horse's flanks, and galloped away.

"We'd better get the cows now," Ellen said. She started toward the shed before Salty could speak.

"We're not going anywhere until we've had some sleep," he said. "After that, I intend to build the chicken pen and finish Jared's crutch. We'll see about our cows tomorrow."

"But what if he shoots them before then?"

"Then he'll have to pay for them. Don't worry," he added, when Ellen started to protest. "I can take care of Mr. Wallace."

Sarah shooed the children into the house. It was only then that Salty was left prey to his own doubts. Anybody could stand up and get run over or killed. The real question was: could he succeed? Wallace was a bully, the kind of man who talked a big game and didn't usually have to follow through because he scared people so much they didn't test him. Salty couldn't afford *not* to test Wallace. His future as well as that of Sarah and her children depended on it.

"What are you going to do about Wallace?" Sarah had returned, her brow furrowed with worry. He wondered whether she was worried about him or just the ranch.

"I can't answer that until I see what he's talking about. We ought to ride together tomorrow. You can show me the ranch, where to find the best graze, and where to look for trouble."

"Maybe you should take Ellen. She knows almost as much as I do."

"I don't need 'almost as much.' I need to know every detail of what went on in the past and how things stand now."

What he didn't add was that he wanted to ride with her. He wanted that more than he would have thought possible.

━━━━━━

"Did you get a nap?" Jared asked as Salty tried to fit the armrest onto Jared's crutch. Salty carved a curl of wood from one side of the hole in the armrest. When he tried to insert the crutch, it slid right in.

"I wasn't very sleepy after all."

"Why would Mr. Wallace want to shoot our cows?"

"To force your mother to sell him her land. Hand me that piece of cloth."

Jared watched as Salty wrapped the cloth around the armrest several times to make a thick pad. He drove a small nail through it on the underside to hold it in place.

"Mama can't sell him all our land because half belongs to you."

"Only if I can find a way to make a living out of this place."

"You will, won't you?"

Satisfied the padding was secure, Salty fitted the armrest onto the crutch and reached for the small wedges he'd made earlier. The boy watched him use the wedges to make the armrest secure. "I'm going to try, but it may take several years."

"I don't care. Will you stay?"

Salty paused. He looked up to find Jared eyeing him rather than the longed-for crutch. "Your mother has made me promise to give her a divorce when she asks for it."

"If she doesn't ask, will you stay?"

"According to our agreement, I don't get the land unless she gets a divorce."

Jared looked disappointed. "Mama didn't tell us that."

Salty couldn't imagine his father having shared that kind of information with him when he was seven. Or when he was seventeen. He wasn't sure how he should have answered, but it was too late to change now. "Stand up. I need to figure out where to put the footrest." Jared's withered leg was capable of bearing a little weight, but it wasn't as long as his good leg. Once Jared had secured a comfortable grip on the crutch, he hobbled around the yard, turning right and left, walking faster and faster. "Slow down," Salty said. "I need to attach the footrest."

Jared turned and gave him a brilliant smile. "I can walk almost as fast as Ellen!"

Salty had spent so many years living with his father's bitterness over the loss of his ability to walk, the boy's gratitude took him aback. But of course it would be an amazing gift, to be able to walk without assistance.

Jared turned toward the house and yelled, "Mama, come see!" The moment she appeared in the doorway he called, "Watch." Then he hobbled rapidly in one direction and then another. After he looped several more times he was winded, but that didn't diminish his happiness. "Salty says I can walk even better once I have a rest for my foot."

Sarah's expression changed from surprise to happiness to tearful joy as she watched her son show off. Her hand went to her chest as though her heart was beating too fast. She blessed Salty with just a brief glance before turning back to her son, but that expression was more than enough to set his own heart to pounding, to tighten his own chest until he found it hard to breathe. He wasn't very good at interpreting a woman's glance—Rose had always said he was hopeless—but that brief glance had been filled with so much sizzling warmth he was dizzy from the force of it. His whole body was filled, energized, overwhelmed. If he hadn't known it was impossible, he'd have said it was a look of love.

Just the thought of a woman like Sarah being in love with him was enough to finish off his fading ability to think. If George had felt even a tenth of this when he met Rose, Salty couldn't understand how he'd held out as long as he had.

He had to be careful not to read too much into Sarah's look, though. She loved her son deeply, had agonized over his inability to be like other boys. She probably would have been thankful to any man who gave the child back a fraction of what that quirk of Nature had taken away. Salty suddenly wondered why Arnie hadn't taken the time to make a crutch for Jared. Surely that would have been a quicker and surer way to her heart than spreading rumors about her.

"Have you thanked Salty?" she asked her son. The boy looked crestfallen for not having thought of it.

"Just seeing him gallop around the yard like that is thanks enough," Salty said.

Jared hung his head. "I'm sorry. I *should* have thanked you."

"Wait and see if you feel the same way in a couple of weeks. I intend to give you so much work you'll be wanting to throw this crutch onto a fire."

The boy's smile peeped through. "Then you'd have to make me

another one."

Sarah glanced from Salty to her son and back again with a wondering look. Salty wasn't sure, but he thought she was pleased. He cautioned himself that he wasn't any good with women.

"I need you to help me with supper," Sarah said to her son.

"Can't Ellen help?"

"She's going to help Salty with the chicken pen."

"I can help him," Jared argued.

"I'm sure you can, but I've already promised Ellen. She has to round up the chickens afterward, and you know how much she hates chickens."

"She hates everything except horses and cows," Jared reminded Salty.

The girl emerged from the house looking sleepy. "I don't like milk cows, either."

"But you like butter and milk," her mother said, "so I guess you'll have to put up with her."

"Okay, but I'll never like chickens," Ellen declared. "They're disgusting."

"Unless they're on your plate," her mother said. "Now, no more silly talk. You help Salty with that chicken pen while Jared helps me with supper."

"Shall we have a race to see who gets done first?" Salty asked.

Both children brightened. Like he'd expected, it seemed competition made any task more welcome.

―――――――

Sarah smiled as she watched Jared struggle to use his crutch in the confined space of the kitchen. He was happier than she'd ever seen him. She didn't know how she was going to thank Salty for making the crutch—or for the other differences he'd already made in her children's lives. She didn't doubt that both children loved her as much as ever, but something had been missing. It seemed that space had been filled.

She tried again to decide what it was that had made them take to Salty so quickly. He was nice and kind. He could be funny as well as serious. He talked to them and did things for them. But it was more than that. It was the quality of the attention he gave them, the genuineness of his interest, the honesty in his answers to their questions. He listened to them and seemed to understand how they felt. Most important of all, he clearly liked them in return.

Jared was setting the table. He was slowed by being able to use only one hand, but he had insisted his mother let him take the dishes from the cabinet. She was worried that he might break something, but so far he hadn't.

"Do you think we're going to beat Salty and Ellen?"

"I don't know, but it's more important that we make sure supper is good."

"Can't we beat them *and* make supper taste good?" The poor boy was so used to being second to his sister in everything that this opportunity to best her had assumed enormous proportions.

"I think we just might do it. Salty has to dig a lot of holes, and that takes time."

Jared's worried look was replaced by a broad grin. He started working faster.

"If you drop or break anything, we'll be disqualified," Sarah said.

Jared stopped and faced her. "Will they be disqualified if the fence falls down?"

"Definitely."

"Okay," he agreed. "I'll be careful, and you shouldn't burn anything, because that might disqualify us, too."

Sarah couldn't suppress a smile. "Stop worrying so much about winning and finish setting the table. There's water and milk to be poured."

Sarah's thoughts turned to Salty. What, beyond physical attraction, had made her choose him? Had she done it for her children, for herself...or had she done it in the hope he was so different from her father and husband that she could learn not to be afraid of men? She had thought she was impervious to emotional appeals, but Salty was different in ways that were threatening all of her preconceived ideas about men. And herself.

"Do you like Salty?" Jared asked.

The question punctured her thoughts. The unexpectedness of it was like a physical blow. "Of course I do. I wouldn't have married him if I hadn't."

"You said you only married because you had to."

"Yes, but I wouldn't have married a man I didn't like or didn't trust."

Jared had finished setting the table and putting out the bowls for the food, but he hadn't put out the glasses. "Do you want him to stay after he fixes things so we won't starve? He said he couldn't get the land until you divorce him."

Sarah didn't know what had prompted Jared to ask these questions. She had always tried to be forthcoming with the children, but maybe she'd told them too much. "That's a long way in the future."

"Would you let him stay if he wants to?"

Sarah dragged her attention back to the stove. She moved the potatoes off the heat and checked the bottom of the corn bread to make sure it hadn't burned. "Why are you asking this?"

"Because I want Salty to stay. Forever."

Sarah forgot her potatoes and corn bread. She looked at her son. "Do you like him that much already?"

"I wish he could be my papa. Arnie said he wanted to be my papa, but I didn't want him. I want Salty."

Sarah pulled her son close and gave him a swift hug. "Honey, I know how important your crutch is to you, but anybody could have made you one."

"But nobody did."

And Salty had indeed made one, had made it a priority despite staying up all night. He'd taken them to eat in a restaurant, bought them a dog, and let them stay in a hotel. No wonder Jared wanted him to stay.

"He might decide to sell his land once he gets it," she cautioned.

"He won't." It wasn't a question. It wasn't even an opinion. Jared spoke as though his belief were an established fact.

"Why do you think that?"

"He doesn't like Mr. Wallace."

"Did he say so?"

"No, but I can tell."

And that apparently settled the question for Jared, because he started setting out glasses.

Sarah hadn't let herself think about what Salty might do when it came time to sign over half of the ranch—not lately. He had become part of her plans nearly as quickly as he had done for Jared. She was more attracted to him than ever. But that's not what worried her. She *liked* him. That wasn't in her plans.

It was okay to like him as a co-worker. It was okay to like him as a friend. It was even okay for her to start to depend on him for physical labor, seeing as he was her husband. However, it was *not* okay to want him around all the time. It wasn't okay to think of him touching her, holding her, even kissing her.

She'd been on edge so long she probably wasn't thinking clearly. She was simply grateful to find someone who might actually solve her problems. As a result, she had started thinking she'd like him to stay around forever. But was she so grateful, so relieved, she'd forgotten what her father was like, or Roger? Had she forgotten the men who'd worked for her, who were more interested in getting into her bed than in doing the work they were paid to do? Rose Randolph might have found a man she could love in a fairy-tale way, but Sarah didn't trust any man that much.

But maybe she could take him as a lover?

The thought shocked her so much she nearly dropped the pan of corn bread she was taking off the stove. She'd never had such a thought in her life. What was wrong with her? But the thought of being held and kissed by Salty caused her temperature to rise. Something deep inside her longed for the physical contact, and it wasn't just a sense of safety she might find in his arms. She sought something much more fundamental, something she hadn't felt with Roger or any other man. It was as though she needed him. She could understand want, could even understand lust, but where had *need* come from? It wasn't physical. She could take care of herself. It was an emotional need, one she'd never been able to fulfill, only deny.

"Hurry up with the corn bread, Mama. Ellen and Salty are almost here."

Sarah's impulse was to run to her bedroom. How could she face Salty with her thoughts in such disarray? She stood frozen while the pair entered the house. Then she did something she'd never done before. She fainted.

FIFTEEN

SALTY WAS MOVING TOWARD SARAH BEFORE THE FRYING PAN HIT THE floor. He sent a chair careening across the room and banged his thigh against the corner of the table, but he reached her in time to catch her. "Ellen, bring me a cloth and a basin of cold water. What happened?" he asked Jared.

The boy stared at his mother's crumpled form, his eyes wide with shock. "I d-don't know," he stammered. "Sh-she was just standing there. Then she dropped the corn bread."

Bones had followed Salty and Ellen into the house. He gobbled up two pieces of scattered corn bread before Ellen shoved him out and closed the door.

Sarah had lost color, but she didn't seem to be in any distress. Salty was less worried that something might be medically wrong than that a woman with Sarah's strength of mind would faint. What could have upset her so badly? Had Jared said something without realizing its significance?

Salty wasn't so worried, however, that he was unaware of the pleasurable sensations that came from having such an attractive woman in his arms. He felt guilty about it, but that didn't stop him from thinking how nice it would be to hold her under different circumstances. She was so soft. She seemed slight compared to him, even fragile. Her upturned nose, her generous mouth, eyelashes that seemed too long to be real; her bones were smaller, her features more finely sculpted.

She stirred in his arms and her eyes opened. She struggled against his embrace. "What happened?"

"You fell down." Ellen had finally arrived with the water.

"She didn't fall down," Jared corrected. "Salty caught her."

"You fainted," Salty explained. "Are you sick?"

"I'm fine. Let me up."

"Maybe you should wait a bit longer. Until you feel steady enough to stand."

"I feel fine. Besides, supper is getting cold."

Ellen was gathering up pieces of corn bread. "Bones ate some," she complained.

Sarah struggled to sit up. "I'll make more."

"There's no need," Salty assured her. "He only got a piece or two."

"But it's all been on the floor."

Ellen rubbed a piece against her shirt. "I brushed the dirt off."

Salty reluctantly released Sarah as she struggled into a sitting position and argued, "You can't eat dirty corn bread."

"Then we won't eat any corn bread at all," he told her. "You're not doing anything until I'm sure you're all right. Let me help you up."

"I can stand on my own," she said.

"I'm sure you can, but there's no reason not to let me help you. Is there?"

Sarah looked like she wanted to say something but thought better of it. "I'm not used to being helpless."

Salty chuckled. "I never saw a less helpless woman in my life—but it's nice to depend on somebody else once in a while."

Sarah allowed herself to be settled in her chair but didn't look happy about it. "I've always been responsible for everything. It was the only way I could be sure things would get done."

"Well, I'm here to help now."

"I can help," Ellen said.

"Me too," added Jared.

Sarah reached for her son with one hand and for Ellen with the other; her eyes glistened with unshed tears. "You know I couldn't do without either of you." She hugged both children, and they threw their arms around her.

Watching, Salty understood why he couldn't be part of this family unit, but he felt like he belonged in that huddle of warm bodies. Maybe it had happened last night while they processed that pig. Maybe it happened when Jared got his crutch. It didn't really matter *when* it happened, he supposed, just that it had. He felt it. He wondered if anyone else felt it, too.

Sarah released both children, kissed them then stood. "We've got to feed Salty before he starves."

Her reaction confirmed to Salty that he still wasn't a member of her family, was in reality just a hired man like all the others. She had to take care of his physical needs so he would be able to do the work necessary to put her ranch on a better financial footing; she wasn't thinking of anything else. He could accept that, he decided. He'd only been here one day.

Still, one day was long enough to know he was part of this family. They just didn't realize it yet.

"I want to go with you." From the moment Salty announced that he and Sarah were going to spend the morning looking for the cows that had strayed onto Wallace's land, Ellen had lost interest in her breakfast.

"I need you and Jared to begin planting the garden," her mother said.

"I don't want to be a farmer," Ellen protested. "I want to be a rancher."

"A rancher has to eat," Sarah reminded her. "Vegetables are

important. Someone has to plant and tend the garden."

Ellen put down her fork and dropped her hands to her lap. "Why does it have to be me?"

"Who would you suggest?" Sarah had eaten little, subsisting mainly on coffee.

The answer was obvious to all of them. Salty had to go after the cows because he knew the most about ranching. Sarah needed to go because she knew the most about the ranch. Besides, she might be able to talk some sense into Wallace if they saw him.

"I hate chickens and I hate gardens," Ellen declared.

"If you want to have your own ranch someday, you're going to have to know all about both," Salty said. "Pigs and milk cows, too."

Ellen took a swallow of milk before answering. "I'll hire somebody to do it for me."

"A topnotch boss should know how to do every job as well as the men he hires." At her look, Salty amended his statement. "Or *she*."

Ellen picked up a piece of corn bread but didn't take a bite. "Why?"

"So you'll know if the men you hired are doing a good job."

The girl looked disgusted. "Maybe I'll just be a cowhand. Zac told me a real cowhand won't do any work he can't do from the back of a horse."

Salty laughed. "Zac was pulling your leg. He doesn't like cows or horses. He says he's going to New Orleans as soon as he grows up."

Ellen shook her head. "And I thought he was smart."

Salty decided it probably wouldn't do any good to tell her there were lots of smart people who didn't like horses and cows. He finished the last of his fried potatoes and corn bread. Sarah got up to refill both their cups.

"What are we supposed to plant?" Jared had eaten his breakfast in silence.

"What do *you* think we ought to plant?" But the moment Salty spoke, he realized he should have let Sarah answer. She didn't appear upset when he turned to her, though.

"Mama has a book of what we planted last year. I'll look there. I'll also see what seeds we have."

"That's an excellent idea. Once you decide, talk it over with Ellen so she'll know what kind of rows to dig."

"I hate digging. I always get blisters." Ellen wrinkled her nose in disgust, but she didn't appear too upset. Maybe she just wanted to make sure everyone knew she was a real cowhand and that she was doing this garden stuff only because somebody had to do it.

"Wear your gloves," Salty suggested.

"I don't have any."

"Wrap an old cloth around your hands or around the shovel handle."

"Will you show me how?"

"If you've finished eating, get Salty to help you find the best place for the garden," her mother interjected. "He can show you how to wrap your hands then. Jared, you can start sorting our seeds and deciding what to plant. I'll clean up. Then we can ride out."

"Are you sure you don't need help?" Ellen asked. It surprised Salty that she wanted to do anything like women's work.

"It won't take but a few minutes."

Salty took a couple of big gulps to finish his coffee then pushed his chair back. "I'll have the horses saddled by the time you're done."

Ellen was up from her chair and out the door ahead of him; she had the same boundless energy that seemed to inhabit Zac Randolph. Jared was slower to move, but he used his crutch so easily it was hard to believe he'd had it less than a day. He was soon out of his chair and headed to the storage cabinet for seeds.

"Are you sure you don't need any help?" Salty asked.

Sarah smiled. "What would you say if I asked you to wash the dishes or dry them?"

"I did it all during the war. I even cooked." He didn't add that he'd cooked and cleaned during the years between his mother's and father's deaths, too. The memory of having his efforts constantly belittled and the food thrown at him on occasion was something he'd rather no one knew.

Her smile vanished. "I don't know why I keep forgetting you were in the war."

"I'm glad you do. I keep trying." It had been easy to believe in a cause. Still was. Everybody believes in something. The hard part was having to kill a human being on behalf of it. He would always wonder if what he'd done was worth it.

"Are you sure the children will be safe while we're gone?" he asked.

Sarah nodded. "No one would hurt them. Not even Arnie."

"Why didn't you marry Wallace?" Salty asked Sarah. "Seems like a perfect answer to your difficulties."

They'd been riding for more than two hours. The sky had been overcast early, but the sun had come out to burn off the chill. It had grown so warm it felt like early summer rather than the tail end of winter.

"If you knew him as well as I do, you wouldn't ask that question."

Wallace and his wife had been good neighbors to Sarah's family while she was growing up, but he'd changed after his only child died of fever. Maybe he thought being the richest man, the biggest rancher, the most influential man in the county could compensate for the loss of his son. After his wife died, he'd gradually became so irascible no one wanted anything to do with him. When he couldn't force Sarah to sell her ranch, he'd tried to acquire it through marriage.

"Has he complained about your cows getting on his land before?"

"Yes, but he never threatened to shoot them," Sarah said. "He doesn't act like himself anymore."

Salty apparently sensed her sadness. "Forget Wallace. Tell me about your ranch. How much land do you control? Who are your other neighbors? What kind of water do you have? Where is your best graze? What's the size of your herd, and what's its condition?"

Sarah was relieved to have something to think about rather than Wallace—or Salty's nearness. She still couldn't believe she'd fainted. She hadn't been able to sleep last night for thinking about him and her feelings for him. The waves of desire that washed over her had shocked her. Where had they come from? Why hadn't she ever felt that way about Roger?

It wasn't as if she had the excuse that she was in love with Salty. She liked him and had confidence in him in a way she never had with her husband, but that didn't translate into love. It took far more than being kind to her children for a woman to fall in love with a man. Didn't it? But even if she wasn't talking about love, these flashes of desire that constantly assailed her were just as unexpected and unexplainable.

"From what you've told me, I don't understand why your ranch is in such difficulty," Salty said.

Sarah tried to recall what she'd been saying. She was hardly aware that she'd been talking, but apparently she had been filling him in on the details for some time. They were approaching the stream that divided her ranch from Wallace's. Cows had punched out several paths to the water through the large patches of bushy growth and tangled vines that bordered the stream.

"My father never seemed to have a problem," she told Salty, "but Roger never wanted to do the work necessary to make a go of this place. After he left, I thought all I needed was a dependable man, but we could never find enough cows when it came time to sell them. At three dollars a head, I never made much."

Salty snorted. "We'll send our cows with the Randolphs when they go to Kansas. A man there is opening a market and says we can make twenty dollars a head if they're carrying good flesh."

Twenty dollars a head? Sarah could hardly believe her ears. She'd never heard of anybody getting that much for a single cow, not even a big five-year-old steer. If she could sell her cows for half that, she'd be able to pay off the arrears on her debt and be on the way to holding the ranch free and clear. "Are you sure of that?"

"There's a railhead coming through Kansas right now. It'll be easier to trail a herd north through Indian country than try to ship them to New Orleans or fight our way through the farmers in Missouri. They're so afraid of a fever that comes from a tick on some of our cows that they've passed a law banning Texas cattle from the state."

"I don't know if I have any steers ready for market." She had often wondered why they couldn't find more cows, but she hadn't been able to ride the range herself. The children had been too small to be left alone when Roger left. It was only in the last year that she had started to feel it was safe to leave them alone at all.

"After we deal with Wallace, I want to ride over all of your range," Salty said. "Once I know what kind of stock you have, we can start branding and choosing which to send to market."

"We?" His comment surprised her. None of the men she'd hired had ever asked her to participate.

"Yes. Me, you, and Ellen—I even have tasks for Jared. You didn't think I could do all of this alone, did you?"

"I really hadn't given it much thought. I don't have any experience."

He laughed. "It's easy to learn. It's just hard as hell to do."

That was probably a reason the men she'd hired had found so few of her cattle. She should have asked more questions, been more vigilant, more involved, but it had been all she could do to take care of her children as well as the milk cow, pigs, and chickens. Now Salty wanted to teach her.

"Is the stream the only boundary between the two ranches?" he asked.

"Yes. There was never any trouble when my father was alive, but now Wallace is trying to claim both sides."

"Cows go to a stream to drink," Salty mused. "It's not likely more than one or two will cross unless the grass on the other side looks a lot better. Has he said anything about your bulls crossing to breed with his cows?"

"No. Our stock's the same."

"It won't be once that calf I'm getting from George Randolph is big enough to start fathering calves. The future of ranching in Texas is dependent on finding an inexpensive way to get our steers to market and improving the quality of our herds. Steers that carry more meat bring a higher price," Salty pointed out.

Sarah's father had never worried about improving his herd. He had been content to sell his cows for tallow or to someone wanting to trail them to market. Roger wouldn't have seen the point of buying a bull when there were already dozens on the range. Sarah had been too concerned about survival to give much thought to improvements.

"Why isn't that cow branded?" Salty asked.

"Which one?"

Salty pointed to a cow with a spotted calf.

"I guess it's not mine."

"That's not what I mean. *Every* cow on the range should be branded. It's the only way you can identify your cows. If it's on your land and has no one else's brand, it's presumed to be your cow. She should be carrying your brand."

"My cows are branded every year. I guess that's one that was missed."

"Missed long enough to have a calf?" Salty asked.

Sarah didn't have an answer.

They eyed the stream that separated her land from Wallace's. Salty rode his horse into it then stopped. "This looks like good water. When does it dry up?"

"It runs all year. My father said it's spring fed."

"I expect that's why Wallace is trying to claim it. Not many Texas streams run all year, even ones fed by springs. Do you have any other streams on your ranch?"

"Yes."

"How many and where are they?"

"I don't know." Sarah could feel his gaze home in on her. She was beginning to feel very ignorant—and it wasn't just because of not knowing how many cows she owned, why one of them wasn't branded, and where exactly to find water. There was a lot more, she imagined. "My father thought it was improper for women to ride horseback, work cows, or to know anything about the ranch beyond how to run the house and take care of things like chickens and the garden. Roger felt the same. By the time I had any freedom to go where I wanted, I couldn't, because I had two babies."

Salty seemed unperturbed. "That's something we can rectify in a few days. As soon as it's practical, I'll teach Ellen and Jared as much as I can about the ranch, too. The more all of us know, the better we can manage."

Sarah rode her horse through the stream. "We'd better start looking for those cows Wallace complained about and get them back. I don't like leaving the children longer than necessary."

Salty rode a little farther and looked around. "You've got better grass. I'd expect Wallace's cows to cross, rather than the other way."

The only time Sarah could recall being at this stream was for a picnic when Roger was courting her. Comparing the quality of grass on each side hadn't been on her list of things to do. She said, "None of the men I hired reported any trouble."

"Well, cows that aren't fenced in are going to wander. That's another reason why I don't understand Wallace's complaint." Salty shrugged. "It's probably just another way for him to aggravate you into selling your ranch."

"The bank owns as much of it as I do."

"That wouldn't be his problem. Let's see what we can find."

They rode at least a quarter of an hour before they found one of her cows. "If this is the only one, Wallace can't complain that your cows are eating up his grass. I counted seven of his on your land on our way here," Salty pointed out. Stopping, he moved his head from side to side and sniffed the air.

"Someone is branding cattle."

SIXTEEN

Salty didn't know why the smell of singed hair and scorched cowhide should send warning signals to his brain. Because of the generally mild winters, Texas cows could give birth at virtually any time, so why should this raise a question in his mind? Probably because of his previous encounter with Wallace, and his natural suspicion of any man who was a bully.

No man branding cows on his land would be breaking any law. Still, his instincts told him something wasn't right.

"What's wrong?" Sarah asked.

"I don't know that anything is."

"Then why are you sniffing the air like a hound dog and frowning like a rancher whose daughter has just told him she wants to marry a farmer?"

That surprised a laugh out of Salty. "I didn't know I looked so forbidding."

"Something is bothering you," Sarah pressed.

"Yes, but I don't have a logical reason for it."

She seemed to accept this, and urged her horse forward. "Then let's find out what's going on. I don't believe in ignoring instincts."

Sometimes she acted just like Rose Randolph. Salty grinned and followed.

The stream flowed through a meadow with low, unevenly forested hills on both sides. Oaks and maples were interspersed with cedar, hackberry, and cactus. The meadow was thick with a profusion of plants heavy with swelling buds ready to burst into flower at the first sustained warmth of spring. The air was crisp, the day sunny, and the breeze gentle enough to give a feeling of stillness. How could anything be terribly wrong on such a day? But the feeling that something wasn't right reasserted itself.

"The smell is coming from somewhere up on the ridge," he said to Sarah. "Probably by that grove of live oaks."

As they grew near, Salty could make out the voices of three men. A calf that seemed less than a week old hovered on the periphery of the group, bleating for its mother. A moment later a cow burst into sight and raced away from the three cowhands, her still-bleating calf in pursuit. One of the men noticed Salty and Sarah's approach and said something to the others.

"Howdy," one of the men called. "Who might you be?"

"I'm Salty Benton, and this is my wife, Sarah."

"I don't know no Salty Benton with a wife named Sarah," one of the hands said.

"I used to be Sarah Winborne," Sarah replied. "I own the neighboring ranch, the F&P. I just got married."

The youngest cowhand winked at Salty. "Congratulations."

"What are you doing over this way?" the first hand asked.

"Your boss said some of our cows were on his land."

The man regarded Salty. "I ain't seen any today, but if we do, we'll be glad to run 'em back for you."

"It sure would make it easier on me. There's only one of me, and my wife's ranch is right large."

The cowhand nodded. "You got to get some help. None of the men your wife hired before could do half the work it took to run that place. I've seen Arnie wrestle a cow down before he could brand her calf. I doubt he could brand as many as half the calves."

Salty had already come to the conclusion that much of Sarah's herd had gone unbranded. The question in his mind was whether they were *still* unbranded. It was perfectly legal for a rancher to claim any unbranded cows on his land even if he knew they didn't belong to him.

"I see you've been doing some branding," he remarked.

"Yeah. The boss was away during the war. We're still trying to catch up on the cows that went unbranded. The hands that ran the place back then weren't worth a damn."

It wouldn't do any good for Salty to accuse him of branding F&P cows even if he'd known for a fact they were doing so. Even if this man suspected not all these cows belonged to his boss, he had a right to brand all of those found on his boss's land. So Salty said, "Tell you what. I'll run your cows back if you'll do the same with ours. I want to do everything I can to make your boss happy, but I can't be everywhere at once, and you know what cows are like."

"He ain't never going to be happy," the youngest cowhand said with a grim look and a shake of his head. "I ain't never seen a man with a temper like his. You'd think someone had done shot his favorite horse."

"The boss has had his troubles just like everybody else," the first hand said.

"Maybe, but he don't have to take it out on us."

"If you don't like working here, you'd best look for another job."

"I'm thinking about it," the youngster said. "Been thinking about it for a while."

"We'd better be going," Salty spoke up. "We've got a lot of ground to cover."

"You take care," the older hand said. "We'll be sure to run back anything bearing your brand."

But would they do the same if the cow wasn't branded?

Sarah didn't know it was possible to be so angry and feel so stupid at the same time. She and Salty had ridden over as much of her ranch as they could cover in six hours, and with each clearing they entered, each group of cows they flushed out of the trees, the brutal truth hit home with greater force: maybe as much as a third of her cows were unbranded. There was no way to estimate how many had wandered off and been collected by other ranchers. She reminded herself of all the reasons she hadn't overseen the ranching herself, but that didn't change the fact that it was ultimately her responsibility to see that the men she hired actually did the work she hired them to do.

"What are we going to do?" she asked Salty. He was nearly as angry as she.

"We're going to start branding every cow we find without a brand."

"What about the calves?"

"They'll stay with their mothers for most of the year. Anyone who owns a cow owns the calf at her side and the one she'll drop the next spring."

"How are we going to do it?"

"I'll show you, starting first thing tomorrow. Now let's see if we can haze these cows away from the borders of your ranch. I don't want any more of them wandering off to be stolen."

"Do you think that's what happened?" Sarah asked. It seemed probable.

"I'm sure of it—which makes it difficult for me to understand why Wallace complained about your cows being on his land. I suspect he has instructed his men to brand any unbranded cows they find there. Why would he complain if he was getting free cows? It would only be illegal if he chased them off your range onto his."

"His cowhands didn't look guilty," Sarah pointed out.

Salty nodded. "I agree."

Sarah didn't know much about moving cows, but they were so wild they wanted to avoid all humans. The difficult part was getting them to move in the right direction. For each step the cows took, her horse took a dozen. She was beginning to understand why all of her hired men had kept asking for more horses, as well as why it was impossible for one person to do all the work of running the ranch.

Talk broke off while Salty went after an unbranded yearling that tried to leave the group, and it was a while before it began again because they collected more unbranded cattle as they worked their way home. The cows didn't like being moved off familiar range.

"What are we going to do with them?" she shouted at Salty over the heads of more than two dozen steers, cows, and calves.

"Put them in the corral."

Sarah wondered how the two of them were going to get that done. There were so many cows!

Apparently the children had been watching for their return. Ellen came riding up even before the ranch house came into view. "I can help."

Sarah wasn't sure her daughter knew enough to herd full-grown steers, but she soon proved so adept at handling her horse that Sarah was filled with pride. Her daughter was fearless as well as talented.

Jared, figuring out what they intended, had gone to the corral and pulled down the bars. After that he positioned himself to one side, apparently intending to haze runaways back with his crutch. But a boy with a crutch was no match for an angry cow.

"Get up on the fence!" Salty shouted.

Sarah turned in time to see a steer heading straight toward Jared. Her breath caught in her throat.

With the help of his new crutch, Jared scrambled out of the steer's path. At the same time, Salty brought his horse alongside the runaway. He used the greater size and weight of his horse to knock the steer off balance and turn him in the direction of the corral. Much to Sarah's relief, several animals followed, and it didn't take long for the three riders to corral the rest of the small herd.

"That was fun!" Ellen was so happy she was almost laughing. "Are you going after some more tomorrow?"

"We have to figure out how to brand these," Salty said.

"Can we start now?" Jared asked.

Salty grinned, clearly pleased by his enthusiasm, but shook his head. "The cows need time to settle down. They don't like being driven from their home ground. In the meantime, I want to see what you did in the garden. Then we have to find the chickens that are roosting in trees and feed the pig."

"And I have to start supper," Sarah said.

"After we eat, you can help me start on the chute," Salty said to the children. "We'll need it for the branding and build it when it's too dark to ride."

Salty packed dirt around the last of ten posts he'd set into the ground. The muscles in his shoulders and arms burned from the work of cutting trees to form them, digging the holes in the hard ground, and packing the soil back so tightly the posts wouldn't move. He sighed with relief then turned to Ellen. "We can finish this chute tomorrow night. We'll start branding the day after that. Now you'd better head to the house and go to bed."

"You promise I can help with the branding?" Ellen asked Salty.

"I promise. Now scat."

He'd never realized a child's head had so much room for questions. Earlier, Jared had shown Salty the work he and Ellen did in the garden then went inside to help his mother with supper. While Salty and Ellen completed the rest of the chores, she'd pelted him with a steady stream of questions. "Can I brand a steer? Can you teach me to wrestle a steer to the ground? How do you build a chute? What is a chute? Can I go with you tomorrow? Can I ride one of your horses? Did Mr. Wallace shoot any of our cows? Do you think he will? Why did Arnie want to kill our pigs? If we go to Austin again, can we stay in a hotel?" Salty had been relieved when Sarah called them inside for supper, but of course the girl had come out to work on the chute. She'd been a help, too. Salty absentmindedly massaged a sore shoulder as he watched her run to the house. Didn't the child know how to walk?

"Come on, Bones," he said to the dog who'd watched him work while resting comfortably on an old blanket. "You have to earn your keep tomorrow. No more lounging around."

Bones got up and trotted over, apparently untroubled by the gash in his side. Salty carried on a meaningless conversation with the dog as he washed up and headed back to the shed. He thought longingly of his comfortable bunk at the Randolph ranch, but he might as well put a soft mattress out of his mind until he had sold the first group of steers. Maybe not even then, depending on how much money Sarah owed the bank. He'd have to talk to her about that. He didn't like having something like that hanging over his head.

He opened the door to the shed. "In you go," he said to Bones, "but don't get used to it. You're supposed to be a watchdog, though I can see how getting a knife in your side might sour you on the job."

He tossed the dog's blanket into the corner. Bones trotted inside the shed, ambled over to the corner, circled a few times, then lay down on the blanket. He then looked up at Salty as though expecting something better.

"Be thankful for the blanket. Tomorrow it's the cold ground."

Salty dropped onto the pile of blankets that comprised his bed. As soon as he had the energy, he'd wash them. He knew nothing about the men who'd slept here before him, or about the insects and rodents that undoubtedly had tried to make this their home. He'd sleep more soundly once he knew all trace of them was gone.

He needed to clear his mind of everything. He needed sleep, and worrying about the challenges that would face him in the coming days wasn't going to help. But the longed-for sleep didn't come, because images of Sarah getting ready for bed filled his mind. He felt like a Peeping Tom, but he couldn't stop himself. Spending the whole day with her had heightened his awareness of her presence.

Thinking of her in bed, her body clothed in a loose gown that probably clung to her every contour, caused him to harden. He was surprised by its force, the wave of desire that surged through him. He'd always had an appreciation for women, but four years in the army had taught him how to live without them. He didn't understand why being around Sarah had caused everything to change so quickly. Fantasies not unlike the ones that had invaded his dreams during his teens assailed him, but he couldn't afford that now. He had too much work to do. Rounding up and branding cows required large reserves of energy and alertness.

Bones's head came up and he whined.

"Be quiet. I don't need you keeping me awake."

The dog ignored him.

"Don't tell me your side is hurting."

Bones got to his feet, walked to the door, and pushed against it with his nose.

"I'm not getting up to let you out. You'll have to hold it until morning."

But Bones's whine changed to a growl deep in his throat, and Salty decided this wasn't a call of nature. The dog heard or smelled something outside he didn't like.

"Okay. I'm getting up, but stop growling," he whispered. "I don't want you to scare off whoever's out there."

Bones's growl turned into a snarl, and Salty figured he knew who was prowling around the ranch. Arnie. It was stupid of the man to come back. What did he hope to gain?

Salty didn't take time to dress or put on shoes. "You have to stay here," he said as he pushed Bones back toward his bed. "I need to talk to Arnie, not have you chew him up." He reached for his rifle and eased the door open a crack. It wasn't big enough for him to see much.

It was big enough for Bones to stick his nose through, and Salty pushed the dog away again. "I told you to get back. And don't start barking when I leave. This isn't like chasing cows out of the brush. Sometimes you have to sneak up on your quarry."

Salty opened the door just enough to stick his head out. He didn't see anyone or hear any movement, but someone was out there and Bones wasn't happy about it. Salty squeezed through the door and closed it behind him despite the dog's protests.

"Stop it!" he hissed as Bones started scratching against the door. "If you keep making so much noise, he'll get away." He didn't know why he was talking like the dog could understand him. Bones's ears told him somebody was outside, and his nose told him it was somebody he didn't like; that was as far as the dog's understanding went. Now it was up to Salty.

The moon was momentarily behind a cloud, but there was enough light for Salty to see any intruder and for the intruder to see him. He only guessed it was Arnie. It could be anybody. Thieves. Rustlers. He was concerned about the pig, the chickens, and the milk cow, but the horses would be the most difficult to replace. Most important was the house, because that's where Sarah and the children lay asleep, unaware of any potential danger. Salty was sorely tempted to loose Bones, but he didn't want the intruder to escape before finding out who it was.

Moving on silent feet, he covered the distance between the shed and the trees surrounding the house as quickly as possible. Crouched in the deep shadows of a post oak he listened intently but couldn't hear any sound. That in itself was ominous: animals moved about, snorted, made small noises on nights they felt safe. They fell silent when they perceived danger.

Salty moved through the trees toward the house. It sat in quiet solitude, silhouetted against a darker backdrop of trees. Being careful to make no noise, Salty circled the dwelling while staying in the shadows. Twice he stopped to peer through the blackness before he could be certain no one was there.

He'd almost finished the circuit when he stubbed his toe. It hurt so badly it surprised a grunt out of him, but he held back the curses that sprang to his lips. Too late to decide he should have taken time to put on his boots, and he finished his circuit of the house at a hobbling gait.

He wondered if he should wake Sarah. He didn't want to worry her until he was sure he had a good reason. Besides, he didn't want Ellen or Jared deciding they had to sit up all night keeping watch. Imagining the things Ellen might do was enough to cause Salty to break out in a cold sweat.

Once he felt certain no one in the house was in danger, Salty headed toward the corral. He went by way of the chicken pen. There was no noise from the hens roosting in the two trees encircled by wire. All was quiet in the pigpen, too, the pig asleep on its side. The milk cow had been staked out in the open. She was lying down, chewing her cud, and looking in the direction of the corral. Bones was still scratching and whining at the shed door when Salty passed.

The corral was in an area that was relatively flat, open enough to have good graze, but with enough trees to provide shade during the hottest days of summer. It was good for the horses. It was also good for anyone trying to avoid detection.

The horses showed no signs of agitation, which meant the person out there was familiar to them—or there was nobody out there. Since Bones had convinced Salty at least one person *was* out there, it must be someone they knew. *Arnie.* Which left Salty with the problem of having to find him, find out what he intended, and decide what he was going to do about it.

Moving carefully, Salty approached the corral fence at a point deep in the shadow of an oak tree. Once there, he searched every part of the corral, attempting to penetrate every shadow with his eyes, whether that shadow was cast by a horse or a tree. Arnie was out there somewhere, likely with the intention of doing something sneaky. A movement in the shadows near several horses caught Salty's attention, but despite staring as hard as he could, he couldn't make out any particular shape.

He was about to turn another direction when a dull flash caught his eye. The moon had crossed behind the darkest part of a cloud and was moving gradually to emerge from the wispy edge. Had that flash been from a button or belt buckle? A gun barrel? A knife? It was too high to have come from spurs and unlikely to be part of a bridle. Just then the moon cleared the edge of the cloud and the horses parted enough for Salty to make out the silhouette of a man next to a black and white paint. He appeared to be patting the horse, apparently trying to calm and reassure it.

The man continued to pat the horse, running his hand down its neck, across the withers, over its back, and down the hind leg. Puzzled but unwilling to wait longer, Salty rose to enter the corral. At that moment, the man bent down and lifted the horse's leg. The flash of a knife meant he intended to maim it.

SEVENTEEN

WITH A SHOUT OF FURY, SALTY CLIMBED THROUGH THE RAILS AND started forward at a run. The paint threw its head up, jerked its foot from the man's grasp, and trotted away. Equally startled, the man started running for the far fence.

The riding boots he wore impeded his quarry's progress, but the rocky, thorny ground was brutal on Salty's bare feet; it would be impossible for him to catch the man unless he could mount. Hoping his horses remembered their lessons, he stopped long enough to whistle. A horse separated itself from a group ahead and turned, but it didn't come to him. Apparently it was only curious about the sound.

Hearing something approach from behind, Salty turned to see both of his horses coming toward him at a trot. "Good boy," he said to the calico, which reached him first. "Now hold still while I climb aboard."

It was never easy to mount a horse bareback, and it was even more difficult when Salty didn't have anything to give him a leg up. His feet were so sore that merely putting his normal weight on them was painful, but he dropped his rifle, took a firm grip on the horse's mane, bent both knees then virtually leapt onto its back. Despite the skin moving loosely under him, he managed to pull himself up and drove his heels into his mount's flanks. The animal responded with a satisfying burst of speed.

He'd almost forgotten the lessons of his childhood. Not since he was a boy on his father's farm had Salty had occasion to ride a horse bareback, but using pressure from his knees and tugging on the mane, he was able to turn the horse in the direction of his fleeing quarry. The distance between them narrowed with satisfying quickness.

They ran the risk of coming together at the fence. Calling on his mount for more speed, Salty was able to head the man off. His quarry turned a shocked face upward, and Salty recognized Arnie.

"Stop," Salty shouted. "If I have to shoot you to stop you from getting away, I will."

Apparently Arnie had enough presence of mind to know that a man in his long underwear riding bareback was unlikely to be carrying a weapon, because he skidded to a stop and headed in a new direction. Unable to turn as quickly, Salty's horse made a big loop before zeroing in on him. Arnie stopped and changed directions twice more before he was exhausted.

"Stop," Salty called again as he rode up alongside. "If you don't, I'm going to throw you to the ground." Arnie didn't waste energy responding, just continued stubbornly onward with ever-slowing steps.

Frustrated, Salty guided his mount close enough to plant his foot in the middle of Arnie's back. Giving a shove, he knocked Arnie to the ground then ordered, "Get up. I want to know why you're trying to ruin Sarah. We can go to the shed and talk like civilized human beings, or I can beat it out of you."

"I hate you," Arnie muttered.

"I'm not too fond of you just now," Salty countered. "My feet are covered in bruises, and I have a thorn in my foot that hurts like hell."

"I wish you'd broken your neck."

"Full of well-wishes, aren't you?"

Arnie grunted.

"Get up, or I'll ride my horse over you."

Arnie was slow to get to his feet. He cast Salty a look of loathing, but it lacked anger. The expression more closely resembled resignation. Salty hoped that meant Arnie could be talked into giving up his efforts to win Sarah back, though Salty had never understood the logic of the man's plan. Whether they succeeded or failed, Sarah was still his wife. But then, maybe a man in love was incapable of reason. His own thinking hadn't been all that rational of late. After all, he'd just threatened to ride his horse over a man.

As they moved in the direction of the shed, Salty remembered that he'd cast his rifle aside when he mounted his horse. Arnie spotted it and broke into a labored run. Salty gave chase and, grimacing at the necessity of what he had to do when his horse arrived a stride behind, launched himself into the air. He landed atop Arnie, driving the breath out of both their bodies.

Pushing the older man aside, he rolled toward the rifle and scooped it up. His quick thinking had been rewarded by a thorn in his shoulder. If he lived to be a hundred, he was going to get Arnie back for this.

He struggled to his feet, careful not to put his full weight on the foot with the embedded thorn. "Get up, and don't cause me any more trouble! If I end up with another thorn in me, I'm liable to lose control of my trigger finger."

Arnie rolled over and sat up. "You were a Johnny Reb. You won't shoot me. You're too honorable."

"I wouldn't test that theory if I were you. Idealism takes a backseat to pain."

"What kind of soldier are you to complain about a couple of lousy thorns?" Arnie growled.

"A bad-tempered one." Salty prodded the ex-hand with his rifle barrel. "Now get up."

"What will you do if I don't?"

Salty lifted his rifle into the air. "After I slam this rifle butt into your hard head, I'll drag your mangy carcass over to that shed. Then, if I'm feeling particularly charitable, I might consider untying you so you can pick the thorns out of *your* hide."

Arnie slowly got to his feet and started toward the shed.

Salty was surprised to see Sarah waiting for them when they reached it. "What are you doing here?" she asked Arnie.

"Trying to lame our horses," Salty said. "Show her your knife."

Arnie was reluctant, so Salty prodded him with his rifle. "Give it to her, handle first." Arnie pulled the knife from his waist and handed it to Sarah.

"I'd appreciate it if you could get the lantern in the shed," Salty said to Sarah. "I've got a couple of thorns that need removing." He held up a foot to show her that he wasn't wearing shoes.

"What made you go after him barefooted?" she asked.

"He was poised to use that knife on one of your horses."

"You ran him down with a thorn in your foot?"

It would have been nice to be able to claim heroic ability, but Salty settled on the truth. "I rode one of my horses."

"You mounted bareback with a thorn in your foot?"

"I couldn't let him get away."

There wasn't enough moonlight to be sure he understood Sarah's look correctly, but he was sure of some approval in her eyes.

"Where is the lantern?" she asked.

"Just inside the door. There are some sulfur matches on the shelf above it. You," he said to Arnie, "follow her, but don't do anything stupid."

He hadn't reached the shed before Ellen came racing up, still in her nightgown. She took in the scene and asked, "Are you going to shoot Arnie?" Her eyes were like pie plates.

"I'm thinking about it."

"What did he do?"

Salty didn't get a chance to answer. Sarah opened the door to the shed, and Bones went straight for Arnie, a growl deep in his throat and his bare fangs flashing in the moonlight. "Stop him!" Salty yelled.

Ellen threw herself at Bones, managing to get her arms around the dog. Bones wasn't willing to give up easily, but he obviously didn't want to hurt the little girl and she was equally determined. After a brief struggle Bones stopped fighting, but he kept an angry gaze on Arnie, the growl continuing to rumble from his chest.

"What's going on?" With the help of his crutch, Jared could now move almost as fast as his sister. The pair looked so young in their night-clothes, Salty wanted to tell them they ought to be in bed dreaming of rich desserts instead of being dragged out in the middle of the night by some addlebrained swain.

"Arnie is causing trouble again," he said.

"What did he do?" the boy asked.

"Nothing. Salty got to him first." Sarah had returned with the lantern, and she asked Jared to hold it for her.

"Why?" Did children ever do anything without asking why first?

"I have to take a thorn out of Salty's foot."

"There's one in my shoulder, too."

It hurt almost as much coming out as it had going in—one more thing to add to Arnie's list of infractions.

"Now let's see your foot," Sarah commanded.

Rather than sit down and risk Arnie trying to get away, Salty held his foot up behind him.

"The thorn has broken off under the skin," Sarah told him. "I'm going to need a needle to get it out."

He'd learned to sew during the war. "I have one in my bedroll."

"I'll get it," Jared volunteered. Carrying the lantern in his free hand, the boy limped over to the shed and disappeared inside.

"Why did you come back?" Sarah asked, turning to Arnie.

"You know why." The naked hunger in his eyes would have been embarrassing if it hadn't made Salty angry. No man had a right to look at his wife like that.

"Were you planning to do something to my husband after you killed my livestock and lamed my horses? I'm married now."

Arnie cast Salty that now-familiar look of loathing. "We don't have to be married for you to run away with me."

Bones lay down on the ground, apparently convinced he wasn't going to be allowed to take a bite out of the man who'd stabbed him. He stopped growling, but he didn't take his eyes off Arnie.

"What are you going to do to him?" Ellen asked Salty.

"Take him into Austin," Salty said. He sighed. "People have been hanged for stealing horses. I don't expect laming them is much different."

"He hasn't done anything awful enough for *that* kind of punishment," Sarah gasped.

Salty had moments of softheartedness, but he was also practical. "If he'd had his way, he'd have killed both pigs—maybe the milk cow as well—and lamed I-don't-know-how-many horses. What are you waiting for, him to burn down your house?"

"I'd never do that," Arnie insisted.

"Sorry if I find it difficult to believe you," Salty snapped. "I haven't had much experience with men who attempt to destroy everything that belongs to the woman they claim to adore."

"I wasn't trying to destroy nothing. I just wanted to make Sarah love me."

Jared returned with the needle. "I found it."

Salty felt sorry for Arnie, but he didn't want to hear any twisted explanations. The man was a lunatic. A dangerous lunatic. "I'm going to sit down," he said. "If you try to escape, I won't hesitate to put a bullet in you. And if I miss, Bones has a score he's anxious to settle."

The dog growled and attempted to rise. Ellen tightened her hold on him.

Sarah picked up a water bucket, which she placed upside down in the dirt. "Sit here."

Salty hobbled over and settled on the bucket. The rim cut into his flesh so deeply he stood up again. "Either you tie Arnie to the fence so he can't escape, or you'll have to do this with me standing up."

"Where is your rope?"

"I know," Jared volunteered. "I'll get it."

"What do *you* think we ought to do with him?" Salty asked Sarah, staring at Arnie. "You can't just let him go."

"We can keep him tied up," Ellen suggested.

"That would mean someone would have to watch and feed him," Salty pointed out.

"Bones could watch him."

"I need Bones to help roust steers out of the brush."

"I could watch him." Jared had returned, dragging a rope behind him.

"I need you to heat the branding irons."

"I'm not watching him," Ellen said. "I'm going to help with the roundup."

"You're going to do the branding," Salty told her. "Your mother and I will drive the steers into the chute."

"Sarah doesn't have a chute," Arnie snapped.

"She does now," Salty said. "Or she will tomorrow, as soon as I finish it."

"Arnie can help us," Jared said. "After what he did, he owes us."

Salty thought that was a crazy idea. "How?"

"He can pen the cows in the chute," Jared said.

Ellen shook her head. "He'll get away."

"Not if you tie him by his leg," Jared explained. "It wouldn't have to be a long rope, because he wouldn't have to move much."

"You don't have to tie me up now," Arnie said, eyeing Bones. "I won't try to escape."

"I don't trust you," Sarah said, "but I'll agree to just tie your legs to the fence." It didn't take her long to make sure he was securely tied a few yards away. "Now, your turn," she said to Salty.

Salty lowered himself to the ground and rested his foot on the water bucket. He kept a hand on his rifle.

"Hold the lantern still," Sarah told Jared.

Salty knew having a needle stuck into his foot was going to hurt. He just didn't know how much. He jerked his foot back before he could stop himself.

"It's in deep," Sarah told him.

"Sorry. I know."

He wasn't going to flinch. In the war he'd watched too many boys have mangled arms and legs cut off without benefit of anything more than whiskey to dull the pain. Besides, Jared's gaze was glued to him. That boy had to live with a withered leg every day of his life and did so with calm acceptance and good cheer. Salty wasn't going to be humiliated by one stinking little thorn.

But it wasn't easy to appear stoic when Sarah was digging a hole the size of a hen's egg in the tender flesh of his foot. She might as well have been using a butcher knife.

Ellen was watching her mother intently. "I've had lots of thorns way bigger than that."

Sarah didn't stop digging. "I'm sure it was a lot bigger before it broke off."

A particularly painful probe of the needle nearly destroyed Salty's resolve. He clenched his fists, took a deep breath, and held it until the wave of pain receded. Then Sarah held up the needle. "I got it."

Ellen peered at the thorn. "It's *tiny*."

"It was deep in his foot. Digging it out had to be very painful."

"He didn't cry," Jared said.

"Men don't," Sarah said.

Salty remembered men who were in so much pain they couldn't cry; all they could do was scream. "Yes, they do. One more jab of that needle, and I'd have been blubbering like a baby."

The children laughed, and Sarah favored him with a look so warm it threatened to heat up the night. Now he was sure her feelings for him were more than mere physical attraction. And if that look measured the intensity of her feelings, she liked him a lot.

Despite the throbbing in his foot, he felt his body begin to react to his desire for her. He fought against it. He suspected Sarah thought men only cared for women because of their physical needs, and he didn't want her to think that of him. He needed to redirect everyone's attention. "We should decide what to do about Arnie," he announced. He talked so the man couldn't hear.

"Let's shoot him," said Ellen.

Sarah laughed, surprised. "I thought you liked him."

"He was trying to hurt our horses." In the little girl's world, horses were more important than people.

She turned to Salty. "What do you suggest?"

"We have to round up and brand a lot of cows in the next several days, and we don't have anybody to help us. He can help us for the next week and prove he's changed his ways. If he doesn't agree, or runs away before we finish, we should turn him in to the sheriff."

"How will you catch him if he runs away?" Ellen asked.

Salty eyed Bones. "I have a feeling he wouldn't get very far. What do you think?" he asked Sarah.

She leveled a harsh gaze at her would-be suitor. "Why did you stab Bones?"

"I didn't mean to. I was just trying to keep him from biting me."

"How about killing our pig and trying to lame my horses?"

Arnie hung his head. "I was hoping if you thought this man couldn't protect you, you'd take me back."

"You've done a terrible thing, Arnie, but we're shorthanded. I'll accept Salty's suggestion if you agree to it, but you have to understand that he is my husband and my children's stepfather now."

"What if he shoots Salty?" Jared asked, suddenly horrified.

"I'd shoot *him*," Ellen declared.

"He's not going to shoot Salty," Sarah said.

Jared wasn't convinced. "But what if he did?"

"Then I'd let Ellen shoot him and we'd leave his carcass for the coyotes."

The children laughed, but Salty thought he detected an edge of steel in Sarah's voice. While he doubted that's what Sarah would *really* do, it pleased him to know that's what she'd *want* to do. Once they got the branding done, he'd have to explore the change in her feelings toward him more fully. In the meantime, he'd better make sure he knew what his feelings were.

He turned his attention back to Arnie. "It looks like you have a choice: work with us or go to jail. What will it be?"

It was impossible to know what was going on in Arnie's mind. Any man who thought he could win a woman's affection by running down her ability to survive and attacking her livestock suffered from thinking that was plain twisted. Salty wasn't sure working with Arnie was a good idea. He wouldn't have suggested it if they weren't in such desperate need of help.

"I'll help with the branding," Arnie said. "At least I'll get something to eat, right?"

Salty hadn't thought of how difficult it might be for a man like Arnie to find work. "I can't turn a fellow soldier out, but you'll have to sleep outdoors. I wouldn't feel comfortable with you in the shed next to me."

Arnie's gaze narrowed. "If you're married, why aren't you sleeping with Sarah?"

It was impossible to offer the real explanation. "Bones and I are sleeping out to watch for thieves."

Arnie looked like he wanted to ask more questions. Instead he asked, "What if it rains?"

"You can sleep in the wagon," Sarah suggested.

"I'll lend you my bedroll to keep dry," Salty offered.

"He'll run away," Jared said.

"No, I won't. If I go to jail, I'll never get a decent job." Arnie looked at the ground. "Or find a woman who'll marry me."

That would probably be a good thing, Salty thought. Texas didn't need children cursed with Arnie's thinking processes.

He declared, "It's time for everyone to get back to bed."

"I need to bandage your foot," Sarah said.

"It's not necessary. I'll be sure to keep my boots on."

Sarah didn't look convinced, but she didn't argue; she took the children and headed toward the house. Arnie watched them just as intently until they disappeared through the trees. "You'll be a lot happier if you can put those thoughts out of your mind," Salty told him.

Arnie took a deep, slow breath then exhaled so completely he seemed to shrink in size. "I guess I was stupid to think it ever would work."

Salty couldn't disagree, but he felt sorry for the man. He knew what it was like to fear no woman would ever love him.

"What about your dog?" Arnie asked. Bones had stopped trying to get to him after Sarah tied him to the fence, but he hadn't stopped watching.

"I'll keep Bones in the shed with me."

"Put him inside before you untie me. I don't like the way he's looking at me."

"Right now he's just watching you. Don't give him reason to change his mind. I'll give you a couple of blankets for the wagon. Get some sleep. We all should."

But after Salty had gotten Arnie settled and crawled back into his own bed, Bones lying near the door, he was wide awake. Was he stupid to keep Arnie around, even though they desperately needed the help? The man suffered from seriously dysfunctional thinking. Wouldn't it be safer for everyone if he was in jail?

He turned onto his other side. It wasn't more comfortable, but he liked his thoughts a lot better. Sarah had called him the children's step-father. That was the first time she'd included the children in their relationship. Rather than being her partner in a business arrangement, it sounded like she was indeed thinking of him as part of the family. He was very fond of both children. Their lives so far had been shaped by circumstances beyond their control. He wanted them to have a chance to discover what they wanted for themselves, not just what was necessary for survival.

Didn't he want the same things for Sarah? Not quite. He wanted her to discover what it was like to live her life without being afraid of going broke, or of a man who'd abuse her emotionally if not physically. He wanted her to know what it was like to go to bed without fear, to wake up without feeling desperate, to be able to face the world without feeling inferior in any way.

He also wanted *her*. He wasn't sure whether it was love or infatuation, but he did know it wasn't mere lust. He'd had enough experience with that to know. What he didn't know was love. His mother had claimed she loved his father, but she'd lived in fear of his rages. His father had said he loved Salty's mother, but he'd treated her like a servant. He'd told the world he loved his son, but Salty had never felt loved. Seeing Rose and George had restored Salty's belief in the possibility of real love, but he wasn't a war hero like George. He was just a lowly foot soldier who wasn't sure he was worthy of that kind of love.

But he wanted that kind of love. He wanted it enough to risk failure.

―――――

"Iron," Salty shouted.

They had been at this for a week. They rose every morning before dawn, ate the first of only two meals they would have that day, then headed out to round up the animals to be branded. Jared would have the fire going and the branding irons hot by the time they returned. Salty had been required to show Jared only once how to tell when a branding iron was too hot or not hot enough. The boy was as smart as he was sweet-tempered.

The boy chose an iron from the fire he was tending and brought it to where Salty stood next to the chute. Inside, a four-year-old steer fought against the boards that held him prisoner.

"Pin him," Salty shouted.

Arnie shoved the steer against the side of the chute, held him steady for the time it took Salty to work the brand without smearing it. The smell of singed hair and scorched hide assaulted Salty's nostrils, but he had grown so used to the stench over the last week he hardly noticed it any longer. Satisfied the brand was clear and lasting, Salty stood back and said, "Let him go."

Arnie pulled away from the steer and, while the animal was regaining his balance, removed the bars that had locked it in the chute. Salty gave a shout and slapped the steer on the rump. The angry creature shot from the chute at a run. Giving a bellow of rage, it headed for the open range.

Returning the branding iron to Jared, Salty mounted his horse to cut another animal from the herd Sarah and Ellen were holding. This time he chose a cow with a calf at her side. This would give him a chance to do two at once. The cow would be caught in the chute; he would lasso the calf and Arnie would wrestle it to the ground.

Salty doubted he would ever learn to like the man, but Arnie was as good as his word. He wasn't a skilled cowhand, but he did whatever Salty told him to do as quickly and as well as he could. With more experience he'd probably turn into a good hand. Salty was already trying to decide whether to keep him on to deliver the steers they were going to send north with the Randolphs.

"When can *I* brand a steer?"

Ellen had been hankering to wield the branding iron, and Salty had tried to explain that it wasn't easy to make a clear, readable brand. You had to have the iron at the right temperature, you had to know how to make the design, and you had to know how hard and how long to press to get a mark that would be clear but not burn through the skin. Unfortunately, it looked easy.

"Stop plaguing Salty," Sarah scolded. "We need you where you are."

After the excitement of the roundup, keeping cows in a herd wasn't enough action for Ellen. "You don't need me. You've got Bones."

The dog had been worth his weight in gold when it came to flushing cows from the brush and tangles of thorny vines, and he was proving almost as valuable as a herd dog. Let a single steer break away, and Bones was after him in a flash.

"You need a crew of at least ten for branding," Salty told Ellen. "We have half that. I thought you wanted to spend your whole day on horseback."

She did, but she also wanted to be in the middle of the excitement, and to her that meant branding, not sitting a horse waiting for something to happen.

They had only ten more to brand today. Salty was wondering if he'd done enough for the time being. His lumber had arrived. He was anxious to start building an extra room onto Sarah's house. It was well past the time Ellen should be sharing a room with her brother.

He had branded the cow and wrestled her calf to the ground when Jared said, "Someone's coming."

Salty glanced up to see several riders approaching. Henry Wallace was in the lead, and he was coming at a fast canter.

"Hand me an iron," Salty said to Jared. He didn't want to face

Wallace while he was holding the calf, and he intended to brand the animal while it was down.

Jared handed him an iron. Salty had it poised over the calf's flank when Wallace shouted, "Stop. That's my calf!" With that, he pulled a rifle and aimed it at Salty.

EIGHTEEN

OVER THE LAST SEVERAL DAYS, THE GROUND HAD BEEN CUT UP BY hundreds of hooves and every blade of grass in a circle of a hundred feet ground to fragments. Generous sunshine and a lack of rain had produced a fine dust which coated the inside of Sarah's nose and penetrated the fabric of her clothes all the way to her skin. Much to Ellen's amusement, the dust had combined with sweat to turn Salty's face slate gray. Jared said he looked like he'd been dead for a month.

"You and Bones hold the herd until I get back," Sarah told her daughter. "Don't worry if a few get away. We'll catch them again." She could understand Wallace wanting to own her land, but she couldn't understand him making such a serious accusation when there was no way he could prove it.

She hated to leave Ellen, but she couldn't allow Salty to face Wallace alone. Not after all the work the man had done in the last week. She didn't know how he managed to get out of bed each morning, or how he seemed to have more energy than any of them at the end of the day. She rode to where Salty still held the branding iron suspended over the calf and positioned herself between him and Wallace.

"Put that rifle away," Sarah ordered Wallace. "I won't have you threatening anyone on my property."

"That's my calf," Wallace shouted.

"Its mother is over there, and she's wearing my brand."

"It's a fresh brand."

"So was the brand I saw your hands putting on a cow last week."

"It was on my land."

"And this cow is on my land. The brand is the only one the cow has ever had. Check it out," she said to the man who she'd seen branding Wallace's cow.

Wallace pointed to the man, "Gary, check it out," before pointing an accusing finger at Salty. "He ran that cow off my land."

"Nonsense. How do I know the cow Gary was branding wasn't one of *mine* that had wandered onto your land?"

"It's like she says, boss," Gary said to Wallace upon inspecting the cow. "That cow's never worn another brand."

"Everybody knows you have to brand a calf with the brand its mother wears." Salty hadn't lowered the branding iron, and he didn't release the calf. Now, without waiting for Wallace's response, he slapped the iron on the calf's flank. The calf bleated, and the nauseating smell of burned hair and hide assailed Sarah's nostrils. Sarah was sure she'd never again encounter that smell without feeling queasy at the memory of branding and castrating so many animals in such a short period of time. She was beginning to question whether she was cut out to be a rancher. Even a rancher's wife.

Salty stood and released the calf, which went bawling to its mother which was still imprisoned in the chute. After Salty handed the branding iron to Jared, he turned to face Wallace. "Every rancher has the right to brand any unbranded cows, steers, or bulls on his land. That's the law, and you can't change it." He made a sweeping gesture that encompassed Ellen, Arnie, and Sarah. "We've spent the last week gathering maverick stock from the outlying parts of our ranch so we can avoid confrontations just like this."

"What if my cows wander onto your land?" Wallace asked.

Salty turned to Gary. "Haven't you been given orders to brand any maverick stock on your boss's range?" Gary glanced uneasily at his boss.

"You don't have to hesitate," Salty said. "I know you have. Every rancher has been doing the same since the end of the war."

Wallace turned to Sarah. "If you'd married me, this would never have happened."

She couldn't tell Wallace the real reason she'd married Salty because she didn't want to say anything that would be disrespectful to Salty or hurt his feelings. In the short time she'd known him, she'd come to believe there *were* men in the world who understood kindness and gentleness, who didn't hesitate to show they cared for others, and who delivered more than they promised. Men women could depend on, could actually learn to care for, without having their emotions used against them. He deserved her support no matter what words were necessary to provide it.

"I don't love you. I do love him."

Those weren't the words she'd wanted to say, but she figured it was the only thing she could say that would come close to making any sense to Wallace. Not that she expected him to understand that, either. Men like him didn't know how to love. All they understood was ownership and control. If they cared about anyone beyond themselves, it was other men they wanted to impress with their power or wealth, on occasion with the youth and beauty of their wives, or the number of their sons.

"But he's just a cowhand."

Wallace apparently considered Salty to be on the same level as one of his cowhands. It would never occur to him that a man he paid to work for him could have the same intrinsic value as he had.

"He's not *just a cowhand*." Jared looked indignant enough for both of them. "He's my stepfather, and I love him, too. He made this crutch for me and taught me how to heat branding irons."

"Anybody could do that."

What Wallace was incapable of understanding was that by taking the time to make the crutch and teach Jared how to heat branding irons, Salty had helped him believe he was worthy of Salty's time and attention.

Seeing himself valued in the eyes of a man he admired was something Sarah couldn't do for her son, and that had warmed Sarah's heart toward Salty in a way that Wallace's money and power never could.

"Maybe anyone could," Sarah said to Wallace, "but no one did."

"I'd have been happy to do that and more if I'd known."

Therein lay one of the important differences between the two men. Wallace had seen Jared many times since the end of the war but had never been interested enough to talk to him or learn anything about him. Salty cared just as much about Ellen as he did Jared. The only time Wallace had noticed Ellen was to tell her she had to act more like a girl if she ever intended to get a husband.

"We've wandered from the point of the conversation," Salty said. "I think we can agree that each of us has the right to brand any maverick stock we find on our individual ranges. I gather you've already been doing that."

"You're right, he has," volunteered a young man Sarah remembered from a week ago. "When I asked if we shouldn't try to find out where they came from, he said they were on his land now so they were his."

"That's the law," Wallace declared. "Your man just said so."

Sarah knew Wallace was within the letter of the law, but in her eyes it violated the spirit of cooperation that should exist between neighbors.

"I haven't branded any cows I saw wander onto our land," Gary said. "Only ones I found already there."

Sarah was tired of this conversation. It wasn't getting them anywhere. "There's no point in discussing what's been done or what might have been done. I would like to think we'd both drive back any unbranded cows we saw wander onto our ranges."

"If you'll give me a couple of your irons, I'd be willing to put your brand on any mavericks I see wander off your range onto Mr. Wallace's," Gary offered.

"As long as you're working for me, you ain't putting any brand but mine on a cow." Wallace was so worked up, he was red in the face.

"That's okay," Salty said. "Just drive it back and we'll brand it."

"I'm not driving any cows off my land," Wallace declared. "If it's on my land, it's mine."

"Using that same argument, a cow will become ours as soon as it crosses onto *our* land."

"If you brand even one of my cows, I'll have the sheriff down on you before the fire is cold." Wallace was furious, but he'd backed himself into a corner.

"Thank you for coming over," Sarah said to Wallace. "I would ask you to stay for supper, but we have more cows to brand before we can quit for the day. Now I have to get back to work. Ellen is too young to be left in charge of even a small herd for long."

Wallace was reluctant to leave, but his cowhands had already turned and were heading home. There was little he could do but follow.

"I'll be watching you," he said to Salty.

"Feel free to come by any time," Salty said. "I can always use an extra hand with the branding. I'll be happy to teach you everything I know."

Wallace was so offended anyone could think he would do his own work it was comical. He doffed his hat to Sarah, wheeled his horse, and galloped away.

"I don't like that man," Jared said.

"You don't have to like everyone," Salty said, "but you have to treat everyone fairly and kindly."

Jared looked up at Salty from where he was seated on a low bench next to the fire. "He's not being fair to Mama. Why do I have to be fair to him?"

Salty sat down next to Jared, put his arm around the boy. "You'll be fair to him because it's the kind of person you are."

"Why do I have to behave better than other people?"

"You don't base your behavior on what other people do. You base it on what you feel is right, what makes you feel good about yourself."

Jared looked at Salty with a question in his eyes. "Do you think Mr. Wallace feels good about himself?"

"I don't know, but I'd guess he's too angry right now to feel very good about anything. Now you'd better get back to the fire before some of those irons get too hot to use." Salty stood, ruffed Jared's hair making the boy smile up at him, his eyes filled with trust. "I don't know about you, but I want to get the rest of the branding done in a hurry. I'm hungry."

In a few minutes, everyone was back in place and the branding took up where it left off before the interruption, but Sarah felt there had been a shift in the relationships that connected her family to Salty. He was taking his position at the head of the family without pushing her aside. Ellen already thought he could do anything. Now Jared was turning to him for guidance. He'd even managed to turn Arnie into a cooperative worker. What about her?

She wasn't ready to put her relationship with Salty into words because her feelings were evolving too rapidly to be quantified. She did know Salty had become a very important part of her life in a way that didn't involve the children, and that scared her senseless. She didn't want to fall in love.

———

The next afternoon, Wallace's youngest cowhand rode up. Sarah recognized him straight off and wondered what he was doing there. It seemed unlikely her neighbor would have sent a message with him.

He rode up to the house and dismounted, then removed his hat before he spoke. "Howdy." He colored slightly, as though unsure how to start.

"Can I help you?"

He looked around at the house and the surrounding trees before glancing back at her. "I was wondering if you could use an extra hand."

"Don't you work for Henry Wallace?" she asked.

"He fired me. Said I didn't have any loyalty. He didn't like what I said when we was here yesterday."

Sarah sighed. "I'm afraid you'll have to look elsewhere. I can't afford to pay you."

"I'm not asking for much," he admitted. "Wallace is going to make sure nobody else gives me a job."

"You don't understand. I can't afford to pay you *anything*. Until my...husband and I sell our steers later this summer, I can't even pay Arnie." She stumbled over the word *husband*. "I don't even have a bunkhouse for you to sleep in."

"Where does Arnie sleep?"

Sarah was caught in a quandary. How could she tell this boy that her husband slept in the shed while Arnie slept in a wagon?

"Arnie sleeps in one of our wagons. He covers himself with a bedroll if it rains."

Much to her surprise, the boy burst out laughing. "You don't pay him, and he sleeps in a wagon. Do you feed him?"

She felt herself grow warm from embarrassment. "Of course we feed him! We're not so poor I can't manage to put food on the table." She was so unused to saying *we*, she stumbled over it every time.

"Well, I have a rain slick to keep me dry, so I'll be satisfied with the same deal."

She'd always made the decisions about who worked for her, but that hadn't always worked out so well. Also, she was no longer the sole arbiter of what happened on the ranch. Despite what she'd said about maintaining control, she wanted Salty to make some of the bigger decisions. "You'll have to talk to Salty. He's out by the corral, teaching Jared to ride."

Her heart had caught in her throat when Salty told her son it was about time he learned to ride a horse. Only the look of happiness on

Jared's face had kept her from objecting to the danger.

"That the little boy who was tending the fire?" the young cowhand asked, squinting as he turned to look through the break in the trees to the corral. "He spoke right up, didn't he, when Mr. Wallace said those things about your husband? That's what made me decide to come here. I figured if a kid with a bad leg liked him, he must be right decent. Er, no offense."

"You figured right," Sarah said. "Now, I have to get started cooking if there's going to be any supper to put on the table. You need to see Salty."

"Salty? That's a right peculiar name for a man."

"It's a nickname. I don't think he much likes Benton."

The youngster grinned. "Don't like my name, either. Maybe that's why I didn't introduce myself earlier. Dobie. Dobie Carlisle."

Sarah didn't see too much to like about the name Dobie, but she guessed it didn't matter. A man was what he made of himself, not what he was called.

"Be looking forward to supper," Dobie said before heading toward the corral.

Sarah couldn't help but think how much had changed in her life. A month ago, no one would work for her; now Salty and two other men were working without pay, her herd was being branded and her son taught to ride. She shook her head to dislodge the sense of unreality. It seemed impossible that one man could make so much difference in such a short time. She still needed to sort through all the changes and how she felt about them, but more important was fixing supper. She couldn't imagine what would happen if five hungry workers showed up at her table to find it empty. That was one change she didn't want.

Once she'd cleaned up after supper, Sarah was so tired she felt like she could go to sleep standing up, yet she was too restless to go to bed. It was the same as the last few nights, actually. She'd tried to ignore the pressure building inside her by concentrating on work. But now things had changed. While they would probably be branding mavericks off and on for the rest of the year, they no longer had to be in the saddle from dawn to dusk. Salty had time to turn his attention to other projects.

The arrival several days ago of so much lumber had disconcerted her. She hardly knew how she felt about his decision to build an extra room onto the house. Three people in three bedrooms seemed extravagant, especially when Salty was sleeping in the shed. Should she suggest a different arrangement? She could share a room with Ellen, Salty share one with Jared, and Arnie and Dobie could share the third—but she wasn't sure how she felt about having the two men sleep in the house or having Salty so close.

She could insist that he use the lumber to build a bunkhouse… but Salty ought to be the one to decide how it was used, she admitted. He'd spent his own money for that lumber. She felt guilty about that, too. She didn't know how much money he'd earned working for the Randolphs, but he must have spent all of it on her and the children now. It was impossible to question his attachment to her family or his will to succeed. So, just what was her attachment to him?

Neither Arnie nor Dobie had commented on Salty sleeping in the shed, but they had to think it was odd, despite their excuse. She had begun to think it was odd, too. Salty was her legal husband. He ought to be sleeping in the house. He ought to be sleeping in her bed, to be honest. And she *wanted* him to sleep in her bed. She was finally able to admit that.

Unable to stand the confinement of the house, she wrapped a shawl around her shoulders and went outside. The night was full of the coming spring. The air was soft and warm. Moisture promised dew in the morning if not rain before.

The sound of a snorting horse emerged from a multitude of tiny indistinguishable night noises. She could almost hear the sap rising in the trees, flower buds swelling, and blades of grass pushing up through softened soil. Mother Nature was just as restless as she, eager to get on with the work of shedding her cloak of winter and revitalizing the land. Calves would be born, her sows would give birth to litters of six to ten pigs, the chickens would turn broody and look for places to build nests. The desire for change was all around. The earth would soon be resplendent with new beginnings. What about her? Did Sarah want a new beginning—one she hadn't originally planned? Or was she too afraid to take the chance?

She settled on the front steps, her bare feet on the cold ground. She liked Salty. From the way he'd been smiling at her lately, following her with his eyes, she was certain he liked her. All she had to do was let him know she would be receptive to a closer relationship. It would be good for the children, too. If they developed a closer relationship, maybe he really would stay attached to their family if and when she asked him for a divorce.

There was no question the kids had become so attached to Salty they would be devastated if he left. He'd taught Ellen how to use a rope, how to ride better, and how to use Bones to roust a steer out of the thickets where they liked to hide during the heat of the day. Teaching Jared to ride had guaranteed her son's lifelong devotion. He wasn't able to do much more than stay astride, but Salty had promised they'd experiment with different kinds of saddles. Watching her son glow with pride when he did things people had said he'd never be able to do had brought tears to Sarah's eyes on several occasions.

It was harder to evaluate exactly what he'd done for her. For so long she hadn't allowed herself to feel anything for anyone except her children. She hadn't had room for real emotions, because fear of failure overrode everything else. She'd drawn her lines of defense closely around her, closed out the rest of the world. She had hidden herself on an island of three in a sea of desperation…but Salty had changed that.

How lucky she was! She was married to a man who liked her, who thought she was beautiful, and who respected her right to decide what to do with her property, her life, and her person. It was inconceivable that he was so strong, both physically and emotionally, and she sometimes wondered if she was losing her mind.

She shivered and tucked her feet into the bottom of her nightgown. The ground was cold and the air smelled like rain, but she didn't want to go inside. The house was a prison, restricting her growth, confining her to old ideas of what was possible. Intellectually she realized it was a metaphor for the past that had caused her to withdraw into herself, and emotionally it felt like some living, breathing organism that had wrapped itself around her and wouldn't let go. And fear held her in place: fear that what she had learned about her possibilities was only a mirage. Once she left it, she'd never be able to retreat to her island of safety again.

Ignoring the cold and the first drops of rain, she got to her feet and walked across the yard. Salty's lumber was neatly stacked under the trees and covered by a tarp. At supper he had said he wanted to start building her bedroom in the morning, if it wasn't too wet. *Her bedroom.* No one had ever bought or done anything specifically for her. Everything had always been handed down from someone else. Even the clothes she wore had once been her mother's.

Things had changed, and she was glad. She wanted more for herself. She was no longer willing to just sit by and make do, not when she had the opportunity to have what she wanted. She didn't know how her body and emotions had been able to stage this successful revolt, or why her body longed for something it never before had, but she couldn't turn back. Not now. Whatever the reason, she wanted to be open to these changes—and to Salty's interest in her. It might yet be as much of a mistake as Roger had been, but she'd never know if she didn't try. She had to find the courage to reach for it.

She turned back to the house. It was starting to rain in earnest.

NINETEEN

SARAH HAD MADE IT CLEAR AT THE BEGINNING THAT SHE DIDN'T want to be attracted to him. What confused Salty was that she seemed to be sending intermittent signals that she desired a closer relationship. He had never been very good with women, so he'd been inclined to attribute it to wishful thinking every time she sent a positive sign. Dobie had recently changed his mind.

"I wish a woman would look at me the way your wife looks at you," the young man said one afternoon when he and Salty were working on the extra bedroom. Sarah and the children were working in the garden, and Arnie was digging holes for a fence to keep the cows out.

Salty didn't look up from where he was nailing together the frame for one of the walls. "How's that?" They'd all been working so hard and were so tired at the end of the day, he hadn't given much thought to anything other than how soon he could crawl into bed.

"Like she wants you to share this bedroom with her when it's done."

Salty laughed. "You ought to pay more attention to your work and less to Sarah. She doesn't trust men, and she only married me because she couldn't see any other way out." Salty hesitated to offer this explanation, but it was nearly impossible to keep secrets when they worked so closely together.

Dobie helped him raise the wall and hold it steady while he nailed it to the house. "She might have felt that way at first, but she's changed her mind."

Salty nearly smashed his thumb with the hammer. He needed to pay more attention to his work instead of letting this youth get his hopes up. "How old are you?"

"Seventeen. Why?"

Salty grimaced. "I'm ten years older, so I've had plenty of time to learn that attractive women aren't interested in me. Whatever it is they want, I don't have it. Now let it drop."

"I don't believe that," Dobie said.

"Well, you're not an attractive woman, so your opinion's not worth a dead coyote's hide. Fetch me another load of two-by-fours. I've got two more walls to frame before supper."

That conversation had taken place four days ago. Salty had tried without success to forget it. Since then, he'd weighed every word Sarah said to him and compared her every glance to those she gave Dobie and Arnie. He struggled to prevent his wants from affecting his judgment, but...Dobie was right. Sarah was definitely warming up to him. He had to figure out what to do about it.

"Are you losing your hearing, or do I have to turn myself into a horse to get your attention?"

He had been standing at the corral, staring vacantly out at the horses enjoying a late evening frolic before settling down for the night. He turned to see Sarah standing a short distance away, a mysterious smile playing across her lips.

"Sorry," he said. "I was lost in thought."

She moved a step closer. "Anything you want to share?"

Salty's throat closed. He was about as capable of communicating as one of the corral rails he was leaning against. Did he dare tell Sarah what he'd been thinking? Why not? If she wasn't happy about it, she couldn't throw him out any farther than he was right now. Besides, he was tired of Bones as a nighttime companion. He was tired of wanting to know what exactly she felt toward him.

"I was thinking about us."

Framed in a halo of golden light cast by the sun that sank toward the far horizon, Sarah took another step closer. "In what way?"

She had just put the pony squarely in his corral, so he decided to tell her the truth. "I was thinking that my feelings for you had changed, and I was wondering if yours had changed, too."

She stepped so close he could practically feel the heat of her. Maybe it was his own heat, or maybe he only imagined it—but he didn't imagine the fire in her eyes. "How? How have your feelings changed?"

There was no trace of disapproval in her tone, yet he felt he was about to take the biggest gamble of his life. "I promised to make you dislike me if I noticed a softening in your attitude. I don't want to do that anymore."

"I'm glad," she said.

He breathed an inward sigh of relief.

"Is that all?" she asked. She moved to the corral fence and looked up at him rather than at the horses. The heat of her presence was like a brush fire.

"Before I say anything else, I need to know if your feelings for me are the same."

She hesitated. When she spoke, it sounded like a sigh. But her answer was, "Yes."

Yes? Damn. That's what he got for listening to a seventeen-year-old kid's advice about women. He and Dobie were just two frustrated men with so little to occupy their minds that they were indulging in fantasies of what they wished were true. Everything he'd seen in her eyes was a projection of his own desire.

"Yes, I'm still attracted to you," she said. "But now it's a lot more than just physical."

He was silent, surprised.

"Do you like more about me than my looks?" she asked. "Roger told me that's the most important thing about a woman."

He thought she was the prettiest woman he'd ever seen. Entranced by her nearness, he murmured, "A man appreciates beauty in all things, whether it's his horse, spring flowers, or the woman he hopes to marry."

In the nearby pen the pig snorted.

Sarah's smile became one of amusement, and her eyes danced. "Hopes? We're already married." Was that an invitation, or merely a statement of fact?

Salty shook his head. "I guess I wasn't very clear. I see my horse as a valued partner in the work I have to do. I appreciate flowers for the lift they give my spirits. I look for all that and much more in a woman, especially if she's my wife."

"How's that?"

He wasn't sure what he was saying. He was rambling. He'd compared her to a horse! He wished Rose were here; he was sorely in need of advice. "I've never been married nor kept regular company with a woman, so my ideas about what I want are so vague I'm not sure I can put them into words."

She seemed unperturbed. "Except for being married to a man my father chose against my wishes, my experience hasn't been that different from yours."

"You have two children and have managed a ranch for six years."

She shrugged. "You fought a war, watched people die, and lost everything you had—all without losing your basic decency, honesty, and love of life. And you have a wonderful ability to care deeply for others."

"It's easy when others care about you."

"People don't care about people who aren't worthy," she pointed out. "They might fear them or feel a duty toward them, but they don't care about them the way you care about Jared and Ellen."

Why *did* he care so much for her children? Was it because it was natural for adults to care about children? Was it because they'd suffered misfortune with bravery and cheerfulness, and he wanted to somehow make their bad luck up to them? Did he care because they were Sarah's children? It was all of that and more. They were people with different personalities and needs. They'd shouldered the responsibilities of adults yet still looked at the world with the openness of children. They'd accepted him without reservation and looked for reasons to be with him.

He was distracted by the sound of the chickens squabbling over the best tree limbs as they searched for a place to roost for the night. That reminded him of the fun he'd had building the pen with the children's help, of Ellen chasing down escaped chickens, of Jared's relief that he no longer had to search through bramble patches for eggs. He hadn't realized it until now, but he loved them. The two children had drawn him into their family, giving him the love and acceptance he'd never had. He'd have to be stone-hearted not to love them in return. His feelings for Sarah were like that, too, but with some very important differences.

"I never knew what it was like for two people to truly love each other until I went to work for George Randolph," he said. "Rose runs that family with an iron hand, and the others let her because they know she does it out of love. They're such a strong-willed bunch, the boys can get into an argument over the shape of a cloud, but they'd each face the world alone to defend Rose. I didn't know that kind of love was possible. It's like a circle. Inside, everyone is allowed to be himself, no matter how obnoxious, but they all stand together to face the outside." He paused. "I'm not saying it very well."

"I think you're doing just fine."

He wasn't. How could he describe what he'd never experienced? "I didn't have brothers or sisters, and my family did its best to tear itself apart. I want the love that keeps the Randolphs together despite their differences."

"Jared and Ellen love you," Sarah said.

He nodded. "But they're children. A man needs the love of a woman to make his life complete."

There was a brief pause. "Are you asking if I love you?"

They'd stood close to each other for the last several minutes, but they hadn't moved closer. Salty eyed the horses being swallowed by lengthening shadows, then the darkening sky. Now, when he needed to see her face, to be able to read her expression, he couldn't. It was that awkward time between dusk and dark, when there was no longer any reflected light from the setting sun, when the sky was still too light for the moon to achieve its full brightness. Everything was shrouded in hazy shadow.

The chickens had settled in for the night; the pig was quiet. The horses glided noiselessly through the gathering twilight. The breeze had died, leaving the dry grass stiff and motionless. He hadn't intended to ask Sarah anything, but now, even if he was in danger of pushing for an answer too soon, he wanted to know. "No, but I won't stop you if you want to tell me."

Sarah turned to face him, reached out to rest her hand on his forearm. "Until I married you, I thought all men were like my father and husband. I didn't want to be with a man again because I had found it distasteful and humiliating. I was certain I could never care for any man enough to join my life with his." She paused. "Do you care for me enough to help me change my mind?"

Salty hadn't expected a bald statement of her feelings, but her words were clear enough for him. He traced the outline of her jaw with the tip of his finger. "I don't care what you think about other men. Just about me."

"I have no more experience with men than you do with women," she explained. "I don't know what to say."

"I don't want you to say anything," he replied. "I want you to show me how you feel."

"How?"

"Like this."

Salty had nothing to guide him except his instincts and a powerful desire to take Sarah in his arms. Remembering Rose's admonition not to be shy about letting a woman know how he felt, he reached for Sarah and pulled her into his embrace. He hoped she couldn't tell that his heart was pounding in his chest and, brushing aside all worry, he kissed her. The effect was so powerful it nearly took his breath away. He had held women in his arms and kissed them, but it had never been anything like this. Before, it had been more like having a plan and systematically following through. This time he acted on impulse. His reward was a feeling that he'd never really been alive until now.

What was he supposed to do next? Was one kiss enough? Should he stand back and wait for her to make the next move? He didn't know what he was supposed to do, though he had no doubt about what he wanted to do, and that was to keep right on kissing her. He could never get enough of Sarah, because every little bit left him wanting more.

Her mouth was soft, her lips sweet, her kiss firm. It took him a few moments to realize she was neither shy nor reluctant; she was kissing him back with an eagerness that matched his own. Rather than attempt to hold herself apart from him, she had pressed forward until their bodies were connected from chest to thigh. The effect on him was so rapid and pronounced he was certain she would pull away. Much to his surprise, she actually leaned closer, pressing herself against his hardness until he felt he would burst.

It was hard to keep his mind on something as simple as a kiss when his body felt like it was on fire. He felt like he was losing control, even losing contact with reality. He was on sensory overload. Not even the heat of battle had affected him so forcefully.

It took every bit of willpower to break the kiss and hold her at arm's length, and she looked bewildered and hurt. "Did I do something wrong?"

He could only shake his head. It was impossible to find words to describe her effect on him. George had never appeared to be rendered senseless when he kissed Rose, so why should it affect him this way? Was it because this was the first time he'd kissed Sarah? Because the situation was so unexpected?

"Something *is* wrong," she pressed.

"No." He managed to force his brain to focus. "I was just surprised. I'm not sure my heart can stand it."

Her smile was teasing. "I've seen you wrestle a steer to the ground."

"That was easy. The steer wasn't kissing me." Taking her hand, Salty turned her so they could both lean against the rails.

Sarah's laughter hung in the air like the sound of chimes in the wind. Funny how everything sounded and felt better after a kiss from the woman you loved. "*That's* something I'd like to see."

Salty shivered at the unintentional image he'd created. "Not a chance. I much prefer kissing you."

"Then why aren't you?"

He didn't waste time trying to answer. Pushing off from the rail, he wrapped her again in his embrace.

Their second kiss didn't affect him as powerfully, but he was able to enjoy it more for that very reason: he could explore the softness and sweetness of her mouth, revel in the sheer ecstasy of having the woman he loved welcome his kisses. He didn't have to follow some protocol he didn't understand, like he'd sometimes felt with other women. It wasn't like a reward for good behavior; it didn't seem that if he didn't do it right he'd fail some test. All he had to do was kiss her.

He loved embracing Sarah. It was a simple act, and yet he couldn't explain why it felt so good to wrap his arms around her. He didn't know whether it was feeling like she belonged to him or that she was giving herself to him; all he knew for sure was that he wanted to do it for the rest of his life.

He thought of her as strong and independent, but Sarah felt small and fragile as he held her. In contrast, he felt big and powerful. He liked feeling that she'd turn to him when she needed a shoulder to lean on. He liked that she had surrendered her physical self to him. Yesterday he'd have said all of this was too much to surmise from a single embrace. Now he realized he'd been given only a glimpse of what love could make possible.

"I'm still waiting for the answer to my question."

The intrusion of Sarah's voice startled Salty. He'd been so caught up in the moment that he'd forgotten there was a question. There was no way out; he had to confess. "Uh, I've forgotten what you asked."

She laughed. "Then I guess I have my answer."

He was more and more lost. "Answer to what?"

"I wanted to know if you cared enough about me to change my opinion about men."

He shrugged. "I don't care what you think about other men, just me."

"You already said that."

"Then what do you want to know?"

"I want to know how you feel about me."

"Haven't I shown you?"

"You've shown me you want me, but that's not what I'm asking."

He flushed. He didn't have to be an experienced lover to know that showing Sarah he wanted her physically before he even said he liked her, much less that he loved her, was the perfect way to kill her affection before it had time to put down enough roots to take hold. It was time to put his cards on the table and to play out his hand.

"Sarah, I don't know if you want to hear this, but I've fallen in love with you. I liked you from the beginning. I knew you didn't want that, but I wanted so badly to have the chance to own my own land that I thought I could deny my feelings and my attraction. If not deny them, control them. It wasn't long before I realized I was wrong on both counts."

Evening had deepened, but the light of a full moon now flooded the corral. The fence rails looked like black ink across a silvery-gray background, the horses like weird splotches of color, their true shapes morphed by the shadows of trees. Heat radiating from the ground clashed with the cooling air above to create drafts that eddied about them like swirling water. In the moonlight, Sarah's face took on a luminous quality that made everything about the evening seem surreal.

"I knew I was attracted to you, too," she said. "I was determined it would never be more than that...but you aren't like other men."

"I'm pretty ordinary."

Sarah smiled in a way that did uncomfortable things to Salty's stomach. "There's *nothing* ordinary about you. You're kind, generous, hardworking, straightforward, and honest. My children adore you, Arnie and Dobie respect you, and Rose Randolph made it clear she thought you were the best cowhand on the place."

It was nice to know other people liked him, but he wasn't interested in other people. Not right now. He was interested in only one person: the woman in his arms. "Is that what you think of me—that I'm a good cowhand?"

"Yes."

He'd been hoping for more, a lot more. Was it so hard for her to say she loved him? She might as well have said he was the family's faithful hound dog. It was pretty much the same as a pat on the head. He should take his arms from around her, but he couldn't make himself give up the chance to hold her a little longer. It might be the only chance he ever got.

"That's what I *think* of you, but it's not what I *feel* for you."

Salty's spirits revived. The door hadn't slammed shut. He wouldn't give up hope until she actually said she didn't love him. He was sure those words would kill him. "What do you feel?" he asked.

"Love."

It was only one word, a single syllable, but it was more potent than the most masterful speech ever given. It had the power to change his life.

"Are you sure?"

Sarah looked startled at his question. It was obviously the wrong thing to ask, but he couldn't help himself.

"Yes, I'm sure. Why do you ask?"

"Because no one has ever said that to me."

"Didn't your parents—?"

"No." The word was spoken softly but firmly.

"My parents didn't, either, but I was sure everybody else's did…"

Neither one of them had grown up surrounded by love, so how could they be sure this wasn't merely a strong liking driven by physical attraction? While it wouldn't be the worst marriage in the world if only one of them was in love, he didn't want to settle for that.

"I never thought I would feel love for anyone except my children," Sarah went on. Moonlight caused the tears glistening on her cheeks to sparkle like diamonds. "I thought only a woman could feel such depth of emotion. That's why I intended to choose Walter over you."

He stared at her. "You never told me why you changed your mind." She appeared reluctant to explain. "You don't have to answer if you'd rather not." But how could he believe her feelings were genuine if she didn't?

"It's not that," she said. "I just don't want you to think I fell in love with you only because of my children."

"Why would I think that?"

"Because of the way you were drawn to them, the way they became attached to you. Right from the start. It's what caused me to change my mind."

He wasn't exactly sure how he felt about that. He'd grown very attached to Jared and Ellen. He'd caught himself thinking of himself as their father, even someday playing with their children as his grandchildren. But as much as that picture appealed to him, it lacked an ingredient that would make this marriage everything he wanted: Sarah's love.

"At least, that's what I thought at first," she said.

Salty had always thought he was unable to experience the strong feelings that plagued other people. Now he realized he was just like everybody else, at least when it came to falling in love. He wasn't sure he could take many more emotional ups and downs.

"The attraction I felt for you scared me so badly I made up my mind to choose anybody but you," Sarah explained. "I opened my mouth to say his name that night. Yours came out instead."

Salty turned away to look at the horses. It was less painful. "You could have said you made a mistake. I was sure you had."

She took his face in her hands and turned it back toward her. "You haven't understood what I'm saying. My brain wanted to take the safe course, but my heart overruled it. I *thought* I chose you because of the children. It took several days before I could admit I'd chosen you for myself."

Salty wanted to believe her, but it was difficult. Yet believing was necessary because being in love had offered him the chance for a kind of happiness he'd believed was forever beyond his grasp.

Sarah studied him carefully. "You don't look like you believe me."

His smile was probably too weak to be reassuring. "I suppose I'm afraid to believe, because I want this so much." He sounded weak, like he was pleading for her to love him. How could she respect and admire a man like that? He was supposed to be strong, the rock-solid support for the family when there was any kind of trouble, the one who didn't allow emotion to cloud his judgment no matter how gut-wrenching the difficulty.

"I feel the same way half of the time. How can you love a woman whose husband left her, who has a crippled son, and who's managed to run what was once a successful ranch into the ground?"

"Any husband who would leave you is a fool. Any father who would turn his back on Jared is hardhearted and cruel. You're both better off without him."

Sarah nodded and planted a quick kiss on his mouth. "I'm sorry Roger died, but I'm thankful it made me free to fall in love with you."

He stared into her eyes. "I'm thankful your ranch was failing, or you never would have come to the Circle Seven."

Sarah gave him another quick kiss—he could grow used to them—and said, "It's enough to make me believe misfortune truly can have a silver lining." She paused, her brow creased. "You really do love me, don't you? You're not saying this because of the land or my children?" It was as if she were afraid to admit the possibility.

Salty was almost relieved to know she had the same fears. "I want land of my own, and I adore your children, but *I'm in love with you*. I would love you just as much if you were penniless and alone. Being able to have all three things at the same time, well, that's just a blessing."

Sarah's face cleared. "I know you love me. I believe you. I just needed to hear you say it. Roger was so—"

Salty's arms closed around her and pressed her hard against him. "I want you to forget everything he said or did. You don't have to worry about him ever again."

Sarah gave him another quick kiss. "I can't forget him, because he's my children's father. But I never felt for him what I feel for you. There's simply no comparison."

Salty didn't want to think about Roger. This family would start over, start afresh. He pulled her closer in his arms. "Let's make a promise to each other to put the past behind us. Its disappointments, its failed promises, its harsh lessons—from now on everything is possible, because we want it to be."

"Do you really believe that?"

"We're the most important part of each other's lives. As long as we have each other, nothing else really matters."

Sarah didn't appear entirely convinced, but that would change. She had given him a family to love and who loved him in return. He would do everything in his power to give her the love she needed and the security she deserved. He wasn't the best man in the world, but he knew how to work hard and he knew how to keep his promises. He would earn her love.

She frowned. "You look so solemn. What are you thinking?"

It was his turn to give her a quick kiss. "I was making a promise to myself, one that makes me very happy."

"You didn't look happy."

"Just determined you will never be unhappy again."

Sarah laughed. "I expect to be unhappy many times, but I'm depending on you to make me forget."

Salty couldn't think of a better request, or a better time to set about the task. The thought of being able to kiss her every night in the future made him almost light-headed.

He was dragged back to earth when she broke their kiss, pulling away from him to say, "Let's go to the shed."

"Why?"

"I've slept with a man who believed he owned me. Now I want to sleep with a man who loves me."

TWENTY

WAS THE CHILL SHE FELT FROM THE FALLING TEMPERATURE OR FROM fear? Had she shocked Salty? Not even the imperfect light of the moon hid his stunned look. His arms had lost their tight hold on her, and his body drew back as though he was unable to believe she could be so forward.

Sarah had known she was taking a chance, but this was something she needed. She had disliked being married to Roger. She had especially disliked when he forced himself on her. She had no doubt that she loved and wanted to spend the rest of her life with Salty, but she didn't know if she could make love to him. It would be impossible if she reacted the same way as she had with Roger.

"Do you know what you're asking?" he whispered.

"As well as you."

"I'm not sure you do."

"We're married!" The awkwardness that existed between them often caused her to forget that.

"I know, but..." She knew Salty wanted to be with her, because she'd felt the evidence against her thigh, yet he seemed lost as to what to say.

"You hesitate. Why?"

"Probably because I've been telling myself at least a dozen times a day that this would never happen. My brain is still struggling with the change."

"What about your heart?"

He stroked her cheek with a feather-like touch. "My heart was never in doubt."

"Then you should learn to trust your heart. I know I do."

It was endearing to see the reflection of his struggle in his eyes. Though his body shook with desire, he was holding back because he was concerned about her feelings, about her happiness. Nothing could have made her love him more. Nothing could have made this union with him more important.

"The shed isn't a suitable place for our first night together," he said. He was avoiding a decision, looking for reasons to object.

"It's where you've been sleeping," she pointed out. "That makes it fine with me."

"Aren't you tired?" he asked.

"I'm never tired when I'm with you." That sounded silly, but just seeing him across the table or talking to him sharpened all her senses until her very skin felt alive. Having him touch her, hold her in his arms, kiss her, had aroused every fiber of her being until she felt incapable of sitting still.

He seemed to have reached a decision. His grip on her arms tightened; his gaze intensified. "If you spend the night with me, I won't give you a divorce." It seemed an ultimatum.

Luckily, it was an easy one. "I don't want one."

His eyes drilled into her. "I'll move into the house when I finish the new room."

"You can move in now."

A smile slowly spread across his face, a smile so joyous, so luminous, that it outshone the moon. If she'd had any doubts he loved her, she had them no longer. She'd had men look at her, but no one had ever done so as Salty did now. There was desire and there was hunger, there might even be need in his gaze, but all were wrapped in a radiant happiness that enveloped rather than coveted her. There was a promise of days and nights beyond this evening, of months and years stretching far into the future. It was a smile that assured her this time would be different. Salty wanted them to be a family.

"We can wait until I finish the extra room," he said.

"As long as I'm with you, it doesn't matter whether we're in the shed, in the wagon, or on the ground. Being with you is the important thing. Where doesn't matter."

He drew her to him and kissed her. Much to her surprise, she wanted something more forceful, more demanding, more possessive. She wanted him to want her so badly he could barely contain himself. She wanted to feel he was laying claim to her, that he was proclaiming her off limits to every man who might cast a glance her way.

"Kiss me harder," she begged.

He did. But now that they had declared their love, he was treating her like a precious jewel, like a fragile flower, as if she would break if he held her too tightly. She didn't want to be treated like someone who needed to be handled with care, or who couldn't take care of herself. For the past six years she'd managed her ranch alone. She'd done virtually everything a man could do. She wanted Salty to realize that, but she didn't want to have to tell him.

He drew back until he could look into her eyes. "Are you sure you're ready for this?"

She almost laughed. "Don't you think I know my heart?"

"I'm sure you do, but I know my heart, too. I love you so much I can't be with you just once then go back to the way we were before. I can't pretend it's just an itch that needs to be scratched. I want this to mean there'll be no divorce. I want this to mean I can adopt Jared and Ellen, that we can be a real family. I want this to mean you love me, that you need me, that you want me. Forever."

"I want the same." It amazed her that she could feel this way after so many years of wanting just the opposite, but when she saw the way Salty smiled, and the look that came into his eyes when he stared at her, she wondered how she could possibly feel anything else.

He took her hand, the same question in his glance. She nodded, a motion so slight as to be virtually nonexistent, yet he saw and understood. Acting with one mind, they turned and walked toward the shed.

Sarah hadn't set foot inside the shed since she hired the first man to help her after Roger left. She was surprised to see Salty had transformed it into a comfortable, if masculine, space. His newly-constructed bunk had been pushed into one corner, providing room for a cane-bottomed chair and a crate that acted as a table. The walls were plastered with pages from magazines and catalogs, which served a double purpose of helping keep out drafts and providing pictures and reading material for a dull afternoon. Salty had used some lumber to put in a floor now partially covered with a rag rug. A lantern had been suspended from the ceiling; a newly constructed window provided natural light.

"As long as Bones is on duty, I don't need to sleep with the door open," Salty explained.

Sarah experienced a new twinge of doubt as she stepped through the doorway. She wanted what was to come, had even asked for it, but she was again afraid the act would be the same as before. She couldn't stay married to Salty if she hated sleeping with him. It wouldn't be fair to either of them. And what made her think it might be different? All men made love the same way.

She struggled against a rising panic. She felt confined, restrained, even constrained, and she folded her arms across her chest in defense—against what, she didn't know—while Salty lit the lantern and turned the wick down. He closed the door gently, yet hearing the dull click of the latch caused her to flinch. He turned to face her, a smile warming his face.

The subdued light, the flickering flame, caused shadows to dance on the wall. He peeled her right hand from its grip on her left arm and took it between his two hands. "You're afraid, aren't you?"

"No. Yes. Not exactly."

He tilted his head in query. "How 'not exactly'?"

"I hated being with Roger this way. It was painful."

Salty's smile stayed so gentle, so understanding, so comforting, Sarah wanted to retract her words, but she felt better for having voiced her fear. Things weren't so terrible when she could share her feelings. When she'd tried to explain to Roger, he'd called her a silly little girl and said a *real* woman would have appreciated him.

Salty caressed her hand. "If anything makes you uncomfortable, tell me and I'll stop."

"Roger said a man can't stop once he starts. He said that goes against Nature."

Salty brought her hand to his lips and kissed it. "I'll *always* stop if you want me to."

She wasn't sure it was fair to ask that of him, but the offer made her love him all the more.

"If it doesn't make you feel so good that you want to do it again and again, we won't do it at all."

Sarah didn't believe she could ever feel the way he wanted, but she wouldn't tell him that as long as it didn't hurt.

"Anything else bothering you?" he asked.

She shook her head. Saying no didn't feel so untruthful that way.

"Then let me hold you."

She was a lot shorter than Salty, but she didn't really mind because she enjoyed resting her head on his chest. There was something about being held by a tall, strong man that made her feel protected. She wrapped her arms around him, held him tight. He wasn't a big man like Roger or Arnie, but his lean frame was strung with powerful muscles that rippled when he worked. The feel of those same muscles under her fingertips sent tiny electric charges racing through her until her whole body felt energized.

Salty murmured, "This is nice, but a kiss would be better."

She signaled her agreement by lifting her face.

Each kiss seemed better than the last. Sarah didn't know how it could be happening. Maybe it was the feel of his work-hardened body pressed against her; maybe it was the sensations aroused by his hands moving over her back. Maybe it was the anticipation generated by the hardness pressed against her thigh. Most likely it was knowing he loved her, and that his feelings would never change.

She was disappointed when he broke away, but the letdown didn't last long. He relaxed his hold on her so that she was soon back on her own feet and ran his hands along her from elbow to shoulder and back again, all while scattering kisses over her forehead, ears, the side of her neck and even the end of her nose. And while she loved the kisses, the feel of his hands moving over her generated a heat that flooded her whole body. She wanted to move closer, to feel his body against hers. She wanted something she couldn't define, yet she also knew her life could never be complete without it.

When he moved his hand between them to cover her breast, her breath stilled; her body grew rigid. This was part of what Roger did that hurt. But Salty simply cupped her breast while he continued to kiss her, caressed her arm and shoulder. It wasn't long before pleasure overcame fear and she was able to relax. She was only mildly concerned when he started to unbutton her dress from the back. For the first time she *wanted* to feel a man's skin against her own.

When she opened her eyes, the look of hunger on Salty's face scared her. She'd seen that same look on Roger. It always meant he'd lost notice of her, that from this point on his satisfaction was the only thing of importance. She felt herself tense, the heat flowing through her beginning to cool, and her previous fears threatened to return.

If Salty noticed, he didn't show it. He continued to undo the buttons of her dress, to cup her breast, to kiss her. Gradually, Sarah's anxiety calmed. It spiked again when he untied her shift and placed his hand on her bare flesh, but it was quickly opposed by the delicious feeling of his fingertips skimming over her back, tracing circles and drawing patterns. She nearly forgot his hand on her breast. How could a man's touch be so calming, so reassuring, so stimulating at the same time? How could it make her want to touch him in the same way?

She shivered when he pulled her dress and shift aside to place kisses on her bare shoulder. She was so distracted that she didn't realize he'd freed her arm until he placed kisses down its whole length. She didn't have a single thought of resisting when he freed her other arm, and she soon stood bare to the waist.

Despite the heat building inside her, the air felt cold on her bare skin, like that of a winter morning when she climbed out of a warm bed and had to shed her nightclothes before dressing. Salty's fingertips were rough against the soft skin of her breasts, but his touch was light, feathery, almost liquid, and at last his heat flowed into her and banished the cold. A sigh of contentment escaped.

"Did I hurt you?"

"No." She shook her head for extra emphasis. Was it possible for the rest of what would come to be just as good?

She flinched when his thumbs started to massage her nipples, which quickly became engorged and hard, so acutely sensitive it was nearly painful. Yet a spear of pleasure lanced through the discomfort until all she felt was the desire for more. When he bent down to take one nipple into his mouth, Sarah thought she would rise right off the ground. Her body was bombarded with so many diverse sensations, she didn't know which to pay attention to first. She compromised by letting them all wash over her in a great wave.

When she was sure she couldn't stand any longer and would sink to the floor in a helpless heap, Salty picked her up, carried her over to the bed, and laid her down upon it. He laved her nipple with his tongue then nipped it with his teeth, and she felt dizzy from the assault on her senses. She'd never guessed her breasts could be the source of so much pleasure! But the same could be said for her shoulders, her arms, her neck... Salty was awakening her body in ways she'd never dreamt possible.

A wisp of thought passed through her head that she'd like to see if his body was equally sensitive, but it was swept aside by the sensations shooting through her body like sparks from a Chinese rocket. They were so powerful that she didn't realize Salty's hand had moved to her leg until it had reached her inner thigh. She wanted to tense, to be afraid, but she was incapable of anything beyond a mild curiosity about what came next. She had never thought she would lose control, but she had no control over what Salty was doing. Nor did she want any. Yet, her fear wouldn't go away entirely, either. It circled like a wolf just beyond the light of a campfire, its eyes burning with uncertainty, wary of the fire burning inside her.

"Lift up, so I can slide your dress under you."

Sarah didn't know when Salty had removed her shoes, but she was acutely aware of every motion he used to slip her dress and undergarments off her body; each movement that brought his hand into contact with her bare skin brought the wolf of fear closer. When he started to remove her stockings, she thought the wolf would pounce...but Salty's touch was gentle, unhurried, unthreatening. It gave the wolf no opportunity.

He slowly rolled each stocking down and laid it aside, and what Salty did next surprised her: he started to massage her feet. He placed her left foot in his lap then began rubbing the top with gentle pressure from his thumbs. As his fingers moved down to the sides then past the ankle to the tendon that ran from the back of her heel, it felt so good Sarah nearly moaned. Better still, the wonderful feeling was gradually moving up her leg to her thighs, even her belly. As he turned his attention to the bottom of her foot, she thought she would turn to jelly.

By the time he had treated her right foot the same, the wolf had been driven deep into the shadows. Nothing hurt. There was nothing to fear. Sarah was happy.

Salty moved to her calves, which caused a wonderful lassitude to invade Sarah's body. It was as if she was losing contact with the physical world in order to become more deeply sensual. The bed was softer, her body lighter. Her skin felt warm, the air tinged with the masculine smell of Salty himself. The sound of her breathing was magnified, the beat of her heart more pronounced. Every part of Sarah felt more alive, waiting, anticipating all that was yet to come.

The wolf came rushing from the shadows as Salty's hand on her inner thigh revived memories of the times Roger had taken his pleasure from her by force. But Salty's fingertips traced halfway up the inside of her thigh, circled around to the outside of her leg, and returned to her knee. They made the journey again, circling, comforting, arousing. And as her fear receded, Sarah felt her muscles relax and her legs move apart on their own. It was as though her body was welcoming Salty's attentions.

She wasn't prepared for him to drop kisses on her abdomen, or for the fire that flared up inside of her with the speed of a lightning strike in dry grass. When the burning in her belly spread out to join the smoldering heat encompassing her inner thighs, the result was a conflagration of desire that she'd never dreamed possible. For the first time in her life, she wanted a man. She *needed* one. The urge was so primal, so bone-deep, she didn't cringe even when she felt his fingers move from her inner thigh.

"Relax. I promise not to hurt you."

She hadn't expected his fingers entering her to ignite such sweet discomfort. It seemed impossible that the two feelings could coexist, but each continued to grow and swell until they joined with the fire already threatening to consume her. Then Salty did something that sent a jolt through her so powerful she felt it would lift her off the bed. She didn't understand why her body was a quivering mass, why her brain was rapidly becoming a useless jelly, but she didn't care. She didn't want it to stop. And when it didn't, she wanted the sensation to grow more powerful. And when it did, she was certain she would never survive. The coil inside her tightened until she was sure she would scream. Every part of her was being drawn into a tight knot of sensual pleasure that was so agonizingly wonderful, so suffocatingly powerful, she was sure she would die.

She was preparing to take her last living breath when the tension broke and flowed from her like water from a ruptured dam. The descent was both a relief and a letdown. While she'd been carried to heights that scared her, she didn't want to sink back to where she'd started. After this moment, nothing could ever be the same. From now on sweets would taste sweeter, bitter tastes more bitter. She would want more of life and demand that she get it. Everything would be—

She had been so consumed with what was happening to her, with what she was feeling and what it meant, that she hadn't paid any attention to Salty. Now she realized he was looming over her.

"This might be a little uncomfortable at first. If it is, let me know and I'll pull back."

It was about to happen: the part that was painful. The wolf had reappeared, bigger than ever, its eyes glowing red, its fangs prepared to rip apart all the wonderful memories of the last few minutes. Sarah felt Salty push against her. He was bigger than Roger, so surely it would hurt even more. The wolf snarled and bared its teeth, but Salty drew back before pressing forward again.

Nothing hurt. All she experienced was a gradual feeling of fullness. And as Salty penetrated deeper, as he filled her to what she was certain was the limit of her ability to contain him, that feeling faded, replaced by the same sensations she'd experienced just minutes before. This time the wolf wasn't just driven back into the shadows; it was exploded, destroyed, all trace of it obliterated from the face of the earth. Never again would she fear Salty's touch. She would welcome it, embrace it, rejoice in it.

Things were different this time, she realized, because she was sharing the experience with Salty. *Everything* was different. She was no longer married merely by a document. She was joined with her husband in spirit and body. Wherever he invited her to go she would proceed without fear. Where he led, she would follow. Gladly.

As she began to surrender to the demands of her body, so did Salty. She could see reflected in his face the pleasure that consumed her. She could sense his rising need for gratification, felt the increasing power of his thrusts, the gathering and releasing of the powerful muscles that were driving them both toward a goal he alone seemed to know. Then she gradually became aware of a need centered deep within her, so deep she was certain Salty could never reach it.

"More." Was it a groan or a moan she emitted? "Deeper."

The deeper Salty plunged, the deeper she needed him to go. The more her need became concentrated, the more it spread throughout her whole body until she felt like a single ball of longing. Desperation drove her to throw her legs around Salty's middle in an attempt to force him to reach the need that was tearing at her mind with talons of iron. Her arms closed around him, pressing him against her breasts, yearning for as much contact as possible. She wanted to feel she was part of him, wanted to absorb him and to be absorbed by him, wanted to let their common need mold them into a single being.

Oh! She lost her ability to think, abandoned all attempts at control and let the tide of passion sweep her away. She wrapped herself about Salty, letting his heat stoke hers to greater intensity. Her reality became their two bodies. Nothing existed beyond the sensual shield that surrounded them, guarded them, encased them. It was white heat that threatened to incinerate them, bursting into showers of white flame that scorched the edges of her consciousness.

The longed-for release buffeted them, allowing them to float down from the peaks.

———————

Next morning Sarah sang as she prepared breakfast. It didn't bother her that Jared watched her with wondering eyes or that Ellen had asked her three times what was wrong. She had never felt better or happier in her entire life.

"What are we going to do today?" Ellen asked.

"You'll have to ask Salty, but I expect he'll want to work on the new room. It's almost finished."

"Do I have to help him? Can't I go with Dobie?"

It amused Sarah to see her daughter developing a young girl's crush on the cowhand. It was even more amusing to see Dobie had no idea what was happening. "You'll have to ask Salty."

"Why do I have to ask him?"

"Because he runs the ranch now." Jared interrupted setting the table long enough to give his sister a how-can-you-be-so-dumb look. "Besides, I'd think you'd be glad for him to work on the house. You'll have your own room when he's finished."

"I don't care about that," Ellen declared. "I want to sleep out like Dobie."

"He snores." Jared resumed setting the table.

Ellen, who was mixing the eggs, stopped. "He does not."

"Arnie says he does."

"Stop arguing and hand me those eggs," Sarah said to her daughter. "I expect the men to be here any minute."

"They won't come until you call them," Jared said.

"How do you know?"

"Salty says it's not polite to crowd the cook or drag your feet when it's time to eat."

Sarah smiled. Here was one more sign that Salty was a cut above other men. "Go ahead and call them now," she told her son. "Everything will be ready by the time they get here."

She poured the eggs into the hot pan and handed the bowl to Ellen to wash. Everything was on the table except the biscuits, which she was keeping warm in a pan at the back of the stove. She looked forward to seeing Salty after last night. It'd be the first time. She'd slipped away while he slept.

"Pour the coffee," she said to Ellen. "Pour Salty's first. He likes it to cool a bit."

"I know, Mama. You tell me the same thing every morning."

Now that she thought of it, she had. She smiled to herself. Maybe she'd been in love with Salty for longer than she'd thought. Why had she been so stupid? She could have enjoyed experiences like last night long before now. Instead of dreaming of last night, she'd better pay attention to the eggs before they burned. She could hear the men outside.

Dobie came in first. He smiled, said good morning, and moved to the table. Arnie followed closely.

"Where's Salty?" Sarah asked when he didn't enter right behind Arnie.

"He's coming." Dobie winked. "He's shaving."

Sarah was certain she blushed. She tried to hide it by turning back to the eggs.

"Why's he shaving?" Ellen asked. "He's just going to work on the new bedroom. Does he need to look good for that?"

Dobie rubbed his downy-smooth cheeks. "I wouldn't know."

"Wouldn't know what?" Salty asked as he entered the kitchen.

"Wouldn't know anything about shaving."

"Not much to know. You need help with anything?" he asked Sarah.

She was too embarrassed to meet his gaze right away. "No. The eggs are done, and Ellen's putting the biscuits on the table." She put the eggs into a large bowl which she carried to the table. She moved to her place and sat down, eyes on her plate. "Sit and eat."

Breakfast was usually a meal dominated by the children. Today the children were uncharacteristically quiet, which made the surreptitious glances she cast Salty's way even more noticeable. Still, soon she couldn't stop looking at him, couldn't even stop smiling after Dobie noticed and grinned. She had never known what it was like to be in love, had never thought it could be so wonderful. Her body was still glowing with the memory of last night, living it over and over again.

Yet, last night had been far more than the widening of her physical horizons, and more than just the extension of her emotional boundaries. She couldn't think of a way to put everything into words, because her feelings and thoughts were so interconnected it was impossible to think of it in parts.

Without warning, the door opening broke her train of thought. A man who looked eerily familiar entered the kitchen.

"Who are you?" Salty asked.

"I'm Roger Winborne," the man replied. "Who the hell are you?"

TWENTY-ONE

SARAH STRUGGLED TO BREATHE. IT WAS AS IF SHE WAS UNDERWATER, suffocating. Her body felt incased in iron, her chest unable to expand. Then quite suddenly, the paralysis gave way, and life-giving air rushed into her body so rapidly she felt dizzy.

Her eyes were still unable to focus, however, her mind incapable of grappling with the claim made by this stranger. All thought retreated behind invisible barriers, leaving her suspended between oblivion and the impossible. She stared mindlessly at the man in the doorway. He couldn't be who he said he was. Roger was dead. If he hadn't been, he'd have come back when the war ended two years ago.

The man was about the same height as Roger, but he was bigger through the body; he probably weighed fifty pounds more. His hair was coarse and long, his beard thick and untrimmed. Roger had kept his hair well-groomed. He shaved every day. He would never be seen in such threadbare clothes. He—

Dawning recognition, horrifying in its implication, deprived her of breath. Roger's appearance had changed drastically, even his voice sounded different, but those eyes destroyed Sarah's newborn happiness and hopes for the future: she would never forget how they'd glared at her when he was angry or frustrated. Underneath the fat, the hair, and the clothes, this man was indeed Roger Winborne.

"I'm Benton Wheeler," Salty said. "This is my wife Sarah and her children, Ellen and Jared. These men are—"

"She's not your wife, you son of a bitch," Roger growled. "She's *my* wife, and those are *my* children."

Sarah tried to speak, but the words refused to come. Her body had turned to stone.

"I don't know what your game is," Salty said, "but Sarah is my wife. I have a marriage certificate to prove it."

Sarah didn't understand how he could remain so calm. The children stared at Roger like he was some kind of apparition. Dobie's jaw was in his lap, and Arnie looked downright furious.

Roger dropped the shoulder pack he'd been carrying. "She's my wife, and I can prove it."

"Sarah was married to a Roger Winborne," Salty agreed, "but he died in the war. Showing up with his marriage certificate won't enable you to steal his property."

Why would Roger even have kept their marriage certificate? He'd hated being married to her.

"I'm not trying to steal anything! I *am* Roger Winborne. What's wrong with you?" Roger had turned a wrathful gaze on Sarah. "Why don't you speak up? Don't you recognize your own husband?"

She felt the strength drain from her like water from an overturned bucket. What was she going to do? She couldn't go back to being Roger's wife. Her children deserved a father who loved them, who cared for their happiness as much as his own. They deserved to feel wanted, appreciated, valued. They deserved to be happy. And so did she.

From somewhere she found the strength to sit up straight, square her shoulders, and look Roger full in the face. "I didn't recognize you at first," she said. "You've changed a great deal."

Some of the anger in Roger's face cleared and he started toward her, but Salty blocked him. "I don't know who you are and I don't care, but you will do nothing to upset my wife."

"She's *my* wife!" Roger shouted. He attempted to shove Salty aside, but Salty didn't give so much as an inch.

"Move one step closer and I'll throw you out. If you don't change your attitude, I'll escort you to the edge of our land and order you never to come back."

"I'll help." Arnie's look was so black, Sarah thought he might attack Roger on the spot. Apparently he could forgive a fellow soldier for having usurped her affections, but he couldn't forgive Roger for having abandoned her.

"Me too," Dobie added.

Roger looked stunned. "This is my ranch. You can't order me off."

"You don't hear very good," Arnie said. "Or maybe you're just stupid." He started to rise out of his chair as Roger moved toward him.

Sarah intervened. "Stop it! I appreciate your feelings, Arnie, but I won't have fighting in my kitchen."

"I wasn't going to fight him inside, ma'am," Arnie replied. "I wouldn't want Miss Ellen to see that much blood."

Why was it that during a life-altering crisis her mind should suddenly focus on a detail of daily life? All she could think to say to Roger was, "Have you eaten anything today?"

He blinked at the abrupt change of subject. "It's barely past dawn. What do you think?"

Long practice helped her ignore his rudeness. "You can eat with us."

Jared reached for his crutch, which he'd leaned against the wall behind him. "He can have my chair."

"Stay where you are," Salty said. "He can have my chair. I'd rather sit by my wife." He picked up his plate and cup of coffee then turned to Roger. "Roger Winborne has been officially declared dead. Sarah is no longer your wife. Now sit down."

Jared had been seated on one side of Salty, Dobie on the other. Neither looked pleased at the prospect of sitting next to Roger.

Roger looked like he might refuse. Sarah had no idea what had happened to him since he left for the war, but he'd used to be hotheaded as well as selfish. He'd never have settled for being told what to do.

He remained standing until Salty set a plate, cup, and cutlery before him. After Salty took a seat next to Sarah, he seemed to realize he was the only one standing, that everyone was looking at him and waiting. With a visible shrug of his shoulders, he sat down.

"Why don't you tell me where you've been since the war ended?" Sarah said.

"I've been in California, prospecting for gold."

Sarah could hardly have been more surprised if he'd said he'd started his own dirt farm in the Indian Territory. Roger had never liked work that got him dirty, took much effort, or involved danger.

Apparently, from the tale he now spun, the army had chipped away at his self-image until he felt the only way to restore it was to strike it rich in the gold fields. The picture he painted of life in the gold fields was unlike anything he'd endured before. "You couldn't turn your back on anybody," Roger was saying. "They'd kill you for a square yard of ground or an ounce of gold."

"What did you do?" Ellen asked.

"You had to have a partner to watch your back," Roger told them.

"Did you find any gold?" his daughter asked.

"Sure I did. Lots of it."

"Are you rich?"

"You only have to look at him to see he's not," Jared spoke up.

Roger bridled. "Everything costs ten to a hundred times as much in the gold fields. An egg would cost you two dollars. Beef was almost impossible to find at any price."

"You should have done without," Jared said. "We did."

Sarah didn't know where Jared had gotten such antipathy for his father. She'd done her best to say nothing that would give either child reason to be ashamed of him.

"I had to eat," Roger said. "Prospecting is hard work."

Jared refused to back down. "So is running a ranch."

Roger laughed, causing a bit of sausage to fall from his mouth. "What's so hard about sitting a horse?"

"Nothing," Jared said. "Even a cripple like me can do that. It's knowing what to do when you're on the horse that's important." Jared had already formed an allegiance to Salty. Roger's return threatened his new-found sense of security and self-worth.

"Prospecting and ranching—both jobs are difficult in their own way," Salty spoke up.

Roger scoffed. "How would you know?"

"I grew up in Georgia. Worked briefly in a gold mine. Georgia was the major source of gold in this country before California."

"I don't believe that."

Salty shrugged. "It's a fact, so what you believe is of no importance." Jared beamed at his reply. Dobie did much the same, though Arnie's expression was unchanged.

Sarah wasn't sure what was to be done. She didn't know what the law might try to force her to do, but she knew she would never be Roger's wife again. Last night had made that impossible.

"What do you plan to do now that you're back in Texas?" Salty asked.

Roger flushed. "This is my ranch. I plan to stay here."

"I can let you stay for a few days or weeks while you figure out what to do next, but you'll have to work for your keep."

"I'm not working with him," Dobie announced.

"He'll work with me," Salty said.

"Who'll I work with?" Jared asked.

"You can work with me," Arnie said.

"How about me?" Ellen wasn't going to be left out.

"You can work with me and Dobie," Sarah said.

"I'm not working with him," Roger said, indicating Salty.

"I'm not forcing you," Salty replied. "I'm sure you'll find something in town."

"I'm not going to town! This is my home!"

"If you stay here, you work," Salty said.

"Salty and I run the ranch together," Sarah told Roger, "but he makes most of the decisions about what needs to be done and who will do it best."

Roger glared at her with dislike. "I don't know why my father thought you'd make a good wife, but I never thought you'd turn yourself into—"

Salty interrupted him. "Before you say something that might lead to a great deal of unpleasantness, you should remember that you neither wrote to your wife after you joined the army nor did you come home when the war was over. She had no way of knowing you were alive. After waiting two years, you were declared dead and Sarah and I were legally wed. She's done nothing wrong."

Salty didn't sound like himself, but Sarah guessed that he, like she, was struggling to come to terms with the fact that Roger was alive. She reached over and slipped her hand into his. She wanted him to know that no matter what happened, he was the man she loved.

Salty turned to her, smiled and squeezed her hand. That was all the assurance she needed.

"I can't believe you would bring him *here*." It was a moderate response, atypical of the Roger that Sarah remembered.

"Where else would my husband be?"

"At his own place. You'd be there, too."

"Sherman destroyed my home," Salty told him, "so I came to Texas with the commander of my troop."

"You were in the army?"

"I served in a cavalry unit. We harassed the enemy behind their lines."

It was amusing to see Roger reassess Salty. Sarah didn't know whether it was the war or his time prospecting, but Roger now realized he didn't know more than everybody else, that he couldn't have everything he wanted just because he wanted it.

"Have you been home to see your parents?" she asked. She was surprised he hadn't said anything about them.

"They're dead."

"What happened?"

"Died in a fire."

"I'm sorry." His parents' treatment of her and their attitude toward her children had made it impossible to like them, but no one deserved to die such a painful death. "Do you know what happened?"

Roger shrugged. "They were old. They probably knocked over a lantern or went to sleep without banking the fire. The fire destroyed everything. I had just enough money to get here."

So that's why he'd returned to Texas; he had nowhere else to go. Apparently being broke trumped hating your wife and children.

Arnie pushed back his chair. Glancing at Salty he said, "I'm done. What do you want me and Jared to do today?"

"See if you can find Sarah's hogs. I want to know where they're dropping their litters."

"Any idea where we should start looking?"

"I know," Jared said. "Mama told me where she found them last year."

"Then let's get going," Arnie said. "Time's a-wasting."

Roger turned his gaze on his son. "He can't even walk. How's he going to look for hogs?"

Salty's expression hardened. "Jared not only gets around nearly as well as the rest of us, he can ride. He's been a big help with rounding up cows and branding them."

"That kid will do nothing but get in the way," Roger insisted.

Salty favored the man with a faint smile and stood up. "I'm sure this isn't the first time you've been wrong. If you want that breakfast, you'd better eat in a hurry. We start work in ten minutes."

"You haven't finished your own!"

"I've lost my appetite." Salty turned to Sarah. "See if you and Dobie can find any more stock that needs branding."

Ellen appeared hurt that he didn't mention her by name. "I'm helping, too," she reminded him.

"I know. I'm depending on you to make sure Dobie doesn't run off with my wife."

The child giggled. "Dobie doesn't like girls."

Dobie winked. "I like girls just fine when they're as pretty as your mama."

"I told you so," Salty said. "Make sure you keep a sharp eye on him." He walked out the door.

Roger was stewing. Sarah was thankful Salty had been able to handle the situation thus far, but it wouldn't last long. Roger's mere presence would continue to be a source of tension. They needed a permanent solution, but she didn't know what that would be. She hadn't petitioned for a divorce, so she was afraid that, as far as the law was concerned, she was now married to two men.

"Why did you marry that man?" Roger asked when everyone was gone.

Sarah got to her feet. "Finish your breakfast. When Salty says ten minutes, he means it."

"You didn't answer my question."

She picked up two plates and carried them to the sink. "I don't have to."

"You're my wife. You have to do what I say."

She shook her head. "I don't have to do what you say ever again."

Roger slammed his knife against the table. "I'm your husband. I have the right to make you obey me!"

Sarah turned to face him, her hands on her hips. She was pleased she could promise, "If you so much as touch me, Salty will tear you apart."

Roger laughed. "You must think a lot of yourself."

She picked up two more plates. "I don't, but Salty does. If you don't believe me, just call me a whore. That was what you were going to say, wasn't it? If there's anything left of you when he finishes, Arnie will feed it to the pig."

Roger's look was scornful, yet it contained an element of surprise and uncertainty. "What's gotten into you? You were never like this before."

Sarah had lifted the plate of sausage, intending to put it away, but she turned back to Roger. "That was before I was left to manage a ranch by myself for six years. Before I raised two children from infancy on my own while doing all the chores. Before I married a man who respects my intelligence as much as my person, a man who believes my wishes and desires are just as important as his."

"No other man is that crazy."

Sarah turned to the stove. "I would have agreed with you before I met George Randolph."

"Who the hell is *he*?"

"He commanded a troop during the war. He's married to a woman he adores. And it was Salty who made me believe I was worthy of being loved the same way George loves his wife." She picked up Roger's plate and took it to the sink.

"Bring that back! I haven't finished."

"Your ten minutes are up. Salty's waiting."

"How do you know?"

The sound of a hammer was clearly audible.

"That's how I know. Now get out there and start helping him.

Nobody eats at my table without having put in a full day's work."

Roger sat motionless, staring at her, apparently caught between the impulse to treat her as he had so long ago and a feeling that something important had changed, something he didn't understand and didn't believe was possible. But he harbored just enough doubt that he finally got to his feet and stalked out of the room and through the door.

Sarah hadn't realized how tense she was until practically every muscle in her body started to relax. The change was so abrupt she felt vaguely dizzy and nauseous. Anger as well as shock coursed through her. The shock was new, but the anger was old. Roger had turned his back on her because he'd felt she was unimportant. He'd ignored his children because he didn't value girls and couldn't accept a handicapped son. He'd gone to California because it looked like an easy way to get rich. He hadn't cared enough for his family to find out if they were well, were in need, or even if they had survived. Now, when he'd run out of options, he'd come back.

She started to put the food away. The meat could be used again and the hominy could go into gravy, but she'd have to think of a way to use the leftover eggs. They couldn't afford to throw out any food. Roger's return hadn't changed that.

Switching gears, she tried to put her children's father out of her mind and plan where they would ride today. Roger Winborne would be no more a part of her life than was necessary as the father of her children. There was no question about herself: she would do whatever the law required, but when all was said and done, he would no longer be able to claim her as his wife. She already had the only husband she wanted, and his name was Salty.

———————

The moon and stars were so bright, and the sky so cloudless, there seemed virtually no chance of rain. Salty picked up his bedroll, grabbed a blanket, and headed for the front of the house. He'd made it clear that Roger was going to be sleeping in the shed from now on, but he didn't trust the man to stay there. Hoping to catch him off-guard if he was going to do anything stupid, and to confront him away from the children, he'd decided to sleep on the ground outside.

Despite the complications that Roger's return had made in his life, Salty had gotten over his bottled up anger. Working everything out about the two marriages was going to be tedious and unpleasant, but legal issues were involved, not issues that could be swayed by individual feelings. Salty was bone tired, because dealing with Roger Winborne for a whole day had been the most exhausting thing he'd ever done. The man would exhaust the patience of a saint, and Salty had never pretended to be a saint.

He checked to make sure the cows Sarah and Dobie had collected weren't pushing on the corral poles looking for a way out. It would be a couple of days before they could get around to branding them. He'd have to see about reinforcing the corral and making it bigger, especially for when George Randolph sent that bull calf. He would have to be kept in a pen and the cows brought to him; he was too valuable to let run wild.

The chickens were roosting in the tree in their enclosed yard. The pig was rooting around, looking for more food. He was putting on weight quickly. Salty had to decide whether to pen up the wild pigs when they got old enough to be weaned, or leave them to fend for themselves. He doubted he could provide them with enough food to fatten them up the way he wanted, but he didn't want to lose them to coyotes or wolves. Six people were depending on them for food for next year.

The garden was up and growing nicely. He was looking forward to fresh beans and peas, and his mouth watered when he thought of fresh tomatoes. There would be corn and squash. With luck, the squirrels wouldn't get all the pecans from the grove of trees along the creek. There was a lot of work still to be done, but on the whole everything was looking more prosperous. Having Arnie and Dobie had made a tremendous difference. Roger was another story.

With good help, Salty should have been able to finish the extra room in a couple of days. He'd figured any man would know how to do basic carpentry. If not, at least he could help. It was probable that Roger could do both with a reasonable degree of skill, but he was the laziest, most trifling man Salty had ever met. All he had done was talk. And ask questions. And make assumptions. And try to convince Salty that he was Sarah's *legal* husband, that her marriage to Salty was an easily correctable accident. It had taken nearly every bit of Salty's patience to ignore him.

Having reached the house, Salty stopped to decide on the best place to make his bed. He didn't want to sleep in front of the steps, but he didn't want to be more than a few feet away, either; he wouldn't put it past Roger to attempt to sneak inside. He finally settled on a spot about six feet from the stoop and laid out his bedroll. Settling his pillow, he folded the blanket double. He expected it would get a good deal colder outside than it did in the shed.

Despite being tired, he was too keyed up to sleep. He still had to figure out how to fix things. Roger had ruined supper for everybody. Everything he said seemed calculated to offend or anger someone. Jared was tight-lipped and sulky. Arnie smoldered silently, while Dobie tried to parry Roger's jibes. Sarah got so upset she turned pale. Even sunny-tempered Ellen had turned quiet. Salty had finally told Roger to shut up. Dobie said he talked more than a woman. Jared said he wished he'd never come back from California. Sarah said he'd have to eat outside by himself if he couldn't stop upsetting everyone.

Clearly Roger was learning to accept a lot of things he wasn't used to, but having his ex-wife tell him he'd have to eat outside wasn't one of them. The man lost color. He probably would have said something terrible if Dobie hadn't threatened to shove a knife between his ribs. That's when he said, "I never thought I'd see the day when a woman thought she had the right to tell her husband what to do."

"You're not her husband." Arnie said. "Salty is."

Roger had lapsed into a brooding silence then stalked off after everybody was done eating. Salty didn't know where he'd gone and didn't really care, as long as he stayed away from the ranch house. He hoped he wouldn't have to see him until morning.

The wish wasn't fated to be fulfilled.

"What are you doing out here?"

Salty looked up to see Roger approaching, bedding under his arm.

"Something wrong with your bedding?" he asked.

Roger's steps slowed. "I decided I don't want to sleep in the shed."

Salty felt his muscles tense. "You can sleep outside if you want, but it's warmer in that shed. Still gets chilly some nights."

"I don't want to sleep outside, either. I'm going to sleep in the house."

"I already explained why you can't sleep in the house," Salty said. "Ellen and Jared have their bunks in one room, and Sarah sleeps in the other."

"You want to sleep with Sarah when you finish the extra room, don't you?"

"Of course. She's my wife."

"Why aren't you sleeping with her now?"

"That's between me and Sarah."

"Doesn't sound like she wants to be your wife, if she won't sleep with you."

He was clearly trying to aggravate Salty, to goad him into action. Salty decided to frustrate him by not commenting. The strategy was successful, because Roger's lips thinned and his eyes grew hard.

"Can't be much of a man if you can't convince your wife to sleep with you. Hell, I'd sleep with her every night whether she wanted me to or not."

"I'm not you," Salty said.

"You sure as hell aren't. I'd never be under the thumb of any woman, much less my wife."

Roger obviously didn't understand love, or didn't believe it was possible—certainly not the kind that required mutual respect and consideration of your partner before yourself. "There's no point in talking about it. Now turn around and go back to the shed."

"I wasn't planning to force myself on Sarah," Roger pointed out. "Ellen can sleep with Sarah, and I can have her bunk."

"You're not sleeping in the house," Salty repeated.

"I guess I'll have to change your mind."

Roger threw aside his bedding and approached Salty, his fists balled up and ready to strike.

TWENTY-TWO

SALTY HAD EXPECTED THE CONFRONTATION BETWEEN HIMSELF AND Roger to come to blows at some point. Reluctantly, he got to his feet and tried one last time to make peace. "Why don't you make it easy on everyone and just go sleep in the shed?"

"That's my house, Ellen and Jared are my children, and Sarah is my wife. It's my right to sleep in the house. Hell, it's my duty."

"I'm not going to let you enter."

"How are you going to stop me?"

"Any way I have to."

The man rushed Salty like a bull, head down and arms flailing. Salty didn't know if that had worked for Roger in the gold fields, but it never worked for him in fights with other boys in town when he was growing up. He stepped aside and simply let the man rumble past.

Roger pulled up and turned, a surprised grin spreading over his face. "You're afraid of me."

Salty shook his head. "I'm just giving you a chance to go back to the shed. You're *not* sleeping in the house."

The grin stayed in place. "I think you're afraid."

"If you can stand up and fight like a man, I guess you'll find out."

The insult wiped the grin from Roger's face. Raising his fists, the man stepped forward to meet Salty, who was trying to determine what kind of fighter he was. Did Roger rely solely on punches? Would he go for more body contact mixed in, or would it turn into a wrestling match?

He stood poised in front of Salty, apparently waiting for him to strike first. "Aren't you going to fight?"

"You're the one who wants to fight," Salty said. "All I want is to keep you from entering the house."

"So you're just going to stand there?"

"Until I need to do something else."

It appeared that Roger was unsure how to start a fight besides rushing blindly at his opponent. He hesitated before moving closer, then threw a tentative punch.

Salty blocked it. "If that's how you fought in the gold fields, no wonder they drove you out."

"They didn't drive me out. I left." Roger threw another punch, which Salty blocked as easily as the first.

"You make a habit of running away early, don't you? Did you leave the army before the war ended?"

"You bastard!"

Roger attacked in a flurry, but landed only glancing blows because Salty feinted left or right while offering a few punches of his own.

"Stand still and fight," Roger shouted. "Are you a coward?"

"I can win this fight a half dozen ways," Salty said. "I'm just trying to decide which will be the easiest."

Roger charged a second time. It wasn't difficult to avoid him and land a sharp jab in his ribs as he lumbered past. The man's stride faltered, but he turned and attacked again almost immediately. The blows were weak, and both men soon backed off to take a breather with little visible hurt.

"If you want to win a fight," Salty pointed out, "you have to apply steady pressure." He danced forward, offering a series of quick shots to Roger's various body parts. "You don't try for the deciding blow right away." Two more quick jabs to the stomach and he moved out of range. "You keep your opponent off balance and on the defensive, never knowing what you're going to do next." He landed a quick uppercut and feinted left to avoid a body blow.

"Stand still, you son of a bitch!" Roger panted.

"If your opponent is bigger, stronger, or heavier, it's important to keep moving," Salty continued. "Getting suckered into a slugging match is the dumbest thing you can do." They exchanged some quick punches, and Salty danced away again.

"All that stuff you're saying is a bunch of horseshit. You're just dragging this out."

Salty grinned, which so distracted Roger that Salty was able to land a punishing blow to the man's gut followed by another swift uppercut. Roger staggered. Salty pummeled him with a half dozen shots before moving out of range.

"Quit now," Salty offered. "I'm not going to let you in the house."

Roger closed with him and they grappled, and at close range they pounded each other with blow after blow. Stomach. Ribs. Jaw. Nose. Chest. No part was spared. Roger wasn't a good fighter, but he was strong and his punches hurt.

A boy's voice rang out: "Hit him again. That's not hard enough!"

Salty was so startled, Roger was able to land a punch that staggered him. He moved back a couple of steps. "Get back inside," he said to Jared.

"Not until you pound him into the ground."

Roger put all his weight behind a punch. It made him just slow enough that Salty was able to avoid him and land a punishing blow of his own.

"That's right!" Jared encouraged. "Knock the bastard out."

"Why are you pulling for *him*?" Roger asked. "I'm your father."

"You've never been my father, and you never will."

His son's disloyalty angered Roger so much that he turned, giving Salty an opportunity to land several punishing blows. Roger stumbled badly but didn't go down. He staggered upright and glared, bleeding from his nose and mouth.

"Why don't we stop now?" Salty asked. "I don't want to humiliate you in front of your son."

Roger's response was to close in once more for another series of punches. He was growing weaker, but he wasn't ready to give up. It looked like one of them was going to have to be knocked out. Salty was determined it wouldn't be him.

As he lost energy, his punches lost power and Roger started to lean on Salty, to wrap his arms around Salty's middle and rain ineffectual blows down on his back. Salty finally punched him in the kidney, causing the man to fall to his knees.

"Are you ready to quit now?"

Roger got to his feet and attacked, but his swings lacked direction.

"Knock him down," Jared said. "I hate him."

Salty struck twice. "You don't hate him. You're just angry at him."

"I *do* hate him. I want you to knock him dead."

Out of the corner of his eye, Salty noticed Arnie approaching from the direction of his wagon. He was followed by Dobie. That unsettled him so much Roger was able to land a punch.

"Pay attention," Arnie shouted.

"It would be easier without an audience," Salty grunted.

The prospect appeared to have energized Roger. He came in with a flurry of punches so forceful it took Salty a moment to regain his balance.

"Quit being easy on him," Dobie called. "Put an end to this so I can get some sleep."

"We *all* need some sleep." Sarah had come out of the house. An excited squeal told Salty Ellen had come out, too. This was turning into a farce. He had to bring the fight to an end, and as quickly as possible.

He waited for an opening. When Roger took a swing, missed, and was off balance, Salty moved in. He landed another series of punches to Roger's gut. When Roger doubled over in pain, Salty kneed him in the jaw.

"Way to go. Hit him again!"

Roger was all but beaten, but he still wouldn't go down. As he rose and swung, Salty finished with a direct shot to his throat. The man fell, gasping.

"Is he going to die?" Ellen asked.

"Naw," Arnie said. "He'll live to make some other woman's life hell." And with that, he turned and walked away.

"You want me to help drag him back to the shed?" Dobie asked, eyeing the wheezing and bloody Roger.

"Go on and get your sleep," Salty replied. "He can make it on his own."

"Doesn't look like it to me," Ellen said.

"I wish you'd killed him," Jared growled. With that, he tucked his crutch under his arm and went back inside.

"Is he hurt bad?" Sarah asked.

Salty eyed him. "No. He just needs a few minutes to get his wind back."

"I've never seen a fight," Ellen said. "Do you think he'll want to fight again?"

"Let's hope not," Sarah said. "Now it's time for you to go back to bed."

"But I want to see what happens when he gets up!"

"Nothing's going to happen," Salty said. "Your father's going back to the shed and to sleep."

Such a tame ending obviously disappointed Ellen. She went inside without further protest.

"I'm sorry this had to happen," Sarah said.

Salty shrugged. "There was nothing you could do. Roger had to try to get inside, and I had to stop him. Now that we've settled that, things should be easier."

Sarah knew Salty was trying to reassure her. Maybe they would be easier in some respects, but there wouldn't be any true relief until they came up with a legal solution. It was possible for Sarah to divorce Roger and marry Salty again, but that would take a lot of time and money they didn't have, and it would put everyone through an emotional nightmare. He wanted to avoid that.

"I knew he'd try to come inside," Sarah admitted. "I put a loaded shotgun next to my bed."

Roger had managed to sit up. "You wouldn't use a shotgun on me."

"Only as a last resort."

"But I'm your husband. We were married."

"You ran off and left us. Now, I'm going to bed. If you want any breakfast, you'll do the same. If you get into another fight with Salty, you'll have to leave until I can get a divorce. I won't allow you to upset my life again."

"I have a right to be here," Roger insisted. "No matter what you and this man think."

Sarah had already gone inside, so Salty answered. "Then don't make it impossible for me to allow you to stay. Now go back to the shed." When Roger showed no sign of picking up his bedding he asked, "Do you need some help?"

"This isn't over," Roger snarled.

"It will take a judge to decide which marriage is legal, but until then you'll sleep in the shed and do your share of work. You'll show respect for Sarah, and you won't make any more belittling remarks about Jared. That boy has shown more courage and determination than all of us combined."

Roger snorted. "He's a cripple."

"His limitations are only physical. One of these days he's going to make you proud to call him your child."

Roger laughed. "How?"

"There's not much he can't do when he sets his mind to it. I'd be proud to have him for a son."

"Then you can have him." Roger bent down to pick up his bedding. The beating he'd taken made it hard for him to stand up again, but Salty had no sympathy.

Roger turned, a look of surprise on his face when Salty growled, "You son of a bitch! What you've suffered is nothing compared with what Jared goes through every day, yet he endures it with grace and courage while you whine about your misfortune and bully anybody weaker than you. I'm glad Jared got nothing from you but his looks. He's already twice the man you think you are."

"You don't know a damned thing about me," Roger shouted.

"I know you were too blind to realize you'd married a wonderful woman. I know you were too shallow to know children like Ellen and Jared are gifts to be cherished. I know you were too lazy to keep a successful ranch running. I saw at least a hundred boys shot to pieces who should have come home to their families instead of you."

"Is your vision so impaired you can't see anyone except yourself? Are you incapable of caring for anyone, or do you merely think it's unnecessary?"

"You don't know what—"

"How could you squander so many advantages? You had a working ranch handed to you, a beautiful wife who was willing to do virtually anything to earn your respect, and two wonderful children anxious to love you for no reason at all. Why would any man who wasn't criminally stupid throw all that away?"

"What kind of soldier were you?" Roger demanded angrily.

"A damned good one, but that appalling waste of life taught me at least one lesson you never learned. *Everybody*, young or old, plain or beautiful, is just as important as I am and therefore worthy of my respect. You spent years thinking you were better than others because you were handsome, but look at you now. You probably thought you were going to win the war by yourself only you never rose above the level of foot soldier. You chased the dream of easy riches and ended up with nothing. You never valued your family until you had no one else to turn to."

Roger started to speak then changed his mind.

"You could have been a hero to your children just by coming home. You didn't have to win battles, be rich, or handsome. All you had to do was be their father."

"They were babies."

"Babies grow up. But you couldn't see beyond Jared's withered leg any more than you could see Sarah was more than just a wife, a possession to be owned like livestock. In your blindness, you wasted the two most valuable blessings a man can have, a faithful wife and loving children."

"I know I didn't do everything I could—"

Salty didn't let him finish. "You didn't do anything except think of yourself."

"I did come back."

"Why?"

Roger seemed to be searching for an answer. For the first time in his life he might be about to admit he'd made mistakes.

"I felt like I belonged here. Nowhere else seemed like home."

Salty wasn't sure he didn't really mean that nowhere else could he continue to live without regard for anyone but himself, but he was willing to credit the man with a small degree of self-realization. The war had changed him. It probably changed Roger, too.

"This ranch can never be your home again, but that's something to work out later. Go to bed. We both need some sleep."

He sighed as he watched Roger hobble back to the shed. He was tired of Roger. He'd much rather think about Sarah, about the way she'd felt in his arms, the way she'd responded to his kisses, the way she looked when he said he loved her. Roger was a more serious obstacle to their happiness than holding the ranch together, but he'd nonetheless figure out a solution. He'd found everything he wanted in life here, and he wasn't about to let a worthless piece of cowhide like Roger Winborne take it away.

———————

Sarah couldn't sleep. It annoyed her that Salty felt forced to sleep outside on the ground to protect her from Roger. It angered her that Roger thought he still had a right to her body or any part in her life. It made her furious that he'd forced Salty to fight.

Growing more restless by the minute, she got out of bed and put on a robe. Salty's nearness was another reason she couldn't sleep. She couldn't stop thinking about last night. Not just the physical pleasure, though that had been a revelation; she found it hard to believe how much she loved Salty, and how happy she had been upon learning he loved her back. She knew she ought to go to sleep, that she ought to stay in her room—or at least not venture from the house—but she didn't bother trying to argue herself out of what she had decided to do. She put on sturdy slippers, tied the robe, and left her room. She was going to see Salty.

She eased the front door open in case he was asleep, not wanting to wake or worry him. She just wanted to feel close to him, to feel his warm and comforting presence. She'd never imagined a man could have such an effect on her.

Salty lay on his side facing away from the house. He'd pulled the blanket up under his chin to ward off the night chill. Seeing that made her want to hold him, to keep him close and warm.

"You ought to be in bed. You'll be exhausted tomorrow."

She smiled. "I should have known you'd hear me."

"You shouldn't have come out."

"I couldn't sleep."

"Next thing you know Jared will be here. Then we'll have Ellen up. Once she starts asking questions in her usual quiet, understated manner, the whole ranch will be up."

Sarah laughed. Only Salty would make a joke of this situation. Was it any wonder her spirits had been raised lately? "I have a lot on my mind right now, and being with you helps me feel calmer."

Salty turned over. "This is the first time anybody's felt that way," he said.

She shook her head. "I doubt that. But you've made everything better for me and the children. I don't know how I can ever repay you."

"You keep making leading statements like that, and I won't be able to stop myself from showing you." A salacious look had come into his eye.

"I was thinking about that, too," she whispered. "Is it awful for a woman to admit that?"

He shook his head. "It's natural for a woman to enjoy being with the man she loves, so I don't see any reason why she can't say so."

She sat down on the steps, tucked her robe around her legs and over her feet. "Women don't talk about what it's like to be with a man."

He grinned. "Boys don't talk about anything else."

"Do you think I'm different from most women?"

"It's normal for a woman to enjoy being with a man. If she doesn't, it's because she's too afraid."

"I was afraid, but I'm not now," she said. Salty had made all the difference.

Even in the moonlight, she could see his eyes soften. "You're not afraid of anything. You're the bravest woman I've ever known."

No one had ever thought she was brave, or smart, or dependable. That a man who'd lived through the war would say such a thing made it even more wonderful. "I just did what I had to do."

"Without help from anyone. You're a remarkable woman, Sarah Wheeler."

Sarah Wheeler. She still found it difficult to stop thinking of herself as Sarah Winborne. Sharing Salty's name made her feel closer to him, made her want to *be* close to him. Physically. She needed his touch, his warmth...his confidence in the future. For the first time in her life, she didn't feel alone.

"You should go in," he repeated.

"I will in a little while." She got to her feet. "I just want to spend a few more minutes with you."

"Let me come to you." Salty wrapped the blanket around himself, and when he noticed her smile said, "Got to preserve decency. Me in my long johns? I wouldn't put it past Ellen to be looking out the window and treat everyone at breakfast with her version of what she saw."

"I *want* her to see us holding hands, even kissing—so she'll know not to be afraid of love." Sarah moved to make space on the step next to her.

"Ellen isn't afraid of anything." Salty slipped his arm around her. "Why should she be? She has you for an example."

Sarah leaned into his embrace. It was odd that she could more easily believe Salty loved her than she could accept that he admired her, but she was going to work on it. She liked the feeling. "Ellen looks to you to be an example, too. So does Jared."

"You've been the important influence." He gave her a quick kiss. "You did a great job. They're great children."

She preferred to be kissed for herself, not for the way she'd reared her children, but she'd take any kiss, anytime, for any reason, as long as it was from Salty. "Can I have a little of that blanket? It's chilly."

"And have you see me in my long underwear? Not a chance."

She giggled. "I've seen you in less," she whispered. "I want to see you that way again."

"So do I, but I think the front yard probably isn't the place."

She tried to stop it, but another giggle escaped. "You know what I mean."

"Of course I do, but I'm trying not to think of it. Besides..." He didn't finish the sentence, but there was no need. They both knew Roger's arrival had changed everything.

Though Roger was the biological father of her children, Salty would be a much better father and husband. She had to find a way to get Roger out of their lives for good. "I don't want to think about him. He's not important anymore. Just us."

Salty hugged her. "That's my girl."

"I am your girl, aren't I?" She glanced at him hopefully.

"The only one I've ever had, and the only one I'll ever want."

"That's good. I'd scratch out the eyes of any woman who looked at you twice."

"Every other beautiful woman in the world could fall at my feet, and I'd never notice. I'd never take second best."

Sarah knew she wasn't that pretty, but it was nice Salty thought so.

In the beginning she'd found him not especially handsome. Now she wondered how she could have been so blind. There was a sweetness in Salty's face that was balanced by strength of character and body. His eyes were open and kind, his mouth firm yet supple. His lean face reflected a life of discipline and hard work, his slow smile a confidence in his abilities and belief in the goodness of others. It was all so simple, so ordinary...yet so rare. She understood the value because she had experienced their absence.

She squeezed Salty. "I expect you'd notice those other women, but it would be okay as long as you stayed with me."

They sat in companionable silence for a few moments, taking the time to enjoy the quiet of the night and the pleasure of each other's company. It was something Sarah had never experienced. Her whole life had been a race to get something done, or to avoid something else.

Everything was different now that Salty was here. She didn't feel as overwhelmed. She had the help of the man she loved, and who loved her and her children. After so many years of watching her life unravel, it had come together in the best possible way.

"Do you like sitting out at night?" Salty asked.

"I don't know. I've never done it before."

"I did it growing up and especially during the war. It feels like the world has pulled back at night, taking away its pressures and demands and leaving me all alone. Gives me a chance to decide what's important."

"What's that?" she asked.

"You. The children. This place."

Bones came ambling out of the shadows from the direction of the shed. "What are you doing here?" Salty asked. "I told you to watch Roger." Ignoring him, the dog walked over to Salty's bedroll, gave it a good sniff then settled down.

Sarah laughed. "Apparently he misses you."

"That's kinda nice to know, but not if he thinks he can take my bed."

"You could share mine." She hadn't meant to say that, hadn't meant to push, but she hadn't stopped thinking about it all evening. "Sorry, I shouldn't have said that." She looked down, somewhat contrite. "I mean, I want you to sleep with me, though I know we can't because—"

Salty tipped her chin up and silenced her by pressing his finger to her lips. "I feel the same way."

"I've tried not thinking about it but I can't stop myself. I want to go to sleep with your arms around me, snuggled up against you, my head resting in the crook of your neck. I want to wake up and see your head on the pillow next to mine. I want to be able to reach out and touch you whenever I want, to grasp your hand, to kiss you. I can't do any of that because Roger is here now, and that makes me angrier than ever."

Salty drew her close and placed a kiss on the top of her head. "We'll soon be able to do all of that—and more."

"When? I don't want to wait. I feel like every minute Roger is here stretches into an hour."

"I don't know. We need to consult a lawyer."

Sarah pushed close. "I know. But I'm scared. I feel like everything is being taken away just as I've found it."

He shook his head. "Nothing is being taken away. Just postponed."

"Then why does it feel the same?"

"Because we both want it so much."

"Do you think Bones wants something?"

Salty looked surprised. "Why?"

"He's staring at you and whining."

Bones's ears were pricked, his gaze focused on the trees. Salty turned to him and said, "Be quiet. Can't you see we're…" He stopped, looked toward the dark circle of trees around the house then back. "You hear something, don't you?"

Tail wagging, the dog got to his feet. He walked over to Salty, stuck his nose in Salty's hand, and whined again.

"Show me where it is."

Bones turned toward the trees. His hackles were up, and his whine changed into a growl. He trotted a few steps then turned back, his growl rolling deeper into his throat.

"He wants you to follow," Sarah said. "Do you think Roger is trying to sneak back to the house?"

Salty had reached for his pants. "If he is, I'll chain him to a wall."

Bones had moved halfway across the yard, his growl deepening.

"Maybe I should just tell Roger I don't love him. I could give him a dozen reasons. Maybe that will make him go away." Sarah knew she was clutching at straws; she doubted Roger cared.

Bones turned back and barked. Salty snapped, "Be quiet, dammit, before you wake everyone. I'm coming as fast as I can." He grabbed his boots and jammed his feet into them.

"A hundred reasons wouldn't be enough," he said to Sarah. "I'll come back as soon as I find out what he's up to."

As he reached for his rifle, which lay beside his bedroll, Bones broke into a volley of barking and disappeared into the darkness.

"Damned impatient dog. Maybe he'll take care of Roger for me."

"Don't shoot him," Sarah begged. He was still her children's father.

Salty laughed. "I'm more likely to take this rifle butt to his head. It's about time someone taught him—"

A pistol shot broke the quiet, and Salty headed across the yard at a run.

"If that bastard has shot my dog, I'll kill him."

TWENTY-THREE

A VOLLEY OF BARKS TOLD HIM BONES WAS UNHURT, BUT SALTY STILL swore with each stride. If he had to do any more running, he would have to buy some shoes. These boots were going to cripple him.

He passed through the belt of trees and out into the open beyond. He turned in the direction of the shed, but Bones's barks were coming from the direction of the corral, so he changed course. What could Roger be doing at the corral? Surely he wasn't stupid enough to try to steal the unbranded cows. He couldn't get away with that many cows alone, much less brand them.

He met Dobie coming from the direction of the wagon he shared with Arnie.

"What the hell is going on?" the young man asked. "I never heard Bones act so crazy." Arnie followed at a distance, putting on his shirt as he ran.

"I don't know, but he's over by the corral."

"You think Roger's trying to steal the horses?"

Roger could sell Salty's two horses for at least a hundred dollars each. He didn't look as though he'd brought any money back from the gold fields, so maybe he was desperate enough to turn horse thief.

"If he touches mine, he's a dead man," Dobie muttered.

Salty felt the same way. Still, it wouldn't look good for Sarah's second husband to shoot her first husband, regardless of the provocation. People were bound to think the accusation was just a cover for murder.

"We can't be sure Roger is involved," he said. "He could be asleep."

"Not if he was telling the truth when he said he could hear a man take a deep breath when he was in the gold fields."

Salty's lungs were starting to burn as he ran. He could work as long as any man in or out of the saddle, but he wasn't a sprinter. His legs were starting to feel wobbly, and he began to wish the corral was closer to the house. The wind hardly ever blew from that direction anyway.

A second pistol report made him forget his burning lungs and wobbly legs. A single gunshot might have been unintentional, but a second wasn't. Something was seriously wrong.

"What do you think's going on?" Dobie asked.

Salty didn't have an answer, so he didn't waste the breath he needed to keep up with the younger man.

Once past a grove of post oaks, he could see the corral. There seemed to be a disturbance inside, but milling animals blocked Salty's view. One thing he could make out, there was a man astride a horse in the center of the melee. That man was Henry Wallace.

"What is that bastard doing here?" Dobie asked.

Salty didn't answer, because he was more concerned about the man in long underwear who appeared to be clinging to Wallace's saddle. It could only be Roger Winborne, and Wallace was pointing his gun at him.

Without breaking stride, Salty brought his rifle to his shoulder and fired. He knew there was no chance of hitting Wallace without stopping to take aim, but he just wanted to stop Wallace from shooting Roger.

The rifle shot deflected Wallace's attention from Roger, but it directed it toward Salty and Dobie. Wallace fired two quick shots at them. Fortunately, both went wide. "Son of a bitch!" Dobie exclaimed. "He's shooting at us."

Salty didn't reply. He was trying to figure out how to capture Wallace. If the man got away, he'd probably force his cowhands to swear he'd been at his ranch all night and avoid justice.

"Let's separate," he said to Dobie. "Since you're ten years younger and more limber, see if you can crawl through the corral poles on the other side and come up behind him."

"He'll shoot you if you get any closer," Dobie said.

"I don't plan to give him an easy target."

Apparently realizing that he would soon be facing two armed men, Wallace pushed Roger away with his foot, turned his horse around, and headed toward the breach in the corral fence. Roger disappeared into the milling animals. Salty decided to let Wallace escape. If he didn't get to Roger fast, the man might be trampled to death. He didn't stop to ask himself why he was protecting this man.

Climbing over the corral fence, Salty ran, yelling at the top of his lungs, scattering cows and horses and nearly stepping on Roger, who lay sprawled on the cut-up ground. The blood on his long underwear made it plain he'd been shot. Dirt on his clothes implied he'd been stepped on several times, too.

Laying his rifle aside, Salty knelt next to him. "What were you doing out here?"

Roger's eyes were open but laced with pain. His words came in snatches, each phrase a physical effort. "I heard that…damned dog… barking. I came out to make him shut up. I saw Wallace…pulling down the poles in…the corral."

"You shouldn't have tried to tackle him by yourself."

"Couldn't let the bastard…steal…my children's cows… Had to stop him."

"You should have called me."

"Wanted…to do something…for them…myself."

"Not without a gun."

"Didn't think he'd shoot me. Shot…at the dog…first."

Arnie arrived. "Stop what you're doing," Salty said to Dobie, who was trying to drive the remaining livestock away. "Tell Sarah that Arnie and I are bringing Roger up to the house. He's been shot. He may have some broken bones as well."

"Get Wallace," Roger gasped.

"I'll get him. Right now we have to take care of you."

Roger tried to talk, but his words became so slurred Salty couldn't understand him. The man groaned in pain when he was lifted. With Salty holding his arms and Arnie his feet, they started Roger toward the house.

"You think he's going to make it?" Arnie asked.

"I won't know until I can get a look at his wound. He'll need a doctor. Is there one nearby?"

"The closest is in Austin or San Antonio."

"No doctor," Roger told them. "Saw...too many...during the war."

It would take more than a day in a wagon to reach either town. Salty wasn't sure Roger would survive the journey. "Sarah can take care of you. She'll know what to do." He would have said more, but Roger had fainted.

He didn't want Sarah taking care of Roger. He didn't want her having to do anything for the man, even spend several minutes with him, but he had to put his personal feelings aside. Whatever he felt, Roger was a human being.

Ellen catapulted toward them out of trees and darkness near the house and came to an abrupt halt. She stared at her father with wide-eyed curiosity. "Is he dead?"

"He just passed out from the pain," Salty explained.

"Dobie said Mr. Wallace shot him. Why would he do that?"

"I don't know," Salty said.

"Did you ask him?"

"Wallace left before I could ask him."

"Why?"

The difference between the twins continued to surprise Salty. Jared would have been silent and figured everything out. Ellen responded to events with barely controlled bursts of energy, and her thinking came afterward.

"I don't know why he was here," he told her, "but he left because he shot your father and knew that would get him in trouble."

"Are you going to shoot *him*?"

He supposed that equation made sense at seven; you shoot someone, you get shot in return. Unfortunately, or fortunately, nothing in life was that simple. "Hold the door for us," he said to the girl. "He's heavier than he looks."

"Put him in my bed," Sarah said as they entered the house.

It was the first time he'd been inside her bedroom, and Salty was surprised by its austerity. Other than her bed and a chifforobe, it was empty of furniture and barren of decoration, not even pictures on the walls or curtains at the window.

Sarah's face was drained of color, but she seemed in control. "How badly is he injured?"

"I don't know yet."

"He's going to die." Salty hadn't noticed Jared standing in the corner, the boy's gaze focused on his father.

"We don't know that," Sarah said.

"I know it."

Salty and Arnie laid Roger on the bed, and Sarah unbuttoned his shirt. Blood welled up from a wound in the upper right side of his chest. It was impossible to tell if the bullet had hit a vital organ. Salty lay his hand on Roger's chest then bent over to listen to his breathing. "His heart is still beating and his lungs sound clear."

"Can you remove the bullet?" Sarah asked.

"I've seen it done, but I've never done it myself," Salty replied.

Sarah turned to Arnie. "How about you?" The man took a step back.

"Don't look at me," Dobie said. "I don't even know how to cut up a chicken."

Sarah studied Roger for a moment. He was so pale he looked like an albino. His breathing was shallow and labored. There was an unnerving stillness about him that whispered of death. "He won't survive a trip to Austin," she decided. "And I don't think he'll last long enough for a doctor to reach us if we don't get the bullet out."

Six people were crowded into the small room, and Salty could feel five sets of eyes staring at him, waiting for his decision. He felt a moment of panic. "Having watched doctors remove bullets doesn't mean I know how to do it," he said. "I could just as easily do something to cause him to die."

"Are you afraid someone might accuse you of trying to kill him so you can stay married to Sarah?" Arnie guessed.

"Nobody would think that," Dobie insisted.

Salty wasn't so sure.

"I think all of us know the only chance Roger has is for you to remove that bullet," Sarah said. "If he should die, Wallace will bear the blame."

Salty knew he had to at least try.

"What do you need?" Sarah asked.

Knowledge he didn't have. Experience he didn't have. Tools he didn't have. A little more courage wouldn't hurt, either. "A sharp knife and the brightest lantern you own," he said. "And you might as well heat some water for cleaning up."

"I'll get some rags," Ellen volunteered.

"He's going to die," Jared repeated.

The boy's pessimism was starting to annoy Salty. "I'm going to do everything I can to keep that from happening."

Roger's skin was getting a chalky tinge Salty had seen too many times as a presage of death. His heartbeat was growing weaker, too. Salty wasn't a doctor, so he couldn't guess what might be going on inside

Roger's body; he could only try to remove the bullet and hope the man could heal.

"This is the sharpest knife I have." The knife Sarah held out looked big enough to carve a ham.

"I've got one." Dobie reached into his pocket and pulled out a pocket knife with a long, thin blade.

"I need some way to clean it."

"Why?" Ellen asked.

"During the war, doctors figured out that washing everything seemed to help prevent infection."

It took several minutes to build a fire and heat the water, minutes that gave Salty too much time to question what he was about to do.

Sarah placed her hand on his arm and gave it a squeeze. "Stop questioning yourself," she said. "You're the best chance he has."

"How can we be sure of that?"

"We can't be sure of anything. We can only do the best we can."

That didn't feel like enough.

"Jared, come wash your hands," Salty said.

"Why?" Sarah asked.

"Because his fingers are a lot smaller than mine. The less cutting I have to do, the better Roger's chances for recovery."

Neither Sarah nor Jared looked happy, but neither voiced any opposition. Finally the water was hot and Salty had washed his hands, Jared's hands, and the knife. He couldn't put it off any longer. Roger's condition continued to worsen. His heartbeat was weak, his breathing erratic. He was so white he appeared entirely drained of blood.

"I'm going to do as little cutting as possible," Salty said to Jared, feeling guilty about asking for his help. But the boy was Roger's best chance. "As soon as I feel the bullet, I want you to reach in and try to pull it out."

Jared looked nearly as white as his father, but he nodded.

The first incision was the worst. After that, it got easier. Thankfully there wasn't much bleeding. Salty inserted an index finger into the wound. It gave him an uncomfortable feeling in the pit of his stomach to know his finger was inside another person's body, how everything inside felt soft, warm, and moist.

Pushing aside the disquiet, he searched for the bullet. After a few tries, he found it. It appeared to be lodged in soft tissue rather than bone. "It's in deep," he warned Jared. "Reach in and over to the right. See if you can feel it."

Jared hesitated only briefly. With a gentle steadiness like his mother's, the boy eased two tiny fingers into the wound. "I feel it," he said.

"See if you can wiggle it loose."

Jared wore a look of deep concentration. "I can move it," he announced, "but it's not coming out."

"You'll have to reach in and pull."

"There's something hard in the way."

"Keep trying."

The hardness was likely a rib. If Jared couldn't get the bullet out with his fingers, Salty would have to try to get it out with the knife. He didn't want to do that because he would risk doing more damage.

Jared reached deeper into the wound, though trying not to enlarge it. "It keeps slipping out of my fingers."

"You'll get it," Salty said.

Everyone else held their places around the bed, their gazes intent on the scene before them, their bodies tense with apprehension and expectation. A lot more hung in the balance than the successful removal of a bullet.

"I got it!" But Jared's concentration remained focused until he withdrew the bullet and held it up.

"Is he supposed to bleed that much?"

Ellen's question drew Salty's attention back to the wound. It had filled with blood, which was running down his side.

"He's bleeding internally," Salty said. "There's nothing we can do for him, unfortunately, just bandage him up. You did a good job," he told Jared. "Better than I could have done."

The boy looked at the wound then turned bleak eyes to Salty. "But he's going to die anyway. Isn't he?"

Salty looked at the wound. It looked bad, but for some reason he didn't want to give up hope.

"You don't need me," Arnie said. "I think I'll go."

"Me too," Dobie said. "Come with me," he told Jared. "I'll help you wash up."

"You're messy too, Salty," Ellen pointed out.

Salty looked down at the blood-covered knife in his hand. Sarah said, "Go with Jared and clean up. Ellen can stay with me."

In the kitchen, Jared was letting Dobie wash his hands. The boy watched in silence while Salty washed his hands and the knife. Dobie glanced down as though unsure whether he should speak.

"What is it?" Salty asked.

"Do you want us to start digging a grave?"

Salty wondered how old you had to be before death stopped being something that happened to other people. For him, the incalculable waste of war had done nothing to inure him to it. It seemed particularly inhumane to talk about burying Roger while he was still alive, and in front of his child, but life seldom waited for the dead. "Not yet. Sarah should be the one to decide where he will be buried."

"Then I'm going back to sleep."

"You ought to go back to bed, too," Salty said to Jared. "There's nothing more you can do."

"I want to sit with Mama and Ellen."

"We can all sit together," Salty said.

Little had changed when they returned to the bedroom. Sarah still held a blood-soaked pad to Roger's chest. Ellen remained at her mother's side. Roger looked the same.

"Want me to take over for a while?" Salty asked.

"I already offered," Ellen spoke up. "She wouldn't let me."

Salty wanted to speak but was afraid anything he said would be wrong. Sarah hadn't wanted Roger to die, even though his return had complicated her life and her children's. Salty wished the children weren't going to witness their father's death, but it seemed an inevitability. At least they'd had a chance to see him again. He had come back and claimed them. Maybe that was enough to balance against his abandonment.

Salty had been so caught up in his thoughts he didn't notice Roger stop breathing. He only noticed when Sarah sat up, lowered her head and whispered a short prayer.

"Is he dead?" Ellen asked.

Her mother nodded.

"Do you want me to lay him out?" Salty asked.

"No. I should be the one to do it."

"Can I help?" Ellen asked.

"No," Sarah said. "This isn't something you should have to handle."

"Come on," Salty said to Ellen. "It's long past your bedtime."

Sarah cast Salty a weak smile of thanks. "Come back when you're done."

It didn't take long for Ellen and Jared to get back into bed. Salty hovered over them for a few minutes, stroking their hair and calming them. They were taking the death rather well. Salty supposed they hadn't known Roger very well. He also supposed it was for the best.

He was back about five minutes later with Sarah. "What can I do?"

"Sit with me and listen while I talk."

He did.

Sarah purged. She talked about how she hadn't wanted to marry Roger, how she'd begged her father to no avail not to force her. She talked about Roger as a spoiled youth, when he was an irresponsible adult, when he was a thoughtless husband. She also talked about how her independent streak had run counter to everything Roger wanted in a wife, how her attempts to change had failed because she didn't *want* to change. She talked about his unhappiness with Jared, about his family's rejection of her and her children. She talked about the anger she'd felt for him, anger that increased with each growing hardship.

She then talked about realizing how Roger couldn't change any more than she could. The marriage had been as wrong for him as it was for her. She explained her feelings of rage when he returned, about her guilt that his death had removed the greatest impediment to her happiness. She talked about being sorry he'd never got to know his own children, yet was also relieved they would never know his true character.

Finally, she fell silent. Salty didn't know whether he should say something or stay quiet. This was uncharted territory for him. No woman had ever poured out her heart to him. Not in this way.

Unable to do nothing, he reached for her hand. It was rough from hard work but warm and supple in his grasp. With a sigh Sarah looked up at him and smiled then allowed herself to lean against him. They sat like that for some minutes, Salty wondering if she had more to say.

When she finally did speak, she seemed to have regained her composure. "I'm going to lay him out now. When I finish, I want you to take him to the sitting room. We'll bury him in the morning."

―――――――

Ellen yanked at her dress.

"Stop before you tear it," Sarah scolded. She and the children were ready to leave the house. The men had already placed Roger's body in a box next to the open grave.

"Why do I have to be dressed up?"

"People always dress up for funerals. It's a sign of respect."

"Why should we respect him?" Jared asked. "He was mean."

It was a hard question to answer. She felt like a hypocrite asking her children to honor the man who'd abandoned them. Maybe it wasn't Roger's fault his parents had pampered him because of his looks, leading him to believe he deserved things just because he wanted them, or maybe he should have had the strength of character to overcome that fault. She couldn't say. All she knew for sure right now was that she wanted her children to think the best of their father, at least in all ways that would affect how they thought about themselves.

"People don't always do what they should when they're alive. We just have to trust your father did the best he could."

"Maybe he did," Jared conceded grudgingly, "but Salty would never have been like that."

"I'm sure you're right," she admitted. "Now, we can't keep everybody waiting."

It had taken most of the night to decide where to bury Roger. Sarah had settled on a spot inside the band of trees that circled the house. That would honor his position as part of the family, but he would be also separated from the new family she was forming.

Once outside, they walked together, Ellen on one side and Jared on the other. Ellen would grow up to be a lovely woman, but Jared was going to be a heartbreaker. She found it ironic that the child Roger had rejected should end up being even more handsome than his father. She was proud of both children. They had inherited the best of both parents without the flaws.

They all gathered at the grave. Salty, Arnie, and Dobie stood opposite her and the children. She knew she had to say something, but Sarah was still searching for the right words. The silence lengthened.

Roger didn't look so handsome now, but there was a humanity to him that had been lacking before. Maybe the war and two years in the goldfields had taught him some of the lessons he'd failed to learn earlier. After all, he had come back to them. Maybe he'd intended to make good on his marriage vows and hadn't really been grasping at straws financially. Maybe the reason he'd been so angry was surprise at finding another man in his place.

She cleared her throat. It was time.

"We're gathered here to remember the life of Roger Winborne, son of Anson and Jessica Winborne, first husband of Sarah Pettishall Winborne, and father of Ellen and Jared Winborne. He was a delight to his parents and a favorite of many who knew him." That wasn't too much of an exaggeration. He had gotten along fine with anyone who wasn't married to him. "He was a good soldier who survived the war to return to his family. He died trying to protect their home."

She debated saying more, but her mind was blank. Roger looked so calm and peaceful, so *ordinary*, not like the man she remembered. He seemed to be indicating that he understood, that it was time for him to rest, that it was time for them to move on. Perhaps in death he was giving her the understanding he'd been unable to provide in life.

"Are you ready to bury him?" Salty asked.

"Yes."

Salty and Dobie fitted the top to the coffin and nailed it shut. They were preparing to lower it into the grave when they were interrupted by the arrival of several riders. Wallace's foreman was in the lead. He eyed the coffin with an odd expression.

"What are you doing here?" Sarah asked.

"Mr. Wallace rode out last night, said he was heading over this way. He never came home." He indicated the coffin. "That wouldn't be him you're fixing to bury, would it?"

TWENTY-FOUR

"That's my pa," Ellen told the foreman. "Mr. Wallace killed him."

The foreman cast a scornful glance at Salty. "It looks to me like your pa is doing just fine."

"Mr. Benton is my second husband," Sarah told the foreman. "Roger Winborne was my first. He was the father of my children."

"The lady we all thought was a widow woman suddenly has two husbands?"

Sarah had been so focused on the foreman she hadn't realized Salty moved until he stood between them. "If you have questions, ask them in a civil manner and we'll answer. If you can't do that, you can ride out of here right now."

The foreman regarded them with a fixed expression for a moment then relaxed into an apologetic smile. "Sorry if I've been rude, but we've spent the morning searching the ranch without finding my boss or his horse."

"I don't know where Mr. Wallace is, but he was here last night, all right—attempting to scatter our cows and horses. Roger, Sarah's first husband, tried to stop him. Three of us saw Wallace shoot him. We didn't try to stop him from getting away because we were more concerned with Roger. He died a short time later."

"I never heard much about your first husband," the foreman admitted to Sarah. "Where's he been all this time?"

Salty started to protest, but Sarah put her hand on his arm to stop him. "People have to know the truth, regardless of how awkward it might be," she said. Turning to Wallace's foreman she explained, "When my husband didn't come home from the war, I thought he'd died. Yesterday, he came back. It was quite a shock."

The foreman didn't say anything. He kept looking at the coffin, though, and Sarah knew what was on his mind.

"Salty, please open the coffin to show Mr. Wallace's men that we're not burying their boss."

Salty uttered a pithy curse but took the hammer from Dobie and pried the lid off the coffin. "All of you come look," he said to Wallace's men. "I don't want any question about who's in here."

"I've never seen Roger Winborne," the foreman pointed out.

Two of Wallace's other men apparently had. They dismounted and walked over to the coffin. It took only a single glance for both to agree it was Roger.

"And you say Mr. Wallace shot him?" the foreman asked. "That doesn't make sense. Why would he do that?"

Jared pushed forward. "He was stealing our cows."

"He thought we were stealing his," Sarah said.

"Why would he think that?" the foreman asked.

"You heard what he said the other week," Salty reminded him. "He was angry about the whole situation. We gathered up some unbranded cows today—from *our* land—and put them into the corral with the horses. Wallace was apparently trying to drive them out. Our dog alerted Roger. Wallace shot Roger when he tried to pull him out of the saddle. I can only assume Wallace hasn't come home because he'll be arrested for murder."

"He's telling the truth, Gary," Dobie said to the foreman.

"I was a little ways behind those two," Arnie said, "but I definitely saw Wallace shoot Roger. When he saw us, he kicked Roger and took off."

"Don't expect me to do anything about it," Gary said. "I won't turn my own boss in for something I didn't see. How do I know you're telling the truth?"

"I don't like the idea of working for a murderer," one of Wallace's men said.

"Me neither," said another.

"You don't know he's done any murdering," a third man said. "You only got these folks' word for it."

Dobie addressed the last speaker. "You know I don't lie, Tully."

"Why should I believe a quitter?" Tully demanded.

"I quit working for Wallace because he ordered us to brand any cow on his land even when we knew it didn't belong to him."

Salty turned to Gary, raising an eyebrow.

"I never did that," the foreman said. "Whenever I saw one of your unbranded cows wander on our range, I hazed it back."

"Tully told Wallace about it," Dobie said, pointing a finger at the cowhand. "Gary had to make up a story to keep from getting fired."

"Talking is getting us nowhere," Sarah said. "You need to find your boss and we need to bury Roger. Why don't you send for the sheriff?"

"If you want to set the law on him, you ought to be the ones to send for the sheriff," Tully growled. Sarah sensed Gary felt the same.

"That seems fair," she decided.

"I don't mind going to Austin," Dobie volunteered. "I might even manage to meet a sympathetic senorita," he added, winking.

"Then we'll be off," Gary said. "I'll act like nothing's changed and let the law handle everything."

Sarah didn't like it, but she wasn't too surprised. The man had only their word to go on, and Wallace was his boss.

"I'll leave as soon as we're done burying him," Dobie said, indicating Roger's coffin. "Expect to see the sheriff in two days."

In actuality, it was three days before he returned. Sarah spent the time trying not to think about Mr. Wallace and the evil he'd done, trying not to worry that he might attack them again. Something had been disturbing their herd. Longhorns were never comfortable around people, but their cows had been more skittish than usual. They couldn't discount the possibility that a wolf had moved into the area—or that Wallace was continuing his harassment.

"Dobie's back." It was a warm day, and Jared had been sitting on the steps in the sun shelling dried peas for supper. "He's got somebody with him."

Sarah didn't stop churning. It was a treat to have enough milk to make butter again. She was planning on making a cake, the first she had made in more than a year. She had to get this done.

"Do you know where Salty went?" she asked.

Things had changed once Salty finished the extra room. Sarah had moved into it, and Ellen had moved into her mother's old room. Deciding it was better to wait until Roger's death had been officially cleared up, Salty had opted to share a room with Jared rather than Sarah. That enabled Arnie to move into the shed, which he would share with Dobie until they could afford to build a bunkhouse.

"Salty said he and Arnie were going out to sweep the range for more unbranded stock. They were also going to look around to see if they spotted any tracks."

Dobie and the stranger rode up. The man accompanying Dobie introduced himself as John Willis, deputy sheriff. He appeared quite young for the job, but he gave the appearance of a man confident in his abilities.

"Did you arrest Mr. Wallace?" Jared asked.

"He's disappeared again," Dobie said, his expression one of disgust.

"What do you mean *again*?" Sarah asked. "Sorry, I'm being rude. Please come into the house. It won't take but a few minutes to make some coffee."

The deputy sheriff dismounted. "Thanks, but I don't want to stop your butter making."

"We're going to have a cake," Jared informed him. "Mama's going to put blackberry jam between the layers!" Sarah felt embarrassed that something as simple as a cake should cause the boy such excitement, but she was excited, too. She was glad they were able to enjoy such a treat again.

"Sounds good," the deputy said. "Maybe you'll save me a piece for when I come back."

Jared shook his head. "Salty said he was going to eat everything left over for breakfast tomorrow."

"That's enough," Sarah spoke up. "It's not kind to tease the man about what he can't have."

"I wasn't teasing," Jared protested. "I was just telling him."

"Did you have something you wanted to tell us?" Sarah asked the deputy.

"Mr. Wallace went home two days ago."

"He brought in a bunch of cows and ordered Gary to brand them," Dobie spoke up. "Gary wouldn't do it because of what we said. He didn't know where they'd come from."

"Some of them looked too young to be weaned," the deputy added.

"I bet he stole them from us," Jared said.

"One of Mr. Wallace's men told him that you all saw him shoot your first husband who everybody thought was dead. Mr. Wallace swore it was a lie. He tried to talk his men out of believing it."

"He told Gary he had come over here to talk to you about doing a roundup together," Dobie inserted. "He said Salty must have seen that as an opportunity to shoot Roger and blame it on him. He said we'd been trying to steal his cows. But after that, he disappeared and no one has seen him since."

"I can assure you there's no truth in his accusations," Sarah said to the deputy. "Why would he come over in the middle of the night to discuss a roundup?"

"I already told him Arnie and Salty would swear to what they saw, too," Dobie said.

"What do you want us to do?" Sarah asked the deputy.

The deputy shook his head. "Nothing yet. Dobie has sworn out a complaint against Mr. Wallace. That's all I need until I find him. Now, I'd better be getting along. It's a long ride to Austin, which is where I think he went." He mounted up. After settling into the saddle he said, "Wallace is a rich man with some powerful friends. Don't be surprised if they try to charge your second husband with murdering your first."

"How can they?" Sarah asked, outraged. "No one saw what happened but us. And it's not true!"

"I don't know what these folks might do, but...witnesses can be bought." Willis seemed embarrassed to admit the possibility.

"I ain't changing my story," Dobie stated. "Not even if somebody offers me a hundred dollars."

Salty wouldn't face false charges if Sarah could help it. "My husband has powerful friends, too. Contact the Randolph family. They have a ranch in—"

Willis laughed. "I know where their ranch is. After the parade last year to honor their father, everybody knows the Randolphs, and that they're friends with Richard King."

"Salty also knows Jake Maxwell. He served with George Randolph in the war."

Raised eyebrows showed the deputy was duly impressed. "The support of these men will stand your husband in good stead if any charges are brought," he said. "But be prepared for Wallace to cause as much trouble as possible." With that, the lawman turned his horse and rode off.

"They won't put Salty in jail, will they?" Jared asked.

"Not a chance," Dobie said. "By the time Arnie and I get through telling what we saw, they'll be building a gallows to hang Wallace."

Sarah doubted Wallace and his friends could succeed in sending Salty to jail, but she was concerned about the rumors that might start. Being accused of murdering Roger so that he could stay married to her would follow him like a bad smell, and she hated the idea of anything sullying his reputation. He was the finest man she knew.

"I hate Mr. Wallace," Jared said. "If he's really saying those things about Salty, I want him to hang."

Sarah was upset that her son should want anyone to hang, but she didn't know what to say. He was just seven, too young to understand the damage that hate could do. He only understood that their neighbor was trying to take away someone who was very important to him. "Mr. Wallace isn't a nice man, but we shouldn't hate him."

"Why not?"

Hate was a useless and destructive emotion that would do far more damage to Jared than it could ever do to Wallace. Besides, it was hate and jealousy that had made Wallace what he was. But before she could explain that to him, Ellen came running up, still smeared with dirt from working in the garden. "Who was that man that rode away? What did he want? Did they find Mr. Wallace? Why didn't you call me?"

"That was the deputy sheriff," Sarah told her daughter. "He hasn't found Mr. Wallace yet, but they're looking for him."

"Mr. Wallace said Salty killed Roger," Jared told his sister. "He wants to put Salty in jail and hang him."

Ellen turned to her mother, her eyes filled with a fear Sarah had never seen. "They can't do that, can they?"

It was impossible to be unaware of the importance of Salty in her life and the lives of her children, but the threatened loss was pushing both her children to the edge of panic. She drew them close and promised, "No one is going to put Salty in jail, and no one is going to hang him."

"But the deputy said—"

"He said Mr. Wallace would try to cause trouble, Jared. He may try, but he won't succeed. Salty's friends are rich and powerful, too. But he doesn't need them because he has the truth on his side." She prayed that was true.

"He'll have them anyway, won't he?" asked Jared.

"Yes, he'll have them anyway."

"He'll have Arnie and me, too," Dobie assured the boy. "Ain't nobody going to make us say anything against Salty."

"Now that *that's* settled, we need to get back to work," Sarah said. "Salty is going to expect the garden to be done and supper ready when he and Arnie get back. And you," she told Dobie, "ought to go help him."

"I feel like I've been in the saddle for three weeks instead of three days," Dobie pleaded. "My butt's got blisters on top of blisters."

The children giggled. Sarah was glad.

"How much of those three days did you spend chasing senoritas?"

Dobie grinned at the children. "Sympathetic senoritas are not easy to find. Deputy sheriffs are much easier."

Sarah laughed in spite of herself. "Get going, you rascal. A few hours of honest work won't kill you."

"I like working for Salty better," Dobie said. "He's not as tough as you." He winked before turning and heading to the corral for a fresh horse.

A short time later they were all back at their allotted chores, but the haunted look remained in Jared's eyes. Sarah knew it wouldn't go away until Salty was home. Maybe not even then.

For the next week Sarah lived in daily hope of hearing that Henry Wallace had been captured, but they heard nothing. The deputy returned twice, but all he could tell them was that Wallace's attempt to accuse Salty of having killed Roger had fallen flat.

His friends had indeed stood by him. George Randolph said anybody who believed Salty could be a stone-cold killer was a fool. Rose, who'd been in Austin because George insisted she see a doctor at least once a month, was even blunter. She said anybody who accused Salty of killing Roger was a bald-faced liar.

Other good news followed: the Randolphs' lawyer stated that he believed being officially declared dead was practically the same as a divorce, and that he could make that stick in court. That meant there wasn't much more to fear except where Wallace was hiding.

But fear it Sarah did. The man could remain hidden only so long before he got desperate. She knew only too well that desperate people did stupid and dangerous things. She had begged Salty to promise he wouldn't ride out alone, and she kept both children in the house unless she was with them. While Jared accepted his confinement with stoic calm, Ellen would have rebelled if Sarah hadn't gone riding with her once a day.

She hurried to finish folding the clothes she'd been washing and putting them away. She could never enter the "boudoir" Salty had built for her without shaking her head in amazement. It was as big as the other two bedrooms combined. She felt guilty having so much space to herself, but she was looking forward to the time when the two of them would share it. Every night it got harder to watch him enter the room he shared with Jared and close the door.

She carefully folded one of the dresses Rose had given her and thought about the closet Salty had built her. It had shelves! She now had more than enough room for her few garments. She laughed to herself. They'd never fill half the closet. Still, it was nice to have the extra storage space. And the new room… Whenever she entered it, she didn't feel quite so poor.

But she did feel lonely. The room reminded her of the one night she'd spent in Salty's arms, and the many nights since that she'd been separated from him. Her bed looked lost in its new setting, much the way she felt without Salty. She tried to tell herself to be patient, that she wouldn't have to wait much longer, but that only worked until she was settled in bed and had nothing to distract her mind. She would start to remember the taste of Salty's kisses, the feel of his hands on her body, the magic of her emotional and physical awakening. Her whole body would come alive. She would start to feel his kisses on the side of her neck, feel his tongue on her breasts, feel him invade her body, and a fire would kindle inside her that would soon have her squirming. She tried to drive the images from her mind, but they were like a fire that fed itself: the more she remembered, the more she wanted to remember.

Sarah shook her head to dislodge the unsettling images. She needed to finish putting her clothes away and get back to the kitchen. Jared was shelling peas, and now that she had milk and cream again, it would be nice to make a custard for dessert. She and Ellen would have to go for eggs.

When she reached the kitchen, Jared was still working. She didn't see Ellen. "Where's your sister?" she asked.

"She said she was going to milk the cow."

The girl had to be desperate to get outside to offer to milk the cow. "She knows she's not supposed to leave the house without me!"

"That's what I told her, but she said nothing was going to happen."

It irritated Sarah that Ellen should go out alone, but the men had told her repeatedly that she was being overly cautious. "Wallace would never come near this house again," Dobie had said. "He knows any one of us would shoot him."

Sarah had wanted to err on the safe side, and Salty had backed her up. He'd supported her restrictions when Ellen complained to him. Apparently a week was the limit of her acceptance.

"How long has she been gone?" she asked.

"Just a few minutes."

Sarah went to the front door. Through the opening in the trees that surrounded the house she could see Ellen leading their milk cow toward a spot where she had left her stool and bucket. She ought to go out and watch, but it seemed foolish to stand around when she needed to be inside starting supper. "Don't dawdle," she called.

Ellen waved, a big smile on her face. She was so thrilled to be outside, she was happily doing a chore she usually hated.

Sarah went back into the house. "Your sister doesn't follow rules very well," she muttered.

"You've made her stay inside all week," Jared replied. "I'm surprised she hasn't snuck out before."

"What about you?"

"Oh, I don't mind."

"Well, once they find Mr. Wallace, you can go just about anywhere you want," Sarah promised him. Since Salty had been teaching him to ride, he'd been pushing his mother to give him a horse of his own.

"Can I ride out with Salty?"

"Maybe," she allowed. "When you get more secure in the saddle."

"I won't learn by sitting inside."

"I know. Just be patient." It seemed she'd been saying that to Jared his whole life. Still, things were better than they'd ever been.

Sarah took a quick peek out the window. Ellen was tying the cow to the tree, so she turned back to the kitchen. Fixing supper for six people, three of them grown men, took at least an hour of hard work. She'd completely lost track of time when Jared said, "Ellen should be back by now."

"Look out the window and see what she's doing." Sarah kept working on the biscuit dough.

"I see the cow, but I don't see Ellen."

Alarm battled with exasperation. Sarah was cleaning her hands when she heard the door open. "It's about time you got back," she said. "I was about to—"

"I'm not your daughter."

Sarah turned to see Henry Wallace standing in the doorway, a gun pointed at her.

TWENTY-FIVE

Sᴀʀᴀʜ's ꜰᴇᴀʀ ᴡᴀs sᴏ ᴇxᴛʀᴇᴍᴇ, sʜᴇ ᴄᴏᴜʟᴅɴ'ᴛ ᴛʜɪɴᴋ, ᴄᴏᴜʟᴅ ᴏɴʟʏ ask the question uppermost in her mind. "What have you done with her?"

"She's safe. I won't hurt her."

Her dread only partially allayed, Sarah's brain started to function. Wallace had nothing to gain and everything to lose by hurting Ellen. She had to remain calm and find out what he wanted.

She had known Henry Wallace all her life, but she had never really *looked* at him until now. He had just been there, a neighbor who grew more annoying each year, whom mostly she pitied for having lost his family. But now he'd placed himself outside the law. To what further extremes would he go?

Being forced to spend a week in hiding had robbed him of his well-groomed appearance. His shirt was dirty and its collar frayed. He hadn't shaved. She guessed he'd combed his hair with his hands, though she didn't know why he'd bothered. His pants were dirty and creased, his boots discolored by dust. His eyes were cold and unfeeling.

He stepped inside and closed the door behind him.

"What do you want?"

"I want your men to swear I didn't kill Roger."

"Who would we say killed him?"

"I don't care. A robber or a rustler. Anybody else."

"The deputy has written statements from all of us."

"It was dark. You could have made a mistake."

"I don't think the deputy would believe us."

"It won't matter," Wallace said. "He can't charge me if he has no evidence, and those statements are all the evidence he has."

Sarah had been so focused, she hadn't noticed Jared move. The boy was on his feet, however, and noiselessly approaching Wallace from behind. She desperately wanted to tell him to stop, that she would handle Wallace, but she didn't want to do anything to startle Wallace. If he thought he was being threatened from behind, he might shoot before thinking.

"I suppose I can do what you want," she said, hoping to keep his attention on her, "but it's going to take some time."

"Why?" He looked puzzled. "All you have to do is tell the deputy you made a mistake."

"It won't be easy to convince the men to change their stories. Both Arnie and Dobie dislike you."

It was all she could do to keep her gaze on Wallace. Jared was only a few feet behind him. Her eyes pleaded with him to back up, but Jared didn't even look up.

"They'll do it for you," Wallace laughed. "Arnie is already sweet on you, and Dobie is young enough to be dazzled by you if you put your mind to it."

Sarah wasn't sure what Wallace meant, but she didn't intend to ask. She just wanted to keep his attention on her. Jared had stopped moving. Hopefully, he'd changed his mind about what he intended.

"Maybe I can convince them to change their story," Sarah allowed, "but you know how hardheaded Texas men can be." Jared was just standing behind Wallace, testing his balance without the cane. That didn't make any sense. He couldn't walk without the cane.

"You'll do it if you want your daughter back."

"What are you going to do with her?"

"She'll be with me. If I get rained on, she'll get rained on. If I get cold and hungry, she'll get cold and hungry. Tell that to your new husband. Tell that to—"

Jared swung his crutch and hit Wallace in the back of the head. He staggered and dropped his gun, which went off when it struck the floor. The bullet struck Sarah in the leg, knocking it out from under her.

"Mama!" Jared's voice and the pain came at the same time.

"I didn't do that!" Wallace shouted. "Make sure you tell the deputy it was your damn son's fault." He picked up his pistol and ran out the door.

Sarah didn't care whose fault it was. Uppermost in her mind was that she couldn't get up and Wallace was leaving with Ellen.

"I'm sorry. I didn't mean for him to shoot you." Jared had crawled to her on his hands and knees, and his tears fell on her clothes and face as he clutched her.

"It's not your fault," she assured him. "It all started with Mr. Wallace. If he hadn't taken Ellen, none of this would have happened."

"Are you going to die? Your leg looks real bloody."

"No, but I can't get up. You have to find Salty. If Mr. Wallace takes Ellen to his hiding place, we might never find her. *Hurry.*"

She hated to ask Jared to undertake such a long trip, but there seemed no alternative. And while her son and Salty found Ellen, she had to bind up her leg, try to keep the wound from bleeding too much.

Salty would get Ellen back. He would take care of both of them. He would take care of everything.

Salty was looking forward to his supper. It had been a long and tiring day, and he was relieved that they had found only eleven cows that needed branding and no signs of a wolf or of Henry Wallace. He was heading home ahead of Arnie and Dobie to watch the children enjoy some time outside before it got dark. He thought Sarah was being overly cautious, truth be told, but it was better to be safe than sorry. To hear Ellen tell, it was practically solitary confinement.

When it was all over and there was no question about the legality of his marriage to Sarah, he was going to move into the new bedroom with Sarah. Just thinking about that made his body tighten. The nights had been hell, and the days weren't any better. It was agony to see her, to be able to touch her and even steal an occasional kiss, but do no more. Dobie had said he was foolish to force on himself such restraints, but Salty knew he'd never be comfortable being Sarah's husband the way he wanted to be her husband until the ghost of Roger Winborne was wholly laid to rest.

It seemed Nature had conspired to make everything around him remind him of her. Today the clear blue sky matched her eyes, the sun's warmth her radiant smile, and its rays her golden hair. The wind was the sound of her sighing, the noise of the stream the sound of her laughter. The clip-clop of his horse's hooves reminded him of her beating heart when he held her close. The down that lined a duck's nest was as soft as her cheeks, the swelling buds of the Indian Paintbrush her lips. His memory of her was so vivid he could almost believe he was seeing her, touching her, holding her in his arms...

He had to stop! He was becoming so uncomfortable in the saddle he'd have to walk home, and he didn't need Ellen to tell him that no self-respecting cowboy walked when he could ride. Thinking of Ellen made him smile. She was so much like her mother. When she grew up, she was going to give fits to every boy within a hundred miles. It would take a special man to win her heart. Ellen swore she didn't want to get married, but he was sure she would change her mind. She was a girl who needed family to—

His thoughts broke off as he saw a horse and rider coming toward him at a fast canter. At first he thought it was Jared, but that was impossible: the boy couldn't capture, saddle, and mount a horse by himself. But no sooner had he convinced himself it was impossible than he realized it *was* Jared, who was riding bareback. That meant something was terribly wrong. Salty was caught between fear and pride that the boy was riding the horse.

Spurring his horse into a gallop, he rode to meet Jared.

"Mr. Wallace shot Mama and stole Ellen!"

The boy's face was wreathed with determination, his hands gripped the horse's mane. Their mounts came together. Jared couldn't turn his, so Salty reined around alongside him. "What did you say?" he asked, crowding Jared's horse to face him back in the direction of the house.

"Mr. Wallace shot Mama! She said I was to come get you so you could get Ellen back. Mr. Wallace ran off!"

A wave of relief swamped Salty, so powerful he swayed in the saddle. He'd been imagining Sarah dead. But she was obviously wounded, and he didn't know how bad. He started picturing how he would make Wallace suffer before killing him. If Sarah was not seriously wounded, he might take pity on Wallace and just shoot him.

Jared looked exhausted. Salty wasn't sure the boy could make it back to the house on his own. He moved closer until their two horses were almost shoulder to shoulder. He reached over and put his arm around Jared's waist. "Let go," he commanded. "You're going to ride double with me. Sit behind me, put your arms around my waist and hold on tight."

He lifted the boy over. Jared pressed his head between Salty's shoulders; he wrapped his arms around Salty's waist and locked his fingers. Salty felt a rush of warmth at the way the boy clung to him, at the way he trusted that Salty would make everything right. The love Salty felt for Sarah was strange and wonderful, but what he felt for this boy and his sister was just as powerful in its own way. It was humbling and wonderful at the same time.

"Tell me what happened," he said after the boy was safely settled behind him. He left Jared's horse to find its own way home.

Salty couldn't catch all the words, but he heard enough to understand. He was glad Sarah had only been shot in the leg, though that was still dangerous. He wasn't surprised that Ellen had sneaked out on her own, but he was shocked that Wallace would kidnap her. Had the man completely lost his sanity?

"Did he say why he kidnapped Ellen?"

"He said everybody had to say some stranger killed Papa if we wanted her back."

"What did your mother say?"

"She told him the deputy probably wouldn't believe us if we lied. Then she said she'd try, but I think it was just so he wouldn't hurt Ellen."

Salty had to find her. The deputy's hands would be tied if the men changed their stories, and the little girl was one of the things Salty loved most in the world. He didn't know how he was going to find Wallace in one afternoon when no one had found his hiding place in more than a week, but first things first. Right now all he could think about was making sure Sarah was okay.

It seemed like hours rather than just a few minutes before he rode into the yard. He brought his horse to a halt, jumped down, and lifted Jared from the saddle. He ran into the house through the open door, the boy in his arms. Sarah was sitting in a chair, her leg bound with strips torn from her petticoat.

"You've got to find Wallace," she said before he could take a single additional step toward her. "He's got Ellen."

Salty put Jared down. "I need to make sure you're all right."

"I'm okay. Find Ellen."

He crossed the room. "In a minute, Sarah. First—"

"If you don't go after my daughter this minute," Sarah nearly shouted, "I'll get out of this chair and do it myself."

The expression on her face was a mixture of rage and fear. Her voice vibrated with an urgency that only a mother could feel, and behind it all was a spine of iron, a will that had refused to break despite everything life at thrown at her. If he didn't go after Wallace right now, Salty knew Sarah *would* do it herself. How could he leave the woman he loved, knowing she'd been shot and not knowing how bad the wound was? Yet, how could he not try to find Ellen?

Salty had never expected to have to make such a difficult decision, but he didn't have to. Sarah had already made it for him. She chose her daughter.

He turned to Jared. "I need you to go back up the trail. When you find Arnie, tell him to take care of your mother. Tell Dobie to ride for a doctor and notify the deputy sheriff." He turned to Sarah. "I don't know when I'll be back. If you start to feel—"

Sarah shook her head. "I don't matter."

Wallace would pay dearly for what he'd done. The pain in her eyes wasn't a pain caused by any physical injury but rather one in her heart. He'd never seen her eyes so bleak, so empty. So scared.

"I'll find Ellen," he told Sarah. "I won't come back until I do."

It didn't take him long to saddle a new horse for Jared. While he did that, the boy explained how he'd taken the bars down, lured the first horse to the fence with corn and managed to climb onto its back. He apologized for any of the other horses that got out, but he couldn't put the bars back up without getting down off the horse again.

"I'm really proud of you," Salty said. "I'd round up a hundred runaways if I could have been around to watch you pull off that trick."

Jared rode off a tired but proud boy.

While he caught and saddled his own mount, Salty tried to think of where to look for Wallace. He couldn't stop worrying about Ellen. She was a brave little girl, and bright, but she was only seven, still a child. She had to be frightened and wondering if anyone was going to find her. He wondered if she regretted having ignored her mother's wishes. Would he find Wallace before it became too dark? It was fortunate he'd come home early, but he wouldn't have more than a couple hours of daylight.

The trail wasn't as difficult to follow as he expected, and he headed in the direction of Wallace's ranch. The standard route between the two ranches was little more than a faint track. They'd had rain the previous day and the ground was still soft enough to show hoof prints. Some were deeper than others, indicating an irregularity of stride. Nor did that horse keep a straight path. It turned toward the hills. Now Salty had to depend on bruised grass and fresh growth that had been broken off.

He was surprised to come to a spot where the ground was badly cut up; he didn't understand why the horse should act up just because Wallace had changed direction. But when it happened a second time, he grinned broadly. Every time Wallace changed direction, Ellen found a way to cause the horse to mark their track. The girl was bright as well as courageous. He just hoped Wallace didn't figure out what she was doing.

The rancher was heading to a part of his land that merged with a group of low hills composed of jumbled boulders and covered with stunted trees. If Salty lost the trail, it would be difficult to pick up again. He followed the path carefully, looking for broken branches, marks of shod hooves on stone, any disturbance in the new growth that even these barren hills couldn't entirely discourage, and he reached the other side more quickly than he expected.

The land that lay before him was rock-strewn and veined with dry streambeds carved by swift running water. Covered by a combination of dry grass and isolated stands of oak and tangled vines, it was a perfect place for Wallace to hide; he could change thickets every day to avoid detection. The lengthening shadows made it hard for Salty to find the trail. He thought he knew where Wallace had come down from the hills, but he couldn't find anything to tell him where he had gone. He was stymied.

For the next half hour he searched one thicket after another. During that time, the evening shadows progressed from twilight to darkness. The decision became whether to stay for the night or go home and come back tomorrow. He hadn't brought any food, water, or his bedroll; he'd have to sleep on bare ground, hungry and thirsty. That prospect didn't appeal to him, but he knew he couldn't go home. Not yet. Not leaving Ellen to Wallace's questionable mercy.

He might not be able to do anything by staying here, but he *surely* couldn't do anything if he went back to the house. In the meantime, needing to find a place to rest, he checked out several thickets. None was both dry and offered a carpet of leaves to keep him from having to lie down directly on the rocks. He had just rejected a fourth thicket when he saw what he thought was a faint glimmer of light in the distance. It vanished immediately, but he took heart. If he was lucky, he'd just seen a flicker of light from Wallace's campfire. At the very least it might be someone else who had seen Wallace and Ellen. But he wanted to see it again, just to make sure he wasn't imagining things.

The light remained invisible for so long Salty began to wonder if it had been moonlight reflecting off a fleck of silica embedded in a stone or a piece of broken glass, but then the light reappeared, and it flared forth with such a burst of color there was no doubt it was real. Within a few moments it had assumed a formidable size. One of the thickets was on fire! Salty drove his tired mount into a gallop. He didn't know what had caused the blaze, but if Ellen was there, she was in danger.

There were perhaps as many as fifty trees in the grove when he reached it, and the perimeter was composed of an impenetrable tangle of thorny vines that would cause serious damage even to the most careful rider. Salty searched for the break in the barrier that Wallace must have used, assuming he hadn't hacked his way in with a bush ax. His search became even more intense when he heard a voice which he identified as Wallace's followed by Ellen's high, clear, penetrating sound. The girl was alive and in fighting form, but he would have to get her out quickly. The fire was growing. It wouldn't be long before the whole grove was on fire.

Despite the moonlight, Salty almost missed the break in the vines that proved to be the only way to enter. He turned his mount toward the opening, but its fear of fire was so great it refused to enter. Salty dug his heels into the horse's side, but the animal squealed in fright, wheeled, and tried to run away. Salty managed to stop him, but he'd never get the horse inside. With a curse of frustration, he leapt to the ground. He didn't look back as the frightened animal ran away, instead headed straight into the thicket.

At first he couldn't see in the nearly total darkness. Then he was blinded by the light from the fire. He nearly knocked himself down on a couple of low-hanging branches, but at last he reached where Wallace was struggling with Ellen. She bit Wallace's hand, which caused him to scream curse-filled threats. She kicked and scratched as well. Wallace had tangled with a wildcat.

The fire had gained such a strong foothold, Salty was more concerned about getting Ellen to safety than apprehending Wallace. After running into several more limbs, one that came perilously close to putting out his eye, he reached the kidnapper.

The noise of the fire had covered the sound of his footsteps, but a sixth sense must have warned Wallace of Salty's approach. He struck Ellen a savage blow that knocked the child to the ground; then he turned on Salty, gun in hand. Fortunately, he was as blinded by the fire as Salty. His shot went wide. A second shot passed so close to Salty's ear he could hear the whine of the bullet. The next sound, the hammer falling on an empty chamber, was music to Salty's ears.

Wallace stood before him, silhouetted against the fire. Rather than waste time, Salty ran to Ellen and lifted her to her feet. "We've got to get out before the fire traps us."

The little girl was still groggy from the blow, but her anger-filled eyes searched for her abductor. "Where's Mr. Wallace?"

Salty looked to where the man had been, but he was gone.

"He probably ran away to escape the fire—something we'd better do." Taking Ellen firmly by the hand, Salty rushed for the way out.

"He'll get away!"

"Not for long," Salty promised. He searched for the exit to the thicket, but it was impossible to see past the blaze all around him. He told himself not to panic. Wallace had found a way out. They would, too.

The fire had leapt from dry leaves and dead limbs on the ground into the treetops; Salty could hear the sound of wood popping and splitting over its roar. They had only seconds to find the way out, he knew. Stumbling over fallen limbs and dodging low-hanging branches, Salty fought to stay ahead of the blaze while struggling for the opening that would lead them to safety.

Ellen started to cry. "We're going to burn up. I'll never see Mama again."

"We're not going to burn up." He and the little girl were going to get out of this if he had to go headfirst through the worst tangle of thorny vines in Texas. He snatched up a dead branch and told her, "Get behind me."

"What are you going to do?"

"Use this branch to force our way out."

He might as well have been confronting a solid wall for all the good his pushing on the branch did. The fire was getting closer, hotter. Salty thrust the end of the limb into the tangle of vines to pry an opening. While the vines had refused to break or be uprooted, they did bend to either side. The tangle was more than six feet in depth, but he managed to make an opening large enough for Ellen to scramble through. By now the fire was in the trees directly overhead and smoldering in the leaves at his feet. The heat was terrible, and the smoke was making his eyes water. He could hardly breathe without gasping, which only made things worse. He had to get out now or it would be too late.

Using his bare hands to pry the vines apart, despite the thorns that tore at his flesh and snatched his hat from his head, he fought his way through the resistant web. His feet got tangled and he fell to his knees. He nearly screamed at the pain of something that felt like a dagger being driven into his thigh, but he continued to push toward the fresh air he could smell despite the heat and the smoke. The pop and hiss of green leaves and vines over his head exploding from the heat drove him to one last superhuman effort. Gulping in a lungful of life-giving air, he dove out of the thicket and rolled.

When he came upright several feet away, he found himself face-to-face with Wallace.

TWENTY-SIX

HE MANAGED TO AVOID THE RANCHER'S FIRST ATTACK BY ROLLING, but his body felt like a pincushion and he was weak and disoriented from having inhaled so much smoke. He couldn't have avoided Wallace a second time, but Ellen threw herself in the way. When the rancher tried to shove her aside, she bit him. Howling in pain and fury, he would have backhanded the child, but Salty managed to grab one of his ankles and throw him off balance. Unfortunately, Wallace aimed a kick at Salty's head that was a glancing blow but enough to knock him onto his back.

Ellen attacked again. Wallace retaliated, and it was clear from the way he was hitting the child that he meant to put her out of the way. Salty fought to clear his head and regain some control over his body. Despite the burning pain from what felt like hundreds of needles buried in his flesh, he had to stop Wallace from hurting her. He climbed to his knees and managed to throw himself at the back of the rancher's legs. The man went down with a crash, momentarily stunned.

Salty crawled to where Ellen lay sprawled on the ground. She looked lifeless. "Ellen, wake up. Are you hurt?"

The little girl opened her eyes. "I'm going to kill that bastard!"

Despite the pain that racked his body from one end to the other, Salty grinned. "That's my girl. You practically saved my life. Just don't let your mother hear that word. She'll swear you got it from me."

"Turn around real quick," she whispered.

Grimacing from pain, Salty turned to see Wallace pulling himself into a sitting position. If Salty didn't get to his feet now, he'd lose all advantage. Something inside of him snapped. Roger was myopic, Arnie delusional, but Wallace was just plain evil. There were times when a man simply had to ignore the consequences and fight. Remembering what some of his fellow soldiers had suffered during the war, he ignored the pain in his thigh. Still, it took every bit of mental toughness he could summon to stand up.

He gritted his teeth and staggered over to where Wallace was attempting to get to his feet. Summoning all his energy, he slammed his fist into the man's jaw. The blow sent Wallace sprawling; it left Salty panting for breath.

"That's for shooting Sarah, you son of a bitch. Now get up. I intend to give you another for hurting Ellen. If you're still able to stand after that, I'll give you one more for this damned pain in my thigh."

Wallace didn't move.

"Wake up, you yellow-bellied coward. I'm not through with you."

Wallace still didn't move.

Ellen appeared, peering down at him. "I hope he's dead."

"He's just out cold." Salty was rather proud that, in his weakened condition, he'd been able to hit Wallace so hard. He just wished his fist didn't hurt nearly as much as his thigh.

"What do we do now?" Ellen asked.

Salty started to say they needed to watch the fire to make sure it didn't leap to the next thicket, but the ground out here was wet from recent rain and the next nearest copse was a good distance off, a clump of trees about a hundred yards away. "We need to find my horse," he said. "It's a long walk home, and I don't think I'll make it with this thorn in my thigh."

"We can use Mr. Wallace's horse," Ellen said.

"We could if we could find it."

"We can." She pointed to the nearest copse. "He hid it over there."

Having used up the nearby dry fuel, the fire was beginning to die down. Salty ran over to the copse and found Wallace's horse. On it was a length of rope. He made a split-second decision to tie Wallace up and tell the deputy where to find him; that seemed easier than figuring out how to get him and Ellen back to the ranch.

"Let's go," he said to Ellen. "I'm worried about your mother."

―――――――

Recounting to Sarah the way her daughter had fought against her kidnapper helped distract Salty's mind until the doctor finished bandaging her wound and told them she was in no danger. Ellen's description of how she caused the horse to leave a trail Salty could follow entertained them all when the doctor switched patients.

He spent longer with Salty than he did with Sarah. "I've never seen anybody with so many embedded thorns!"

"It's becoming an occupational hazard," Salty joked. "You should have seen my foot several days ago." He was trying to make light of the situation, but he hurt worse now than before the doctor removed the thorns. He did all right until the one in his thigh. Then it was all he could do to keep from embarrassing himself in front of the children. Not even Ellen's description of how she'd intentionally started the fire had been able to keep Salty's mind off the pain.

"Both of you should stay in bed for at least the next day," the doctor told them. "It's important for Mrs. Wheeler to stay off her feet until that wound has time to heal. She's fortunate it's only a shallow flesh wound."

"How can I do that when I have six people to feed?" Sarah asked.

"I can cook some," Arnie volunteered.

"Me too," Dobie added.

"If it comes to that, I can cook," Salty said, "but I doubt anybody will want to eat it."

"I'll figure out something," Sarah said, giving him a fond smile. "I want you to get better, not worse."

"I'll send Mr. Wallace's cook over," the deputy said. "I imagine he'll be looking for new work soon."

The deputy had been present when Salty returned with Ellen. He'd collected Wallace and taken him back to his ranch, ordering the men there to watch him until he could be transported back to Austin. He'd warned them all of the penalty for helping a wanted man escape. None had seemed likely to risk that, not even Tully.

"Someone's coming," Jared announced. "I hear a wagon."

Salty couldn't get used to Jared being able to hear things long before anyone else. The boy's senses appeared to have sharpened to compensate for his leg.

Ellen jumped up from where she'd been watching the doctor remove Salty's thorns. "I'll go see." She was out of her seat and through the door with the speed of a gazelle.

"I think she's recovered from her ordeal," the deputy said.

Salty tried to laugh. "If you'd seen what she did to Wallace, you'd know he suffered more than she."

The door was flung open and Ellen burst in. "It's the Randolphs," she announced, a little out of breath. "And they've brought two calves!"

Rose, looking big enough to give birth at any moment, bustled into the room moments later. "George wanted me to stay in Austin until I had the baby, but I told him I wouldn't get a minute's rest as long as I knew you were in trouble." She took one look at Sarah's leg and turned to her husband, who had followed her through the door. "I told you she needed me. What can I do?"

Salty's body was covered in wounds, he had gone without sleep, and he had endured his most stressful twenty-four hours since the war. Nonetheless, he started to laugh. Well, it wasn't exactly a laugh; it was more like a choking noise. But when Rose looked bewildered and then slightly miffed, it became a laugh. And the twinkle in Sarah's eyes finished off what was left of his self-control.

"Benton Wheeler," Rose intoned, "don't you dare laugh at me. I'm the one who told Sarah you were the best possible choice for a husband, that if she chose you, nothing would go wrong."

At that point he simply howled.

EPILOGUE

"I HATE TO LEAVE SO SOON," ROSE SAID AS SHE ALLOWED HER HUS-band to help her into the wagon, "but George won't get a minute's peace until I'm back with a doctor. You'd think a woman never had a baby without a sawbones standing over her."

Sarah had enjoyed Rose's company as well as her help during the last three days, but she was also anxious for life to return to normal. The friendship of the Randolphs was a blessing, but they had so much energy they overwhelmed everybody around them. She wanted to get back to just her family—Jared, Ellen, and Salty. Maybe Arnie and Dobie, too. She was also anxious for Salty to take his rightful place as her husband. She'd given up her room so Rose and George could have her bed, but then she'd shared with Ellen, Salty with Jared. Considering their respective wounds, they didn't trust themselves to be in the same bed. That would happen tonight.

"I expect Salty would feel the same if I were having a baby," she said.

"You can be sure I would." Salty had entered the room, and from the look in his eye it was possible another baby or two might be in her future. That was all right with her. She wouldn't mind a couple of little boys who looked like him. Now that they finally would be sharing the same bed, that was a real possibility.

Salty winked at her. "If we get to buy Wallace's ranch, I'll need extra cowhands. Of course, they'll have to grow up real fast."

Seeing the work that had been done here, George had offered to lend Salty the money to buy the neighboring ranch if he could get it at a decent price. Just thinking about this caused Sarah to shake her head in wonder. Only two months before she had been on the verge of losing everything. Now it was possible she and Salty would become the biggest landowners in the area. With the two bull calves George had given them, they would definitely have the best herd. And all because Salty's name had fallen from her lips when she meant to say Walter.

"If you have any more trouble, I'll lend you Monty," George said as they all went outside. He climbed up next to his wife in their wagon. "He's been bored ever since the McClendons stopped stealing our cows and Cortina was driven back across the border."

"Can you bring Zac next time?" Ellen asked.

"I'll let you have him." Rose laughed and patted her stomach. "I'll soon have a replacement."

Sarah and Salty stood waving until the Randolphs' wagon passed through the trees surrounding the house. Ellen ran alongside it—she would probably run all the way to the main trail—but Jared took up his favorite place: at Salty's side.

Sarah put her arm around Salty's waist and hugged him. He placed a kiss on the top of her head.

"Tired?"

"A little," she said. "I love Rose, but she wears me out."

Salty laughed. "She's a perfect wife for George. She's probably the only woman alive with more energy than his brothers."

"I prefer you." She looked up at Salty. It scared her to think how close she'd come to choosing someone else, how the difficulties of the past had almost closed her up to the possibilities of the future. If she hadn't taken a chance on Salty, she would never have found her dreams. "I can't believe how lucky I am."

"How can it be lucky to have a husband who's so full of holes he looks like he lost a fight with a cactus?" Salty joked.

"Because he got those holes protecting my daughter."

"*Our* daughter." He put his arm over Jared's shoulder. "With quite a bit of help from *our* son."

The look of happiness on Jared's face filled Sarah's heart to overflowing. Roger had given her children, but Salty was both her husband and their father. He loved her, and she him. Together, the future was theirs.

No one but you could have done that, she thought. No one but you.

ABOUT THE AUTHOR

Leigh Greenwood is the award-winning author of over fifty books, many of which have appeared on the *USA Today* bestseller list. Leigh lives in Charlotte, North Carolina. Please visit his website at www.leigh-greenwood.com.

Read on for a sneak peek of the first book in the
brand-new Men of Legend series by *New York Times*
bestselling author Linda Broday:

To Love a Texas Ranger

Central Texas
Early Spring 1876

WIND SIGHING THROUGH THE DRAW WHISPERED AGAINST HIS FACE,
sharpening his senses to a fine edge. A warning skittered along his spine
before it settled in his chest.

Texas Ranger Sam Legend had learned to listen to his gut. Right
now it said that the suffocating sense of danger that crowded around
him had killing in mind. Deep in the Texas Hill Country, he brought the
spyglass up to his eye and focused on the rustlers below. All fifteen had
covered their faces, leaving only their eyes showing.

Every crisp sound swept up the steep incline where he hid in a stand
of cedar. "Hurry up with those beeves! We've gotta get the hell out of
here. Rangers are so close I can smell 'em!" a rustler yelled.

Where were the other rangers? They hadn't been separated from
each other long and should've caught up by now.

Letting the outlaws escape took everything he had. But there were
too many for one man, and this bunch was far more ruthless than most.

He peered closer as they tried to drive the bawling cattle up the
draw. But the ornery bovines seemed to be smarter. They broke away

from the group, scattering this way and that. Sam allowed a grin. These rustlers were definitely no cattlemen.

A lawman learned to adjust quickly. His mind whirled as he searched for some kind of plan. One shot fired in the air would alert the other rangers to his position if they were near. But would they arrive before the outlaws got to him?

Or...no one would fault Sam for sitting quietly until the lawless group cleared out.

Except Sam. A Legend never ran from a fight. It wasn't in his blood. He would ride straight through hell and come out the other side whenever a situation warranted. As a Texas Ranger, he'd made that ride many times over.

From his hiding place, he could start picking off the rustlers. With luck, Sam might get a handful before they surrounded him. Still, a few beat none. Maybe the rest would bolt. Slowly, he drew his Colt and prepared for the fight.

Though winter had just given way to spring, the hot sun bore down. Sweat trickled into his eyes, making them sting. He wiped away the sweat with an impatient hand.

A half second from taking his first shot, cold steel jabbed into his back and a hand reached for his Colt. "Turn around real slow, mister."

The order grated along Sam's nerve endings and settled in his clenched stomach. He listened for anything to indicate his fellow rangers were nearby. If not, he was dead. He heard nothing except bawling steers and men yelling.

Sam slowly pivoted. Cold, dead eyes glared over the top of the rustler's bandana.

"Well, whatd'ya know. Got me a bona fide ranger."

Though Sam couldn't see the outlaw's mouth, the words told him he wore a smile. "I'm not here alone. You won't get away with this."

"Well, I reckon we'll just see." The gun barrel poked harder into

Sam's back. "Down the hill."

Sam could've managed without the shove. The soles of his worn boots provided no traction. Slipping and sliding down the steep embankment, he glanced for anything to suggest help had arrived, but saw nothing.

At the bottom, riders on horseback immediately surrounded him.

"Good job, Smith." The outlaw pushing to the front had to be the ringleader. He was dressed all in black, from his hat to his boots. "Let's teach this Texas Ranger not to mess with us. I've got a special treat in mind. One of you, find his horse and get me a rope. Smith, march him back up the hill. The rest of you drive those damn cattle to the makeshift corral."

The spit dried in Sam's mouth as the man holding him pushed him up the steep incline toward a gnarled oak high on the ridge.

Any minute, the rangers would swoop in. Just a matter of time. Sam refused to believe that his life was going to end this way. Somehow, he had to stall until help arrived.

"Smith, do you know the punishment for killing a lawman?" Sam asked.

"Stop talkin' and get movin.'"

"Are you willing to throw your life away for a man who doesn't give two cents about you?"

"You don't know nothin' about nothin', so shut up. One more word an' I'll shoot you in the knee."

Sam lapsed into silence. He could see Smith had closed his mind against anything he said. How far would he get if he took off running? He'd be lucky to make two strides before hot lead slammed into his leg. Even if he made it to the cover of a cedar, what then? He had no gun. No horse.

His best chance was to spin around and take Smith's weapon.

But just as he started to make a move, the ringleader rode up beside on his horse and shouted, "Hurry up. Don't have all day."

Sharp disappointment flared, trapping Sam's breath in his chest. His fate lay at the mercy of these outlaws.

They grew closer and closer to the twisted, bent oak branches that resembled witch's fingers. Those limbs would reach for a man's soul and snatch it at the moment of death.

Thick, bitter gall climbed into his throat, choking him. The devil would soon find Sam'd already lost his soul, a long time ago.

The steep angle of the hill made his breathing harsh. The climb hurt as much as his looming fate. He'd always thought a bullet would get him one day, but to die swinging from a tree had never crossed his mind.

The outlaw sent to find and bring Sam's horse appeared as they reached the top. The buckskin nickered softly, nuzzling Sam as though offering sympathy or maybe a last good-bye. He stroked the face of his faithful friend, murmuring a few quiet words of comfort. He'd raised Trooper from a colt and turned him into a lawman's mount. Would it be too much to pray these rustlers treated Trooper well? The horse deserved kindness.

"Enough," rasped the black-clothed boss with an impatient motion of the .45. "Put him on the horse and tie his hands."

Sam noticed a crude drawing between the man's thumb and wrist—a black widow spider. Not that he could do anything with the information where he was going.

One last time, he scanned the landscape anxiously, hoping to glimpse riders, but saw only the branches of cedar, oak, and cottonwood trees swaying gently in the breeze. He strained against the ropes binding him, but they wouldn't budge.

Thickness lodged in his throat as they threw him on Trooper's back. His heart pounded against his ribs. He sat straight and tall, not allowing so much as an eye twitch. These outlaws who thrived on violence would never earn the right to see the turmoil and fear twisting behind his stone face. Advice his father had once given him sounded in his ears. *"When trouble comes, stand proud. You are a Legend. Inside you beats the heart of a survivor."*

Sam Legend stared into the distance with unseeing eyes, the muscle working in his jaw.

The ringleader threw the rope up and over one of the gnarled branches.

Bitter regret rose. Sam had never told his father he loved him. The times they'd butted heads seemed trivial now. So did the fights with big brother Houston over things that didn't make a hill of beans.

Yes, he was going to die with a heart full of regret, broken dreams, and empty promises.

The rope scratched, digging into his tender flesh as the outlaw settled the noose around Sam's neck. "You better find a hole and climb into it, mister," Sam said. "Every ranger and lawman in the state of Texas will be after you."

A chuckle filled the air. "They won't find us."

"That wager's going to cost you." Sam steeled himself for pain, wondering how long it would take to die. He prayed it was quick. He wondered if his mother would be waiting to soothe him in Heaven.

"Say hello to the devil, Ranger." With those words, he slapped the horse's flank. Trooper bolted, leaving Sam dangling in the air. The rope violently yanked his neck back and to the side as his body jerked.

Choking and fighting to breathe, Sam Legend counted his heartbeats until blackness claimed him. As he whirled away into nothingness, only one thing filled his mind—the tattoo of a black widow spider on his killer's hand.

TWO

A MONTH AFTER TEXAS RANGER SAM LEGEND ALMOST DIED, AN ear-splitting crash of thunder rattled the windows and each unpainted board of the J. R. Simmons Mercantile. The ominous skies burst open, and rain pelted the ground in great sheets. A handful of people scattered like buckshot along the Waco boardwalk in an effort to escape the thorough drenching of a spring gully-washer.

Sam paid the rain no mind. The storm barely registered—few things did, these days. The feeling of the rope around his neck was still overpowering. He reached to see if it was there, thankful not to find it.

The nightmare had him in its grip, refusing to let go. More dead than alive, he moved toward his destination. When he reached the alley separating the two sections of boardwalk, he collided with a woman covered in a hooded cloak.

"Apologies, ma'am." He glanced down by rote, then blinked. All at once, the world and all its color came rushing back as Sam stared into startling blue eyes.

She nodded and opened her mouth to speak. But before she could, a man took her arm and jerked her into the alleyway.

"Hey there!" Sam called, startled. He'd been so focused on those blue eyes he hadn't realized anyone else was there. "Ma'am, do you need help?"

He received no answer, as her companion forced her toward a horse at the other end of the alley where a group of mounted riders waited.

The hair on the back of his neck rose.

Intent on stopping whatever was happening, Sam lengthened his strides. Before he could reach them, the man threw her onto a horse, then swung up behind her. Within seconds, they were gone.

Sam stood in the driving rain, staring at the empty street. It had all happened so fast he could hardly believe it.

Hell, maybe he'd imagined the whole thing. Maybe she'd never existed. Maybe the heavy downpour and gray gloom had messed with his mind...again. Ever since the hanging, he'd been seeing things that weren't there. Twice now he'd yanked men around and grabbed for their hand, thinking he saw a black widow spider between their thumb and forefinger. The last time almost got Sam shot. Folks claimed he was missing the top rung of his ladder. Now his captain was sending him home to find it.

Crippled. The word clanked around in his head, refusing to settle. But even though he had full use of his legs, that's what he was at present. The cold fear washing over him had nothing to do with the air temperature or rain. The sudden appearance and disappearance of the woman seemed suddenly so fantastical that it couldn't possibly have been real. What if he never recovered? Some never did.

His hand clenched. He'd fight like hell to be the vital man he once was. He had things to do—an outlaw to hunt down, a wrong to right...a promise to keep.

Sam drew his coat tight against the wet chill, forcing himself to move on down the street toward the face-to-face with Captain O'Reilly. It stuck in his craw that they thought him too crazed to do his job. The captain thought him a liability now, a danger to the other rangers. Wanted him to take a break.

His heart couldn't hurt any worse than if someone had stomped on it with a pair of hobnail boots. Maybe the captain was right. If he'd imagined that woman just now—and he really couldn't be certain he hadn't—then maybe he *needed* the break. Sam Legend, who had brought in notorious killers, bank robbers, prison escapees and the like, had become a liability.

But one thing he knew he hadn't imagined, and that was the blurred figure of Luke Weston standing over him when he'd regained consciousness that fateful day. There had been no mistaking those green eyes above the mask. They belonged to the outlaw he'd chased for over a year—he'd stake his life on it.

When his fellow rangers had ridden up, Weston disappeared into the brush, leaving Sam with questions. Who cut him down from the tree? Was Weston with the rustlers? Why had the outlaws left Trooper behind? Awful considerate of them.

So what the hell had happened, dammit?

Rangers who'd ridden up told Sam they'd seen no one. He lay on the ground with the rope loosened around his neck, drifting in and out of consciousness.

Those questions and others haunted him, and he wouldn't rest until he got answers. Somehow he knew Weston was the key.

At ranger headquarters, he took a deep breath before opening the door. He pushed a mite too hard, banging the knob against the wall. Captain O'Reilly jerked up from his desk. "What the hell, Legend? Trying to wake the dead?"

"Sorry, Cap'n. It got away from me." It seemed a good many things had, recently.

The tall, slender captain waved him to the chair. "I haven't heard this much racket since the shoot-out inside that silo with the Arnie brothers down in Sweetwater."

"I hope I can talk you out of your decision." Sam sat down.

O'Reilly sauntered to the potbellied stove in the corner and lifted the coffeepot. "What's it been? A month?"

"An eternity," Sam said quietly.

"Want a snort of coffee? Might improve your outlook."

"I'll take you up on your offer, but doubt it'll improve anything. I need this job, sir. I need to work." Revenge burned hot. He'd not rest until he found the men who'd hung him and when he did, they'd pay with their blood.

"What you *need* is some time off to get your head on straight. I can't have you seeing things that aren't there." O'Reilly sighed. "You're gonna get yourself or someone else killed. I'm ordering you to go home for a while, then come back ready to catch outlaws."

"Finding the rustlers and catching Luke Weston is my first priority."

"That wily outlaw has been taunting you for the last year." O'Reilly's eyes hardened as he handed him a tin cup. "It seems personal."

"Hell yeah, it's personal!"

Weston had been there, that much he knew. The outlaw could have strung him up himself. Why else would Sam remember those green eyes?

In addition to that, and though it sounded rather trivial when compared to a hanging, a year ago Weston had taken his pocket watch during a stagecoach holdup. Sam'd tried to protect a payroll shipment, but Weston'd done the oddest thing. The outlaw had only taken exactly fifty dollars, a paltry sum compared to what he'd left behind, and the passengers' belongings untouched. But he'd seemed to take particular delight in pocketing Sam's prized timepiece. Memories of the intent way Weston had flipped it open and stared at the inscription before tucking it away drifted through Sam's mind.

"Makes me mad enough to chew nails, and him calling himself Luke Legend half the time! Does it just to taunt me. I have a reputation to protect." The thought filled Sam's head with so many cuss words, he feared it would burst open.

The captain leaned back in his chair and propped his boots on the scarred desk that Noah must've brought over on the ark. To make up for a missing leg, someone had cut a crutch and stuck it under there.

The line at the bottom of the poster, also in heavy bold print, read: *Armed and Extremely Dangerous*. As with all the others, it didn't bear a likeness, not even a crude drawing. There were no physical features to go on. Frustration boiled. The lawman in him itched to be out there tracking Weston. The need to bring him to justice rose so strong it choked Sam. Weston was *his* outlaw to catch, and instead he'd been ordered to go home.

Hell! Spending one week on the huge Lone Star Ranch was barely tolerable. A month would either kill him or he'd kill big brother Houston. The thought had no more than formed before guilt pricked his conscience. In the final moments before the outlaw had hit his horse and left Sam dangling by his neck, regrets had filled his thoughts. He'd begged God for a second chance so he could make things right.

Now it looked like he'd get it. He'd make the time count. He'd mend bridges with his father.

Family was there in good times and bad.

Despite his better qualities, Stoker had caused problems for him. Sam had driven himself to work harder, be quicker and tougher, to prove to everyone his father hadn't bought his job. Overcoming the big ranch, the money and power the Legend name evoked, had been a continuing struggle.

Captain O'Reilly opened his desk drawer, uncorked a bottle of whiskey, and gave his coffee a generous dousing. "Want to doctor your coffee, Sam?"

"Don't think it'll help," he replied with a tight smile.

"Suit yourself." The hardened ranger put the bottle away. The white scar on his cheek had never faded, left from a skirmish with the Comanche.

Sam studied that scar, thinking. Although Sam had intended to keep quiet about the woman he may or may not have bumped into on the way over out of fear of being labeled a lunatic for sure, he felt a duty to say something. He wouldn't voice doubts that he'd imagined it. "Cap'n, I

"I'll take a ride over there while I'm home."

"No hurry. Give yourself a few weeks."

"Sure thing, Cap'n." The clock on the town square chimed the half hour, reminding him he'd best get moving. Relieved that O'Reilly had softened and allowed him to still work, Sam set down his cup. "Appears I've got a train to catch."

O'Reilly shook his hand. "Get well, Sam. You're a good lawman. Come back stronger than ever."

"I will, sir."

At the livery, Sam hired a boy to fetch his bags from the hotel and take them to the station. After settling with the owner and collecting his buckskin gelding, Sam rode to meet the train. He shivered in the cold, steady downpour. The gloomy day reflected his mood as he moved toward an uncertain future. He was on his way home.

To bind up his wounds. To heal. To become the ranger he needed to be.

And he would—come hell or high water, mad as a March hare or not.

Right on time, amid plumes of hissing white steam, the Houston and Texas Central Railway train pulled up next to the loading platform.

Sam quickly loaded Trooper into the livestock car and paid the boy for bringing his bags. After making sure the kerchief around his neck hid the scar, he swung aboard. Passengers had just started to enter so he had his pick of seats. He chose one two strides from the door.

Shrugging from his coat, he sat down and got comfortable.

A movement across the narrow aisle a few minutes later drew his attention, as a tall passenger wearing a low-slung gunbelt slid into the seat. Sam studied the black leather vest and frock coat of the same color. Gunslinger, bounty hunter, or maybe a gambler? Bounty hunter seemed far-fetched—he'd never seen one dressed in anything as fine. Such men wasted no time with fancy clothing. A gunslinger, then. Few others tied their holster down to their leg. No one else required speed when drawing. Likely a gambler too. Usually the two went hand in hand.

sense of the thoughts clunking around in his head. When he next looked over at Andrew Evan, Sam wasn't surprised to find the slouching gunslinger's head against the seat with his hat tilted over his eyes.

The hair on his neck rose. Sam felt Andrew's eyes watching from beneath the brim of the black Stetson. Then he saw a muscle twitch in Andrew's jaw, confirming that he wasn't asleep.

Tension sparking between them electrified the air.

As Sam stared at Evan's hands, searching for the tattoo, a woman rushed down the aisle. She came even with them just as the train took a curve, and tumbled headlong into his lap. He found himself holding soft, warm curves encased in dark wool.

Stark fear darkened the blue eyes staring up at him, and her bottom lip quivered.

A jolt went through him. Lucinda? But no—it couldn't be her. But this girl had Lucinda Howard's same black hair and blue eyes framed by thick, sooty lashes.

His body responded against his will as he struggled with the memory. Hell! At last, he realized this girl was not the faithless lover he'd once known.

But she *was* the woman he'd collided with on his way to the ranger headquarters.

"Are you all right, miss?"

"I…I'm so sorry," she murmured.

He felt her icy hand splayed against his chest through the fabric of his shirt, where it landed in breaking her fall.

"Are you in trouble? I can help."

"They're…I've got to—" Mystery woman pushed away, extricating herself from his lap. Then with a strangled sob, she ran toward the door leading to the next car.

Sam looked down. Prickles rose on the back of his neck.

A bloody handprint stained his shirt.

His coloring spoke of Mexican descent, though judging by the shade, he had one white parent. Lines around the traveler's mouth and a gray or two in his dark hair put him somewhere around the near side of thirty. Though he wore his black Stetson low on his forehead, he tugged it even lower as he settled back against the cushion.

The fine hairs on Sam's arm twitched. He knew this man. But from where? For the life of him, he couldn't recall. He leaned over. "Pardon me, but have we met?"

Without meeting Sam's gaze, the man allowed a tight smile. "Nope."

Darn the hat that bathed his eyes in dusky shadows. "I'm Sam Legend. Name's not familiar?"

"Nope."

He'd been so certain the man looked familiar. "Guess I made a mistake…" Odd that the man hadn't introduced himself, though.

"Appears so, Ranger."

How did he know Sam was a ranger? He wore no badge. "My apologies," Sam mumbled.

The train engineer blew the whistle and the mighty iron wheels began to slowly turn.

Sam swung his attention back to the gunslinger. A few more words and he'd be able to place him, surely. "Would you have the time, Mr…?" Sam asked.

"Andrew. Andrew Evan." The man flipped open his timepiece. "It's 10:45."

"Obliged." Finally, a name. Not that it proved helpful. Sam was sure he'd left his real one at the Texas border, as men with something to hide tended to do. By working extra hard trying to make himself invisible, Evan had as much as declared that he had things to conceal.

Worse, the longer Sam sat near Andrew, the stronger the feeling of familiarity grew. And that was something Sam's brain had not conjured up. He glanced out the window at the passing scenery, trying to make